THE COLTONS of MUSTANG VALLEY: *Guardian*

JENNIFER MOREY

LINDA O. JOHNSTON

MILLS & BOON

Jennifer Morey is acknowledged as the author of this work
COLTON FAMILY BODYGUARD

First Published 2020
Second Australian Paperback Edition 2024
ISBN 978 1 038 90866 7

Linda O. Johnston is acknowledged as the author of this work
COLTON FIRST RESPONDER

First Published 2020
Second Australian Paperback Edition 2024
ISBN 978 1 038 90866 7

Published by
Mills & Boon
An imprint of Harlequin Enterprises (Australia) Pty Limited
(ABN 47 001 180 918), a subsidiary of HarperCollins
Publishers Australia Pty Limited (ABN 36 009 913 517)
Level 19, 201 Elizabeth Street
SYDNEY NSW 2000
AUSTRALIA

Printed and bound in Australia by McPherson's Printing Group

CONTENTS

Colton Family Bodyguard

Jennifer Morey

Two-time RITA® Award nominee and Golden Quill award winner **Jennifer Morey** writes single-title contemporary romance and page-turning romantic suspense. She has a geology degree and has managed export programs in compliance with the International Traffic in Arms Regulations (ITAR) for the aerospace industry. She lives at the foot of the Rocky Mountains in Denver, Colorado, and loves to hear from readers through her website, jennifermorey.com, or Facebook.

Books by Jennifer Morey

Harlequin Romantic Suspense

The Coltons of Mustang Valley

Colton Family Bodyguard

Cold Case Detectives

A Wanted Man
Justice Hunter
Cold Case Recruit
Taming Deputy Harlow
Runaway Heiress
Hometown Detective
Cold Case Manhunt

The Coltons of Roaring Springs

Colton's Convenient Bride

The Coltons of Red Ridge

Colton's Fugitive Family

Visit Jennifer's Author Profile page at millsandboon.com.au, or jennifermorey.com, for more titles.

Dear Reader,

Welcome to another fun-filled Colton series book! I don't have the opportunity to do bodyguard books very often, especially one where a child witnesses a murder. This one was special for me. The plot fell right into place with characters who really moved the story for me. Little Evie is as adorable as can be!

One of the elements I liked most—and hope you find enjoyable as well—was the heroine's and hero's past heartbreaks and how that played into their reluctance to get involved. Writing their emotional growth felt honest and rewarding. And of course, who doesn't love a good Colton book?

Sincerely yours,

Jennifer

For my family, for always supporting me and
the time I spend writing.

Chapter 1

Why did every woman he met and thought might be the one always announce at the worst possible time that she wanted babies? Callum Colton walked along a street at the edge of Mustang Valley, Arizona, on a sunny, early spring day. He had just left his now ex-girlfriend, Cindy, in tears because he'd had to tell her he was never going to have any children. He'd explained that to her at the beginning but she must have thought she could change his mind. He'd had to remind her he meant what he'd said. In truth, he felt so rotten, ending the relationship like that. She'd told him she understood and held no animosity toward him, but she was obviously very hurt.

Callum stepped into Executive Protection Services, LLC still lamenting what had happened. What else could he have done? He would have hurt his ex-girlfriend more had he continued on with her. When Cindy sat him down for The Serious Talk, she'd told him she wanted children and she wanted them with him. She loved him, and her biological clock ticked on and she felt she had to move now. That convinced him they weren't right for each other. She had hoped he felt the same as her and that he would give her children. She hadn't anticipated how unbending he was on the matter. And the truth was that he did not love her. They would have ended their relationship eventually, since she wanted a family. Why drag it out? He never had serious relationships with women he dated. How had she gotten the impression he would with her? He had told her as much. He almost shuddered as the door closed behind him and he walked through the entry with its vacant reception desk toward an office in the back.

He had enough going on without having to now feel guilty for hurting Cindy. He was still reeling from the news that his half brother, Ace, had been switched at birth and wasn't really his biological sibling. Not by blood. Who would do such a thing and why? The why of it really twisted his mind. Charles, the owner, chief executive officer, president and whatever other titles a guy like him liked to have, looked up from behind his metal-and-glass desk. The lack of clutter and nearly bare walls pretty much described him. Focused. Nothing personal. Good business head. That's why Callum had agreed to work for him. Callum had no liking for paperwork. Charles did.

"It's about time you got here." Charles stood and moved around his desk.

"I had to take care of something." Cindy's tear-damp cheeks flashed through his mind. Chaos had reigned recently in his life, ever since an email had made the rounds of his family's company, Colton Oil, saying that his oldest brother, Ace, was not a biological Colton. Since then, his father, Payne, had been shot—and now the cops even suspected Ace.

Charles stopped before him and cocked his head. "Well, that sounds like you. When you need to take care of something, nothing keeps you from doing it—not even your boss."

"I broke up with my girlfriend," Callum said.

"Another one? The hot blonde? What's wrong with you?"

Callum put his hands up. "She wanted kids."

Charles's brow creased a little. "What is it with you and kids? They're harmless and adorable. Who wouldn't want them?"

"Not me."

"Why not? They can be challenging sometimes but the rewards far outweigh that."

Charles had two young kids. He had a wife and a nice house. A real family man. "Why did you call me here?" Callum asked in irritation.

After considering him awhile, Charles said, "You never talk about anything, do you realize that?"

Callum angled his head in silent warning.

"Keeping things bottled up is unhealthy. I worry about you."

Callum said nothing and continued to look at him.

"Why do you think I called you here?" Charles asked.

Callum had a pretty good idea why. And he also thought this was going to be a waste of time. "I got the job done and the client is alive." He'd done a job as a bodyguard for an executive who had a stalker.

"I'm not telling you to change your ways." Charles scoffed. "I couldn't anyway. But for the welfare of this company, I am telling you to be more careful. I almost couldn't convince the police you didn't break the law."

The stalker had gotten too close to his delicate female client and Callum had given him a clear…message. Someone must have called 911 because the police had arrived after Callum and his client left.

"You were lucky the stalker was wanted for sexual assault on another woman. If they hadn't been able to arrest him, they probably wouldn't have let you go with just a warning," his boss said.

Callum walked over to the window and passively watched cars go by and a man walking his dog on the sidewalk.

"Seriously, Callum, you can't make up your own rules as you go."

Why was Charles rambling on so long about that? Hopefully Callum had knocked some sense into him. Charles was just uncomfortable about employing a man who wasn't afraid to cross boundaries.

"I'll be careful, Charles," Callum said.

"Why does that sound so half-baked?"

Callum glanced back with a rueful grin. "Because it is. Stop worrying so much. You're not the one who would have been arrested, and protecting our clients won't damage our reputation. If anything, it will get us more business."

"You can't protect anyone if you're in jail."

Turning back to the window, Callum said, "I didn't cross the line. We advertise elite services, don't we?" The view distracted him a moment. Charles had rented an office in an attractive one-story mall with a restaurant and a gas station beside the parking lot. The back of the building faced a quiet, tree-lined road. Across the street an upscale subdivision sprawled.

"Okay, but just don't get caught."

"I knew that stalker was wanted for assault. I found out two days ago."

"You still could have been arrested, Callum. Even criminals have rights."

"I'll keep that in mind." Or not. Callum's first priority was protecting his clients. He had a strong conviction about that. Victims didn't deserve to be forced into being victims. The menace that threatened them was a cancer that had to be carved out and stopped. That's what had led him to a career as a bodyguard, and back home to support his family in a time of crisis.

"It turns out that's not the only reason I asked you to stop by. I've got another case for you. Ever hear of the country singer Blake Reynolds?"

"No." Callum liked country but didn't pay attention to the artists' names.

Outside, a black Mercedes SUV—one of the more economical versions—pulled to a stop on the side of the street. Callum caught sight of a woman with long dark hair in the driver's seat.

She had a fantastic profile. At the same time, a car stopped on the side of the street about two houses down.

Callum listened to Charles explain the new case while he turned back to the woman, who climbed out of the SUV and opened the back door. She worked to free a little girl from a car seat. Normally this was when he would have turned away from the sight of a mother and her child, but something about the woman made him keep watching—and stop listening to Charles. Maybe it was that tight body in those dressy black pants, or the curve of that slender waist, or the way her those perfectly shaped breasts strained against the white blouse.

She lifted the girl from the seat and lowered her to the ground. Holding a stuffed Cookie Monster in one arm, the child looked up at her mother and said something, to which the woman shook her head. The little girl didn't appear to like the answer, an adorable pout forming beneath scrunching eyebrows, and she hugged the stuffed toy against the white top of a cute flaring black skirt. He felt an automatic pang at the adorable mother-daughter duo.

The mother went to the back of the Mercedes and lifted the hatch. Callum got a really nice view of her frame as she leaned in and retrieved two recyclable grocery bags. Setting those on the pavement, she reached in again and handed a plastic container to the little girl, who still frowned and continued to argue with her mother.

The beautiful woman crouched before her, her facial features striking him to the core. She spoke to the girl, whose frown finally smoothed.

Standing, the woman closed the hatch and lifted the bags, talking with the young girl. The child walked with short, clumsy steps beside her mother up the driveway to the front door of a house. When they disappeared inside, Callum realized how immersed he'd become in watching the woman and child. His stomach fell.

Then he looked down the street and saw the car that had

pulled over was still there, with someone sitting in the driver's seat. A man. He appeared to be watching the woman's house, though he was too far away to get a good look inside. Out of habit, Callum checked the license plate but it was too far away to make out.

Charles appeared beside him, looking from the house across the street to him. "Have you heard a single word I've said?"

"Sorry, no." Callum turned away from the window.

"The singer had a girlfriend who's gone off the deep end. He's afraid she'll go after him."

"Another one of those cases?" Only this time it would be a man he protected.

"They were together for six months and she started to get too clingy, so he ended it. He said he noticed other things, too, like catching her in lies. She told her friends they were getting married. She also told him she was pregnant but she wasn't. He made her do a test and it was negative. When he asked why she lied, she said she was afraid she was going to lose him."

"Does he have any kids?" Callum asked.

"No. You've made it perfectly clear you don't want those kinds of cases—which you still haven't told me why." Charles looked out the window again. "I meant what I said about keeping things bottled up, Callum."

"When do I go?" He didn't like talking about why he never took mother-child cases. Charles tried to get him to every once in a while and Callum believed that Charles was concerned about him. He had become a good friend, aside from being Callum's boss.

"He's local. That's how he heard of you."

"Me?"

"Yeah. He asked for you by name. You'll be working with his usual security team."

"He doesn't think his own team will be enough?" What kind of woman had this new client broken up with?

Charles walked back to his desk and picked up a folder. "I

printed these out for you. I also emailed them. You'll understand more after you read it. He's out of the country right now, but asked if you could stay at his place next month."

Callum took the file. "Thanks." Charles knew he liked studying cases on paper more than on a screen. Some things were still better offline, like holding a book instead of a tablet.

"Any news on your father?" Charles asked.

"He's still in a coma. I'm heading over to the hospital after I go see my brother." Payne Colton had been shot after receiving a bizarre email containing the shocking news about Ace. He didn't say which brother he was going to see, since Ace was still a suspect in Payne's shooting. When Callum and his twin sister—current Colton Oil CEO Marlowe—had visited Mustang Valley General Hospital last month, they were told that a fire broke out the morning of Ace's birth and destroyed all records.

With one more look out the window that told him the car and the man were still there, Callum bade Charles farewell and left the building. But he couldn't stop thinking about that parent and child. He couldn't explain why he needed to make sure she was all right. A sixth sense told him something was off about the stranger in the car. Even though he had sworn off guarding families, he couldn't ignore this. He'd make sure the woman and her daughter were okay and then he'd be on his way.

Hazel Hart took her now-cheerful daughter's hand and walked with her toward the SUV. Earlier Evie had fussed about being told she could not go for ice cream today. Hazel's schedule was far too busy. But Evie liked passing out cookies to Hazel's clients. Hazel had told her five-year-old she could sample one with them. That had taken care of the ice cream tantrum.

Hazel glanced around. The street was quiet. This area of town didn't get much traffic. On the edge of Mustang Valley, there was a lot of new development and not much commercial business. The back of the strip mall across the street hid most of the activity there, though landscaping along the sidewalk made it more palatable for residents. The client she'd just left enjoyed the convenience of Hazel's home deliveries, especially since she had been taken ill with breast cancer. The woman was going to be all right, but had hired Hazel to provide her meals while she recovered. The woman had family but they all lived out of state and she didn't like the food her neighbors prepared.

Hazel had left her job at an upscale restaurant several months ago to go off on her own as a personal chef. She preferred the independence and not having to work under someone else's thumb. Plus, she could always be with Evie, which was her most favorite thing in the world.

Reaching the SUV, Hazel unlocked it and had her hand on the back seat door handle when Evie said, "Mommy, what is that man doing?"

Hazel looked in the direction Evie pointed and saw a man in a blue sedan, wearing sunglasses and a baseball cap.

"Why did he hit that man over the head with a rock and put him in the car?"

Hazel turned sharply to Evie. "What?" She looked around and didn't see anything.

Evie pointed. "That man put another man in the trunk, Mommy."

Hazel felt a wave of apprehension sweep through her as she stared at the sedan. If the driver had struck a man unconscious and put him into the trunk, he could not have any good intentions. He started pulling out into the street way too quickly for Hazel's comfort.

Hazel memorized the license plate as the man began driving along the street, right toward them.

Reaching for Evie's hand, she went to pull her daughter onto the sidewalk. Evie dropped her Cookie Monster and bent to pick it up. Horror flared up in Hazel. She glanced up and saw the car was almost on them! They'd be run over!

"Evie—" Just then someone swooped Evie up and grabbed Hazel's hand, yanking her backward.

The stranger in the sedan continued to race for them. Hazel screamed, as did Evie, as a man hauled them behind her Mercedes and up onto the sidewalk. The other car whizzed past, taking out her Mercedes' driver-side mirror.

"Are you all right?"

Hazel pulled her hand from the man's, heart flying and struggling to catch her breath. A car had just tried to mow them down! The sound of the Mercedes mirror being torn off kept echoing in her mind.

She reached for a crying Evie. The heroic man handed her daughter over and Hazel held her tightly. "It's okay, baby. We're all right." She looked at the man as she answered his question.

Hazel checked up the street and saw no sign of the driver. Then she turned back to her hero. "Thank you."

He took out his phone and called 911.

Her adrenaline began to abate as Evie's crying softened. Smoothing the few tendrils of brunette hair that had fallen free from the two ponytails sticking out from the sides of Evie's head, she wiped her daughter's cheeks.

Looking over the child's shoulder, she saw the man as more than her rescuer. His reddish-blond hair was slightly wavy and he had strong facial features. He wore dark slacks with black leather loafers that had thick soles, and between the lapels of his black jacket she could see he had on a white shirt with the first two buttons undone. He finished telling the operator where they were and disconnected. Towering above her, he was probably six-three and had an athletic build.

"I'm Callum Colton," the handsome man said.

"Hazel Hart, and this is Evie, short for Evelyn."

Evie turned her head, still pouting, and looked at Callum.

"Hi, Evie. Are you okay?" Callum asked.

Evie nodded.

"That's an awfully cute stuffed monster you have there," he said.

"Her name is Cookie," Evie said, brightening.

He chuckled and glanced at Hazel, who became transfixed by his smile. "That's appropriate."

Well, whether he was a kid person or not, his tactics worked. Ever since Ed ran out on her after hearing she was pregnant, Hazel always wondered whether or not a man who caught her eyes liked children.

"I think Evie saw something," Hazel said. "She said a man hit another one over the head with a rock and put him into the trunk."

The faint sound of sirens joined the gentle hum of distant town movements. Hazel put Evie down and held her hand, needing to have contact with her. Having nearly been run down by a car had rattled them both. To think Evie could have been hurt, or worse…

"Did you see him, too?" Callum asked.

She shook her head. "He was in the car already when I saw him. I didn't get a good look at him. I did get the plate number, though."

"That's great." Then he asked Evie, "Can you describe the man?"

The little girl nodded. "Mm-hmm. He looked really mad."

"Mad?" Hazel asked, prompting her to elaborate.

Evie crowded her tiny eyebrows over eyes that were greener than her mother's. "Yeah." Evie nodded. "He looked like the man at the mall, Mommy."

Hazel met her daughter's round, innocent eyes, heart melting as usual at Evie's adorableness and also searching for the memory. Then she recalled a homeless man they had encountered at the edge of the parking lot. He had been dressed in heavy clothing and had a beard, a dark beard.

"Was the man you saw as hairy as the man in the parking lot earlier?" Hazel asked.

"No, he was not skinny. And no hair on his face."

The homeless man had been slim and had a beard. "The man she saw was average in height and weight," Hazel said.

The sirens were now a blaring howl and seconds later, fire trucks, police cars and ambulances converged upon them.

"I hope this doesn't take long." Hazel had to prepare meals for tomorrow's deliveries.

"You witnessed a crime," Callum said. "The man got away. What if he comes after you again? We need to catch this guy."

Hazel hadn't considered that. Police approached and, filled with intensifying apprehension, she had to turn away from Callum's unmistakable concern. Her meals could wait. She could get up early tomorrow and prepare them.

A woman in a tan blazer approached, her strides graceful, auburn hair flowing.

"Kerry," Callum greeted her. "Good to see you again."

"Callum, what are you doing here?" Kerry's blue eyes were direct and exuded confidence.

"My office is across the street. I saw a man in a car and thought it was suspicious."

He had? Hazel looked across the street at the one-story strip mall. One of the spaces must be where Callum worked.

"This is Hazel and Evie Hart," Callum said. "This is Detective Kerry Wilder. She's also my brother Rafe's fiancée."

Hazel shook the pretty woman's hand.

"Evie here saw the man when he got out of the car," Callum said.

"You did?" Kerry asked in a lighthearted tone, crouching before the girl. "What did you see?"

Evie huddled closer to Hazel's leg, bringing Cookie up to her face. She got bashful sometimes.

"She saw the driver of the car hit another man on the head and put him in the trunk," Hazel answered for her daughter.

Kerry straightened and began writing on a small notepad.

The detective with Kerry went to take photos of Hazel's broken mirror while Hazel described the man who had almost run them down. Then she gave the detective his plate number.

"All right. We're going to talk to neighbors and tenants of the commercial building to see if there are any other witnesses," Kerry said. "Why don't you stop by the station later so we can have a sketch artist draw the man you saw?"

Hazel nodded.

"Callum, you should come, too. You can probably help with the description."

Callum nodded once.

Detective Wilder put away her notepad. "Meanwhile, we'll have officers on the lookout for this car."

And whatever he had done with the man in his trunk. Hazel warded off a shiver. If he could hurt someone like that, what would he do to Evie?

"You should be careful until we locate him. Are you or your husband armed?"

"I'm not married," Hazel said, then saw Callum glance at her at that revelation.

"Maybe you should stay somewhere else," Kerry said. Then to Callum, "I don't think they should be alone tonight."

Callum looked a little startled by the suggestion, or that Kerry had directed the declaration at him, as though he should be the one to take care of them for the night.

"Do you have any family you can stay with?" Kerry asked Hazel.

They were all far away except her brother, but he was a two hour drive from here. She shook her head.

"Friends?"

All out of state. She didn't know anyone well enough here to impose on them like that. Again, she shook her head. "All my close friends are in Colorado and I haven't had time to make any here." She looked down at Evie, who consumed every spare moment she wasn't working.

"That man could have gotten your plate number the same as you got his. He might have a way to find out where you live," the detective said. "Maybe I'm being overly paranoid, but I'd rather you be safe."

That certainly unsettled her.

Detective Wilder smiled. "I'll let you be on your way. Think about staying somewhere other than your house tonight after we finish up with the sketch, okay? Maybe get a room at the Dales Inn."

"Okay."

"What about letting Evie go to the station with Kerry for her safety? In the meantime, I'll take you home to pack bags for both of you," Callum said.

Oh. Hazel hated being separated from Evie under such dire circumstances, but her daughter seemed entranced by Kerry's shiny badge and getting her own detective shield sticker.

Hazel hesitated. "Detective Wilder is the one with the gun..."

Kerry chimed in, "Maybe Callum can help out. He's an ex-Navy SEAL turned professional bodyguard."

Evie looked at Callum. "Are you going to catch the bad man?"

Callum didn't respond, just stared at Evie as though flustered. What about her question had caused such a reaction? He seemed to be frozen.

"What if he comes after us, like you said?" Evie asked.

"I shouldn't have said that in front of you," Callum said.

"Honey, Callum isn't a policeman. He is a bodyguard," Hazel said.

"What's a bodyguard?" Evie asked.

"Someone who protects people from bad men," Callum said.

Evie smiled big and again Hazel noticed a change in Callum, the way his body stiffened. "Then you can protect me and my mommy."

He smiled down at her. "I'll try."

Evie glanced down at her toy. "It's okay, Cookie," she said. "You're all right now. Just remember, it's wrong to hit and push. You should always be nice to other people."

Hazel reached over and put her hand on Evie's. "Now you're going to the station and I will go home and pack clothing for us."

"Okay, Mommy."

It was getting late, past six in the evening. "All right," Hazel said. "Let's go."

Detective Wilder joined her partner and Evie as they walked up the street.

"Let's go to your place," Callum suggested.

The abruptness stopped Hazel short. This man was a complete stranger.

"I'd like to talk a little more," he said. "And Kerry has a point. I'm worried that man will come after you. You got his plate number. He probably got yours. He could find you."

Why was he so concerned about her? He didn't even know her. "I'm a newbie with all this. What kinds of people do you usually work with?"

"My next client is Blake Reynolds."

"The country singer? Really? You must be some bodyguard. Are all your clients celebrities?"

"Oh, all right. Let's go."

The police were still working the neighborhood but the emergency vehicles had left a while ago. Callum drove Hazel in silence to her apartment, located above a bakery. Callum had arranged for someone to take her car in for repairs. She had left a key under the mat. She might drive a Mercedes but it was the lower end model and she had saved for a long time for a decent down payment. The money she made was just enough for her and Evie to get by. So far, being a personal chef didn't earn her huge income. Her business showed signs of picking up but she wasn't quite there yet.

When they arrived at her apartment, Callum passed the front and turned to go around to the back.

The first floor of the older building was a charming little bakery with a neon Open/Closed sign on the door, four old-fashioned, small round tables in the dining area and two booths against the window. The main feature was the display case… and, of course, the kitchen. The owner of Jasmine's Bakery let her cook her biggest batches there for a modest fee.

After Callum parked, Hazel walked from the rear parking space up the iron stairs. Unlocking her apartment door, she flipped on a light and entered, Callum behind her. "It isn't much. Just two bedrooms and not very big." She didn't know why she felt the need to explain that.

Callum didn't say anything as he stepped inside, looking around.

"When my ex, Ed, walked, I started saving for a house, but I also want money tucked away for Evie's college education."

Hazel found herself looking at him, his rugged, stubbly jaw, his thick, reddish-blond hair. Her gaze moved to his bright blue eyes…and stayed. He had been watching her study his face and now his eyes flared with something more than friendliness. A spark of heat flashed inside her.

How could just a look do that to her? Did he feel it too? Granted, he was hot, but she had seen other attractive men, and none of them had caused this reaction.

"So, you're an ex-Navy SEAL and now you're a bodyguard," Hazel said by way of breaking the awkward moment. "If you're going to protect me and my daughter, I should know more than that about you."

"I'm surprised that's all you know about me," he said. "I am, after all, a Colton."

The name did sound familiar but not familiar enough. "I may have heard the name before. I haven't lived here my whole life."

"Given the news lately, you probably have. Payne Colton is my father."

Hazel searched her memory but still nothing stuck. "I'm sorry. I don't watch the news. I try to keep it away from Evie. I don't think it's healthy for a five-year-old to hear about murders and lying politicians. And besides that, I have a very busy schedule. We do watch a lot of family movies and listen to country, though." She smiled. "You might have to introduce us to Blake Reynolds."

He chuckled. "I can't believe it."

What couldn't he believe? That she didn't watch the news or that she didn't know him by name? She couldn't detect conceit. He wasn't bragging about being a Colton, just surprised she hadn't heard of them.

"My father is chairman of the board of Colton Oil and owns Rattlesnake Ridge Ranch just outside of town. But we do all work hard for our money," he said.

Then it dawned on her. She had heard of a man who had been shot and was now in a coma, a prominent local rancher and businessman gunned down for no apparent reason. She hadn't paid any further attention to the story. Until now.

"Oh, I'm so sorry," she finally said. Callum came from lots of money, then. Hazel felt herself stiffen and erect a barrier. She was from a very humble background and her last encounter with a rich guy hadn't turned out so great.

"Don't be."

"I grew up in a small Colorado mountain town where everyone knew everyone and there were no conveniences, no big-box stores, no chain restaurants or movie theaters. We lived outside of town on several acres in a small colonial. I spent my childhood reading or watching satellite television and going to community events with my older brother and our parents."

"Sounds charming."

His handsome grin disarmed her a moment. She should go pack but she didn't feel she knew enough about him to stay with him yet. And if her daughter was going to be near him for the unforeseeable future…

"In some ways. But growing up that way made me a little naive. I met Evie's father, Ed, when I went to college and moved to Arizona with him. When I got pregnant, he left."

"How does that make you naive?"

Edgar Lovett had lied to her about almost everything about himself. The only thing he hadn't lied about was his college degree. "I should have known he wasn't reliable. I had never met anyone so experienced at duping people. He wasn't at all what he pretended to be. He told me he came from an average family and that his parents were dead."

He also told her that he had never been married before. "I didn't find out until after he left that he was the son of a wealthy Arizona senator and his parents were very much alive. He also was married before we met in college. He divorced his secret wife before I met him and we moved to Arizona."

Hazel didn't know why he had lied. She could only guess he had done so because he was afraid she was using him for his money. The last she had heard, he was living in Florida off his trust fund. Hazel had tried to get child support but he always evaded the attempts. Eventually she gave up and chalked him up as a deadbeat dad, albeit a wealthy one. She didn't have to be told he had abandoned her and Evie because he was incapable of accepting any real responsibility. She wanted to thank him for leaving instead of putting her through a life of struggle with a man like him. She also held a lot of animosity toward him, a man who could have easily afforded to help her out but had not. What kind of person did that? And how had she never seen that about him?

"You weren't naive," Callum said. "I bet he liked you, maybe even loved you, but he must have known you had higher expectations than he could deliver on when it comes to making a family. He misled you because he was probably tired of being identified as a senator's son."

Of course, she thought the same, except her expectations were pretty simple. She didn't require anyone rich or anyone with specific personality traits. She only wanted someone decent. She had told Ed she wanted a good and honest man like her father had been, like so many other men she had grown up around.

"Why bother lying, though, about who he was and about his ex-wife?" Hazel still wanted to know, to this day. "He must have known the truth would come out eventually." Hazel would have left him after learning about his deception.

"You're a beautiful woman, Hazel. Any man would be a fool not to want you."

Ed had lied in order to have her, even if for just a little while. He had never talked about marriage with her, a fact she'd only thought of after he was gone. Then she realized what Callum had just said. Did *he* want her?

"What about you?" she asked, flirting back.

"I've never been married," he said, "and I'm not lying about that." He grinned.

She laughed lightly and briefly, believing him. It was easy to talk with him. Feeling much more comfortable with him, she stopped herself from enjoying this too much. Hadn't she just finished telling him about the biggest mistake she ever made with a man? She would never regret Evie, obviously, but Evie's father was nothing to brag about. She'd rather not wind up having to say the same thing about Callum—or any man. And despite knowing she was biased, she didn't trust anyone wealthy.

"You better get packing," Callum said.

Yes. They'd better pack—rather than play on their attraction to one other.

Chapter 2

Callum leaned against the door frame of Evie's bedroom, watching Hazel pack a bag. She glanced up and saw him.

"Bored?" Her eyes glowed a green hint of her name. Long and dark, finger-tempting wavy hair fell over slender shoulders and framed a remarkably pretty face. Tendrils of that silky splendor curled around melon-shaped breasts. He felt his defenses rise. She had a *daughter*. A really cute one.

"No." He would just rather stare at her. This sudden chemistry threw him off balance.

With a soft smile, she resumed packing.

In just the brief time he had been around Evie— rescuing her, watching her fascination with Kerry and then her bravery in going with the detective—the child had already touched his heart. Now he knew more than ever why he tried so hard to avoid protecting kids. The mothers were another issue completely.

Evie had punched her way through his usual, iron-walled barrier. She was about the same age his daughter would have been, had she and her mother survived. Callum shook off the thoughts.

He was better shutting that off, contrary to what Charles said. Despite his cardinal rule never to protect mothers with kids, to leave that up to other bodyguards who didn't share a history similar to his, he could not leave them at the mercy of a man who knew Evie had witnessed him dump a body in a trunk. Now here he was, in Hazel and Evie's apartment, about to take them to the Dales Inn and live with them for however long it took to catch the bad guy.

Hazel finished packing for Evie and went into her bedroom to do the same for herself. Callum followed, she wasn't sure whether out of boredom or because he just enjoyed watching her. The way he did made her acutely aware of him as a man.

"I bet my room is much smaller than the one you sleep in," she said, still self-conscious of his wealth and her bad experience with a man with money.

Callum eyed her peculiarly. "It's a nice apartment. And even though I'm a Colton, I don't dwell on the wealth of my family."

She believed that, but he also must have a sizable bank account, maybe a trust fund or something like that. Just like Ed. That put a sour taste in her mouth.

Taking the bags to the dining area next to the back entry, she saw Callum go to the mantel above the gas fireplace. She had an electronic photo album there. He gestured with his hand to it. "These are great."

There were lots of pictures of Evie doing all things Evie. Evie with a toothy smile and mouth smeared with ice cream. Evie holding a bunny rabbit. Evie riding a pony with Hazel. Evie and a friend dressed identically and striking a pose. Hazel and Evie cheek to cheek in a selfie. And so many more. Vacations Hazel had saved for, trips to Disney World and Yellowstone. Them at community events.

As he watched the pictures change, his expression changed. What about these photos put such a look of sadness on his face? She wanted to ask but didn't.

"She's the best thing that ever happened to me," she said instead. "Ed taking off the way he did doesn't even matter anymore. I mean, it did when I was pregnant. What kind of man can abandon their unborn baby?"

Callum didn't say anything, just continued to look at the pictures.

"As soon as Evie was born, everything changed. I didn't care about Ed anymore. She became my world. And she's such a good kid. Even when she was a baby. She didn't cry much, only when she needed something. She slept all night and still does. She rarely has tantrums and when she does, they're over pretty quickly. I'm a lucky mom."

Callum turned to look at her, some of the sadness leaving his eyes. "She's an adorable girl."

"Do you want kids some day?"

"I travel a lot. Usually I'm out of the country on assignments."

He must be some bodyguard. "Do you protect a lot of affluent people?"

"Yes, and high targets for kidnapping in countries where that sort of thing happens."

Dignitaries, politicians and executives for big companies, she supposed.

"I'm only here now to be near my father."

His father had been shot. That must be so difficult, not knowing whether his dad would wake up or not. Callum must be close to his father if he'd changed his work schedule to be by the man's side. She wondered if he regretted helping her, since she obviously was taking time away from his hospital visits.

"If you need to be with him…"

"I'll visit him. I don't have to be with him all the time. I do still have to work, after all. Just not out of state."

Hazel smiled because this was the chattiest he had been since they met.

"You must be close to him," Hazel said, thinking she had made an accurate observation.

"Actually, I'm not," he said, and regret seemed to come over him.

With him out of the country so much, Hazel could see why, but what about when he had been younger? "Was it always that way?"

"Yes. When I was a kid he was always working, and I had my own ideas about what I wanted to do with my life. I knew early on that I never would be an executive like he was." He paused. "Is."

She felt terrible. "If not for me, you would be with him right now."

"No. I was going to visit my brother, but I saw you and…"

And what? He saw her when? Before she had gone into her client's house? And then he had seen that car. She'd changed his plans for the day.

"Which brother?"

"Ace." He shook his head and scratched his forehead in angst. "He's a suspect in my father's shooting. We were never close, either, like with Dad. He followed my dad into the oil business. But I feel for him, you know? He just found out he's not a Colton by blood and there's this clause in the Colton Oil bylaws that says the CEO must be a Colton by blood, and then Dad got shot and everybody thinks he did it—geez, why am I telling you all of this?" He walked toward the back door and the luggage.

Hazel caught up to him and put her hand on his forearm, stopping him from bending to pick up one of the bags. "Hey, it's okay. I like hearing this."

"You like hearing about all my family drama?"

That's all he worried about? She breathed a laugh. "Every family has drama. Why is your brother a suspect?"

"My father had to fire him because of the bylaws. He did it in front of the board, and Ace didn't react well. He threatened my dad."

"How did he threaten him?" With a gun? Had he said he'd better watch his back or something? Ruin his reputation?

"Ace told Dad he would regret it and stormed out of the room."

"That doesn't mean he shot him."

"I know. I don't think he did, but he shouldn't have threatened him like that, and in front of the board."

Hazel could see he was genuinely concerned for his half brother, despite his claim of not being close to Ace. Just because he had spent a lot of time overseas didn't necessarily mean a family bond didn't exist. Hazel wondered if they were closer than he thought.

"You're easy to talk to," he said after a while, his smile rueful. Did he not open up to anyone? Why had he done so with her?

"Evie doesn't think so."

He chuckled a little. "I saw her arguing with you when you first got to your client's house. I think she does listen to you."

"Like I said, she's a good kid."

"She must have a good mother."

Hazel fell into his eyes, the warm regard there, the attraction. She felt it, too, these underlying sparks that had grown since the moment she saw him.

Once again stopping the sparks, Hazel asked, "So, tell me about this family of yours. You seemed to know that detective, Kerry."

"I come from a large blended family. My father married three times. I have a half sister and two half brothers—including Ace—from the first marriage. He had none with the second, and my mother had me and my twin sister, Marlowe, plus our brother, Asher. Rafe is my younger adopted brother. He's engaged to Kerry. That's how I know her."

"Ah. She's part of the family now. She's very pretty," Hazel said.

"And smart. And tenacious. She's a rookie but Rafe swears she's as good as a seasoned detective."

"I did get that impression of her, well, short of knowing her, that is. She just had a way about her."

"If anybody can find the man who almost ran you down, she can."

Hazel fell silent, not liking the thought of that. A man capable of hurting or killing another human—especially a child—was a dangerous one, for sure.

"You're a twin?" Hazel asked. "What is that like?"

"We're more like a regular brother and sister, but closer. We were close growing up and still are."

"Are you similar?"

He chuckled at that. "Not at all. Her hair is blonder than mine and she has brown eyes. She's now the CEO of Colton Oil, an executive type. Workaholic." Callum was definitely not an executive type. He was driven in different ways. "But she's pregnant and engaged now, so that will probably change. She's still going to keep her job but she's starting a day-care program."

Hazel seemed to ponder that awhile, as though doubtful that a woman like that could change.

"I technically have one less sibling now—even though I still consider Ace my half brother. Ace's switch has caused a bit of chaos in the family," he said.

She breathed a tiny laugh at his sarcastic tone. "It sounds dramatic. Who switched him and why?"

"We don't know yet."

"That must be hard for him to face," Hazel said.

He fell silent and Hazel sensed he had given out enough family information for now. Then he just nodded and said, "Yes, it is."

"What made you decide to leave the navy and become a bodyguard?" Hazel asked to change the subject.

"I was getting too old to be a SEAL."

At his short, simplistic reply, she wondered if he didn't want to discuss this. He seemed reluctant to talk about anything personal.

"How old is too old?" she asked anyway.

"I'm thirty-two. Right now, I'm not taking out-of-state assignments, so I can be close to my dad."

"I'm twenty-five," she said. "Have you been married or in any serious relationships?"

She had confessed her failed serious relationship, so that justified her asking the question. "No to marriage. Yes to a relationship, but it didn't work out."

"What happened?"

"It didn't work out," he repeated, turning his head and not looking at her anymore.

She watched the tension on his face for a few seconds, then said, "Sorry. I didn't mean to pry."

"We should get going to the police station. Why don't we go get her and head to the hotel?" Callum said.

She wanted to get to Evie as soon as possible—and slow down whatever was happening between her and Callum.

Waiting for Hazel to finish getting ready to leave, Callum struggled with what her questions had brought to the surface. Shortly after he had left the SEAL team, he had lost Annabel. He never talked about her and their unborn baby. After she died, he had told everyone they'd broken up. He couldn't bear to face the truth and he didn't like people asking him about her. No one had enquired about her in a long time, which probably explained the heavy emotion he felt right now.

When Hazel joined him at the back door, Callum left the apartment, carrying two of her bags with one hand, leaving the other free. He searched the parking area behind the bakery and at first everything seemed quiet. But then he saw someone sitting in a car parked at the end of one of the rows. It was different than the one that had nearly mowed down Evie and Hazel; this one was white with tinted windows. He couldn't see the person inside, but the shape had the form of a man.

Alarmed that someone might try to harm Hazel again, he said, "Go back inside, Hazel."

"What?" Her eyes searched his face beneath lowered eyebrows.

"I need to check out that car over there. Go back inside." He had to keep her safe and she'd be safest in there for now.

Hazel looked out into the parking lot. "Oh, no."

"It might not be anything. Just let me check it out," he said as reassuringly as he could. He didn't mean to frighten her.

She turned and went back inside. He saw her go to the window next to the door and watch.

Callum stepped down the stairs, leaving the bags on the landing by the door. He walked to his truck and started it, then drove closer to the building. There, he waited a few moments. The driver of the other car pulled out of the parking space and drove down the alley toward the street.

Getting out of the truck, Callum went to help Hazel as she came out of the apartment and locked the door. He searched the parking lot and alley, keeping his body between the direction the car had gone and Hazel. He picked up the two bags and followed her down. At the passenger door, he opened that and waited for her to get in, continuing to watch for the mysterious car.

Putting the bags in the back seat, he got behind the wheel and started driving.

At the street he pulled out into traffic, glancing frequently into the rearview mirror. As he suspected, the stranger had waited for them.

Hazel twisted to look behind them. "Is that car following us?"

"Yes."

"Is it the same man?"

"I don't know." Callum turned a corner to see if the stranger would follow.

He did.

Callum turned another corner and the stranger turned, too.

He was two vehicles behind them. Callum couldn't see the man clearly.

He decided to drive to the police station. Who in their right mind would try anything in front of a police station? Someone out of their mind…?

Hoping to get a better look at the man, Callum slowed down.

"What are you doing?" Hazel asked in a scared tone.

"I want to see if we can identify him." He watched in the rearview mirror as the vehicle behind him got into the right lane and passed them. The second car moved over next. The white sedan slowed with Callum, maintaining distance. Whoever was driving wouldn't risk being seen up close.

Not wanting to incite the man into drawing a gun or doing anything else that might endanger Hazel, Callum sped up and drove the rest of the way to the station. As they made the turn into the parking lot, the other car drove by. Callum stopped his truck and looked out his window. He saw a man who probably was about six feet tall. He had a hoodie and wore sunglasses—at night—and looked right at him, lights from the dash meagerly reflecting on him.

Callum waited until the white car disappeared from view, having memorized the plate number.

He parked. "Wait for me. Don't get out."

Hazel stayed in the truck and Callum opened the door for her, looking for the white car. Then he put his arm around her and walked with her to the front entrance. Inside, he turned to the glass doors and watched for a few minutes. The car didn't reappear.

He heard Hazel ask for Detective Wilder and turned from the door. A short while later Kerry appeared from a hallway.

"Evie is looking at mugshots," Kerry said. "I thought you both should have a look as well. Right this way." She waved her hand in encouragement.

Callum followed Hazel and Kerry down a hall to an office where Evie was perched on a desk chair that all but swallowed her. Seeing her mother, she hopped down and ran over on her little legs.

"Mommy!"

Hazel picked her up for a hug. "Hi, sweetie. Did you have fun?"

"Yes. The artist is really good. He said he likes his job." Her innocent eyes were wide with excitement.

"Oh, really?"

"And I looked at pictures of bad people."

The kid would probably go down hard when Hazel put her to bed. Who needed sugar when you had such an active imagination? Evie definitely needed a lot of stimulation mentally. She would probably do great in school. He often wondered what his daughter would have been like. Who would she have been? What would her personality have been like? His personality or her mother's?

Callum went over to Kerry and told her about the white car, glad for the distraction. She went to the computer where Evie had been "working" and must have navigated somewhere that would tell her about the car.

"Reported stolen this afternoon," she said.

Damn. The stranger was being very careful. Callum didn't like how he had followed them. He had found where Hazel lived. What if he found them at the inn? He felt enormous pressure to keep Hazel and Evie safe, more so than his usual clients. This seemed more personal.

Before that thought could cause him some heartburn, he went with Hazel to the computer, where Kerry brought up the mugshots. They spent about an hour going through those, but none of them looked familiar. They also couldn't say with any certainty that any of those who had the same type of build might be a potential suspect. Evie's assessment was their best shot at this point.

He'd been so consumed with protecting Hazel and Evie that

he hadn't asked Kerry about the progress of the investigation into his father's shooting.

"Hey, have you gotten any further on finding Nan Gelman?" Nan was a nurse who'd been working on the maternity ward at Mustang Valley General Hospital the day Ace had been born—and swapped with another baby. Though the hospital's records had burned, the Coltons were trying to track down Nan to find out what had happened that day.

Kerry made a disgruntled sound. "No. I found a Gelman living in Mountain Valley, but they aren't related to Nan. No one in that family worked at the hospital."

Maybe he'd see what he could dig up. "I might be able to help. My company has resources that you may not have access to."

She brightened. "That would be great."

"Detective Wilder?" Callum looked up and saw an officer in the doorway. "We have a body. It might be related to the near hit and run."

Kerry indicated for Callum and Hazel to follow.

Hazel looked at Callum. "Evie should probably have a tour of the station or something." She should not hear about a dead body.

An officer approached at Kerry's gesture and Evie happily went off to resume her fun-filled day at the police station.

Callum and Hazel went into a conference room, where other detectives had gathered.

"Kerry's here now," the chief of police, Al Barco, said. Fifty-two, mostly bald and with a slight paunch, he had calm, kind green eyes, despite his commanding nature.

And a man started talking through the speakerphone on the long table. "Hi, Kerry. It's Dane Howman."

"Hey, Howman. What have you got for me?"

"A hiker found a body on the banks of a river a few miles from where Evie saw him put in the trunk. Preliminary forensics suggests the cause of death was blunt force trauma to the head. He had a wallet and an ID. It's Nate Blurge."

"I know that guy," one of the other officers in the room said. "He's a wild twenty-six-year-old, been arrested three times for drunk and disorderly conduct. Practically lives at Joe's Bar and always gets into fights."

"Could one of the people he crossed have killed him?" Hazel asked.

"That's a possibility," Kerry said. "It's where we'll start in the investigation."

Hazel looked over at Callum and he could feel her worry. How long would the investigation take? How long would she have to be on high alert?

"I'll find the killer as fast as I can so you and Evie can have your lives back," Kerry said.

Hazel answered with a slight smile that was more of a silent thank-you than anything else. The reassurance didn't alleviate the fear, and Callum's determination to protect them with all the skill he'd gained over the years redoubled.

Rejoining Evie, Hazel flashed back to Callum's reaction when she had asked him about his past relationships. Clearly something bad. It bothered her that he had trouble talking about something personal like that and also made her doubly curious.

Again, both she and Callum added what little information they could to the description of the killer. Right now her daughter was transfixed by Kerry's badge.

"I've booked out one of the two-bedroom suites at the Dales Inn," Callum said.

Hazel looked at him, startled. "You mean…you and me and…" In one suite? "I can't afford that."

"I can. Don't worry."

She kind of did worry, but she decided not to argue. Keeping Evie safe was most important to her. He put his hand over his chest. "I'm a bodyguard. Consider this a professional courtesy. No charge." Now he opened his arms in offering, and oh, what an offering.

She stared at him for long seconds. “Oh, I don’t—”

Hazel felt some trepidation at staying with a man she had only just met. Nearly being killed had frightened her but this was all happening so fast. Her routine had been disrupted.

“Actually,” Detective Wilder said, removing her badge and handing it to Evie, who took it and felt the top, “Until we find Blurge’s killer, I think you should stay at the Dales Inn with Callum.”

More than one night? “I don’t—”

“I’ve already offered my services as a bodyguard,” Callum cut in again.

Hazel hesitated.

“You’re in good hands, Hazel. He is one of the best bodyguards in the country. His company is known for that. They have a solid reputation. You can trust him.”

That made her feel marginally better, but it seemed excessive. And with a stranger.

Bodyguard.

She supposed if she thought of him that way…

“You would be my bodyguard?” she asked him.

“Yours and Evie’s.”

Hazel glanced at Kerry, still uncertain but wavering. “He isn’t a policeman.” Callum might be six-three and solid muscle, but cops carried guns.

“He’s licensed to carry a firearm.” Kerry looked at Callum, who moved his jacket aside to reveal the gun in a hip holster.

When Hazel said nothing, just looked over at Evie, Kerry added, “There isn’t an officer in this department who wouldn’t vouch for him. He does work for a top personal protection agency. Really, I can’t say enough good about him.”

Hazel put her hand to her forehead. “This is so sudden.” She lowered her hand and looked at Evie. The sketch artist handed her a detective shield sticker, which put a big smile on her face. She peeled the back off the sticker and stuck it to the left side of her chest.

"Hey, Detective Evie." Hazel went to her and crouched where she sat at Kerry's desk. Evie beamed, no doubt imagining she was a detective and would go to work just now. "We're going to stay at a hotel tonight. It'll be a vacation."

Evie nodded, looking at Kerry, who had put her badge back on, clearly distracted.

Chapter 3

Having confirmation that the man Evie saw being dumped into a car trunk was dead unsettled Hazel much more than she'd anticipated. Evie had seen the man knocked over the head with a rock. They didn't know if that had killed him. Sure, she had contemplated the possibility, even the likelihood, but having it become fact put them up against a killer. *A killer!*

Callum held the station door for her and Evie, whom she held since her eyes were drooping with the late hour. She saw him scan their surroundings. He put his hand on her back protectively and then his head stopped moving. She followed his gaze and saw a white car drive past the station again and then turn the corner. Apparently the vehicle had been circling the block while they were inside.

"Go and get Kerry," Callum said. "Hurry."

Hazel turned and walked quickly back to the door. When inside, she saw Callum had drawn his gun and was watching the street.

"Is something wrong?"

Hazel heard Detective Wilder and faced her. "The white car

that followed us here is still out there. He's going around the block." Just then Hazel spotted the car in front of the station on the street, driving slowly. Callum took cover behind his truck.

Kerry hollered for two other officers and ran out the front door.

"Mommy?" Evie said sleepily.

"It's okay, honey. Go back to sleep." Hazel hoped it would be all right.

Evie rested her head on Hazel's shoulder and closed her eyes. Hazel didn't have time to savor the sight.

Callum opened the station door as Hazel saw Kerry racing away in her car, two other officers following.

"Let's get you out of here," Callum said. "Kerry's on his tail."

She carried Evie out the door.

Callum stayed close to her side with his pistol. At his truck, he opened the back door and guarded them while Hazel put Evie in the car seat he had thoughtfully put in there. Then he opened the passenger door and guarded Hazel again while she got in. Going around to the other side, he got behind the wheel and drove quickly out of the parking lot.

A few minutes later they arrived at the Dales Inn. Hazel knew it was upscale but she had never been this close before. Its grandeur towered before her, the double wooden doors with oval windows welcoming guests to promised luxury. A parking valet gave Callum a ticket.

"Welcome, Mr. Colton," the valet said and then nodded to Hazel. "Ma'am."

"Callum Colton?" a bellboy asked.

"Yes," Callum answered.

"I'll take care of your bags."

"Thank you."

All Hazel had to do was carry a sleeping Evie inside.

The richness of majestic white columns and dark polished stone floors beneath a high, ornately trimmed ceiling engulfed her. Numbly she walked to the reception desk with Callum.

"We're checking in to a two-bedroom suite, please."

Hazel thought about protesting again, but her anxiety over the driver of the white car stopped her. That and Detective Wilder's unwavering praise of Callum's good character.

He took the room keys, then guided Hazel with his hand on her lower back, something that was becoming a habit for him. Strangely, Hazel didn't mind. She wasn't accustomed to a man doting on her the way Callum did. She had always taken care of herself. He might be doing all of that as her bodyguard, but she still liked it. She felt pampered.

They rode the elevator to the top floor with the bellboy and their luggage. Her luggage. Hazel looked at the cart the bellboy had gotten and saw two additional bags. She looked up at Callum in question, Evie's warm breaths touching her neck.

"I arranged for my things to be brought here."

Who had he called? And when? He must have done so while he waited for her to pack. No doubt his family had all kinds of people who did such things for them. Hazel had a funny feeling about that. Ed had hidden his wealth from her, so he had never taken her to places like this, but his lies had hurt. She wouldn't fall so easily for anyone again. Not that she was falling for Callum. He was extremely handsome, that's all. What woman could be immune to that? It was like staring at a beautiful painting, unable to look away until she'd had her fill of the pleasure.

In the posh hallway, Callum stopped at a room door and unlocked it. Then he held the door for Hazel and the bellboy.

"Go ahead and put my bags in the room with one king," Callum said to the bellboy.

"Yes, sir." The bellboy walked down the hall and Hazel followed.

Going into the other bedroom, Hazel drew the covers back on the far queen bed and gently laid Evie on the sheets. She touched her daughter's sleeping face as the bellboy brought in her bags.

"Thanks," she said.

"You're welcome. Enjoy your stay at the Dales Inn." The young man left and Hazel shut the door before undressing Evie.

It was a bit of a challenge to get her daughter into pj's but she finally succeeded without waking her. The poor kid was exhausted.

Hazel unpacked both of their bags, hanging some clothes and putting some in drawers. She put Evie's toys on one of the chairs in front of the draperies and then spread Evie's favorite soft blanket over her. Leaning down, she kissed her daughter's forehead.

Going out to the main room, she saw Callum on his phone, standing between a four-seater dining table and a sectional that faced a gas fireplace with a TV over it. He talked to someone as he faced the corner windows, Mustang Valley town lights sparkling outside.

There were some things on the table, a computer and other equipment. As she neared, she saw three GPS tracking devices, several USB drives. Some devices looked high tech, others had tiny screens, and she saw bulletproof vests, one small enough to fit Evie. Now she knew why he had two bags.

"All right. Keep me informed," he said and then disconnected.

Hazel went to the four bar stools at a marble-topped kitchen island with a sink in the middle. Three pretty orange-gold pendants hung from the ceiling. A four-burner gas stove with a microwave above was on the other side, and there were cabinets on both sides. It even had a pantry.

She put her hands on the back of one of the chairs. "This is very nice. I'm more of a two- or three-star hotel kind of girl." Not a fiver.

He chuckled. "We need the space and you need a kitchen. Think of it as a home away from home."

Hazel had told him she was a chef on the way to the Dales Inn but not much else. Leaving the chair, she went around the island and began going through the cabinets. The kitchen was fully stocked with all the equipment she would need. "The only things missing are food and spices."

"Make a list and I'll have that delivered in the morning."

With the snap of a finger he'd do that? "Then I'll pay you."

"No, you won't. I want you to relax and have as much semblance of your normal routine as possible. Don't worry about anything other than doing your job and taking care of Evie. I'll do the rest."

Finished checking out the kitchen, seeing it had pretty much everything, she walked to the impressive windows. Mustang Valley looked bigger than she had always thought of it from here.

"Why are you doing this?" she asked.

She heard him walk up behind her and stop beside her. "I was there when the man tried to run you over."

He had already indicated as much, but she wanted to know why he was here with her. Why had he offered his services, free of charge?

"Why this?" She turned as she swept her arm out into the room, facing him. "Why is it so important for you to help us?"

She met his incredibly blue eyes while he considered his reply.

"I don't know," he finally said. "When I first saw you, I had no intention of going out to meet you, but then I saw that car with the driver and instincts kicked in. This is what I do, Hazel."

That sounded truthful enough. Why, then, did she have this feeling that it was more personal than that?

"Kerry called. She lost the white car," Callum said, pulling her thoughts elsewhere. "She said the driver must know the town well. Otherwise he might not have gotten away as easily as he did."

Hazel bit her lower lip in consternation. The killer had gotten away. Where was he now? Lurking outside? Did he already know they were here? Picturing Evie's sweet sleeping face, she released her lip with a long sigh. If the killer knew the town well, he'd know the Dales Inn was the only hotel in Mustang Valley.

Feeling as though someone could see them through the windows, she went to stand by the dining table.

Callum went to the other side. "I sleep light, so don't worry. And if you have any lingering doubt as to why I'm doing this, now you shouldn't. I couldn't leave a dog in danger like this."

She believed that his work was second nature to him, but she still thought there was more to him than that, more that drew him to her and Evie, maybe even something he hadn't acknowledged himself. Yet.

Looking down at all the items on the table, she pointed to the vests. "I take it we're going to be wearing those?"

"Whenever we leave the inn. They're knife- and bulletproof and made with poly-cotton netting that breathes to keep you cool or warm, depending on the weather. You can wear them underneath your clothes. They're comfortable."

Very high tech. And she would feel so much better knowing Evie would be protected as best as she could.

"What will you do with the USB drives?" she asked.

"Some are listening devices, others are cameras. One is for deleted file recovery." He gestured to the USB devices. "We'll put a GPS in your car, purse and Evie's backpack. They all have extended battery life."

Hazel couldn't bear to think she or Evie might be abducted, but Callum would know where they were if it happened. He wasn't taking any chances. She couldn't imagine they would need to recover any deleted files in order to find the killer. Maybe that was another precautionary measure Callum had taken.

"I've got some night vision goggles and extra guns and ammo in the bag. I'll keep those in a safe place."

Out of Evie's curious hands. That was comforting. Hazel met his eyes, thinking she could never get tired of doing so. She could stare at them for an hour and float on a cloud of infatuation. How many other handsome men had she seen and not had such a strong reaction? She had been quite attracted to Ed, but she had never felt this way with him. Callum might be ruggedly gorgeous but Hazel didn't think he'd be a good match for her.

What made a good match? She did not know him at all, at least, not very well. He physically attracted her. What would she do with that? What if she had no control over what was between them?

Why are you doing this?

Why is it so important for you to help us?

Those two questions that Hazel had asked kept repeating in his mind and he couldn't shut off the voice. He was tired of hearing it. Mostly he was tired of wondering why and feeling somewhere deep inside that he already knew the answers.

He opened the drawer of the built-in desk next to the kitchen, looking for a notepad and pen. Hazel had gone to sit on the sectional. It was getting late but she needed to give him a list of kitchen necessaries so he could have everything she needed by morning.

He had been truthful when he had told her instinct had taken over. Instinct had made him walk across the street to check on the mysterious car. He hadn't really thought much beyond that, but now here he was, guarding a woman and her child.

Finding a notepad and pen, he brought it to Hazel and sat beside her. "Here you go. Make your list."

She tapped the pen lightly against her lower lip awhile before finally beginning to write down ingredients.

Callum studied her profile, sloping nose and full lips. Long lashes low over hazel-green eyes. He let his gaze travel lower, noticing a button on her white blouse had come loose and exposed more of her cleavage. She was a stunning woman.

He turned his attention to her growing list.

"Do you have regulars?"

"Yes. I'm a personal chef," she answered without pausing in her writing.

Leaning over he started reading the list. "Are the ingredients all meat and potatoes?"

Smiling she slid a glance toward him. "No. Some are chicken and mashed potatoes."

He chuckled. "I could do that job."

"I also have clients who want things like shrimp and scallop scampi. Roasted chicken au jus. Seafood-stuffed salmon. Steak. Lobster. Vegetable dishes. Fruit."

He would like to try a few of her concoctions. But since he barely knew her, he didn't mention it.

"What made you decide to become a chef?" he asked.

She smiled softly. "My mother cooked all the time. I grew up with delicious smells wafting from the kitchen."

"You never told me about your family. You know all about mine and I know nothing about yours." That wasn't fair. He felt safe asking her, not too personal.

"Not much to tell," she said. "My parents are both from Pagosa Springs, Colorado. They knew each other in high school but didn't get together until after college. My brother is a cop and lives in Phoenix with his wife's family."

"I'm sure there is more to tell than that."

She smiled in that soft way again. "Are you looking for drama?"

"You did say every family has it." He was starting to love this banter.

She laughed once. "Um…let's see…well, there was the time when my brother skipped school to smoke pot with his friends. My parents flipped. They were afraid he would drop out of school or be kicked out and his whole future would be in ruins. But it turned out he just went through a phase. He rebelled for a year and then got his grades back up and went on to college."

To become a cop. Her family drama paled in comparison to his. "What about you? Did you ever rebel?"

"No. I was never good at math or the sciences, but I managed a B average. Art was my forte. I oil painted, drew in lead and colored pencils. My paintings were often displayed in the school hall outside the art room. My parents worried I'd never make a comfortable income. They sat me down for a talk my senior year and said, 'Hey, look, you might not be able to support yourself.' Their way of saying they were convinced I'd be the clichéd starving artist." She laughed. "I suppose I am still, in some ways."

He liked that she smiled and laughed so much. He smiled and laughed, too, at least he thought he did.

"You were an artist and became a chef," he said. "How did you go from one to the other?"

That made her think a moment, tipping her head up a bit, eyes lifting in search of an answer. He could see the flecks of green glowing.

"I think the talk with my parents influenced me," she said. "I went to college for interior design, but one of my optional classes was culinary. That's what changed everything. I loved the art of making plates look like colorful, abstract paintings. And then I fell in love with flavors and aromas. I dropped out of college after the first semester and went to culinary school."

She must have a knack for it, since she was so young and already striving for success. "You're self-employed. That's quite an accomplishment."

"I only recently went out on my own. I did my externship at Flemming's, a renowned restaurant here in Arizona."

"I've heard of it. Where did you go to school that got you that kind of externship?" he asked.

"The Culinary Institute of America."

He whistled. How had she been able to afford that? He didn't know the exact tuition but did know it was among the best culinary arts schools in the country, if not the world.

"My parents saved for my college education. They gave me almost half and I took out student loans for the rest. That and the externship got me my first job at a place called Carolyn's Kitchen. It was an upscale, home-style restaurant. I helped them spiff up their menu and some of the meals I created gave me the idea to go out on my own. Jasmine, the owner of the bakery, lets me cook in her kitchen when I have a big order or several all at once. I cook after the bakery closes at two."

She didn't appear to make a ton of money, living in the small apartment, but she had to be getting along just fine, making a decent income to support herself and Evie. Callum admired that. He admired ambition in anyone. Working hard was rewarding. It didn't matter if the hard work made a person wealthy. If Callum hadn't been born a Colton, he wouldn't be wealthy. He made a good income, more than an average bodyguard, but nothing approaching what his father made.

"What's your favorite food?" Hazel asked, handing him the notepad.

Taking it, his fingers brushed hers. She gave him the pen as their eyes met.

"Seafood. Clams. Scallops. That scallop recipe sounded really good."

"Clams. I could make you an outstanding clam dinner. We'd have to make something else for Evie. She doesn't like seafood."

"Does any kid?"

She took the pen and paper back and jotted down some more ingredients. Then she handed the list back to him. He put it on the coffee table.

"What are you going to make me?"

"Linguine with white clam sauce."

"Mmm." He couldn't wait for that. Spending time with her in the kitchen, too. Doing anything with her. He liked being with her. "How much time do you need to cook tomorrow?"

"Five or six hours."

Taking out his phone, he took a picture of the list then texted it to one of his agency's best personal staff and asked to have everything by nine in the morning. Patsy Cornwall responded a few seconds later. She was a night owl. Callum could always depend on her.

"Just like that, we'll get all the ingredients?" Hazel sounded amazed.

"Just like that. Patsy is paid very well for her services."

"Is she some kind of concierge?"

"She's a personal assistant. She works from home and runs errands for us when we need it. We all keep her pretty busy."

"Nice. Lucky me." Hazel gave him the pleasure of one of her soft smiles and the color of her eyes spellbound him.

She moved her head a fraction closer, as though she couldn't help it, stopping short and looking into his eyes.

Callum lifted his hand and placed his palm against her cheek, then, nearly involuntarily, pressed his mouth to hers. She immediately responded, her warm lips melding with his and sparking much more carnal urges. The intensity of sensations just a kiss caused in him made him withdraw.

She opened her eyes and he found himself transfixed again. He had only known her for about ten hours. With all that had happened, he felt he had known her a lot longer.

"I should get some sleep. Tomorrow is going to be a busy day," she said.

"Right. Yes." He stood with her, seeing her smooth her hair and press her lips together as though she could still feel him kissing her.

He walked behind her toward their bedrooms, she veering to the right and he to the left. When she reached her door, she slowed and looked at him. A moment of electrified attraction passed between them before she disappeared from view.

Callum entered his room and closed the door. While he undressed and got into bed, he imagined what it might be like to be naked with Hazel. On his back, he folded his arm under his head and stared at the dark ceiling, the passionate urges subsiding as the reality of starting something romantic with her set in. Hazel, single mother of Evie, an adorable little girl who reminded him of what his own daughter might have been.

Daughter. He had never formed that word since his girlfriend died. And now an intense sense of dread came over him. Dread and a horrible, defenseless feeling that swirled in his stomach.

Okay. He had gotten himself into this mess. He would treat it like any other job. Watch out for Hazel and Evie. Get them through what they had witnessed. Catch the bad guy. Move on to the next client. No more kissing Hazel.

Chapter 4

When Hazel woke, she didn't immediately know where she was. She had been so exhausted, she'd slept deeply. Now, pushing the covers off, she sat up to be surrounded by the luxury of the Dales Inn room. With white, brown and splashes of color in paintings, the room was immaculate and quiet. She stood and saw Evie had already gotten up.

Checking the time, she saw it was almost eight. Going to the door, she cracked it open and heard Evie chattering happily away. Assured her daughter was fine, Hazel hopped in the shower. Remembering kissing Callum, she tipped her face up into the spray, feeling him all over again. She'd had trouble falling asleep last night because of that. She couldn't even blame him, though, since she was the one who had leaned in. She had been so entranced by him, by his eyes and every feature of his face. The sound of his voice and the things they had talked about, the connection between them.

She dressed in gray slacks and a black blouse and left the room, hearing voices.

"I love strawberries."

"I can seen that you do," Callum said.

"I *looove* strawberries," Evie repeated.

Evie sat at the dining room table with a huge plate of strawberry crepes in front of her. The dish dwarfed her head and upper torso, just her shoulders cleared the height of the tabletop.

"What are you doing to my daughter?"

Callum looked up from the table, where he arranged two breakfast plates that still had silver covers on them.

He chuckled. "She said she was starving. I hope this is okay with you. I sort of winged it by ordering room service." He pointed to the plate at Evie's right. "That's yours. I'm glad I didn't have to wake you before it got cold."

"More than fine. I'm starving, too." She sat next to Evie and lifted the cover.

"It's a Santa Fe skillet," Callum said. "Wheat toast and fruit for sides. Evie picked it out for you. She said you liked food like that. There was a picture on the room service menu."

She did like food like this. Evie knew she loved green chilies.

He poured her a cup of steaming coffee. "Cream or sugar?"

"Yes, please, just creamer."

He handed her two small containers of creamer and she went about adding both to her coffee as Callum sat across from her and removed the silver cover from his plate. He had gotten a ham and cheese omelet with rye toast.

"Do you eat out a lot?" she asked.

With a bite of food, he nodded. Then after swallowing, added, "Bachelor."

She and Evie rarely ate out, but why would they, when Hazel cooked for a living?

"Evie told me the last man you were with was a…what did you call it?" He turned to Evie.

"A nerd." Evie giggled before shoveling another bite of crepe into her mouth.

"Evie was worried you were falling for him," Callum said.

Hazel saw his questioning look. She had dated James for a few weeks. She didn't like talking about him.

"Well, Evie, you're awfully chatty this morning," she said.

Evie giggled. "Cal-em is funny."

"Why is he funny?"

"I don't know. He's funny. He's not a nerd."

Gaze running over his shoulders and chest, Hazel had to agree. When she met his eyes, the same tingles of sexual awareness assaulted her, just as they had last night.

"Who is this nerd? He must have been important to you if you let him spend time with Evie."

"He didn't think Mommy was smart. He called her stupid once."

Callum's lower jaw dropped. "What?"

"She told him to leave. Except she used a bad word."

Hazel remembered the sting of James's condescension all too well. Just when she had begun to trust him, he'd turned on her. He had made her feel the same awful sense of betrayal that Ed had.

"He had a PhD in economics," she said. "Apparently he was very proud of that."

"Why did he call you stupid?" Callum asked, sounding incredulous.

"We were talking about retirement. I didn't have anything put away at the time. My sole focus was Evie, taking care of her, saving for her college, making sure she has medical insurance and good clothes and shoes and healthy food. It escalated to an argument and he called me stupid. He said I didn't know arithmetic or anything about science and all I did know was how to cook."

As she talked Callum's brows gradually rose with each insult. "The man is clearly mad. And completely blinded by his own self-interests."

She wasn't sure she could have said that better.

"Just because you're more inclined to the arts doesn't make

you stupid," Callum said. "A person doesn't have to be a genius in math or any of the hard sciences to be intelligent." He shook his head. "I can't believe anyone would say that to another person."

"I thought he was a decent man, just like Ed." She glanced at Evie. The little girl didn't yet understand what had happened between her mother and father, but some day Hazel would have to have that talk with her. She wouldn't disparage Ed's character, just state the facts. What she dreaded most was that Evie would feel her father never loved her, even though he hadn't. He didn't. He didn't care about Evie. He didn't even know her name. Maybe she could tell Evie someday that her father never knew her, but that if he ever did, or took the time to, then he would love her.

When Hazel turned back to Callum, she saw he had caught her meaning. She was no good at assessing men, at predicting their characters. She had always been trusting, had had no reason not to be, having been surrounded by good people, raised in a stable family.

"I've always thought relationships were based on trial and error," he finally said. "Sometimes the trials go well but you learn the person isn't right for you and you respectfully part ways. Sometimes the trials go badly and end up a mistake. But eventually, with a little luck, you find a person who works."

Works? He sounded as though he believed what he said, or had at one point. "What kind of trials have you had?"

"Ones where I learned something, and some that were a mistake."

"What did you learn?" She'd start with the easier question to answer.

His shrewd mind must be at work. He eyed her with subtle suspicion mixed with intrigue, perhaps, and then his head cocked ever so slightly.

"Too personal?" she asked, half teasing.

A one-sided grin was his initial response, then he said, "I

learned that some women are more interested in their own gain, and others aren't certain enough about what kind of man they're searching for or don't care as long as he is kind and capable of providing. I've learned those kinds of women aren't for me."

Oh, my. This man knew what he wanted. He sounded so candid. She didn't doubt he had learned what he claimed, but what about the mistakes? Maybe there had been only one.

"What about your mistakes?" she dared to ask.

Going still, he just looked at her.

A knock on the door interrupted. Callum went to the door and in came carts of groceries and supplies.

"Whoa!" Evie exclaimed, holding a sticky fork and sporting a strawberry-stained mouth. She put her utensil down, prongs up, on the table, watching the assistant roll bags of food into the suite.

"I'll help put all of this away," Patsy said. A woman of average height with wavy brown hair and blue eyes, she had an energy about her that radiated efficiency.

Evie got off the chair. "Are we going to cook, Mommy?"

"*I'm* going to cook. You're going to go take a bath." She stood. "Come on. I'll get you started."

Hazel saw the assistant begin to put groceries away and Callum lending a hand. The refrigerator would be bursting by the time they finished.

In their en suite, Hazel started the bath and then went to Evie's stash of toys and found her floating Barbie boat and doll. Returning to the bathroom, she discovered Evie had removed her clothes and stepped into the filling tub.

Seeing Hazel had her favorite toys, she smiled and reached up for them. "Yes."

Hazel laughed with the affection that filled her. She handed her daughter the toys and Evie went instantly into playtime mode. Leaving the door open so she could hear her if anything happened, Hazel left the room and saw that Patsy had gone and

Callum was removing cooking pans from a box. Patsy must have brought them, since the inn only had a minimal collection.

"You're going to help?" Hazel asked, going to the sink to wash her hands.

"I wouldn't want to ruin anything. I'll keep you company. I have nothing else to do until I make all your deliveries."

"I make the deliveries. It's good PR."

"No, I'll make them. You stay here, where you and Evie will be safe."

She had spoken without thinking, distracted with getting ready to cook for a few hours.

"I'll tell your customers Evie is sick and you sent me instead," he said. "I'll be charming. You won't lose any business."

Was he a good liar? She wished she could be there to hear him so she could make that assessment. Then again, she was never any good at detecting falsehoods.

While Callum made a call to Kerry to ask her to post an officer outside the inn while he made deliveries, Hazel decided to start with the pork chops. Brining them first, she felt Callum observing her work. While the chops soaked for thirty minutes, she moved on to the chicken and broccoli. Turning on the oven, she put the meat in a bowl, seasoned it and drizzled the cutlets with olive oil. All the while she contemplated picking up her conversation with Callum. She was beyond curious over what mistakes he had made. She knew there was one, probably a big one that he had trouble talking about.

She placed the broccoli on one baking pan and the chicken on another, then put both into the oven. Next, she began preparing spaghetti sauce, cooking the meat first.

"Mommy," Evie called from the room. She must be finished with her bath.

"I'll watch the meat." Callum took her place at the stove.

Hazel hurried to the room and helped Evie dry off, giving her hair a rub with the towel. "Get dressed, honey."

Evie went to the drawers where Hazel had placed her clothes

and began digging through them. She'd make a mess and take forever to find something she liked. For the last year Evie had insisted on dressing herself. Usually she didn't match very well, but she always looked cute.

Back in the kitchen, Hazel took over at the stove, Callum moving aside. He leaned his hip on the counter and again Hazel became aware of his more than casual observation of her. She resumed preparing the meals.

A while later, Evie emerged from the room, half skipping her way toward them, her hair an utter mess. In the kitchen, she stopped next to Hazel.

"Mommy." She lifted the brush.

Callum stepped around Hazel and took the brush. "I'll do it. Your mother is working."

Picking her up, Callum took her to the other side of the kitchen island and sat her on a tall stool. Hazel had a great view of her as he began to brush her long hair. Evie brushed her Barbie doll's hair at the same time.

"How long are you going to be with my mommy?" Evie asked Callum.

"I don't know, Evie. It depends on how long it takes to catch that bad man," he said, struggling with a tangle.

His big body and manly hands running the brush through a five-year-old's hair touched Hazel for some reason.

"Are you and Mommy going to be friends after?"

Callum's hand paused in brushing her hair. "Do you want me to be?"

Evie shrugged. "Are you working for her?"

"Yes, I am."

"But you're her friend, too."

It was Hazel's turn to pause in her task. Why had her daughter asked such a question?

"We just met yesterday, but yes, she is a friend." Callum looked at Hazel with a grin, clearly enjoying this conversation. He began brushing again.

"Mommy needs more boy friends." She tipped her head up. "I don't have a daddy."

"You do have a daddy, Evie, he just isn't here," Hazel said. Why was her daughter bringing this up now? She wasn't prepared to have this talk so soon.

"Where is he?" Evie resumed brushing her doll's hair.

"He...wasn't interested in being with me."

"Does he know about me?"

"Yes, but he has never met you." Hazel glanced at Callum, who looked back at her somberly.

Evie lowered the doll and looked at Hazel. "Why not?"

"He left me, Evie. It had nothing to do with you."

"But...doesn't he want to meet me?"

"You're awfully inquisitive for a young girl," Hazel said.

"Some people aren't prepared to raise kids," Callum said. "Sometimes they aren't ready until much later in life. He doesn't know you, but if he did, he would see what a special girl you are."

Hazel's heart burst with appreciation and awe that, without prompting, Callum had told Evie something similar to what she had thought she would say.

"Do you have a daddy?"

"I do. We aren't very close, though."

That had surprised Hazel when he'd told her before. He seemed so concerned over his father. If they weren't close, why weren't they? Evie had looked up at him with his answer and Hazel could see a connection forming. Did Evie relate her lack of a relationship with her father to his?

"Do you have any kids?" Evie asked, a fountain of questions.

Callum finished brushing her hair and put down the brush. "No."

"Are you going to?"

Hazel watched him tense up. She wondered—if it had been anyone other than a child asking, would he have retorted something to stop this grilling? She also began to worry about Evie's unabashed curiosity about Callum. She seemed to have taken a liking to him rather quickly, which might not be a good thing.

"Evie, that's enough. We barely know Callum. It isn't polite to ask so many personal questions," Hazel said, sure that Evie's Curious George mode was too much for Callum.

Evie's lower lip puffed out a little in a pout, but then she brightened quickly enough. "Can I go watch cartoons?"

"Sure," Hazel said.

Callum helped her get the television on and tuned to the right channel and then returned to the kitchen island. Hazel had put the chicken into the oven and gone to work on the chops, getting a pan ready to sear them.

She busied herself in the kitchen for the next few hours. Callum had gone into the living room to watch television with Evie. The two were getting chummy in there. Callum had found a good family movie that adults could enjoy.

Hazel began putting food into microwavable containers and then into the refrigerator. Her customers could freeze what they wouldn't use in the next day or two. Instant, delicious meals for busy workers or the elderly.

"Will you write down the addresses?" Callum asked. "The officer is outside. I checked."

While that was reassuring, he couldn't keep her penned up in here until the killer was caught. She had a life to live. But dragging Evie around with them wasn't a wise idea, either. Damn that stranger. He was taking her freedom from her. She needed her freedom, but she was no fighter like Callum. Better that he did what he could. He was right. She and Evie were safer here.

"You're doing an awful lot to keep us safe," she said.

Callum stepped closer to her. He put his fingers beneath her chin. Heat coursed through her as she tried to figure out why he had touched her this way.

"It's more than wanting you safe, Hazel. I have a personal reason for doing so. You see, I normally don't take the cases involving women and children. Protecting them. It just so happens that I fell into protecting you and Evie and now I cannot turn my back. I have to see this through."

He seemed to be trying to make her understand why it was so important to him that she stay here in their suite. She still didn't get it. He had to see this through...but why *him*? Why didn't he take cases involving women and children? Why make such a pledge?

"I can't explain it right now. All I ask is you trust me," he said.

After a moment of stunned perplexity, she nodded. She wouldn't press him now, but the need to know would gnaw at her until he told her everything. If he ever did...

Mystified over how close he had come to telling Hazel his darkest secret, Callum began loading the containers of food into his truck. What really got him was that he had felt as though he *could* tell her. And that maybe a huge burden might be lifted if he did. Maybe Charles was right. Maybe keeping all of that bottled up was doing more harm than good.

Memories of when he had first met Annabel flooded him. He had been at a home improvement store looking at wood-saw blades to remodel his bathrooms. Annabel had been looking at the drills. He'd found that interesting. It wasn't every day a guy saw a woman buying tools, unless it was for her man. Callum hadn't seen a ring, so he had gone over to her.

"Are you a carpenter?" he had asked.

Her head had come up and she looked at him for endless seconds. She had long dark hair and dark eyes. Very beautiful.

"No." She had held up a drill in her hand. "Replacing old doors in my house."

"You don't hire out for that?"

"Why? Because I'm a woman?"

From that moment on, he had fallen hard for her. They talked for hours. They spent quiet times together, just comfortable in each other's company. Callum had thought they had the makings of something special, but he hadn't had time to really get to know her. They had only begun to explore. They hadn't been together long before—

He could not let his mind dwell any more on that. A deep sorrow penetrated his usual wall of carefully crafted indifference. He finished putting the food in the truck and closed the door.

As he walked to the rear of the truck on the way to the other side, he spotted a black SUV. That in and of itself didn't alert him, but the man sitting in the driver's seat did. The guy was just sitting in a vehicle.

The passenger window rolled down and he barely noticed the muzzle of a gun before diving for cover. He just made it around the side of his truck before bullets hit the bumper and rear tailgate.

He drew his own weapon and inched up enough to see the shooter. He took aim and fired before ducking as more bullets hit his truck. Hearing the SUV's engine rev and tires squeal, Callum tried again to shoot the driver. He had to take cover again as the SUV raced by and bullets pummeled the truck.

When the volley subsided, Callum got into the truck from the passenger side and crawled behind the wheel, fleetingly seeing a couple crouching at the entrance of the inn, one of them with a cellphone to his ear. Starting the truck, he peeled out of the parking space and chased after the SUV. He veered in and out of traffic, seeing the vehicle several car lengths ahead.

The shooter turned a corner. Callum was slowed by traffic and when he made the turn, he didn't see the SUV. He searched side streets as he weaved, earning honks from a few drivers. Looking left, he spotted the SUV and nearly sideswiped an oncoming car as he swerved into the turn. He gave the truck full gas, no cars in his way, and careened into another turn. The SUV had vanished again, but Callum saw an alley. Swerving into the turn, he gained on the SUV. The shooter flung out into traffic on a busier street. Other traffic veered out of the way as the driver maneuvered around them, Callum not far behind.

There was no plate on the SUV.

The shooter craned back to fire his weapon again and bullets struck Callum's windshield. He crouched low and stuck his pistol out his window, firing back. The shooter drove erratically and made a sharp right turn, causing a delivery truck to brake hard and swerve.

With the delivery truck in his way Callum had to stop and then drive around. People scattered on the sidewalk. The SUV had distance on him again. The shooter turned a corner about a block and a half ahead.

But when Callum reached the street, he didn't see the SUV. He searched until he reached another road. He checked both ways, but the SUV was nowhere in sight. Making a guess, he drove left. A few minutes later it became apparent he would not find the shooter.

His cell rang. Seeing it was Hazel, he answered.

"Are you all right?" she asked. "There are a bunch of police out front and someone said there was a shooting."

"I'm okay. Stay in the room. The shooter came after me. I tried to chase him but he got away."

She was silent for a while. "I'll stay in the room. Be careful."

"I'll be back soon." He liked the concern for his welfare in her voice but not her worry. He thought about rushing back to Hazel, but she was safe in the inn, which had solid security. There were security cameras everywhere and a security team. That was probably why the shooter had waited outside. He knew if he tried to go inside and kill anyone, he'd be captured on video. Besides, the police were there now.

He called Kerry.

She answered on the second ring.

"The killer tried to shoot me just now," Callum said.

"I heard."

He explained what had happened and that he didn't get a plate number this time.

"Well, we can pretty much assume he's stealing vehicles to avoid identification," she said.

"He's getting bold. He waited for us outside the inn. How did he know we were there? How did he find out so fast?"

"Mustang Valley isn't very big. Dales Inn is the only hotel in town. I'm sure he deduced you and Hazel would go there if you weren't at her place."

"What about the ranch?"

"I'm sure he checked there, too."

Callum ran his fingers through his hair as he drove to the address of the first delivery.

"I'll put out a BOLO on the SUV and check for any reported stolen vehicles," Kerry said. "Be careful."

Nobody had to tell him that. Ending the call, he gathered the bag with all the containers for Emily Watson, one of Hazel's elderly clients. With glasses on a chain, her silver hair in stiff curls and a face covered in peach fuzz, Emily smiled her welcome in a floral house dress. Callum was immediately charmed.

She glanced down at the bag he held. "Where is Hazel?"

"She's not feeling well so I'm making her deliveries for her. My name is Callum."

"Come in, come in." Emma stepped aside and checked him out. "My, my, aren't you a handsome fellow."

Callum entered the older Victorian, dark wood floors creaking, letting her comment go.

Emily shut the door and led him into the kitchen. "Go ahead and put them in the freezer. That's what Hazel always does. I still have one of her delicious meals in the refrigerator and with it just being me, that lasts a few days. My Irwin passed a few years ago and the kids don't come around as often as I'd like."

She must be lonely and starved for adult conversation. Callum opened the freezer drawer and began rearranging the contents to make room for a week's worth of meals.

"Irwin was an engineer and retired a vice president of his

department," Emma said. "He was a good provider. What is it that you do, Mr…?"

"Colton. I'm a personal protection officer." That always sounded more palatable than *bodyguard.*

"Oh, you're a security guard?" Emily asked, going to a glass-faced cabinet. "Would you like something to drink?"

She didn't recognize his last name. Maybe it was her age. "No, thank you. No, I'm not a security guard."

Emma filled a glass with tap water. "Hazel never told me about you. She and I have such lovely talks when she's here."

Callum imagined Emily talked anyone's ear off when they visited. Plumbers. Electricians. Maybe the mail carrier. And her kids when they came over.

"She is such a dear," Emily said. "I know she doesn't have to stay when she delivers my meals, but she does. She genuinely cares about me. She's become a friend of mine even if she doesn't consider me one of hers."

"I'm sure she does."

"She's a very good chef." Emily patted her tummy, which wasn't protruding much at all. "She felt so bad for leaving that job of hers, but she belongs on her own."

"She felt bad?" Hazel hadn't mentioned that.

"Oh, yes. Hazel is such a conscientious person. She wouldn't hurt a flea. She worried about the owner of that restaurant… what was it called? Carolyn's Kitchen. She and Carolyn were good friends. Carolyn didn't want her to leave but Hazel followed her heart, and good thing she did. She's going to be very successful someday. You wait and see."

"She already seems to be."

"It's nice to see that she's finally found a husband and father for Evie. I'm going to have to ask her why she didn't tell me."

Husband and father? Callum stood, finished putting the containers into the freezer, feeling a lump form in his throat. He swallowed.

Emily smiled fondly at him, making him more uncomfortable. "I always knew it would only be a matter of time. Hazel is so pretty and nice. And her daughter is sweet as can be. But I'm sure you already know that."

"Hazel and I aren't married," he said.

Emily waved her hand in dismissal. "You don't have to get married to be a family these days. Look at Kurt Russell and Goldie Hawn. They're a model of how healthy families survive without being taken down by old traditions."

Her refreshing outlook did little to calm his inner turmoil. Being a part of Hazel's family would bring heavy responsibility. Callum would go crazy worrying for their well-being. His line of work brought plenty of danger. The people he protected clients against might go after his family to get to him.

Emily stepped closer and gave his forearm a few pats. "If you aren't romantic with her yet, you will be. I'm good at reading people and you seem like a decent man. Unlike Evie's father. Hazel says she won't go for the gorgeous and rich types ever again." She observed him critically. "You're gorgeous, but I bet you aren't rich. Bodyguards don't make that much, do they?"

What did she mean by that? Hazel had told her she would never be with anyone wealthy?

"I don't make millions protecting my clients, but I make more than average," he said, not going into any details of the company that employed him—or the fact that he was a Colton. This woman was already making him talk too much.

"I better get back to Hazel and Evie." He began to back off.

"Yes, I'm sure they are anxiously waiting your return. It was very nice to meet you, Mr. Colton." Emily's face sobered as though something dawned on her. "Colton. You're Payne Colton's son?"

"I am." Maybe she wouldn't be so quick to pair him with Hazel now.

"I heard about the shooting. Who would do such a thing? And how is he doing? Is he going to survive?"

"We don't know yet." Reminded of his father, he planned to go see him in the morning.

Emily's mouth pursed as though mulling over something troubling. "What I said before about Hazel not seeing anyone rich… I didn't mean…"

Callum held his hand up. "Don't worry about it. Hazel and I aren't together that way."

"Are you working for her? She hired you? Is she in danger?"

"Evie witnessed a crime. I'm staying with her until the suspect is captured."

Emily put her hand over her mouth with a sharp inhale. Lowering her hand, she asked, "Is she all right?"

"Yes."

"Because you're watching over her." Emily smiled. "You might come from wealth but you're not the same ilk as Edgar. I can tell."

Right. Because she was good at reading people. Maybe that was true. When a person lived as long as Emily had, they grew wise. She had no magical insight. And Callum would not give credence to anything she had shared with him today. Even if he secretly wanted to.

Evie wouldn't eat her vegetables. Hazel had neared her limit of tolerance just when Callum reentered the suite. She quelled the surge of gladness seeing him made her feel. Evie, on the other hand, did nothing to hide hers. She jumped off the chair and ran to him with a squeal and a loud "Cal-em!"

He bent as she crashed into him, tiny arms going around his torso, reaching his sides and no farther. Callum lifted her and carried her to the table.

"Mommy and I made cookies today. Chocolate."

"Chocolate chip," Hazel corrected.

"And we watched *Frozen*."

"For the thirtieth time," Hazel quipped.

"Hectic day?" Callum asked her.

Seeing his teasing grin, she said, "Evie wanted to go for ice cream. I've been arguing with her all afternoon. Now she won't eat her vegetables."

Callum put Evie down. "Why don't you go do as your mother says? You don't want to grow up short and puny, do you?"

Hazel had to hide a laugh.

"What's puny?" Evie asked.

"Littler than everyone else your age. Go on."

"Will you read to me first?"

Hazel rolled her eyes behind her daughter's back. What a manipulator. But even at her worst, Evie was the most precious thing ever.

"After you do as your mother says and finish your dinner."

With a pout and much slower steps back to the table, Evie climbed up onto the chair and picked up her fork. As she began eating, Hazel opened her mouth in awe and looked at Callum.

"The man with the magical touch," she said, and then regretted letting that slip. It sounded so sexual.

His eyes heated as he appeared to register the same meaning.

"How did it go today?" Hazel asked, going into the kitchen to resume preparing dinner for herself and Callum.

"Good. Emily Watson is quite the character." He followed her, inspecting what she was doing.

She was making linguine and clams. After that exchange she hoped he didn't guess that she had chosen this recipe because he had said it sounded good.

With everything out and ready to go, she started the gas stove burner and cooked the garlic.

"Is that going to be what I think it's going to be?" he asked, standing close behind her and to her left, looking over her shoulder.

She turned her head, her face inches from his. He smelled like outside and subtle cologne.

"Yes." Her voice sounded sultry to her own ears.

His eyes shifted to hers, then lowered to look at her mouth.

"Are you making that for me?"

"We all have to eat," she said.

He grinned, as if to tell her he knew better.

When the garlic cloves browned, she removed them and dumped them in the sink. They had served their purpose. In their place went three and a half dozen clams, some wine and water. She covered the pan and soon the suite began to smell like the beginnings of a delicious seafood plate.

"Can I help?" he asked.

"Sure. I need a big pan of boiling water."

While he did that, she saw the clams had opened and removed them to cool. She reduced the remaining liquid in the pan, feeling Callum watch her.

"The clams need to be removed from their shells," she said, uncomfortable with the manly way he regarded her, eyes warmer than enjoying the preparation of a good meal would cause. "But leave a few of them in their shells for garnish."

"Roger that." He began removing the clams and she salted the boiling water and added linguine.

"Now what?" he asked.

She put butter into the sauté pan, poured in the clams and added seasoning. Once the ingredients began to boil, she reduced the heat and waited until the pasta was al dente. She strained the pasta and combined it with the sauce. After cooking that awhile, she turned off the heat and tossed in grated Parmigiano-Reggiano.

"Voilà," she said.

He reached past her and picked up a clam.

Hazel swatted his hand. "Contamination."

"I used to do that growing up. Drove the cooks mad."

"It drives me mad. You should have sat through the food safety class I had in college." Spooning the pasta onto two plates, she put the clams in shells on each and then sprinkled a little more Parmigiano-Reggiano on top. She handed Callum a plate and took hers to the table.

Evie had finished her dinner and immersed herself in a coloring book. Hazel and Callum ate in silence for a time.

"This is fantastic," Callum said. "Whoever marries you will have a tough time keeping the pounds off."

Whoever? A quick flash of his being that person made her pause in taking her next bite. Cooking for him would be fun. Among other things…like sex.

"It promotes exercise," she said.

"Is that how you stay in shape?"

"Mommy takes me on bike rides," Evie said as she colored. "We go camping, too."

"Horseback riding," Hazel said. "I used to hike when I lived in Colorado." Having a child disrupted a routine.

"You like sports?" Callum asked.

"Not softball or football or things like that. Just hiking, biking."

"I want a horse," Evie said with a glance at Callum. "Mommy says I'm not old enough."

"You probably aren't. You could get hurt pretty bad if you fall off."

"I still want a horse."

Hazel had adored horses when she was a kid, too. What wasn't to love? They were beautiful animals. She had gotten Evie some books on horses, along with some model horses that she played with often.

"Well, when you're old enough to take care of it yourself, then we'll talk," Hazel said.

Evie looked at her mother and saw she meant it and didn't argue. She went back to drawing.

"Why didn't you go back to Colorado after you had Evie?" Callum asked Hazel.

She wondered over the suddenness of his question. He must have been thinking about it before Evie had joined the conversation. Was he trying to learn more about her? Was he interested?

"I like it here. I like the community and the climate. It's

warmer and drier here. We go back to Pagosa Springs to see my parents, usually on the holidays."

"Don't you want to be closer to your family?" he asked. "Especially with Evie?"

He had hit on one of the things that had kept her away. "Actually, I love my parents but they can be intrusive. My mother would be at my house daily or demand I come see her. She already does that now. She complains she doesn't see us enough. It's like she has a hard time letting us go as kids. We're adults now, with our own lives and aspirations. I wish she'd treat us that way."

"Have you told her that?"

"Yes. She just says she loves me and wants to see me as much as possible. It's better that I'm in Arizona and she's in Colorado, at least for now. I might want to change that as Evie gets older. We'll see. What about you? What kind of relationship do you have with your family?"

"You said you would read to me," Evie interrupted.

"Go get your jammies on," Hazel said.

"Aww," Evie complained, but she went to do as told.

"I'm not very close to them, except Marlowe. I never talked much with my parents. I don't know if that's because my father was so busy working at Colton Oil. I would like to change that, though. Ever since my dad was shot, I've thought about that. I want to be closer to him and the rest of my family."

Hazel thought that was quite sentimental of him. She liked that.

Just then Evie bounded into the room in her pj's.

"Are you ready now?" Callum stood and went to the sofa. Evie grabbed a book from the coffee table and sat right next to him.

Evie's easy acceptance of Callum troubled Hazel. What if she got too attached and then the time to part ways came? Regardless, seeing her daughter bonding with a father figure warmed her and made her yearn to give her that all the time.

She watched as Evie tipped her head to the side to see the pages better and listened to Callum's deep voice reading the children's book. She could feel his affection, hear it in his animated tone. She cleaned the kitchen with a soft smile, not wanting to fall for Callum but afraid she would if he continued to befriend Evie.

Thirty minutes later, Evie's head rested on his shoulder, her eyes closed. Callum put the book on the sofa beside him and carefully lifted the child, cradling her and standing. He looked to Hazel, who led the way to their room. She pulled back the covers and Callum laid her down. Hazel tucked her in.

Then she joined Callum at the foot of the bed. He wore an awed look, no sign of his usual tensing. Evie was working her magic on him. Hazel wasn't sure if just any child could have done that for him. She hoped he would someday get over whatever had happened to make him decide not to protect women and children.

"She's something," Callum said.

"Yes. Of course, she is to me. I'm her mother."

"She seems smart for five. Her understanding of words is really good. Advanced."

His fondness sank into her as she sensed his genuine reaction. He sounded like a proud father. Hazel had noticed Evie was a quick learner, too.

They stood there awhile, until Hazel's awareness of him changed. His feelings for Evie melted her, lowered her guard. An intimate connection grew out of their mutual appreciation of her daughter. Her insides reacted, sparked, and instinct nearly made her move closer. But with him she needed to be careful. She would not make the same mistake she had made with Ed.

She couldn't look away. He lifted his hand and curled it behind her neck. Unprepared for this, she let him lean in and kiss her. His mouth pressed firmly to hers as inexplicable chemistry took over. She put her body against his as she slid her hands up his chest. With that encouragement, he turned the kiss into a flaming ball of passion, pressing harder as they added tongues to the erotic play.

Hazel could barely catch her breath as he devoured her. Callum had his hands on her back, holding her against him. He all but danced her around and guided her through the doorway, into the hallway—and away from Evie—until she came against the wall. Hazel had enough presence of mind to be thankful for that.

Now his hands were free to caress her elsewhere, and he wasted no time running them over her breasts. She had a crazy thought that making a baby with him would be wild and wonderful. He unbuttoned her blouse. Exposing her bra, he touched her again.

He worked the front clasp and once he had her bared, he stopped kissing her and lowered his head to her left nipple. Next, he lifted her off the floor to bring her more to his level, planting his mouth on her right nipple. Hazel wrapped her legs around him and gripped his head, urging him to her mouth. She wasn't ready to stop kissing him.

Callum pressed his lips to hers and she fell into a whirlwind of torrid desire. She fumbled with his shirt, needing more than anything to have her hands on his chest—a chest she had only been able to look at up until now. Slipping her hands under the material, using the wall for support, she had to draw away to catch her breath.

As she reveled in the hard panel of muscle under smooth skin, Callum kissed her neck and jaw before taking her mouth again.

"Mommy?"

Jarred from this uncontrollable state of sexual frenzy, Hazel jerked her hands from underneath Callum's shirt as he abruptly stepped away and her feet lowered to the floor. He stared at her, visibly stunned but his gaze still lustful.

Appalled by her behavior—just outside the room where Evie slept—Hazel put her clothes back together and rushed into the room, trying to calm her racing heart and breath.

"Yes, honey?"

Evie blinked up at her sleepily, thankfully oblivious to what had occurred in the hall. "Will you turn off the light?"

Seeing the lamp between the two queen beds was on, she bent and turned it off. Then she went to Evie and kissed her forehead. "Go back to sleep, sweetie."

But Evie had already done so, slumbering peacefully. Hazel pulled the blankets up over her tiny shoulders and then returned to the hall, where Callum still stood. He looked much more composed now. In fact, he looked downright aloof.

"Everything okay?" he asked.

"Yes. She just wanted the light off." She studied him carefully. His eyes were a mask now, almost cold they were so remote. He had withdrawn. Granted, that hot encounter had shaken her to her core as well, but he seemed to have withdrawn much more than was warranted. Didn't he marvel over how spectacular it had felt? She did. And she felt slighted that he might reduce it to something meaningless.

"Look… I'm sorry about…" Callum began.

He couldn't even put what happened into words. Maybe he refused to, because doing so would add meaning to it.

"Good night, Callum." Miffed, she went into her room and shut the door, wishing she could slam it. But she didn't want to wake up Evie.

She jerked herself into her pajamas, muttering, "Imbecile," before getting into bed. She turned on the television. It would be a long time before she settled down enough to sleep.

Emily must have given him an earful about her and Evie, in particular about how Ed had run off after discovering Hazel was pregnant. Emily herself had a blended family, having remarried after divorcing her first husband, whom she had met when she was a teenager. No one should ever marry at such a young age. People, at least in Hazel's opinion, needed time to grow before they made such a huge commitment. Spending your entire life with someone was kind of an important decision. Emily strongly opposed a too-impulsive marriage, saying it was just a legality, when love was the thing that kept couples together, not a piece of paper and a few laws.

Whatever Emily had planted in his head, it had made him think. It had brought him closer to Evie, a child and Hazel's daughter, two things he had for some reason sworn off.

Trying to get distracted by the nature program she had turned to a low volume on television, Hazel failed miserably. Her spirits sank when she considered how she'd celebrated the fantastic feeling of kissing Callum, while he apparently shunned such an emotion. The cops had better find that shooter soon. Hazel needed to get away from a man like Callum Colton. She'd be better off with someone more in her league.

Chapter 5

The next afternoon, Callum arranged for a car rental and went to visit a comatose Payne at the hospital. He brought with him Hazel and Evie, who skipped beside Hazel on their way toward the entrance. Callum had noticed a distinct change in Hazel this morning. He wondered if he had mistaken the way she'd said good night and shut the door before he could even respond. Was she upset that he had kissed her? He'd rather have this resolved before going in to see his father. Some of his family would be there and he didn't need to have to explain Hazel's mood.

He stopped her on the cement in front of the doors. "Is something wrong?"

Evie's head tipped up and she looked at him.

"No," Hazel said.

"Last night…"

Evie turned to her mother.

"Don't worry about it. We'll wait for Kerry to find and catch the shooter and then we can both get back to our lives."

Callum met Evie's eyes as she glanced back at him and then she asked her mother, "Mommy, are you mad?"

"Not now, Evie."

Callum could see Hazel was quite upset, her keen gaze firing arrows at him. "I didn't mean to hurt you. It just—"

"Do we have to talk about this now?" Hazel interrupted.

It might not be appropriate to talk in front of Evie, but he doubted she'd really understand and he wasn't going to say anything grossly offensive. "I'm sorry, that's all."

"Yes, I could tell you were."

She thought he was sorry for kissing her? But was he? "Sorry" wasn't the right word. *Concerned* would be a better choice but he couldn't tell her that.

"Don't worry," she repeated, sounding more sincere now. "Whatever you're going through, I get it. I don't need to get involved with another rich guy, so let's just make the best of this situation, okay?"

"Who is Rich?" Evie asked.

Callum almost smiled. Evie thought Rich was a man.

"You're judging me because my family has money?"

"*You* have money. I don't mean to judge. I don't know you well enough. All I can do right now is go on what I do know."

"My *parents* are rich."

"They don't share any of it with you?" Hazel asked, more of a challenge.

He didn't like what she was implying. "We all have trust funds, but—"

"Well, there you go." Hazel resumed walking toward the door, Evie in tow.

Evie looked back at him and then up at her mother. In the elevator, she asked, "Why are you mad, Mommy?"

"I'm not mad."

Callum watched her as he stood beside her, clearly disagreeing.

Hazel felt a little contrite over her reaction. She couldn't blame him for not feeling what she'd felt in that kiss. Some men treated women poorly, without empathy, and others didn't intend to cause harm. Callum hadn't meant to snub her, humiliate her or make her feel rejected. Even though, absurdly, she had experienced all of those emotions. Or maybe she was just mad for putting herself into a situation that resembled that with Ed far too much.

Callum entered the hospital room first. Hazel was struck by the extent of the medical equipment and the tubes coming from Payne Colton. She had never been this close to someone in such critical condition. She had seen a coma patient on television, of course, but the real thing came with a considerably larger impact.

There were three others in the room, two men and a woman.

"Mommy?" Evie said in a quiet tone, tugging on her sleeve.

"Yes, Evie?" Hazel noticed that everyone except Payne had turned toward Evie, who was oblivious to the attention she'd gained.

"I like Cal-em," Evie said.

"I know you do." Hazel saw a good-looking, dirty-blond-haired man on the other side of Payne's hospital bed smile slightly.

"Don't be mad at him," Evie said, eyebrows arched upward in earnest appeal.

The striking woman with light blond hair looked very businesslike and snickered a bit, while the man next to her in a suit smiled.

"I'm not mad at him," Hazel said, glancing at Callum, whose eyes held a teasingly smug glint.

Evie's expression said she didn't understand. "You were mad."

"Evie, not now," Hazel said sternly.

Evie went into one of her lower-lipped pouts.

"Is my brother stirring up trouble?" the woman asked Evie.

"No," Evie retorted, eliciting a round of laughter.

"How did you manage to make such a fine friend, Callum?" the woman asked.

"Hazel, this is my twin sister, Marlowe," Callum said. "That's her fiancé, Bowie."

"Hello, very nice to meet you. Callum told me about you," Hazel said to Marlowe. She liked that Callum had such a high regard for his twin.

"And this gentleman over here is Rafe," Callum said, "my younger brother. He's also Detective Wilder's fiancé."

The adopted brother. Hazel recalled Callum telling her that. Not only were the Coltons wealthy, they were all so good-looking! Hotness filled the room. And even though Bowie wasn't a Colton, he was also quite a treat for the eyes.

"I'm going to go get a soda," Bowie said. "Does anyone else want anything?"

"Juice," Evie said.

"A punch or mixed berry is fine," Hazel said.

Everyone else declined and Bowie started for the door. "One juice coming right up," he said.

"How is he today?" Callum gestured toward Payne.

"The same," Rafe said.

They all fell into somber silence.

"What do the police think happened?" Hazel asked.

"He received an email saying Ace was switched at birth and isn't a Colton by blood," Marlowe said. "Naturally, Ace wasn't happy to hear about that."

"The police think Ace tried to kill Payne?" Hazel asked.

"He's the only one who appears to have a motive," Callum said. "But I don't think he did it."

"I don't, either," Rafe said.

"He's our brother," Marlowe said. "Of course he didn't try to kill Dad."

"He said he was home the night of the shooting," Callum said. "There's no video surveillance supporting that."

"Isn't Kerry looking for someone shorter?" Callum said.

"Yes," Marlowe answered.

Callum moved closer to Payne. Hazel watched him take hold of his hand.

"I wish you'd wake up, Dad," he said. "You could tell us yourself who shot you."

Could the shooting have something to do with Ace being switched at birth? Maybe the culprit didn't want to be discovered. Then why send an email making that announcement? Unless the one who had actually swapped the babies wasn't the one who sent the email.

"Do you know who sent the email?" she asked.

"No. I have someone from IT at Colton Oil looking into that," Marlowe said.

"Hey, Callum, how long are you going to be in town?" Rafe asked.

"Indefinitely. I have a new job starting at the end of the month but it is local. I'm free until then."

Marlowe turned her gaze to Hazel, appearing to grow more curious. "When did you two meet? Callum never tells me when he has a new girlfriend."

Why did Callum's twin think Hazel and Callum were together like that?

"Kerry is investigating a murder that Hazel's daughter witnessed," Rafe said. "Callum is protecting them."

"Oh." Marlowe looked from Hazel to her twin. "And you already made her mad?"

"Marlowe..." Callum protested.

"Sorry, brother. I'm not buying it. You look at her like she's more than a client," Marlowe said.

Hazel turned to Callum. He looked at her in a particular way? She hadn't noticed. But then, she hadn't glanced at him much since they entered the hospital room. Every time she did she felt an unwelcome spark, which only brought her back to his regrets over kissing her. She could not afford to want something he would never give.

* * *

Later that day, Callum couldn't stop thinking about what Marlowe had said—that he had looked at Hazel in such a way that gave Marlowe the impression they were an item. He hadn't been aware that he had done that. If he had no control over the way he regarded Hazel, wasn't aware of how she affected him, how could he control how he felt about this relationship? Was he calling it a relationship? A zap of alarm pricked him as he realized they were starting to have one. How could he call it anything else? They had kissed. They had almost had sex. They'd have a casual relationship, then.

He walked with her into the inn. They'd go back to their suite and be alone again, except for Evie.

Halfway through the lobby, Hazel stopped, Evie by her side.

"Carolyn?" Hazel asked.

Callum followed her gaze to a woman standing by a cart full of food chafing dishes. A blonde with a bob in a smart black skirt suit with a white top, she seemed surprised to see Hazel.

He stopped next to Hazel as she leaned in for a hug. Obviously the two knew each other, and judging by the catering supplies, they shared food as an interest. Had Hazel worked with this woman in the past?

"What are you doing here?" Carolyn asked, moving back from the hug, smiling as her eyes roamed over Hazel's face.

"I'm staying here."

"We're being protected," Evie said in her cute voice.

Carolyn crouched down to the girl's level. "Well, hello, Evie. You've grown since the last time I saw you."

"I'm five."

Carolyn laughed a little and stood, sending Hazel a questioning look. "Why are you being protected?" She glanced at Callum.

"It's a long story," Hazel said.

"I saw a man get hit in the head with a rock and he died," Evie said.

Carolyn looked down at her. "Oh, my." Then she returned her attention to Hazel. "Are you all right?"

"Cal-em is protecting us," Evie said.

"That's enough, Evie."

Hazel must say that a lot to her daughter. The more time he spent with them, the more he learned of their close connection. He had always thought a mother and a daughter must have a special bond. Then his Annabel had died and he'd avoided anything mother-daughter altogether.

"What happened?" Carolyn asked.

Who was this woman and how did Hazel know her? He waited for Hazel to give a quick summary of why they had ended up here and then she finally turned to him.

"Callum is a bodyguard."

"Oh." Carolyn sounded impressed. "A bodyguard, huh? You must be special now."

"Not really." Hazel smiled humbly.

"Yes, she is," Evie said, hanging onto Hazel's arm.

"Callum Colton." He held out his hand to the woman. "And you are…?"

Carolyn's mouth dropped open. "Colton? As in Colton Oil?"

He had grown accustomed to people recognizing him by his surname. They were sort of like celebrities in town; some regarded them in awe and some in loathing, depending on which Colton's path they had crossed. "Payne Colton is my father."

"Oh, yes. I'm so sorry. I heard about your father. My deepest condolences."

What had she heard? "He isn't dead yet."

"But in a coma, right? That's terrible." Carolyn looked from him to Hazel. "How did you manage to meet up with a Colton bodyguard?"

"Completely by accident," Hazel said. "He was across the street when the man was struck and came to help us."

"Aren't you the lucky one?" Carolyn smiled.

"How long have you and Hazel known each other?" Callum asked.

Hazel put her hand to her forehead. "I'm sorry. How rude of me. Callum, this is Carolyn Johnson. She owns Carolyn's Kitchen. I told you about working for her."

"Yes, I remember. Very nice to meet you."

After a moment where she seemed miffed that her friend hadn't mentioned her, Carolyn looked at Hazel. "She was one of the best chefs I've ever had."

Callum thought she sounded wry, even cynical, and wondered why.

"Thank you, Carolyn. You always treated me so well. Restaurants can be so stressful, but you were always calm and courteous."

Hazel didn't seem to notice her friend's tone. Pleasing customers with food did seem demanding, as did the work hours. Service jobs were unfortunately thankless, most of the time. A shame, given how enjoyable going out for dinner or whatnot was.

"We have to keep customers coming back." Carolyn sounded faintly derisive.

Hazel looked at the cart behind her. "You're making a catering delivery? You normally have others do that."

"Yes, normally."

Hazel hesitated, finally registering Carolyn's sarcasm. "How are you doing? H-how's the restaurant?"

"Oh, I had to close it."

That came as a total shock to Hazel, Callum saw by her rounded eyes and dropped jaw. "No. What happened? You were doing so well."

"Yes. After you left, I couldn't find another chef as good as you. And me?" She lifted her eyes and glanced at Callum ruefully. "I am not a cook. I'm a businesswoman. This lady, however…" She gestured toward Hazel. "She is *amazing*."

She sounded different now, not so brash. Did she mean the compliment?

"Carolyn. I'm so sorry. I had no idea. You should have called me." Hazel seemed genuinely remorseful, as though she felt responsible for the closure.

"You made your decision and you gave me more than enough notice." Carolyn shrugged. "The luck of the draw, I guess. The chefs I hired after you left couldn't prepare the meals the way you did. Customers slowly stopped coming. And then I had a bad review and it was all over. I got out before it ruined me completely. Now I work for a catering company." She gestured back at the cart. "A tough transition, going from entrepreneur to servant."

Callum was good at reading people and he could tell her transition had been especially difficult. Carolyn made a good show of being a good sport but the loss had to be painful. Who wouldn't feel that way after accomplishing so much, just to lose it? He felt bad for her. He couldn't imagine how Hazel felt.

"Is there anything I can do to help?" Hazel asked.

"No. Don't worry about me. It's been really great to see you again. How is your food delivery service going?"

Hazel paused before saying, "It's going all right. I wouldn't say I'm a raging success. I'm staying afloat."

Carolyn smiled. "I'm sure it's just a matter of time before you are a raging success, artist that you are. I know firsthand how your cooking can make a big impact on revenue."

"Oh, my gosh, Carolyn. I never intended to cause you to lose business. I set everything up so the recipes would be easy to follow. You shouldn't have suffered at all."

Carolyn shrugged again. "You made quite an impression for me, you know."

Hazel seemed confused. "No, I didn't know that."

"I don't see how. Patrons asked to thank you personally all the time. They complimented your cooking to me more times than you know. I didn't tell you at the time, but I was very worried about how things would go after you left. I respected your decision, though, and didn't want to influence you. You were my friend more than you were my chef."

"Oh." Hazel leaned in and hugged Carolyn again. "I wish you would have told me. I could have worked part-time for you or something. Anything to help you not lose your restaurant. I know how much it meant to you."

Moving back, Hazel looked at Carolyn with heartfelt sympathy and regret.

Carolyn met the emotion with stiffening aloofness. She didn't like pity, that much Callum could see. Neither did he.

"Really, Hazel. I'm a grown woman. I can take care of myself. I'll do the servant thing for a while and then start up a new venture. You know me. I'm no quitter."

Callum believed that. He didn't really know the other woman but she had an indomitable energy about her. No wonder she and Hazel were such good friends. While Hazel wasn't aggressive, she had tenacity and ambition as well as talent.

"No, you are not. And you are a smart businesswoman. You belong in your own element."

"Ms. Johnson?" a voice interrupted.

Callum saw a hotel worker approach Carolyn.

"We're ready for you," the hotel worker said.

Carolyn turned to Hazel. "Have to go now. So nice running into you."

"You, too." Hazel touched her arm before Carolyn pushed the cart, following the hotel worker, probably to a conference room.

It took Hazel a few long seconds to start walking toward the elevator with Callum. She apparently had fallen into melancholic thought.

"Why do people always think it's their fault when decisions they make result in others having a run of bad luck?" he asked.

That pulled her out of her reverie. "W-what?"

"You aren't responsible for other people's misfortunes."

They stepped into the elevator, Evie holding Hazel's hand,

head tipped back as usual. Her curiosity made her listen intently to everything said by the adults around her.

"I created the recipes," Hazel said.

"Which should have helped her."

"It did, but you heard her. The chefs she hired after me couldn't replicate them."

He took a moment to marvel that she didn't see what he did. "You're an artist first, Hazel."

She blinked a few times as though startled by what he brought to light.

"Your passion went into every one of those recipes, those meals you oversaw in the kitchen," he said.

"But…they had the recipes and I wrote detailed instructions."

"*But* they didn't have the heart. Only you had that. You made Carolyn's Kitchen."

"No. Carolyn made Carolyn's Kitchen," Hazel argued. "She was an aggressive businesswoman. Driven. Smart. She hired me to help her make her dream a reality. She was a good person."

"Then she should have gone to culinary school if she wanted to run a restaurant," he said.

Hazel rubbed her forehead with two fingers.

The elevator doors opened and Evie tugged Hazel toward the exit. Callum wanted to say more, do more about this discussion. But he walked to their suite, mindful of the energetic Evie, and let them inside.

Evie bounded toward the television and Hazel set her up with an animated show. Then Hazel walked into the kitchen—and took out a pizza from the freezer. No gourmet meal for tonight.

Glad Evie's overactive mind had something to keep her occupied, Callum joined Hazel behind the island, where Hazel had picked up a pen and hovered the point over a notepad.

He wasn't fooled. She used idle tasks to help ease her tormented thoughts.

Putting his hands on her upper arms, he asked, "Did you leave on bad terms?"

She shook her head. "I gave her a lot of notice."

"Then why are you beating yourself up over this?"

She put down the pen and ran her hand over the top of her hair. Facing the living room where Evie watched television, she stilled. Callum didn't think she registered Evie's presence all that much, so absorbed did she appear to be in her separation with Carolyn.

Finally, she turned to him. "I left for selfish reasons. I had Evie and…"

"You had to look out for your own."

"Yes, but Carolyn would have never betrayed me."

Callum moved to stand near her, gripping her shoulders and making her face him. "It's okay to want to forge your own way in life. You don't have to work hard to make others succeed. I think, deep down, you knew you had greater potential than what you got working for your friend."

Hazel's captivating, green-gold eyes met his soulfully, and she added a slow and telling shake of her head. He had nailed what she felt.

"Am I right?" he asked to make her confront it.

With teary eyes she nodded.

He drew her into an embrace. "You followed your heart, Hazel. No one can condemn you for that, least of all me. I did the same."

His father hadn't been happy with his decision not to join the Colton Oil team. Neither had his mother. "I know what it's like to want something others don't understand or expect from you."

"I just hate to see good people fail," Hazel said.

"I bet she'll have a comeback. Maybe she won't open another restaurant but she'll find success somewhere."

At last the first glimmer of a smile emerged on her pretty face. She had her hair back today, exposing her expressive eyes, prominent cheekbones and full lips he longed to kiss right then.

"That's better. A woman like you should never be sad," he said.

Her smile expanded. "Why me?"

Why indeed? He had to think a minute as to why he'd even said such a thing. Although he inwardly cringed with the truth, he said, "You're beautiful inside and out."

"Wow, the last man who said something that nice to me probably lied."

He was glad she made light of such a serious compliment. "Ed?"

"Yes. He said sweet nothings to me a lot. He had me really believing I was special."

Wait a second. Was she making light or did she think Callum had just said something nice and was being insincere about it?

"Surely you've had others. I can't be the only one who complimented you over the last five-plus years."

"No." She shook her head and moved into the kitchen. "No one."

He followed her, leaning against the island counter as she began to prepare dinner. "No one?" There had to have been *someone*.

"No one serious," she said.

But she had dated. "How many have you dated?"

She made a funny face. "You make it sound like I slept with all of them."

"Unintended. How many guys have you been out with?" He discovered he really wanted to know.

"Not many. Three. No, four. Two were one date and the other relationships lasted a few weeks."

He reflected on his own experiences. Annabel had died almost five years ago. He and Hazel had been single and getting past old hurts for the same length of time. Maybe for too long. Hazel had a better excuse than he did. She had Evie to keep her busy, and it would be a lot harder for her to find a man suitable to take over a father role.

Father role.

"What about you?"

Hazel's question spared him from painful memories. He had already faced more of those than he could deal with.

"Girlfriends?" Had she capitalized on the direction of their conversation?

"How many have you *had* since your last serious relationship?" She grinned before opening the oven to check on the pizza.

Wily woman. Lucky for her, this was something he could talk about.

"Not many. Seven."

She planted her hands on the counter beside him. "Seven?"

That was a lot to her? "Yes. Minimal dates."

She mouthed *minimal dates* and scrunched up her brow in question. "You cannot tell me that some of those women didn't mean something more than a date."

As she chopped lettuce for what he presumed would be a healthy salad to go with their not-so-healthy pizza, he realized she had concluded he had had not more than a casual fling in the past five years. How could she? She knew nothing about him, really.

"What happened to you?"

Her earnest question put him at odds with how to respond. "Nothing."

She chopped a carrot, the knife hitting the cutting board hard. "Did any of them matter?"

"They all mattered."

She continued chopping and, without looking at him, said, "No. Really matter."

He had to be honest. "They all mattered, Hazel. They just deserved better than what I could give."

"How many were you serious with?"

Why did she ask? Why was that important to her? Was she trying to find out what she was up against?

"Five or six. Some lasted a few months, others a week or two. One pretty recent." When it got too serious, then he walked.

She stopped chopping the poor carrot, her head bowing slightly and her shoulders slumping equally indiscriminately. Still keeping the knife on the cutting board, flush with a carrot, she turned her head to see him. "What happened, Callum?"

He silently cursed. No one had ever pushed him like this. He glanced over at Evie, who was still engrossed in her movie and not paying them any attention.

He had never told anyone about Annabel. Few knew she had been his girlfriend. Back then, he had been mainly in Texas, but he worked a lot. He had drifted away from his family, only seeing them on Christmas and Thanksgiving. He had brought Annabel to both holidays that last year. When asked later if he was still seeing her, he had only said no. Now he was about to tell Hazel. Why her?

He met her eyes and could feel his soul pouring out through his. She blinked solemnly, putting down the knife and facing him. She put her hand on his cheek. "It's okay. You don't have to tell me."

The selflessness of her saying that tore through all of his resistance. She meant it. She respected his sensitivities. The connection between them strengthened, his to her, anyway. She was someone he could trust. Maybe it was timing more than anything else. Maybe, finally, he was ready to put in words what he had so far kept to himself.

"She died nearly five years ago." Saying that felt like a regurgitation, it came up from inside him like sour milk. He felt sick. He put both hands on the kitchen island counter and lowered his head. "I've never told anyone this."

Hazel's hand touched his back, high and on the left. She caressed him in comfort. She didn't press him, just waited. He could go on or he could stop right there. She wouldn't force anything out of him.

"She was pregnant." Callum choked back a powerful wave of anguish.

"Oh," she breathed in heartfelt empathy. Not pity, no sympathy, just a profound understanding. She was a mother. She must know how terrible it would be to lose her child.

"We knew it was going to be a girl," he said, barely getting the words out before his anguish became too unbearable.

Unable to continue, he pushed off the counter and walked toward his room.

Chapter 6

Hazel ordered room service the next morning. She had picked at her dinner the night before while Evie devoured hers. Callum had not come out of his room the rest of the night. Hazel had lost her appetite after hearing his gut-wrenching confession. She could not imagine the awfulness of losing a person you loved and a child all in one fell swoop. She had to assume he had really cared for the woman. Such crushing emotion would not have overcome him had he not.

She prepared Evie's breakfast of cereal and fruit. Evie had complained about the fruit but Hazel said that after junking it up last night, she had to eat healthy today.

Hazel sat down at the dining table and began eating with her daughter. Looking at Evie's innocent face as she scooped milky bites into her mouth, Hazel thought again about how difficult it must be for Callum to be around them. She had thought about that a lot since the previous night. She also had so many questions she would never be able to ask, would not ask. How had the woman died? How long were they together? Were they engaged? Did he love her as much as he appeared to? Now she understood why he usually refused to take cases involving families.

He had broken down just voicing that she had died and their unborn baby girl along with her. Callum was not a weak man mentally. He was tough, fearless. Look at his profession. He was a bodyguard, one of the best in the world. But talking about the woman from his past had brought him to his knees.

And then there were the other thoughts she had. The selfish ones, like, what did his loss mean for her, Hazel? She could no longer deny she had begun to have feelings for him. What would it do to her if he decided to turn away? He had already withdrawn and it had been nearly five years since the tragedy. *Five years.* Something terrible must have happened. Something sudden. A car accident? No one ever got over losing love—or a child.

"Mommy?"

Grateful to be pulled out of her never-ending contemplations, she looked at Evie.

"You're not eating."

Hazel hadn't touched her cereal. She still wasn't hungry. "I know."

"How come?" Evie swung her legs under the chair and table.

"I have a lot on my mind."

"Cal-em?"

"Finish eating, Evie." Dang if her daughter wasn't a perceptive little thing.

"Were you mad at him again?"

"No."

"Good, because I want him to be my daddy."

Where had that come from? Daddy?

"He's not your daddy, Evie."

"But I want him to be. I want a daddy. Everybody else has one. Why can't I?"

"Someday you might." Hazel couldn't predict when and she

wouldn't rush into anything. The man she married would have to prove himself a good person and role model for Evie.

Callum could be.

Hearing Callum enter the room, Hazel hoped Evie would stop asking all her questions and expressing that she wanted a father.

"Good morning," Hazel said.

Callum was all cleaned up and ready for the day in jeans and a long-sleeved white button-up. Sexy as hell. He didn't seem reluctant to see her after what he'd told her. He seemed back to his normal self—and guarded again.

"Good morning." He picked up the box of cereal Hazel had left out and poured some into a bowl she had also had ready for him. Then he sat across from Evie, who sent him a big smile.

"Somebody got plenty of sleep last night," he said to her, smiling back.

Evie giggled as she chewed a mouthful of cereal.

Callum reached over and put his hand over Hazel's, catching her by surprise. She met his sobering eyes.

"I'm sorry for leaving you the way I did last night," he said. "I've never told anyone about Annabel."

Hazel sensed she had a chance to ask questions. She'd be careful not to push him. "Not even your family?"

He shook his head. "They knew I was seeing her, but they don't know she died."

Her heart went out to him. He had suffered for so long in silence. "Callum, why?"

Pulling his hand away, he looked down at the bowl of cereal. "I…couldn't."

Until now, with her. He had told her.

"Were you engaged?" Hazel asked.

"Not yet. I was going to propose the next weekend."

Seeing him drift off into that dark place, Hazel refrained from asking how the woman and the baby had died. This time she put her hand on his. "Thank you for telling me, Callum. I know how difficult that was for you." He looked at her, the darkness fading. "I want you to know if you ever need someone to just listen, I can be that person for you."

He took her hand in his. "I know you can, but I'm not sure I'll ever be able to talk about her again."

After long seconds of staring into his candid eyes, Hazel nodded. "Okay."

"Are you going to be my daddy?" Evie blurted out.

"Evie," Hazel admonished. "That is rude." Clearly she hadn't understood anything Hazel and Callum had just said. Adult talk.

Callum chuckled. "What makes you ask that, Evie?" Callum asked.

"You keep touching my mommy."

"Your mother is a very good friend of mine."

"I would like you to be my daddy," Evie said.

"Evie, that is enough."

Callum chuckled again and Hazel realized he had done so because she repeated "that's enough" to Evie a lot. She smiled at him and then Evie.

The suite phone rang and Hazel went to answer it.

"Ms. Hart?"

"Yes?"

"We have a package that was delivered by courier for you at the front desk."

That was odd. She hadn't forwarded her mail, but was having it held at the post office. She'd pick it up there on occasion.

"All right. Could you have someone bring it up?" She hung up and faced Callum, who looked at her in question.

"There's a package for me at the front desk."

He immediately looked concerned.

Moments later a hotel worker knocked on the door. Callum answered, taking a cardboard overnight delivery envelope.

Well, it couldn't be a bomb. It was too thin, and looked like it contained a letter.

He inspected it and then ripped open the top, taking out a typed letter. After he read it, he handed it to her.

In capital letters it said:

I WOULDN'T GET TOO COMFORTABLE IF I WERE YOU. JUST BECAUSE YOU'RE WITH A COLTON NOW DOESN'T MEAN YOU'RE INVULNERABLE.

She looked up at him. "The shooter knows we're here." This was a small town and the Dales Inn the only hotel, but being stalked like this scared her.

Nowhere she and Evie went would be safe. The shooter would find them. Hazel looked at her daughter, who had moved into the living room and was watching a cartoon. If anything happened to her…

Hazel recalled how devastated Callum had looked when he told her his baby girl had died with her mother. Hazel wouldn't survive losing Evie.

He took out his phone. "Hello, Kerry. Someone sent Hazel a threatening letter." When he disconnected he said to Hazel, "She's on her way."

Hazel looked at her daughter again, imagining the shooter hitting her over the head with a rock or shooting her little body. She dropped the letter and put her hand to her mouth.

Callum came to her and pulled her into his arms. "I won't let anything happen to her."

"We can't stay in this inn forever."

"You won't have to. Kerry will find him."

"In the meantime, what if he gets to us? He seemed certain."

He rubbed her back. "I won't let him hurt you. He'll have to get past me to get to you and I won't let that happen."

She believed him, but even with his expertise, he couldn't be one hundred percent sure. She leaned back and met his eyes. Pressed this close to him, with his arms still around her, and especially with their deepened connection, her sexual reaction to him was stronger than ever before. His eyes grew darker with passion. He had to feel the same.

If Evie hadn't been in the room, she would have kissed him. Last night and this morning, Hazel had been tempted to take a chance on him. She had never met a man since Ed who made her feel they could have something lasting.

Easing away, she took a seat at the kitchen island. Callum bent to pick up the letter and placed it on the counter. They waited a few minutes and Kerry called Callum to say she was on her way up. Moments later, he let her into the room.

"Hey, Evie. I've got something for you." Evie turned from the television as Kerry went to her and handed her a MVPD baseball hat.

Evie inspected it and then put it on her head with a giant smile.

"What do you say, Evie?" Hazel said.

"Thank you!"

Kerry straightened and walked over to the island, where Callum handed her the letter.

She read it and frowned.

Callum gave her the envelope, handling it lightly to preserve fingerprints—if there were any.

"I'll run some forensics on this but my guess is whoever typed this was careful not to leave any traces," Kerry said. "I will check security and can track down where the envelope was mailed from and maybe find out something that way. It might take me some time, though."

"Whatever you can do," Callum said.

The next few days were anticlimactic in that no one sent any more threats and they saw no suspicious characters in the few people who visited their suite. Callum decided it was time for a surprise to break up the monotony—and provide some relief from the constant awareness of Hazel and how much he would like to stop fighting to keep things professional.

A sudden knock on the door signaled the arrival of the surprise.

Hazel looked up from her work in the kitchen, preparing another week's worth of food deliveries while wearing a sexy blue flowing sundress and no shoes. He loved a barefoot chef. He held back a smile as he went to the door to let Patsy Cornwall inside. The assistant led a hotel bellboy into the suite. The bellboy pushed a cart that held a big box and some bags of other items.

"Something for a young girl," he said.

As soon as Evie spotted the packages, she squealed and charged to the entry. The box contained a finished dollhouse mansion. The bags contained everything to furnish it.

He put the box in the living room and let Evie go through all the accessories.

"You didn't."

Glancing up, he saw Hazel had left the kitchen to get a closer look. "I did."

"Callum, this is too much."

"No, it's not. We're cooped up in here. We'll all get a kick out of this." The dollhouse had turrets, curving staircases going up three levels and two porches. The miniature house had incredible detail, from the exterior Victorian trim to interior wallpaper and paint. Evie was going to have a blast.

Callum sent Hazel a mischievous glance.

She looked at her daughter, who was ecstatic over the plethora of doll items.

"You're going to spoil her."

He wanted to spoil her. After seeing her play with her Barbie and how her imagination soon soared, he knew he had to get her one. He had asked Patsy to get every piece of furniture she could find and to include the little things, like dishes. Patsy had it overnighted from a store willing to work with them in a hurry. He had requested it a few days ago. She might break a few things at her age but she'd have this for years, maybe even into adulthood.

It took him a while to set up the dollhouse. Evie had all the accessories scattered on the floor behind the house, which she'd already begun to fill with furniture.

This is what it would have been like with his daughter, had she lived. Callum pushed those thoughts away and went around to the back of the house to help Evie arrange the rooms.

She let him take over and began dressing two Barbie dolls.

"This is Angie," Evie said, showing him the doll dressed in a sparkly dress.

"She's pretty, like you."

Evie beamed up at him before going back to her dolls. He finished arranging furniture and got out of her way.

She instantly dove into playtime, speaking in a low voice, pretending the dolls were talking about going to their new house.

He left her to it and went to the kitchen, where Hazel was cleaning up after a day of cooking. "What's for dinner?"

"Spaghetti."

"Nothing too fancy. Too bad." He dipped his finger into the sauce for a taste.

She swatted the top of his hand. "Raised the way you must have been, you didn't spend much time in a kitchen."

They'd had servants to do the cooking and serving. "Your cooking is irresistible." He could get accustomed to this, a delicious meal every day…and a beautiful woman by his side.

That thought came unbidden. She *was* a beautiful woman, no denying that. And he could get accustomed to a delicious meal every day. What troubled him was much more than how those two things appealed to him. The idea of living with them made him feel good. Too good.

"Why don't you set the table?" Hazel asked.

Callum did so, enjoying the sense of being part of a family unit. Hazel put food on the table and had to force Evie away from the dollhouse. They all sat together, something he hadn't often done with his family growing up. The Coltons had formal gatherings and sat together on holidays. He and his siblings had tremendous respect and love for one another, but Callum had drifted apart from them after Annabel passed. Since he'd been back in town, he had grown closer to Marlowe and Bowie. And he couldn't imagine Ace could ever have shot their father...

He ate dinner without talking, because he feared he could not survive the cost to his heart. Despite all his efforts to steer clear of women with children, he was falling headfirst into a powerfully moving relationship with Hazel and Evie. Where had all his resolve gone?

Hazel tucked Evie in to the sound of Callum cleaning the kitchen. She hadn't missed his joy in seeing Evie's excitement over receiving the extravagant gift. Sharing dinner tonight had been especially poignant. He genuinely adored Evie. He looked at her as though they had been a family for years. When he let his guard down—unaware or not—he was a phenomenal man. Evie could look up to someone like him.

That terrified Hazel.

She had to know more about him before they sank into a lovestruck quicksand.

"I'd like a glass of wine before we turn in," she said. "You?"

A few seconds passed before he said a tentative, "Sure."

After she had two glasses on the counter, she took out a chardonnay from the cooler and found an opener. Manly hands took over from behind her. Putting her hands on the counter, she watched him open the bottle, feeling his arms on each side of her.

After he uncaged her with one arm, she rolled to lean on her lower back against the counter.

He handed her a glass.

Taking it, she said, "Princesses all over the world must have cast a spell on you."

"I've protected many princesses."

His deep, chocolaty voice and intimate tone riveted her. "You have? Like who?"

"They were from Morocco, Spain, Japan and Sweden. Most of them are repeat clients and usually need me when they travel."

Which must be often. He lived such a glamorous life. He came from a wealthy and prominent family and he protected affluent people. But then, he must be used to that way of life.

He was so different from the kind of man she had envisioned for herself after Ed ran off. She couldn't forget the promise she had made. Up until Ed, she had left her fate to chance, believing that everything happened for a reason and that the right man would come along naturally. Well, Ed had come along naturally, all right, but he'd turned out to be all wrong. Nothing should be left to chance. Maybe some things happened for a reason, but finding a good man was not one of them.

After sipping some wine, she asked, "What made you decide to become a bodyguard?"

He took a moment before he answered. "I was on a mission in Ukraine and noticed two men waiting outside of an apartment building. A young woman came out and they abducted her. I followed them. Watched them force her out of the vehicle and into a house. They had her blindfolded and tied."

Hazel listened with increasing horror.

"I went to the door and knocked. One of them answered and I gave him a throat strike." He gestured with his hand, putting his fingers to her throat. "I heard the girl screaming down the hall and the other man yelling for her to shut up. I heard him hit her and tell her he'd kill her if she didn't be quiet. By then I was at the doorway. He had already torn her shirt and was trying to remove her jeans. He saw me and stopped and asked who the hell I was. I told him I would be the last person he'd ever see alive if he didn't get off the girl." He stopped as though back in the scene.

"What happened?" she asked.

"He got off her and lunged for his gun. I threw it out of reach and gave him a good beating. Just before I knocked him unconscious, I told him if he ever hurt another woman again I'd come back and finish him off." He drank some wine.

"Then what?"

"I called the police and told them what happened. The two were arrested and sent to prison."

"What happened with the girl?" Had she been the woman he had lost?

He shrugged. "She thanked me and I never saw her again. That was my last mission before my service ended and I left the navy."

Callum had done a very heroic thing and that woman had to have been so grateful. If that had happened to Hazel, she would have wanted to find the man who saved her from rape and possibly murder, to thank him when she wasn't traumatized.

Looking at him and his handsome face and messy hair and into his blue eyes, she fell for him even more. Although she tried to ward the feeling off, the warmth mushroomed and gave her a tickle in her stomach.

"When I returned to the States, I didn't know what I wanted to do with the rest of my life. All I knew was I didn't want to work at a corporation, especially Colton Oil."

Hazel hadn't expected him to continue talking, but welcomed it.

"Being a SEAL taught me how to fight and use guns and do both really well. That was my skill set. I ran into an old friend who told me about Executive Protection and put me in touch with the CEO."

"And the rest, as they say, is history," she said, admiring his tall, muscular frame and his SEAL background that he put to good use. She sipped wine and put down her glass on the kitchen counter.

"A little more history than I like," he said.

Could it be he'd talk about the woman he had lost?

"I almost stopped working for Executive Protection a year after I joined."

"Because of her?" she asked quietly.

He nodded, the mood turning darker. Putting his glass beside hers, he walked into the living room and stopped before the windows.

Hazel followed, standing beside him and resting her hand on his forearm, urging him to face her.

He did.

"Tell me, Callum." It would help him if he talked about it. And since she was losing her fight not to fall madly in love with him, her best interest was to help him help himself.

"I was protecting a witness in the trial of a drug dealer who murdered someone," he said. "I did my job and saw that the witness made it to court, testified and sent the dealer to prison." He stopped.

Hazel could see he had come to the most difficult part. She stepped closer and put her hands on his impressive chest, encouraging him without words. The painful storm in his eyes eased a little.

"No one knew he wasn't just any dealer. He was high level and dangerous, with ties to one of Mexico's most notorious cartels. Living in the shadows of the underworld. I was seeing Annabel during the trial. She lived in the city where we met. The dealer must have found out. She was run off the road and killed."

Hazel felt his pain, shared it and wished she could take it away.

"I protected the witness but I couldn't protect Annabel or our unborn child," he said, grinding out the words with deep and barely leashed anger.

"Listen to me, Callum." Hazel had to reach him now. He was vulnerable. "You didn't know he would send someone to kill her. It is not your fault."

"The person who ran her off the road was never found. I tried, but..."

Hazel touched both sides of his face. "You didn't kill her. The drug dealer did."

"He did it to get even with me. To make me pay."

"It is not your fault." She stopped him from turning away. "I know people say that too much, but it's true, Callum. An evil man killed her, not you."

"I vowed to never protect women and children after that."

Hazel slid her hands to his shoulders. "But you protected princesses."

"That was different."

"How?" She watched him ponder that. Princesses were women. Some of them had to have kids.

"I don't know. They didn't make me think about Annabel."

She had a question she dreaded to ask because she was pretty sure she'd hate the answer. "Do I make you think about Annabel?"

"You make me have to try very hard *not* to. You and Evie both."

Well, that was better than an all-out yes. "You need to confront your grief, Callum. Have you talked with Annabel's family?"

"Not since the funeral."

"Maybe you should. It might give you closure."

"They blame me."

"That's what they said? Are you sure they really blame you? Any parent would be distraught over losing their child. Have they tried to contact you?"

"They invited me to a gathering they planned on the one-year anniversary of her death, but I didn't go. Even if I'd wanted to, I was out of the country. I didn't get the invitation until after the memorial."

"Do they know about the baby?" she asked.

"Yes. Annabel told them."

"And no one in your family knew you went to her funeral?"

He shook his head. "At the time all I thought about was getting away."

He had submerged himself in work, traveling all over the

world, never taking a break to be with family or friends. What a lonely existence. And the burden he had carried with him must have been suffocating at times. Hazel couldn't believe he hadn't told anyone about the baby. Well, maybe she could. He hadn't been able to talk about them.

Until now. With her.

Hazel became aware of his hands on her hips. At some point during their exchange he'd placed them there. Her body pressed against his. Her gaze melded with his, seeing into him without barriers. He'd opened himself to her and their connection blossomed.

"Why me?" she asked, her voice low with rising desire.

"I wish I knew." He lowered his head and kissed her. His lips touched hers, featherlight, brushing over them and then taking her mouth for an intimate mating.

After he had poured out his heart to her, Hazel felt secure in giving herself to him. Everything.

Chapter 7

Hazel looked up at Callum when he broke from another impassioned kiss. His eyes burned with lust, fueled by the significance of what he had confided, as though freed. She reveled in the deep meaning in his next kiss, and was glad she had put Evie to bed. She had the night with Callum. With his arms around her back, she looped hers over his shoulders.

He lifted her and she wrapped her legs around him as he carried her to his room, kissing all the way to the bed.

Hazel had to fight for a few seconds of clarity before this continued.

"Callum, I'm not on the Pill."

He rose above her, looking intently into her eyes. She didn't want him to stop but they had to behave like adults.

"I don't have anything, either. I have something at home but I didn't bring it."

Neither one of them had thought they'd end up in the same bed, especially this soon. She did some quick calculations.

"I just had my period. We should be safe."

She spent a long moment wavering between temptation and

logic. He had to be thinking the same thing. What if she got pregnant? How would she feel about that? Was this worth the risk?

Her heart charged forward with an affirmative while her brain cautioned to slow this down. Lying here like this, with him hovering over her and her hands on his hard chest and the vision of his face, so manly and full of desire, temptation hummed into a roar. She could feel his member against her. Kissing had made her hot; this wasn't lessening the effect.

"Are you sure?"

He wasn't asking if she was sure about the timing. He asked if she was sure if she wanted to take this risk.

"Are you?"

He lowered his mouth to hers for a soft kiss. "I asked you first."

"I'm sure." Especially now that he had resumed kissing her.

"Me, too." He kissed her harder, lowering his body onto hers and sending lightning bolts of sensation through her.

She sank her fingers into his thick hair and moaned. In response to that sound, he moved against her, teasing, hinting at what would come.

Sliding her hands down to his T-shirt, she lifted the hem. He moved back and removed the shirt the rest of the way, sending it sailing to the floor while his eyes devoured the sight of her. The blue sundress dipped modestly low in the front, but there was enough cleavage to show off.

He lifted the dress up and she sat up as he pulled it over her head and dropped it on top of his shirt. His eyes took their fill of her naked breasts before he came down and sampled one in his mouth, flicking the nipple while his hand ran over the other breast.

Eager to see him, she tugged at his jeans' button. He withdrew and helped her, having to get up to take them off. Convenient that they were both already barefoot. She kicked off her underwear and waited for him to climb back on top of her. She was traditional that way. She loved the feel of a man's weight on her before he entered. While that was her favorite position, it most certainly wasn't the only one she enjoyed.

Callum crawled over her and slowly lowered his body onto hers. A delicious shiver coursed through her. He kissed her softly for endless moments before kneeing her legs apart. She was ready to give herself to him, more ready than she had been for any man in a long time.

He guided himself to her and slowly pushed into her, filling her deliciously. The initial friction against her sensitive spot drove her to near orgasm.

"Wait. Wait," she rasped.

He stilled above her, his breathing faster and his eyes ablaze.

Hazel dug her head into the pillow against unbearable pleasure. She didn't want her first orgasm to end so quickly. But he turned her on so incredibly much!

Callum groaned. "I can barely hold still when you look so sexy and beautiful." He withdrew and thrust into her and then repeated the action over and over, moving her body on the bed and sending tingles of ecstasy radiating from her abdomen all the way out to her limbs.

She bit back a cry as she came on an explosion of orgasmic fireworks. He groaned again and slowed as he experienced his own release.

Then he put his head beside hers, each of them catching their breath.

"That was incredible," he said next to her ear.

"Like the Kentucky Derby, except the most exciting two minutes in sex."

He chuckled, then rolled off her to prop his head on his hand. "Are you usually this responsive?"

"No. Ed had to work at it for at least fifteen." Suddenly disturbed by that revelation, Hazel averted her eyes from Callum. What was different about Callum?

After a moment, she turned her head and saw his thoughts

had taken a sober turn as well. Not wanting this moment or the beauty of what had just transpired to fade yet, she rolled onto her side with her back to him.

"We can at least spoon for a while, can't we?" she asked.

After a few brief seconds, he moved closer and said above her ear, "Yes."

The feel of him against her calmed her and enveloped her in warmth. When his hand caressed her arm and he planted a soft kiss on her cheek, she knew he had fallen under the same spell, the spell that had landed them in bed together. Tomorrow would bring whatever it brought.

Callum ordered room service the next morning. Hazel had gotten up after him and gone into her room before Evie woke. Now Evie was busy with her dollhouse and Hazel was finishing getting ready. He'd heard her shower turn off a few minutes ago.

When he had first awakened to Hazel's sleeping face on the same pillow as his, he had been overcome with affection and arousal. Her ankle was over his calf. Her plump breasts were molded into tempting mounds above the sheet and blanket. He could start every morning like that.

And that was precisely the thought that had sent him careening back to reality. Annabel's face rushed forth. He didn't feel guilty or that he had betrayed her. It had been too long since she had died. It was more of a threatening feeling. He was in danger of welcoming a woman and her five-year-old girl into his life. He had failed at protecting the last mother and daughter he had been involved with. Did he want to take that risk? No. At least not now. He didn't know if he'd ever be ready for that.

Hazel's responsiveness to him had only increased his pleasure and, if he were brutally honest, the bond he felt with her. It was too overwhelming. Too potent.

He had told her what he had told *no one*, not a living soul other than Annabel's family. He recalled the day of her funeral, when her father had asked why no one from his family had attended. He had said they couldn't make it. Annabel's father had looked at him strangely. He didn't know it at the time, but all Callum had wanted was to leave and be as far away from any reminders of Annabel as he could.

Annabel's murder had occurred in another city, not Mustang Valley. Another police force and even the feds had investigated but with no real zest. It had been assumed her killer had fled to Mexico. It hadn't made big news. No one in his family or circle of friends had heard about it, by some miracle. He had needed to be left alone.

No one would have understood. No one who hadn't gone through what he had would be able to understand. The terribleness of her murder. The helplessness of not being able to find her killer. The knowledge that her murder and the killing of their unborn child would never be solved.

There wasn't a day that passed when he didn't think about that. Who was her killer and where was he today? Did anyone know what he had done and could it lead police to him? Was there a way to extradite him to the States if he was abroad?

Maybe that was what he needed. Annabel's cold case solved. Maybe then he could move on. Maybe then he wouldn't think about what was taken from him so violently whenever he spent time around women with children. Pregnant women got to him the most. He had missed out on that.

One could argue he could find another woman and start a family, but for him it wasn't that simple. Not only had Annabel and their unborn baby been taken from him, so had all of the first-time experiences and the happiness. The wonder of the creation of life, the stages of pregnancy, the anticipation of the birth. Looking up names. Imagining being a family—a *close* family.

Everything good about being with a woman who was pregnant with his child had been destroyed. All that came to his mind now in connection with pregnant women was Annabel's lifeless and abused form on the coroner's table, the baby bump still there, but full of death now.

He had put up with enough when it came to family, so why did he have to go through that? His was not an idyllic family. His former stepmother, Selina, loved drama and enjoyed driving wedges between his siblings. Callum never understood why his father allowed her to keep her job at Colton Oil. Everyone thought she must have something on Payne. She also kept jovially reminding everyone of the Colton Oil bylaws that said the CEO had to be a Colton by blood. With the discovery that Ace was switched at birth, that presented a significant problem. Her heartless pokes reminded Callum of his estrangement from his father and how terrible it would be if Payne never woke up from his coma.

He snapped back to the present and poured Evie some cereal. "Evie, come get breakfast."

Saying that made him feel like a father figure. Taking care of Evie came so naturally. How had that happened? Would he ever be the same after this?

Just then Hazel appeared in jeans that hugged her slender hips and a silky white top. She eyed him peculiarly and he knew she wondered why he'd gotten out of bed before she woke. Was she gauging him? Maybe she hoped he was an early riser. More likely she thought he had run away.

He put the room service on the table. "Coffee?"

"Sure."

He felt her continue to evaluate him as he finished getting their breakfast spread out on the table.

"I'd like to talk with Kerry about what we can do to help with the investigation." He watched her ascertain why he was so anxious to help. Or maybe she wondered why he'd so abruptly made that announcement. He needed something to do and he needed to get away from her as fast as possible.

"Okay," she said slowly. She sat and sipped the coffee he'd poured.

He sat across from her. Evie bounded to the table and took her seat, oblivious to the tension between her mother and Callum. She scooped up her cereal and looked toward the television.

"What did you have in mind on the investigation?" Hazel asked.

"Nate Blurge was the murder victim Evie saw being kidnapped. Maybe we can find out more about him."

She nodded a couple of times. "Okay."

"Did you know him or of him at all?"

"No. I never went to bars like Joe's."

Of course, she wouldn't. Not only did she have a young child, she wasn't the kind of woman who would frequent places like that. Maybe he had asked just for something to say that wasn't related to last night.

"You were up early," Hazel said.

"Yeah. I couldn't go back to sleep."

"Something troubling you?" She took another sip, doing a poor job of appearing nonchalant.

"No." He ate his breakfast, hoping she'd just let it drop.

Turned out, she did, but she was way too quiet as they left the inn to go to the police station.

Outside, he gave the valet his ticket.

Evie clung to Hazel, trying to swing off her mother's arm.

His rental arrived and he opened the back door for Hazel to get Evie in her car seat. Then he opened the front passenger side and went around to get behind the wheel. She was still quiet as they headed out, but only for five minutes.

"Did you love her?" Hazel asked.

He had often thought of that. He hadn't known Annabel long before she had become pregnant, but as time passed and the birth of their child drew nearer, he'd thought he could love her. They never had the passion he and Hazel shared last night. That confused him.

"I have to believe I did, yes."

"Do you still?"

That stopped him for a few seconds. He hadn't really contemplated that since she died. Now as he reflected on it, he realized he did not.

"No," he finally said.

"Then…why?"

She was reading too much into him getting up before her. He got it that she was suspicious, but why grill him like this?

"I just woke up before you, Hazel. Did you want me to wake you?"

She didn't answer right away and he let her take her time in contemplating what he'd said.

"I wouldn't have been with you had I thought you'd turn me away the next day," she said at last.

Where had that notion come from? "I didn't turn you away." Was she the cuddling type? He used to be.

Evie's father must have really done a number on her. Was Callum another mistake to her?

"You seem different this morning," she said.

"I don't mean to be." He wished she wouldn't push the issue.

"Are you okay with us?"

He glanced in the rearview mirror and saw Evie fast asleep in her car seat. No wonder Hazel was talking so freely. Now he had to answer, and he hesitated because he had to be honest.

"I take it by your silence that you aren't. I'm sorry for making such a big issue about it, but I need to be sure about how to handle this going forward."

He heard sincerity in her voice. She didn't like asking all these questions. She just felt she had to. "Everything is going so fast between us. I haven't had time to process it. Have you?"

She breathed a laugh of relief. "No. We can slow it down. Is that what you want? I have Evie to think about. She's already so fond of you. I worry about her when it comes time to part ways—if that happens."

"I don't ever want to hurt Evie, so I'll do whatever you think is best when it comes to her."

"What about me? Will you do what you think is best when it comes to me?" She said it lightly, but he sensed she actually needed to know.

"It isn't my intention to hurt you. I'm trying to be honest with you."

"I appreciate that, but I'm a little disappointed in myself for not thinking this through better. We rushed into this and now I wish I hadn't."

They had rushed into sleeping together. Could they have done anything to prevent their attraction? He couldn't blame her for being regretful or concerned. They barely knew each other. About the only things they did know were a little background information and that they had a hot physical chemistry that was apparently uncontrollable.

"I don't regret last night at all," he said. "In fact, that's what has me in such a conundrum today. I have never had such an amazing time, except maybe my first time."

She averted her head, propping her elbow on the door frame and curling her fingers against her chin. "That has me in a conundrum, too."

Her quiet, soft tone revealed her vulnerability. He reached over and covered her hand with his. "We'll cool this off for a while. Get to know each other more."

She looked at him as though having serious doubts as to whether either one of them could cool this off.

Suddenly, the glass of Callum's window shattered as a bullet flew past him and went through the passenger window. An instant later, he realized someone had shot at them, narrowly missing him and Hazel. "Get down!" he shouted, looking in the back at Evie, who had slouched enough in her sleep to be below the door frame but now began to wake.

As he took out his pistol, his heart pounded as he urgently searched for the shooter. An SUV had fallen back in the other lane but sped up as Callum had done the moment the bullet had penetrated.

He weaved in and out of traffic, putting more distance between them and the shooter.

"Call 911," Callum said to Hazel, who had already taken out her phone.

He slowed enough to make the next turn, trying not to frighten Evie more than she already was. She had begun to cry. Cars ahead blocked his way. This wasn't a movie—he couldn't drive up onto the sidewalk.

Hazel finished talking to the dispatcher.

The gunman began to gain on them. Callum's fear that Evie would be harmed intensified.

"Callum." Hazel sounded terrified. "Evie."

"I know."

He tried to veer out into the oncoming traffic to get around a car. He had to steer back into the lane. The car passed and Callum would have tried again but the gunman was beside them in a big black SUV. The shooter aimed. Callum pressed on the brakes. The other man did too and then rammed into them.

"Evie, stay down!" Hazel hollered, dropping the phone.

"Mommy?"

"Just stay down."

Callum didn't want to shoot unless he had to, not with a child in the truck. The traffic began to clear. He drove into the oncoming lane and gunned the truck, passing two cars before getting back over as another vehicle approached, horn honking. With some clear road, Callum raced toward the police station, unable to believe they were being chased again, that he had allowed it to happen.

If he hadn't been distracted by Hazel and their night together, he could have stayed focused and prevented this—at the very least putting Evie in less danger.

He made the last turn to reach the station. In the rearview mirror he saw the SUV pass without turning. The gunman knew they were headed for the police. He also must know the police would come after him if he tried to wait for them again.

"He's gone," Callum said.

Hazel breathed heavily and put her head back.

He drove into the police station parking lot and parked.

Hazel jumped out and hastily removed Evie from the car seat. When she had her daughter in her arms she asked, "Are you all right?"

"I'm fine, Mommy. Did we almost have an accident?"

"Yes, sweetie. Mommy just had a big scare."

Callum put his hand on her back as she scanned the area. "Let's get inside."

They walked inside. Kerry would be expecting them. Callum had phoned ahead. A few minutes later, she appeared, sporting her badge on her belt.

"How are you doing?" Kerry asked.

"We were chased again and shot at," Hazel said, putting Evie down.

"Where is he? I'll get some cars out there."

"It's too late. He didn't follow us all the way to the station," Callum said.

"I'll have them be on the lookout for the vehicle."

Hazel gave her the plate number, surprising Callum with her stealthy observation and thinking. She went on to describe the SUV, including the damage to the passenger side when the shooter had rammed into them.

"What brought you here today? Not drawing the shooter out and trying to run you down?"

"We'd like to help with the investigation. Speed it up if we can."

Kerry looked from Hazel to Callum and then Evie. "We've questioned some of the workers at Joe's Bar. Nothing very concrete has come up. We did learn that Nate Blurge's wife works there and he had a reputation for flirting with a lot of women, many of them the waitresses there. Apparently he made a lot of husbands angry. If the killer was one of them, he might show up. If you could watch the place, see if you can find out anything about who might want him dead. If you help out with that, I can pay more attention to his family."

Callum nodded. "We can do that, but not with Evie."

Hazel shook her head. "No, not with Evie."

"Is there anywhere you can take her?" Callum asked. "Didn't you say you had a brother who was a cop in Phoenix?"

"I did. His wife is a cop, too."

"That sounds about as perfect as it gets," Kerry said. "I agree. Evie is in too much danger if you keep her here. Every time you leave the inn you're at risk. Whoever is after you is watching that place very close."

"I hate the idea of parting company with my daughter but I can't argue she's in danger. She'd be safe with my brother and his wife."

Callum liked that idea. Not only would it keep him from bonding even more with the girl, he wouldn't have to worry about protecting her *and* her mother.

"Why don't you go back to the inn?" Kerry said. "I can have an officer escort you."

"That won't be necessary," Callum said.

"Are you sure? It's too dangerous for you to come and go from the inn and I'm concerned next time you won't get away without being harmed."

Or killed. Although she didn't say so, Callum knew she worried they could very well be murdered.

"I'm sure." He would not let his guard down again.

"We need to come up with a way to get you out of the inn and Evie somewhere safe." She tapped her lower lip with her forefinger and then lowered her hand. "How about if I have someone drop off some disguises so you can get Evie out safely? Then I can arrange for undercover officers to watch you and make sure you get on your way."

Callum grinned. "I like that idea. In fact, I know the perfect disguises." He leaned close to Kerry's ear and told her in a low voice what to get for them.

Kerry smiled and glanced at Hazel.

"What are you up to?" Hazel asked Callum.

"You'll see." Then to Kerry, he said, "Just ask Patsy to pick them up. She'll have fun with that."

He gave Kerry Patsy's contact information, looking forward to the trip to Hazel's brother. All that time they would spend together as a family… And then he would be alone with Hazel after they dropped Evie off. That came with so many conflicting emotions. Leaving Evie would be sad, but being alone with Hazel gave him all kinds of unwelcome thoughts…and welcome ones, too.

Chapter 8

Later the next morning, Hazel couldn't believe what she had allowed Callum to talk her into wearing. She looked at herself in the mirror. The studded leather sleeveless top zipped up to just above her breasts and the low-hipped leather pants hugged her shape. The jewel encrusted shoes with four-inch heels would bring her much closer to Callum's height. A blond wig completed the ensemble.

Beside her Evie giggled. She had a wig, too, also blond, and wore an adorable biker girl T-shirt with leather pants—not skin-tight like her mother's. Patsy had also gotten her a fun metal rivet and leather wrap bracelet and a pair of black boots.

Evie posed in front of the bathroom mirror, only her head above the sink counter.

Hazel chuckled. "Come on, Evie."

They left the bathroom. Callum waited for them in the kitchen, leaning against the island counter, holding his phone. His eyes lifted as they approached, frozen in that pose as his gaze roamed down Hazel and then back up.

"I'm a biker girl!" Evie jumped and stopped in front of him.

"You sure are. Looking good, too."

"Hopefully you haven't ruined her future," Hazel said with humor, enjoying this and feeling like they were a family getting ready to go on an outing. She wouldn't even analyze that right now.

She did have a moment where she had to stare at him, though. Dark blue jeans that cupped his crotch and a leather jacket over a gray T-shirt that had a black print on the front. He also had on glasses to ramp him up from lowly biker to biker with money. She liked his wig, black with a tasteful ponytail.

"Are we ready?" he asked.

"Yeah!" Evie called out cheerily.

"Let me check outside first. I have my rental car waiting in front of the inn," he said.

He had prepared well for this. And even though her disguise was a bit sexy, all of them were convincing. They looked completely different than they had this morning.

In the lobby, Hazel took Evie's hand, and Callum noticed a man walking with another woman staring at her.

She looked away, stopping before following Callum through the doors. He covertly checked the front of the inn and beyond and then turned, still holding the door open, not saying he'd spotted a dark SUV across the street. The driver turned their way, stared a few seconds then turned away. A man and a woman with a child wasn't unusual. They might stand out as a biker family but they looked nothing like they usually did. Callum was pleased the man apparently hadn't caught on to their disguises.

Hazel stepped outside with Evie. The car was right in front of them, a valet having already opened the back door.

Ushering Evie into the seat, Callum let Hazel bend to buckle her in. She looked through the opposite window at an SUV. The driver still wasn't even paying attention to them. Callum saw he wore a cap and sunglasses, so recognizing him was still impossible. Callum thought it might be the same man who'd come after them before.

He saw another man ogling her as she got in the front passenger seat. Callum got behind the wheel, looking over at the SUV. The driver glanced their way but didn't seem to have any peculiar reaction.

"This costume is attracting too much attention," she said.

"Good, nobody is going to guess it's you."

"Evie might have made that SUV driver suspicious," she said.

"Evie won't be with us after today."

As they moved out of the inn's parking area, Callum glanced once more at the SUV. The driver paid them no attention as they passed. Evie would be safe. Callum leaned back, savoring the victory. He didn't understand why or how, but Hazel and Evie were so important to him. His job of protecting them was so important to him. He looked over at Hazel, gorgeous and content in their successful getaway. He'd seen her satisfied in another way, too, and struggled to ward off the temptation to see that again.

"Hazel?"

Hazel's brother was a couple of inches over six feet and built like a linebacker. Off duty, he sported jeans and a Kansas City Chiefs T-shirt. Callum could see the resemblance to Hazel in his thick dark hair and hazel-green eyes.

"Is that you?" her brother asked.

Hazel smiled big. She had called ahead to make sure Owen could take in Evie but she must look so different than her usual self right now. "Yes."

"And Evie?"

Evie giggled. "Yes."

"What's with the look?" Her brother opened the door wider to let them in.

"I'll explain." Hazel entered the house.

After a two hour drive they'd arrived in this neat and tidy

suburb of modern homes, some stucco, some more traditional, all with big front windows. Hazel's brother's house was two stories with a covered porch and a three-car garage.

The grayish-brown wooden floor of the foyer opened to a formal living room, with the kitchen and dining areas to the left. Stairs led up to the second level beyond the dining room.

"Callum, this is Owen and Jessica, my brother and his wife." Hazel introduced them.

Callum shook Owen's hand as his wife walked up beside him, a stunning woman with long dark hair and brown eyes. They made a handsome couple.

"Hi," Jessica said with a wide, toothy smile.

"Hey there, Evie." Owen crouched to Evie's level, who clung to her mother's leg in a sudden show of shyness.

"You remember your uncle, Evie," Hazel said. "Say hello."

"Hi," Evie said quietly.

Hazel laughed, her affection and adoration coming out in the sound.

Callum hadn't thought Evie had a shy bone in her body but meeting new people apparently made her withdraw. She'd done the same to him when they had first met. Kids.

"You've grown since I last saw you," Owen said.

A beagle came trotting up with a wagging tail.

"Do you remember Olive?" Jessica asked.

"Yes." Evie crept out from behind Hazel's leg and knelt down before the beagle.

Eager for attention, the dog jumped up on her, paws on her legs. Evie giggled and collapsed onto her rear. When she crawled on hands and knees into the living room, Callum knew she'd be preoccupied for a while.

"We were surprised you were coming up today," Owen said. "Such spontaneity isn't like you. We were glad we're both off duty today. Is everything all right?"

"There's a good reason for us showing up on such short notice, and looking like this," Hazel said. "Evie saw a man get hit on the head with a rock and his body was found."

Jessica inhaled sharply. "Oh, no. She saw that?" She glanced back at Evie as though wondering if she was okay.

"Evie seems fine," Hazel said. "She seems unaffected."

"She's probably too young to fully understand what happened," Callum said. "The problem is the police haven't caught the killer yet, and he knows where we're staying."

"He's tried more than once to get us."

Owen kept an unreadable but somber face but Jessica's jaw fell.

"Evie?" Jessica asked, incredulous.

Hazel nodded. "That's why we're here." She looked at her brother. "I need a huge favor."

"You want us to watch Evie? You don't even have to ask," he said. "Of course we'll do it."

"And she'll be safe," Jessica said. "We're both armed and have licenses to carry."

"She'll be guarded at all times," Owen said.

Callum saw Hazel's shoulders slump in relief. "I can't thank you enough," she said. "You don't know how much it means to me to know she'll be with two cops. I won't have to worry about her the way I have been."

"Of course," Owen said. "We'll love having her." He glanced over at Evie and Olive, who were rolling around the living room in play. "And so will Olive, it would seem."

Hazel laughed and Callum smiled a little at the cute sight of Evie and the dog.

"Do the police have any solid leads?" Jessica asked.

"We're looking into the murder victim right now. Hopefully that will point us to a suspect," Callum said.

"Where are you staying?" Owen asked. "Is there security?"

"Callum is a bodyguard." She explained how they met and how Callum had saved her and Evie. "He's kindly agreed to protect me until the killer is caught."

"Bodyguard, huh?" Owen said, checking Callum out. "Do you work for a security service?"

"I work for Executive Protection Services. It's an international personal protection agency."

Owen's brow lifted and he seemed impressed. "Sounds flashy."

"He's protected princesses," Hazel said. "Not your everyday bodyguard."

The way she looked at him snared his attention. He doubted she meant to reveal her admiration so guilelessly.

"So it would seem," Owen said.

"We were just about to have lunch," Jessica said. "Are you hungry?"

Callum wasn't but Hazel glanced at Evie and said, "Evie hasn't eaten yet."

"I hope chili cheese dogs are okay." Jessica led the way into the open, bright kitchen.

"*Yaaay,* hot dogs!" Evie bounded into the kitchen and took a seat at the table, Olive right by her side, sitting on the floor beside the chair.

Jessica prepared some paper plates, serving Evie first and then the men at the kitchen island.

Hazel sat at the table with Jessica.

Callum wasn't very hungry so he knifed off one bite and set down his utensils.

"So, a bodyguard, huh?" Owen asked, picking at his food.

"Yes."

"What's your story? How'd you get into that profession?"

"I was a Navy SEAL before that and the opportunity presented itself when I left."

"SEAL. Not many can make it through that training," Jessica said, sounding impressed.

"No." No point in denying it. SEAL training was beyond extreme.

"What made you decide to be a SEAL?" This question came from Hazel.

He hadn't thought about that in a really long time. Growing up he hadn't always aspired to be a SEAL. "I was an aggressive kid. Always getting into fights. Staying out late and getting in trouble. I was never arrested, just kind of…wild. My last year in high school I wondered what I wanted to do with my life. Not follow my father. A friend of mine suggested the military. He had a good point. If I continued on my path of aggression, maybe I would have ended up in jail. When I was a kid, I would play with toy soldiers. The army didn't appeal to me but the navy did. The SEALs always fascinated me. The challenge of becoming one satisfied my headstrong nature. So I tried out and made the team."

"You were wild?" Hazel asked. "You're so levelheaded now. So calm."

"I thank the discipline of training for that. It changed my life." The years he had been active had been enough. When he left, he was ready for something different. Being a SEAL had served its purpose. He had learned how to channel his aggression, put it to good use. Being a bodyguard continued to do that for him. He felt fortunate to have found his true calling in life. Not many people did. He would have been a lost soul if he had chosen to work an office job.

"You said you were staying somewhere together?" Owen asked.

"At the Dales Inn," Hazel said.

"You're staying with my sister?" Owen asked Callum.

"For her protection. And Evie's, up until now."

Owen glanced from him to Hazel and back again. "Are you sure there isn't another reason?"

Was he being a protective older brother?

"Owen," Hazel said in a cautionary tone.

"Are you seeing him?"

"What difference does that make?" she asked.

"So you are?" Owen looked at Callum.

"No. We aren't *seeing* each other. He's helping me, that's all." But Hazel averted her head, a dead giveaway that she wasn't being completely truthful.

"Hazel has been through a lot," Owen said to Callum. "Did she tell you about Ed?"

"She did."

"So you understand she needs a man she can depend on."

"Owen, stop." Jessica laughed a little. "He's always been protective of Hazel. Don't mind him. I'm sure you're a decent guy and wouldn't hurt her."

"I wasn't there for her when Ed left her. That won't happen again." Owen said the last directly to Hazel.

"Everything is all right, Owen," Hazel said. "I'm not doing anything I don't want and I won't do anything that will hurt me or Evie." She turned to Callum. "Especially Evie."

Callum put his hands up. "I am a decent guy and I would never harm Hazel or Evie." He looked at Hazel. "Not intentionally."

He couldn't promise she wouldn't end up with hurt feelings after this was over. He couldn't predict the future, much less their chemistry. That had a mind of its own.

"All I ask is you don't tell anyone Evie is staying here."

"We would never put her in that kind of danger," Owen said, Jessica shaking her head in full agreement.

They finished eating and now it was time to go. Callum saw how difficult this was going to be for Hazel. She watched Evie play with Olive with somber eyes.

"She'll be fine," Jessica said. "We have toys for my nieces and nephews, my siblings' kids, so she'll have plenty to do."

Hazel sent her a grateful but bittersweet smile. "I've never been away from her like this before."

Jessica put her hand on Hazel's shoulder. "You'll see her again before you know it."

Hazel nodded, wiping her eye even though no tears had

fallen. She did look a little misty, though. She went to Evie and crouched.

"Hey, Evie. Mommy's going to go now. I'll be back to get you as soon as I can, okay?"

"Okay." Evie stood and turned to hug her mother, not seeming at all afraid to stay with her aunt and uncle—and their cute beagle.

Hazel kissed her head. "You be good for Aunt Jessica and Uncle Owen, okay?"

"Okay." Evie plopped back down by Olive, whose tail wagged and head moved forward for a quick lick on Evie's face.

Evie giggled and petted the dog.

Hazel stood and walked to the entry where Callum waited. She glanced back once more before saying goodbye to her brother and Jessica.

Just then, Evie bounded over, throwing her arms around one of Callum's legs. "Bye, Cal-em."

Callum knelt before her and she hugged him around his neck. "Bye, Evie. We'll see you soon."

"'Kay." With that, she ran back to the dog.

"How long did you say you two have been living together?" Owen asked incredulously.

"Not long. A week or so," Hazel said.

"You must be good with kids," Jessica said.

"Maybe so. Evie is a good girl," Callum said, seeing Hazel wasn't amused. She was probably concerned over how Evie would react if he left them.

Callum couldn't do anything about how much Evie liked him. He could be careful with her, though—and Hazel.

They left the house.

Outside, Hazel rubbed under her nose as though the sting of tears threatened her composure. "Is she even going to miss me?"

Callum chuckled. "She'll have a lot of new things to keep her preoccupied. But yes, she'll miss you and she'll be so excited to see you again."

Hazel smiled slightly. "And you, it would seem."

"I'll be mindful of that, Hazel."

"She's already so attached to you."

"She likes me. I haven't been around her long enough to make that big of an impact. It will be the same as saying goodbye to a friend at school."

"It *will*?"

He hadn't meant to sound as though he had already decided to part ways with her when this was over.

"If this doesn't end up turning into something more," he said.

She glanced at him with appreciation for the clarification. As they reached the car, Callum wondered why he had reassured her. The prospect of their becoming a real couple—maybe even a family—gave him a sick feeling. He would never forget the way he had felt when Annabel died, along with their unborn baby. His soul had been ripped from him. He hadn't been able to function. He had wondered if he would ever make it through.

No more talk about the future for him and Hazel. He'd make sure she was safe and then that would be that.

Since they were already dressed in disguise, Callum suggested they start staking out Joe's Bar. Nate Blurge was known to have spent a lot of time there, as Kerry had said. Someone had to know something that might lead to a break in the case. Hazel stepped into the dimly lit bar with Callum. Right away her first impression was that the lights were low to conceal the disrepair. A melting pot of people half-filled the place with its dirty, worn floor, and scratched and chipped tables and chairs. The ceiling had water stains and dirt caked the twenty-plus year old trim.

"Have a seat anywhere," the bartender called out.

No Wait to Be Seated sign here.

Two young couples laughed at a table. Solitary patrons at the bar watched the television that hung above shelves of liquor or stared at their drinks. A group of scary-looking biker men loitered around a pool table. The tallest one zeroed in on Hazel, making no effort to hide his ogling.

Callum chose a table in the middle of the bar. Hazel sat adjacent to him. Moments later a scantily clad waitress approached with a name tag that said Shelly. Callum ordered a beer and Hazel ordered a chardonnay.

"Hey, isn't this the place where that man who was murdered hung out?" Callum asked.

Hazel was amazed at how quickly he went to work.

"Nate?" the waitress replied. "Yeah. He was here most nights. Been kind of peaceful without him."

"Oh, really? Why is that?" Callum asked.

"He liked to flirt with all of us girls. Nate wasn't the handsomest man you ever saw. Shame he was killed and all, but I didn't know him very well. I'll be back with your drinks." She left for the bar.

Hazel watched her get their drinks from the bartender and walk back over to them.

"Did Nate sleep with any of the waitresses?" Callum asked.

Shelly slowed as she placed the glass of wine in front of Hazel. "Why do you want to know?"

Callum shrugged dismissively. "Maybe that has something to do with why he was murdered."

"Police already came in asking questions." She set a bottle of beer in front of Callum.

"Did they talk to anyone who had relations with him?"

"Don't know for sure. He bragged to me once that he had a thing going with Candace."

"Candace?"

"Yeah. She works two jobs. Has a day job in town."

"Is she here now?" Hazel asked.

"She only works weekends here," Shelly said.

"Did he engage with anyone else?" Callum asked.

"I didn't keep track of his love interests. He mostly annoyed me and the other girls."

Kerry hadn't mentioned anyone named Candace. Could it be they had stumbled upon something?

The waitress left to visit other tables.

Hazel looked around the bar, at the bikers who gave her an uneasy feeling, at the cheerful pair of couples and the line of solitary men at the bar. She was about to turn back to Callum when she noticed one of the men at the bar was staring at the waitress who had just served them.

The waitress turned from a table and the man quickly averted his head. As she passed behind him, he looked at her again and watched as she retrieved more drinks from the bartender and then walked to the table of couples.

"What is it?" Callum glanced behind him and saw the man. He followed his gaze and also where Hazel looked.

"That man," she said. "He's watching that waitress."

The waitress returned to the bar, going behind it. She smiled at the man who had been staring at her and they began to converse.

"They seem to know each other," Callum said.

The man at the bar reached over and touched the woman's hand and she smiled differently now, much more warmly. Then she glanced at the bartender as though making sure she hadn't been seen. The man seemed to respect that and pretended to pay attention to his bottle of beer.

"The ghost of Nate Blurge?" Hazel said.

Callum chuckled. "Yes. He might be flirting vicariously through that guy." If the woman Blurge had flirted with was the killer's wife, maybe that was why Nate was murdered. And maybe the new man who flirted with her would draw the killer out.

"I have to go to the bathroom." She stood and made her way to the back corner, having to pass the group of bikers on the way.

She ignored the tall biker, aware that he followed her movement. She finished her business in the bathroom, washed her hands and left.

As she walked past the pool table, the tall biker stepped in her path. She stopped.

He wore a sleazy grin, or at least that's how she interpreted it. "Hey, how about a game of pool? You can invite your friend over." He gestured toward Callum. "Is he your boyfriend?"

She contemplated lying. "No."

"Oh." His gaze roamed down her body and back up again. "What's your name, pretty lady?"

"Excuse me." She moved to go around him but he blocked her way.

"If not tonight, then maybe another night?" He gestured toward Callum again. "Maybe when he isn't around?"

"No, thanks."

"At least tell me your name. Can I have your number? I think we should get to know each other."

"Look, I'm not interested." Hazel stepped aside.

The tall biker took hold of her arm and she got a whiff of his breath. He had been drinking for some time.

"Let go of my arm." She jerked her arm and he held firm.

"Tell me your name."

Just then Callum's hand flattened on the man's chest. "What do you think you're doing?"

"Hey." The tall biker stumbled back with Callum's shove. "I was just talking to the lady. She said you and her weren't a couple."

"She also told you she wasn't interested. Is there a problem?"

The tall biker shook his head, feigning nonchalance and acting as though he wasn't afraid. "No problem."

"It looked like you weren't letting the lady pass."

"I would have let her pass. What business is it of yours anyway?" The man stepped forward, as though trying to intimidate Callum.

Callum stood at least an inch or two taller than the biker. "She's with me. And even if she wasn't, I can tell when a woman doesn't want to talk to a man and she doesn't want anything to do with you."

"You don't know that. And you don't own her."

"Come on, Callum." Hazel put her hand on his forearm. "Let's go."

"You gonna hide behind a woman now?" The tall biker stepped even closer. "You should have stayed out of this. If you hadn't shown up, I'd have her number by now."

"She wouldn't have given you her number."

"Well aren't you a cocky bastard. Maybe somebody needs to put you in your place."

"Maybe you should quit drinking and go home. I don't want any trouble. I was a Navy SEAL, so you should think twice about starting something with me."

Callum didn't brag. He sounded calm and as though he had given the man a courteous warning.

But the tall biker smirked and glanced back at his cohorts. "Did you hear that? This jerk is a SEAL. He thinks he's better than all of us."

"I'll warn you once more. You don't want to start anything with me."

Hazel backed up a little. This could get ugly. She had no doubt whatsoever that Callum could take on all of the bikers. Maybe if they were sober the other men would have had a chance, but all of them looked inebriated.

Two of the bikers stepped forward, one holding a pool cue.

"You don't look like you ride. You're too pretty," the tall biker said. "What makes you think you can come in here and get between me and a lady?"

"She doesn't want to talk to you," Callum said.

"I'm getting tired of you saying that." The tall biker took a swing, which Callum easily avoided. He ducked another attempt and then delivered a hard uppercut to the jaw.

The tall biker stumbled backward and the one with a pool cue tried to jab Callum.

Callum blocked that and outmaneuvered him for control of the stick. He swung the cue, knocked the third man on the head and then kicked the taller one, sending him flying back onto the pool table.

This was turning into a real bar fight. And Callum could really move. She almost wasn't afraid, she was so in awe of him.

Hazel backed up some more when the biker who had come after Callum with the cue charged. Using the stick, Callum blocked his punching fists and twisted to high-kick his face. When he landed he used the cue to poke the second man and then tossed it aside to hit the taller biker twice. His opponent fell down.

The other two backed off. Hazel noticed everyone in the bar had stopped to watch, even the bartender. Fighting must be the norm here, because no one interfered.

Callum waited for the taller man to decide what to do. He stared at Callum as he got to his feet, wiping blood off his lip.

"Come on, man. Let's play pool," said a biker who hadn't joined the fight.

The taller biker looked from Hazel to Callum and then finally swatted the air with his hand. "She ain't worth it." With that he faced his friends.

Callum turned and found Hazel, putting his hand on her lower back.

She walked with him toward the exit, Callum tossing money on their table on the way out.

"That was quite a spectacle back there," she said when they were outside.

"They were drunk."

"Clearly. You could have seriously hurt them."

"Yes. I'm glad he chose not to engage anymore."

"Did you learn all those moves in the navy?"

"I refined them in the navy. I got into bar fights a lot when I was young."

"Right. Wild." She smiled and laughed a little, trying not to be so turned on by him.

Nobody had ever fought for her, least of all at a bar. She had not been the type of girl who hung out at such establishments, especially like this one. She had always been more of a wine bar kind of woman. Lunches with her girlfriends. Dates to nice restaurants.

Walking beside Callum, covertly taking in his long strides and his big shoulders, slightly swaying, she had never felt safer.

He caught her looking at him. "What?"

She shook her head, fumbling with brief self-consciousness. "Chivalry isn't dead."

"You liked it that I got into a fight back there?" He grinned teasingly. "I wasn't playing around."

"Oh, I know you weren't." She eyed him again, unable to stop her admiration.

At the car, he stopped her before she opened the door. "Maybe I should get into fights more often."

She tipped her head up, falling into this flirtation far too easily.

"And you in this outfit doesn't help matters." He touched beneath her chin. "I've been dying to do this all day."

He kissed her, soft and slow. Then the flames took over and he deepened the caress. He didn't touch his tongue to hers, just gave her a long and reverent kiss.

She was beginning to think avoiding another tumble in bed would be impossible. And as for avoiding falling for Callum? That was becoming even more impossible by the moment.

Chapter 9

Back at the Dales Inn, Callum saw that same SUV out front with someone inside. Funny, now that he had a closer look, this man didn't appear as large as the one who had shot at them. He must have been mistaken about the suggestion that this was their shooter.

"We should be fine. Just don't look at him." If it was a man. Callum wondered if it could be a female.

Up in the suite, he called Kerry, who told him she was on her way to check on them.

"Is there anyone else you can think of who has a grudge against you?" he asked Hazel.

Her head popped up from the tablet she had been playing around with. "What?"

He went over and sat beside her. "It just occurred to me that the person who's been sitting out in front of this inn might be a woman."

Her brow scrunched in confusion. "But the person who almost ran me and Evie over was a man. I know it."

"I know that, too."

"Well…what are you suggesting?"

"Maybe nothing. I'm more thinking out loud." He ran his fingers through his hair. "I just have this feeling that there is someone else seeking you out. The person who sits outside the inn doesn't shoot at us."

"We were in disguise."

Yes, but every time? What if Callum hadn't noticed the driver of the SUV before today?

"Can you think of anyone who might have a reason to be angry with you?" he asked.

She frowned in confusion. "Callum, I don't understand why you're asking me that. You think there is someone else—besides the kidnapper Evie witnessed—who is after me?"

"Yes, and no. Like I said, I'm thinking out loud, making sure I cover every angle."

After a moment she slowly shook her head. "No."

She seemed hesitant.

"What about your ex-boss? Carolyn Johnson?" The woman had lost everything after Hazel left her restaurant. People murdered for different reasons and revenge was one of them. Not that he could say for certain that Carolyn would try to kill Hazel. Maybe she stewed over her losses and blamed Hazel, but hadn't gone over the edge yet.

"Carolyn wouldn't do that," Hazel finally said. "She isn't that kind of person."

"People respond differently to life situations. What did that restaurant mean to her?"

When Hazel looked away, Callum already had his answer. The restaurant had meant everything to Carolyn.

"That's why I felt so terrible," Hazel said.

And Carolyn had seemed gracious and forgiving. Even accepting, maybe overly so. "Let's talk to her again. Maybe keep an eye on her."

"You mean…do surveillance on her?"

"Yes."

After a while she shook her head. "I don't know. I can't believe she'd do something like that."

"Let's hope not. Let's hope Carolyn is not somehow associated with the killer."

"What if whoever you saw out there wasn't Carolyn and was just waiting for someone else?"

That was possible, but Callum wouldn't take any chances.

"I need to be sure, okay?" He met her eyes in a silent plea to heed him.

She blinked in concession. "Okay." Then she gave him a faint smile that told him she appreciated his careful concern.

He heard his phone go off, indicating he had received a text message. It was from Kerry. She was five minutes out from the inn and she asked him to meet her in the parking lot.

After they each changed into normal clothes, he went back into the main room. "You wait here," he said to Hazel. "There's another officer outside on guard. I'm going to go down and meet Kerry."

"All right." Hazel sounded distracted, possibly weighed down by thoughts of Carolyn retaliating.

Assured that Hazel would stay put and she'd be safe in the suite, Callum rode the elevator down and went outside.

He spotted Kerry getting out of her vehicle. He also searched for the mysterious SUV and didn't find it. The driver must have given up and gone for the day.

He looked around for any other signs of danger. A man wheeled his luggage toward the inn entrance and a car left the parking lot. Movement drew his attention to a tree off to the side of the front doors, where a man smoked a cigarette and looked back at him. He was about the same build as the man he had seen who'd shoved a body into his trunk. It was hard to say, though, because this man stood and the other had been in the car. Could they be the same man?

"Do you see that?" Kerry asked.

"Sure do." He looked like a stalker. A few months ago, a creep had stalked Marlowe until he'd been caught.

"Let's go see if he'll talk to us."

Callum started for the man with her by his side. The man continued to smoke and watch them.

Kerry took out her badge and showed it to him. "Detective Kerry Wilder. Are you staying here?"

The man glanced at Callum and back at her, blowing smoke out and then dropping his cigarette onto the ground.

"No. I'm waiting for someone."

"What's your name?"

"Joseph Smith."

"Do you have any ID?" Callum asked.

The man removed his wallet and showed them his driver's license. It said Joseph Smith but any person, even a man who stole cars and committed murder, could come up with a fake one.

"Who are you waiting for?" Kerry asked.

"No one who's staying here. We just agreed to meet in this parking lot because it's halfway between where we live."

"What is the person's name who you're meeting?" Callum asked.

"You a cop like her?" Joseph asked.

"No. There's been suspicious characters loitering around this inn."

Joseph didn't respond right away but then he said, "Her name is Eleanor and I'd rather not tell you her last name. She's married. I don't want to get her in trouble."

Callum halfway believed this guy. Just when he was about to interrogate him some more, a gunshot rang out and a bullet splintered the bark of the tree.

"Holy…!" Joseph dove for the ground as Kerry and Callum drew their weapons and took cover, she behind the tree trunk and he behind another nearby.

He searched the parking lot and saw no moving vehicles

or anyone inside a vehicle. Most notably, there was no sign of the SUV.

He spotted something in the trees surrounding the inn. "Over there!" He pointed.

Kerry nodded and yelled, "You stay here!" then sprinted for the trees.

Callum followed. He couldn't in good conscience allow her to track down a killer on her own. But she was the detective.

The shooter had a good head start, but he ducked behind a tree trunk and poked his head out to shoot at them. He missed Kerry by inches.

Callum fired back, forcing the man to retreat. He got a good enough look at him to know this person was bigger than the one in the SUV. Whoever this person was, he was very desperate to silence anyone who could track him down.

He and Kerry emerged from the trees where they had taken cover and ran to two others closer to their target.

The shooter fled. Callum didn't have a good shot, but Kerry did. She fired and must have gotten the man's leg because he stumbled and then limped away.

Callum lost sight of him in the trees, but they soon reached a clearing and the highway. An older model Camaro was parked at the side of the road and the shooter got inside. By the time Callum and Kerry broke free of the trees, he had the car racing away. Kerry took aim and fired twice, breaking the back window but missing the driver.

She stood on the side of the highway staring after the vanishing car, putting her gun away.

Callum did the same.

"He's a slippery one, isn't he?" she said.

"Why did he shoot at us?" Callum asked.

"He was trying to shoot you," Kerry said.

He had shot at Kerry, too. Had he gone insane?

The detective called in the incident, which would bring in

other officers. “I’ve got something else to discuss with you. Why don’t you come up so Hazel can listen in?”

“All right. Is there more going on between you two than a mad shooter?”

He walked with her up through the trees—all part of the landscaping of the inn’s grounds. “Unfortunately, yes.” He was more convinced of that than ever.

Hazel heard the door open and looked up from the book she had been reading. She had to keep her mind off Evie. Kerry followed Callum into the suite.

Hazel stood from the sofa as they approached. “Did you find out who was out there?”

“That SUV was gone but someone started firing at us,” Callum said.

“We were questioning a man who was standing outside the inn looking suspicious when we were shot at,” Kerry added.

Hazel looked from her to Callum, confused as to who could have shot at them. “Was it the person in the SUV?” Maybe they had parked somewhere else.

Callum shook his head. “No. I’m sure of it. The gunman was bigger than the person in the SUV. I’m sure they’re two different people.”

“The person in the SUV is watching you?” Kerry asked. “Is it the stolen one from before?”

“No, this one was a charcoal gray and that other one was black. I didn’t get a plate number, but I don’t think that person is the same as the shooter. It’s just suspicious. The gray SUV was parked out there a long time.”

Kerry nodded. “Well, let me know if something changes or you see it parked out there again. And try to get a plate number. If it’s someone different than our shooter, then maybe they won’t be as careful.” She glanced at Hazel. “Like, if it’s someone you know.” Looking back at Callum, she said, “I’ll keep an undercover cop outside. I would suggest going somewhere else to stay, but given how brazen the shooter is, he will most likely come back. We could catch him if you keep drawing him here."

Callum told Kerry about Carolyn.

"Then your suspicion is definitely warranted. She may seem rational to your face but you never know what she's thinking or doing when no one is around."

Hazel didn't like imagining Carolyn capable of stalking her or something more, but she would keep an open mind.

"I should get going," Kerry said. "It's a really busy day." She stopped at the door. "Hey, did you have any luck tracking down Nan Gelman?"

Judging by Callum's frown, he hadn't done anything yet and felt bad. "I'm sorry, with everything going on..."

"It would be great if you could do that."

"I'll see what I can come up with in the next few days for you about Nan."

"Thank you," Kerry said. With that, Kerry left.

Alone with Callum, Hazel began to get uncomfortable, as she usually did, because she had such a hard time controlling her attraction to him. He was just so nice to look at. She even loved the sound of his manly voice. And she couldn't forget the frequent reminders of how good they were together in bed.

"I've got to cook some meals. Can you start looking for this Nan person?"

"I need access to some systems through work. I can call Charles and get something going."

Hazel went into the kitchen to start cooking, ever aware of Callum as he made a call to Charles, who must have been his boss. She listened to him make a request for remote access and Hazel gleaned from the call that Charles would have what he needed delivered later that day. Just like that, he'd be connected.

Callum sat on the sofa and saw her book. Picking that up, he read the title, then the back cover. "You like thrillers?"

"I like any action-packed murder mystery." She watched a lot of the murder case shows on television.

"I like those, too."

She sneaked a look at him. Pretty soon they'd be watching television together like a couple who'd been together for years. It already felt like she knew him that well.

He put the book down and flipped channels, stopping on a local one showing a reddish-blond-haired woman with blue eyes talking on a news program. She stood in front of the Colton Oil offices, so Hazel assumed she was a member of the family. She was quite attractive and looked to be in her late forties. The banner beneath her image read Selina Barnes Colton, VP and Public Relations Director of Colton Oil.

"Ace Colton is innocent until proven guilty," she said to a group of reporters.

"Have you seen or spoken to him since he's become a suspect?" a reporter asked.

"No, I have not, and I am sure he will be exonerated very soon." She flashed a megawatt smile for the cameras.

Hazel got the impression that she liked attention. She did not sound very sincere. One look at Callum and she knew he had similar sentiments about the woman.

She gave a wave to the reporters and walked like a movie star to her Mercedes—a much, much, much more expensive one than Hazel drove. Hazel experienced a few seconds of envy but she knew she would never be happy with that kind of lifestyle. Just looking at the woman gave her more than enough information. That woman thrived on attention and material things, expensive things, unattainable things for most people. Hazel thrived on her daughter and the everyday routine. She paid no heed to what strangers observed in her. They either accepted her or they did not. No bother to her.

Caring about all that would take too much energy. Energy better spent on what truly mattered. Evie. And real life. Real relationships.

Meeting genuine people was rare. Something to be cherished. Dear friends didn't come along at will.

Neither did meeting Mr. Right…

She saw Callum's expression had grown stormier.

Hazel finished with her recipe and put the freezable casserole into the oven. Cooking always lulled her into a state of artistic creation. She believed that the activity warded off stress and prolonged life because of that.

As she finished putting the food she had prepared into containers, she noticed Callum half-heartedly watching the newscast.

She put the Tupperware containers into the freezer, barely fitting them, and decided to delay cleaning the kitchen.

Going to where he sat, she plopped down beside him. "Everything okay?"

She saw his tension release. He leaned back and sighed. "Selina is kind of a loose cannon, in my opinion."

"Who is she to you?"

He let out another stress relieving breath. "Sorry. Selina Barnes Colton. She's vice president and director of public relations at Colton Oil. Also, my father's second ex-wife."

The way he said that piqued Hazel's curiosity. "Not well liked among the family?"

He grunted and looked at her. "No. My mother hates her. None of my brothers and sisters care for her much, either. We always were suspicious of her hold over him, why he keeps her on at Colton Oil."

Hazel saw him drift off into reflection. "She seems very good at her job. She put on a good show on that news segment. She might come across as lofty but I bet people buy into her game."

His demeanor smoothed some more and he looked at her again, this time much more warmly. "Yes, that is exactly how I would describe her. And I do think she is good at her job, but I also think she has something on my father and that is why he had to keep her on as an employee. She creates a lot of friction there—or so I'm told."

"But she's good at her job," Hazel summarized for him.

"She is good at her job."

"And you and your brothers and sisters are stuck with her."

"We are stuck with her." He met her eyes with warm regard.

As their uncontrollable chemistry heated up, he stretched his arm out behind her.

After a few simmering, electrically charged moments had passed, he said, "Selina hasn't let it leak to the press that Ace was ousted from the board."

Hazel didn't understand the significance of that. "Why wouldn't you want anyone to know?" Anyone paying attention to Payne's shooting in the news would know Ace was a suspect.

"The company bylaws say only a Colton by blood can be CEO."

That certainly held significance, but she thought of something else that might hold even more. "He wasn't ousted because he is a suspect in your father's shooting. He was ousted because he isn't a Colton by blood?"

Callum turned his head, his eyes going all shrewd and sexy. "No one knows Ace was let go because of the bylaws. She's trying to protect the company."

"That's a good thing, right?"

"Yes. It would seem so. Although I don't trust Selina. I never have."

"What if she's the one who sent that email?" Maybe she had learned Ace wasn't a Colton by blood. But then why shoot Payne?

Hazel didn't think Ace had a strong enough motive to shoot Payne. All his father had done was remove him as CEO. Having thought about it that way, though, Hazel changed her mind. Maybe Ace did have motive. In the throes of bitter emotions of loss and betrayal, he could have snapped.

"What kind of relationship did Ace have with Payne?" she asked.

"Not bad. Dad can be tough and isn't one you'd want to cross, but Ace was his son in every way. Ace *is* his son."

His cell chimed, indicating a text message had arrived. He read it and then got up to go to his laptop on the table. His boss must have come through with a way to track down the woman named Nan.

She followed, sitting beside him, seeing him navigate from his email to a browser. "What are you doing?"

"I couldn't find her in a regular search. She doesn't work as a nurse anymore, from what I can tell. Charles found a good way to search the web."

"What is that? A search engine?"

"No, it's not a search engine like what you're accustomed to using. It's more like a repository of archived data. It accesses content that search sites can't or that have removed the information because it is old. Hundreds of times more in volume."

That sounded intriguing.

"How can it do that?"

"They're databases, not websites. It's content that is invisible to normal search engines."

She watched as he typed in Nan's name, which produced a daunting amount of results. Callum didn't seem bothered. He worked intently.

In just a few minutes he brought up a file that looked like a photo of announcements. He scrolled to a twenty-year-old wedding announcement for Nancy and Herman Hersh. In the text, Nancy's maiden name was listed: Gelman.

"You found her!" Hazel exclaimed, amazed and impressed.

"Maybe." He went back to searching. "Nancy Gelman might not be our Nan Gelman."

The Dark Web had brought forth information on a Nancy Gelman. Callum needed to find a link to Nan the nurse.

After a few more minutes he found the obituary of Samuel Gelman that listed the surviving family, with Nancy Hersh as one of them. He did additional searches and found that Nancy Hersh was the same person as Nan Gelman, a nurse who'd worked in the maternity ward at Mustang Valley General Hospital.

"She lives three towns over, in Mountain Valley," Callum said. "She's not related to the Gelmans from forty years ago that Kerry found in the census, though."

"We should tell Kerry."

While Callum called the detective, she called to check on Evie. She missed her daughter so terribly.

"Kerry is unavailable." He looked at Hazel after he hung up and she could see him contemplating going to see Nan himself. What could it hurt? They would help the investigation if they did and also save time.

"Let's go," Hazel said.

Nancy Hersh lived in a neighborhood one would expect of an average, everyday working family. Neat and tidy, green grass and no rundown vehicles or junk lying around. Callum walked with Hazel up to the door and rang the bell.

No one answered, so he rang the bell again.

Still, no answer. No one was home. After 6 p.m., it was late enough in the day that someone should be there after work.

"You looking for Nancy and Herman?" a woman called from the house next door.

Callum looked there and walked with Hazel into the woman's front yard. In jeans and an Arizona Cardinals T-shirt, the neighbor was in her forties with dark hair and rectangular glasses. He'd take advantage of her willingness to talk.

"Yes."

"They went to Europe. Just left yesterday. Won't be home for ten more days. Asked me to keep an eye on the place." She eyed them suspiciously. "Who are you?"

"They don't know us. We were hoping to ask Nancy a few questions," Callum said.

"About what?"

Was the woman being nosy or did she plan on reporting back

to Nancy when she returned? Callum wasn't sure how much to reveal at this point. If Nancy had switched babies all those years ago when she worked at the hospital, had she suddenly vanished out of fear of prosecution—if she *was* the one who switched the babies? And why would anyone do that in the first place?

"We're reporters doing a story on the history of Mustang Valley General Hospital," Hazel said.

Callum inwardly cheered at her cleverness. "There was a fire there and we heard that Nancy was working around that time."

The woman's mouth spread into a smile. "Reporters, huh?"

She seemed happy that her friend and neighbor would get a little notoriety for a story about a historic hospital.

"We're freelancers, but yes, the article would appear in the paper," Hazel said.

And again, Callum was captivated by her ingenuity. He had a sudden urge to do something romantic with her tonight. Maybe dinner in a dimly lit restaurant followed by a quiet night at the inn.

"We'll come back when she's home."

"I can tell her you stopped by," the woman said as they headed back for the car. "What're your names?"

Callum waved farewell and didn't answer, hoping the woman wouldn't grow suspicious again.

"Why don't we grab dinner while we're here?" he asked when they were in the car. "I know a great place." He knew they hadn't been followed, so he felt safe in spending a little quality time with Hazel. He wouldn't think about what that meant for the near future, how it might bring him closer to her.

"All right." She smiled over at him, the whole beautiful presentation sending sparks shooting through his chest.

Hazel was still floating on air after dinner. They had talked about opinions on politics and religion. They shared a lot of the same views.

At the hotel, she walked with him toward the entrance and

saw a toddler with her mother. Wearing a cute pink dress with white tights, the girl laughed up at her mother, who crouched before her in the stroller.

Hazel could see and feel the love. Reminded of Evie at that age and younger, a pang hit her. A glance at Callum told her he had fallen into regret, likely thinking of Annabel.

"Evie was so adorable at that age," she said. "I wish I could have recorded the first time she said 'Mommy.' We were at the grocery store and she stared at my face like she always did. I have never seen a kid study faces the way she did. All of the sudden, when I was picking out some apples, I heard, 'Mommy.'" She smiled and a gush of love suffused her.

Callum chuckled. "I wish I could have been there. I can imagine it, though."

"All those moments happen when you least expect them. Except when she learned to walk. I taught her and she picked up on it pretty quickly, taking those first stumbling steps." Now she chuckled.

Callum opened the door for her and they entered the hotel. It was late, so they'd booked a room at this place rather than drive back late at night. The place was a nice one but not a five star like the Dales Inn.

She saw him reflecting again, his lightness gone.

"Are you thinking about Annabel?" she asked.

He turned to her as they headed for the bar. "About what I missed out on."

"You could always have another family, with someone else." With her…

They checked in and then walked to the elevators.

She stepped inside and faced him. He stood before her, still somber over what she had said earlier. She wondered if he was pondering having a baby with her.

"The more time I spend with you and Evie, the more that seems like a possibility," he said.

"The more you feel you can?" she asked.

After a few seconds, he nodded. "Yes."

She met his heated gaze and stepped toward him. Deliberately avoiding thinking about what would happen when the case was solved, she put her hands on his face and kissed him.

She didn't mean for it to turn into a firestorm, but the instant their lips touched, passion flared and they kissed fervently. That made her glad she had gone on the Pill.

The elevator doors opened and that broke them apart.

Hazel saw an elderly couple waiting on the floor outside. They looked shocked.

Callum took Hazel's hand and led her down the hall to their door.

As he swiped the keycard to their room, she moved in front of him, not able to wait. She put her hands on his face again and kissed him. His hands flattened on her lower back and he pulled her against him.

Pushing the door open, he walked forward and she backward into the room, bumping into the door as it swung closed.

Hazel began to unbutton his blue shirt, spreading the material aside to put her hands on his bare chest. He pulled up her blouse and she moved back to lift her arms. He tossed that to the floor and removed his shirt. Then he unclasped her bra and she sent that to the floor as well.

Callum cupped her breasts. "I will never get tired of looking at these."

She liked the sound of that. *Never.* That implied a future.

He returned to kissing her, caressing her nipples as he did.

She ran her hands over his muscular chest and abdomen, then around to his back and up to his shoulders.

Callum lifted her and stepped to the bed, letting her down. He unbuttoned her jeans and she pushed them off her legs, along with her underwear, while he got out of his.

Both of them naked, he crawled on top of her. She wrapped her arms around him as he resumed kissing her.

Hazel lost herself in the feel of her hands on his skin, roaming down his back to his rear. Ending the kiss, he just looked down at her. The wonder of all this entranced her, too.

At last he kissed her again, and she opened her legs as he sought to enter her. For long, slow moments they moved together. Each gentle penetration stirred her senses higher and higher, until they both climaxed at the same time.

Afterward, he pulled her beside him and held her, kissing her forehead.

"What the hell is happening with us?" he asked softly. Although he swore, he sounded bewildered.

"I don't know."

She didn't admit aloud that this could be the makings of true love, and she sensed him doing the same.

Chapter 10

Callum stepped into the lobby of the Dales Inn, holding Hazel's hand. He had taken it after they left the car, ignoring the realization that the action had been automatic, driven by his affection for her and the passionate night they had shared. He also didn't want to hurt her by abruptly letting go.

The reception desk was busy. It was close to checkout time, and people rolled luggage toward the exit and away from the reception desk. People's voices mixed with a ringing telephone. A lone man walked toward the exit with no luggage. Something about him looked familiar. He had on sunglasses and a Stetson. Wrangler jeans and cowboy boots completed the cowboy ensemble.

The man looked at Callum and both of their steps slowed.

Callum knew this man. He approached and when he saw his jawline and nose in more detail he recognized Ace.

"Ace?" Callum checked out his brother. Ace would normally be seen in very expensive suits. About the only thing cowboy about him normally was his slightly unruly light brown hair.

"Yes. Callum." He leaned in for a quick manly hug. "Good

to see you. I didn't know you had a new girlfriend." Ace looked at Hazel.

"This is Hazel Hart," Callum said.

She smiled and shook his hand. "Hello."

"From what I can see, Callum is the lucky one."

"Thanks for the compliment," Hazel said.

And Callum had to agree. He was the lucky one. Or not, if things fell apart.

"What are you doing here?" Callum asked.

Ace sighed his frustration. "I can't believe this is happening to me. I didn't shoot Dad."

Although Callum didn't believe his brother would kill anyone, he often wondered if it was possible Ace had fallen into a rage and acted impulsively. A lot of murderers went to prison that way. They seemed like normal, everyday, rational people but something happened to make them lose control momentarily and in seconds the deed was done. They killed and instantly wished they could undo the act.

"Dad had a long list of enemies," Callum said. "I wouldn't even know where to start to look for suspects." That's why he was a bodyguard and not a detective.

"I can't risk coming out of hiding. There is too much publicity." Ace glanced around as he must do all the time. "I'm going out of my room to get food. Other than that, I stay hidden. I'm a little worried you recognized me."

"I'm family. Anyone who doesn't know you well wouldn't."

"There are rumors all over Rattlesnake Ridge Ranch and my condo, so I'm staying at the Dales Inn until all the nonsense dies down. I'm half tempted to leave town, even though the cops told me not to. I cannot be arrested."

"You should be fine if you lay low," Callum said.

Ace didn't look convinced. "I miss it," Ace said. "Running Colton Oil. It's in my blood." He stopped as though catching himself. "Even if Colton blood isn't running through me, I am a Colton."

Having been raised by Coltons and then entering into the world of Colton Oil, Ace's entire life revolved around the family name. Callum felt for him, that he faced losing so much.

"No argument from me," Callum said. "You're my brother no matter what." Even if his instinct said Ace didn't shoot Payne and he ended up being wrong, Ace would always be his brother.

"I appreciate the support, brother." Then he glanced at Hazel. "What are you doing here?"

"Someone is after Hazel. She and her daughter witnessed a murder." He went through a brief explanation, Ace listening.

"You're working," Ace said when he finished.

"In a way, yes."

"I saw you holding hands," Ace said. "So, it must be more than work."

"In a way," Hazel said, mimicking Callum's response.

Ace laughed, low and brief. "Love at first sight?"

Callum didn't have a comeback for that. Hazel must not have, either, because she also had nothing to say.

"It's about time you had a long-term relationship," Ace said. "It's been, what, almost five years now since Annabel?"

Callum nodded.

"I always wondered about that. She must have done a number on you. Weren't you the one who broke up with her?"

"It was mutual."

Callum half saw Hazel glance sharply at him. He shouldn't lie to his brother. Or his family. Not anymore.

"Actually, I lied about that, Ace."

Ace's expression sobered. "Why?"

"We didn't break up. She died in a car accident. I was protecting a witness testifying in the trial of someone who worked for a drug cartel. They found out I was dating Annabel and had her killed to intimidate me. Annabel was also pregnant."

Ace gaped at Callum in stunned silence.

"I'm sorry. I...couldn't talk about her." He looked at Hazel. "Not until I met Hazel."

Her eyes turned soft with deep gratitude and respect. He felt himself falling in love with her.

"Wow, Cal. I had no idea. You should have told someone."

He nodded. "Probably. But I just couldn't. It devastated me." Hell, it had changed him. He was not the same man as he was before that. He was a lot more cautious now. And better at his job. The one good thing that had come out of the experience.

"He blamed himself for her death," Hazel said to Ace. "She was murdered after the trial, when Callum was no longer watching over her."

"Then clearly it was not your fault."

"I should have checked out the suspect more. I should have known what kind of monster he worked for."

"You can't blame yourself for that. You aren't a cop. You're a bodyguard, and a damn good one." Ace did another check of the lobby and his eyes stopped short toward the entrance.

"Sorry to cut this short," Ace said. "I have to go now."

Callum followed his eyes and saw two police officers enter the lobby.

"You go back up to your suite. We'll bring food to you." Callum nudged his brother with a hand on his shoulder. "Hazel is a personal chef."

"I miss good food. The food here is good, but I mean my favorite restaurants."

Callum chuckled and gave his brother a pat on the back, letting him walk to the elevators. He wouldn't risk anyone exposing Ace.

"I hope I didn't sign you up for more work than you can handle," Callum said as they entered the suite.

Hazel walked in ahead of him, feeling him check out her butt. "It's a slow week. I have some pork chops to make today and that's pretty much it. I'd like some more to do."

"I'll pay you, of course. Can you come up with a week's menu?"

"What kind of food does Ace like?" she asked, turning in the living room to face him.

She saw him take in her face and chest. "He isn't picky. Seafood pasta, burgers, Mexican. Anything but Indian food."

"Easy enough. I'll write up a menu. I know a good week-long plan."

Hazel used the same meals for certain types of people. In minutes she had a list and handed it to him.

"You're going to increase my revenue this month," she said. "There are perks to this relationship." She winked at him, making him want to take her into his arms and show her the other perks.

Hazel made a quick call to Evie, which she did each day. She went into the kitchen, hearing him phone Patsy. Once again she marveled over how quickly he could make things happen. He had people at his service with just a call. Money gave him that. As he talked to Patsy she admired his profile, from his sloping nose to his moving lips, and on down to his strong shoulders and chest, flat stomach…nice ass…and long, manly legs. He'd called Patsy for her. She had almost refused to let him pay her but she needed the money. And she also felt pampered and liked that.

Reminded of Ed, she cut short her too-trusting reaction. *Treat it like a business deal.* He wasn't asking her to prepare meals for his brother because he wanted her sexually. He'd asked for her business.

She started to prepare a pork chops recipe. Chops never turned out well if all you did was cook them in the oven. In culinary school she'd learned that the secret was to brine the pork first. Hazel had already done so and now got a pan out to sear the meat.

As she began to do that, Callum joined her in the kitchen. She retrieved the chops from the refrigerator, where they had been soaking in water and salt for three hours. Removing them from the solution, she placed them on a paper towel, flipping them to dry the other side.

Next, she brushed them with olive oil and then sprinkled them with garlic.

Callum joined in with the onion salt and she said, "Good," when he'd done enough on each chop.

She followed up with pepper, glancing up at him. His playful eyes caught hers. He enjoyed being close to her. The seasoning was just an excuse.

"If I stick with you I could learn how to cook," he said.

If he stuck with her? As in being girlfriend-boyfriend? She decided not to rein in her temptation to play along. This was too fun.

"I hope you're a fast learner, then." She let him interpret that any way he chose. She meant she hoped he'd learn to forgive himself for the deaths of his girlfriend and child and open himself up to new love. And quickly. Before Nate Blurge's murderer was caught.

"I fear you're the kind of woman who could make me one," he said.

He had interpreted what she had said exactly as she meant it. Tickled on the inside, she seared one side of the chops and then the other, feeling as hot as the pan right now.

After placing the chops on a pan, Callum put it into the oven. Then he straightened and faced her, the movement bringing him right before her.

She put her hands up against his chest, a reflexive reaction.

He didn't step away and she found herself melting into his eyes. The seconds ticked on but she was only aware of him and the heat rising.

"What's next?" he murmured.

"I..." Dazed by the fire coursing through her, she at first thought he referred to their close proximity.

"With the pork chops," he said.

"Oh." She breathed a laugh. "Three minutes on each side and then they're done. Then I need to make the vegetable. I already have the potatoes and gravy in the freezer."

Their room phone rang.

Hazel went to answer it. "Hello?"

"Hello," a man's voice said. "This is the front desk. We have a delivery here for Ms. Hart."

"Oh. A delivery?" She glanced at Callum, whose lighthearted expression turned to concern.

"Yes, ma'am."

"Okay. I'll be right down." She hung up and turned the stove off before going for the door. "There's something at the front desk for me."

Callum headed for the door ahead of her. "I'll go with you."

They took the elevator down.

In the lobby she walked with him to the front desk, where she already saw a vase full of flowers and a box of what had to be chocolates next to it.

"I take it you didn't send me those," she said, needing to keep the moment light.

"No, but maybe I should."

At the desk, she told the clerk her name. He slid the vase and box toward her.

Callum took the box and opened it. Inside were what appeared to be ordinary chocolates. She removed the card from the flowers.

Reading aloud, she said, "Thank you for preparing me all the wonderful meals. It's signed Abigail." She looked up at Callum. "That's my client who lives in the house where that man almost ran me and Evie over."

He took the box of chocolates. "We have to tell Kerry."

"Kerry…why?" Did he think Abigail sending these was significant? That had been her first thought, as well, but would the killer be this subtle? He had already tried to run her down and shoot her. He must know Evie wasn't with her now. If the chocolates were poisoned, he would only take out Hazel, not the star witness.

"It may be nothing but we have to be sure. If they turn out to be all right, I'll replace the box of chocolates."

She glanced at the flowers. Was there a way to poison those?

"I think we'd all be dropping dead already if those were casting off any toxins," Callum said, having read her thoughts.

"Abigail is a new client. If these are from her, it's good to know I won't be losing her."

"This doesn't seem like the killer's MO," Callum said. "It's more like what an ex-boss would do for revenge."

"Carolyn?" She still could not imagine her capable of murder. Why would she try to kill Hazel for leaving the restaurant? Even if she blamed her for her ruin, would she really resort to murder?

A few days later, Kerry called with the results of toxicological testing done on the chocolates and they came back negative. She'd also confirmed that Abigail sent them.

Callum asked Patsy to bring a replacement box to the front desk of the inn without Hazel knowing and was waiting for her call.

Hazel stood behind the kitchen counter, where she had worked for hours on a new order. The flowers, now in a vase, were still fresh on the dining table.

"Callum?" Hazel asked.

Judging by her tone he sensed a serious question was on the way.

"Yes?"

"Can I ask you something about Annabel?"

Yup, here they went. Mentally preparing himself, he said, "Yes."

She set down the knife she'd been using in the kitchen. "Do you still keep in touch with any of the friends you had together?"

What made her ask that? "We didn't really have any friends in common, only mine and hers."

"Why haven't you spoken with her parents in all these years?"

"They don't want to hear from me."

"You indicated that before, but I have my doubts. If anything, they'd be more upset that you didn't keep in touch. You were the last person to be close to her. You were going to have a baby together. Don't you think they'd like to talk to you? You could tell them things about her in the days before she died. Was she happy? Maybe some special moment you two had. They probably needed that and you abandoned them."

"I didn't abandon them. I got their daughter killed. Seeing me would only remind them of that."

"Now, see, there's where I think you're wrong. You said they invited you to the one-year memorial and you didn't go."

"I couldn't go."

"Right. You were out of the country, but you could have called and told them that."

He looked over at her, unable to refute her point. "Okay then, I couldn't have gone even if I was available."

"Now *that* I believe," she said. "You've been running all this time. You buried her and your emotions. You didn't even tell your own family about her death."

"I *couldn't*." Didn't she get it?

"But I bet you can now," she said quietly, gently.

It had been long enough now that he should be able to face Annabel's family. And funny how the thought of that wasn't as painful as it had been in the months after Annabel's death. He felt more open to the idea.

"It would help you move on, Callum," Hazel said. "And now that I have a vested interest in you, I encourage you to reach out to them."

She had a vested interest in him? He grinned over her choice in words.

"And I'm hoping you feel the same about me and will work on getting over Annabel's death."

She hoped he had a vested interest in her. Did he? He enjoyed her company. He felt an intense attraction to her. But he still couldn't think about any kind of long-term future with her.

His cell chimed and he was relieved for the interruption. He read a text from Patsy. The returned chocolates were downstairs.

"There's something for you at the desk again," he said to her.

"Again?"

"Maybe it's another admirer. Come on. Let's run down there."

She rinsed her hands and dried them and then adjusted one of the burners to low. Then she rode the elevator with him. In the lobby they were headed for the desk when he spotted a woman who looked vaguely familiar. She wore a baseball cap and sunglasses, but her hair was a blond bob. Carolyn. She wasn't dressed as smartly as when he'd first seen her. She wore jeans and a T-shirt today. Was she trying to disguise her appearance?

She turned her head and saw them. Callum pretended not to notice her and went to the desk with Hazel. The clerk gave her the new box of chocolates.

"Those are from me," Callum said. His voice sounded lower than normal and he had to attribute that to liking giving her something romantic.

Her mouth parted in surprise and she took them. "I didn't think you'd actually do this. Thank you."

He'd have to get her flowers, too, when the others wilted.

Carrying the box, she opened it a crack to retrieve one, popping it into her mouth as she walked away from the counter.

Callum looked toward Carolyn. She watched them. Was she trying to monitor their movements? If so, she was doing a terrible job. He looked through the front windows to the parking area and saw a dark SUV.

Taking Hazel's hand, he steered her toward Carolyn. Might as well confront her. Maybe it would dissuade her from any future attempts to do whatever she might intend against Hazel.

"That's Carolyn over there," he said to Hazel.

She searched the room until her gaze came back to the woman in the cap. "She never dresses like that."

"I didn't think so."

Carolyn stood as they approached, awkwardly removing her sunglasses as though feeling caught. "Well, fancy meeting you here again."

"Carolyn," Hazel said. "Why are you here?"

"I'm waiting to meet the manager about an upcoming catering event."

"Who are you catering for?" Callum asked.

"It's a local business," she said, sounding blasé. "An all-day meeting."

He doubted she had to meet in person to discuss what needed to be done in preparation for a business meeting.

"Why are you still here?" Carolyn asked. "Is that man not captured yet?"

"No, unfortunately."

"Where is Evie?" Carolyn asked. "I never see you without her."

With Hazel's hesitation, Callum knew she was thinking twice about telling her former boss. "She's somewhere safe."

Carolyn eyed her peculiarly, as though not missing that Hazel had chosen not to tell her. "This whole thing must be so disruptive to your business. Without a kitchen to handle all that cooking."

"Oh, no. It hasn't slowed me down at all," Hazel said. "Our suite has a full kitchen and Callum has lined me up with new customers."

Callum wondered if she was aware of how unabashedly excited and happy she sounded to be so busy.

"He has, has he?" Carolyn looked over at him and then back at her.

"I'm supplying one of his brothers with food this week and that has already led to other customers."

Ace had recommended a few to Callum, who had made some calls. Hazel's business was thriving and would continue to do so.

"You always did seem charmed," Carolyn said with a hint of resentment. "Some people are just born with luck, aren't they?

A great start to a new business and a handsome man to boot. Cute little girl. How do you do it? Is there a method?"

"I…" Hazel seemed perplexed. "I guess I just follow my heart."

"That's what I did and look where it got me."

Hazel studied her for several seconds. "Carolyn, you aren't angry with me for leaving your restaurant, are you?"

Carolyn waved her hand through the air. "Of course not. I understand people have their own lives to live."

Her answer fell flat because she seemed to be overdoing her sugary tone.

"Yes, but my leaving put you in a difficult position. I wish you would have told me."

"You were busy doing your thing. People do that. They move on without a second thought to those around them. I'm sure you did what was best for you and your daughter."

"Carolyn. Maybe we should talk. You're angry with me."

Carolyn shook her head. "No. I just understand people."

"People in the restaurant industry can be brutal. Not just cantankerous customers, either," Hazel said. "Executive management and coworkers. It's a highly stressful environment for a career. That was one of the reasons I left it. I'm not in a restaurant environment anymore. Maybe you should consider doing something similar."

Carolyn scoffed. "You told me that was one of your reasons. You had a daughter to look after and wanted to be with her more. But that kind of choice won't work for me. I'm not a chef."

Did Carolyn now feel trapped in an unsatisfying career? She must prefer being the boss. Short of owning a restaurant, she'd still have to report to someone. Nobody liked that but most of them had no choice. Callum was lucky to have a boss who let him do his job and didn't inflict any ego-driven power trips on him.

"The manager must be running late," Callum said.

Carolyn turned to him and he saw that she recognized he didn't believe her.

"I'm early."

"I mean it, Carolyn," Hazel said. "We should talk."

Callum would not allow that unless he was right next to her. Second nature in his line of work was not trusting anyone, especially when there appeared to be a good reason not to. Why would Hazel suggest such a thing? Why did she want to talk to her? He got it that she had empathy for the woman, but maybe she was trying a little bit too hard.

"We have talked. I don't think there's anything left to say."

But maybe there was something to *do*. And what would that be? What would Carolyn do in retaliation for Hazel causing the demise of her business?

Chapter 11

Hazel went with Callum to check on his father. There was still no change in his condition. Callum wanted to sit in the room awhile. Hazel sat on the couch, her bodyguard in a chair beside the bed, just watching his father's still and pale face. Machines hummed around him and lines hung from Payne's body.

Hazel could see Callum genuinely needed another chance to be close to Payne Colton. His tense mouth and eyes said that his thoughts ventured beyond worry.

"Who besides Ace do police think may have shot him?" she asked.

He looked at her, coming out of his deep thoughts. "They considered many, most in the family. They even considered Marlowe, since she is now CEO."

Hazel wondered if all of this was related to Ace being switched at birth. "It seems like too much of a coincidence that he was shot so soon after that email was sent about Ace not being a Colton by blood."

He nodded. "Yeah, I thought about that myself. We're all trying to figure out who switched him—and if that same person sent that email via the Dark Web. Marlowe and I tried to find hospital records, but a hospital administrator told us there was a fire on Christmas morning, the morning Ace was born. All the records were destroyed. We thought it too much of a coincidence that the fire broke out then."

"The person who did the switch must have set it," she said.

"Yes. It would seem that way. What we all can't understand is, why anyone would switch a healthy baby with one who wasn't?"

"The real Colton baby wasn't healthy?"

"No. He wasn't doing well. That's why Ace was called a Christmas miracle, because none of his symptoms were present the next day."

Further proof—if the DNA wasn't enough—that Ace had been switched. Someone really unbalanced must have done it. Hazel could see no other motive for Ace to shoot Payne than anger over being cast out of Colton Oil. Whoever had shot Payne had to have another reason—one related to the baby switching. Maybe she was wrong, she was no detective, but the motive had to be more complicated than that.

"Is there any evidence supporting Ace's innocence?" she asked. All the times she'd encountered him, he had not struck her as a violent man. She had a good barometer when it came to judging people. In the last two weeks they'd stopped by his room four times. Ace had never been anything but kind and gracious when she and Callum had delivered food.

"Not really," he said. "There's video footage showing a person who's around five-nine wearing a ski mask and black clothes near the crime scene. If it's a man he's not very big. Ace also doesn't own a gun. If anything, the evidence points toward him. It might not be Ace in the video but Ace had the resources and the motive to hire someone to shoot Payne. There's no video showing him coming home the night of the shooting but there is video showing other Coltons arriving home at the mansion."

"So, there was nothing wrong with the surveillance equipment." If Ace claimed to be home, which he must be doing, then the video evidence contradicted that. "And then there's the threat that the board all witnessed."

"Yes, the threat. And a cleaning woman named Joanne Bates, who found Payne's body, heard someone say *mom* just before he was shot." He looked back at his father, clearly frustrated that his brother had to be in such a perilous situation.

Hazel stood and went to him, putting her hand on his shoulder. He looked up and put his right hand over hers. Warm tingles spread through her as their gazes met and locked. She could feel him returning what she felt. With just a touch and the invisible energy linking them in a look, she fell into the magic of their chemistry.

If Evie had been there, she'd have acted as a buffer. Without her, there was none. Hazel might as well be floating through rapids toward a waterfall ahead. As soon as she reached the edge, there'd be no turning back.

Callum spent the next two days thinking about what he and Hazel had discussed about going to talk with Annabel's parents. Avoiding them had been a burden in and of itself. Not telling anyone about Annabel's death had, too. He had to agree it was long past due that he go and see them.

He had just finished making a delivery for Hazel. Driving in the car gave him more time to solidify his decision. He had also had time to make a few calls.

Entering the suite, he found Hazel relaxing on the sofa with her feet up. Something smelled really good.

"What's for dinner?"

"Truffled bay scallops with celery purée, buttery potatoes and snap peas."

"You're going to make me fat." He went to her, bent and planted a kiss on her mouth. It was something he had never done before—come home and kiss her, first thing. She looked up at him with startled but heated eyes.

"I made arrangements to fly to San Francisco to go see Annabel's parents. I decided not to tell them I'm coming."

After surprise turned to a warm glow of appreciation, she reached up and touched his cheek. "That's good, Callum."

"You're coming with me." He wouldn't let her out of his sight. "We'll be safer if we aren't here anyway."

"How long will we be there?"

"I got open tickets so we can come back when we need to. In case they aren't home when we go there."

"You want me to be with you? I don't think—"

"Yes. I want you there. You're the one who helped me get to this point. I want you with me."

She tipped her head back, seeking his mouth. Still bent over, he obliged and kissed her. He kept his mouth pressed to hers, feeling her breath and the sparks that always started with just this.

Reluctantly lifting his head, he looked into her sultry eyes. "Keep that up and you're going to rope this cowboy in."

She smiled. "You're not a cowboy."

He chuckled. "I can be for you." Seeing her smile slowly fade, he knew some sobering thought had caused it, something about the two of them. He walked around the sofa and sat beside her. "What's the long look for?"

She sighed and snuggled closer to him. He put his arm around her, feeling this was so right.

"I can see a weight has been lifted off you," she said.

It has. "I do feel that way. It feels good."

"I love this," she said. "You and me relating like we're a couple, like this could last."

He hadn't thought much about the future. He had only acted on how good it felt to look forward to resolving something he hadn't thought bothered him as much as it had.

"Well, what if things don't go the way you expect in San Francisco? What happens after this euphoria fades and you begin to think about how serious you and I are becoming?"

"Are we becoming serious?" He wasn't so sure. They had great sex. How could they know that would translate into compatibility in every other way? How did anyone know that without spending months, or even years, together?

She moved back from him. "Do you have any feelings for me?"

He knew he was falling for her and thought she was extremely beautiful. More. There was something about her that was different from any other woman. "I enjoy being with you." And he truly meant that. He loved spending time with her and Evie. "We seem to be hitting it off really well. You make me feel good and I hope I make you feel the same. So, yeah, I'd say I have feelings for you."

He didn't want to ask if she had feelings for him. He didn't want to know right now. What if something happened to her or Evie? He cringed with even the suggestion. He could not go through that again. Not ever. And given her situation, she was in a lot of danger. Something could easily happen to her.

Best to keep his distance—at least for a little while longer.

After they landed in San Francisco, Hazel drove with Callum to their hotel. They checked in and then Callum drove their rental to Annabel's parents' house. She was probably as nervous as he was, but for a different reason. He was about to face the biggest demon from his past and she would find out if there was any hope for them as a couple.

On the way, she called Evie. Her brother answered.

"Hey, it's me," she said.

"Hazel. How are you?" Owen asked. "Is everything okay? I was about to call you to check."

"We're doing fine. We are going out of town for a little bit, hopefully to find information. How's Evie?"

"She's good. Keeping busy."

"Is that Mommy?" Hazel heard her daughter almost screech in excitement. She missed her so much.

"She's about to grab the phone from me." Owen chuckled as Hazel listened to him hand the phone to Evie.

"Mommy?"

"Yes. Hi, honey, how are you?" Being without her had been a lot harder than she thought. Not having that bundle of energy around all the time created a big hole.

"I miss you. When are you coming to get me?"

"I can't yet, but I hope to real soon. Are you having fun?" She would try to steer her daughter away from talk of when she could go get her and bring her home.

"Yes. We went on a picnic and the movies. I got to see Tinkerbell."

"Oh yeah?" Adoration and love filled her to overflowing. And gratitude for her brother keeping Evie entertained.

"Yeah. And they took me to work. I got to ride in a police car."

"Wow. That's exciting." Owen wouldn't have taken her on any emergency calls. He must have just given her a ride.

"Mommy?"

"Yes, sweetie?"

"I want to be a police girl when I grow up."

Evie had been getting a lot of exposure to policewomen, first Kerry and now Jessica. "That's a good profession. You'd make a fine one. And you're already getting experience." Hazel believed that children could not get enough encouragement. It allowed them to focus more on the positive than the negative, what they could do as opposed to what they couldn't.

"I like Jessica. She bosses all the boys around."

Hazel laughed and saw Callum pull to the side of the street. They had arrived at Mark and Loretta's home.

"She's a good role model for you then. I've got to go, Evie. You be good for me."

"Okay, Mommy."

Hazel would never get tired of her kiddie voice, high and sweet. She'd miss that when Evie grew up. "I love you."

"Love you, too."

Hazel didn't hear any disconnect and in the next couple of seconds her brother came back on. "Hey," he said.

"She sounds really good."

"Yeah. She's a good kid. You're doing an amazing job with her."

"Give her a kiss and a hug for me."

"Will do. Are the police any closer to catching that shooter?"

"No. We're trying to track down information on the victim and hoping that will lead to something. All we know so far is he liked to flirt and he went to a bar a lot. The sooner we find out more, the better." She wanted Evie back by her side.

"Well, don't worry about Evie. She's warm, safe and dry here."

Warm, safe and dry. "I like that. Thanks, Owen."

"Take care."

She ended the call and looked over at Callum, who must have been watching her and listening the whole time. He had a soft expression, his eyes full of admiration or maybe envy. For a man who shied away from mothers and children, he sure seemed to yearn for exactly that type of family life.

"You ready?" she asked.

"Yes." He got out of the car and so did she.

They walked to the house, a three-thousand or so square foot two-story home. A rock water fountain bubbled beside the front door. Callum rang the bell. After a few moments a lanky man with a headful of gray hair appeared. He looked from Hazel to Callum and froze. He was surprised to see him.

"Hello, Mr. Rubio."

"Why are you here?" Mark asked.

"I'd like to talk if you're okay with that."

Mark Rubio stared at him awhile.

"This is Hazel Hart," Callum said without any further explanation as to why she was there with him.

"Who's here, Mark?" a woman called from inside.

A remarkably youthful woman appeared, blue eyes widening and then going rather chilly as she stopped beside her husband.

"Well, you're here, so you may as well come in." Mark moved aside.

"Thank you." Callum stepped in, putting his hand on Hazel's lower back.

She wasn't sure if the contact gave him reassurance or if it was an automatic gesture. Either way, she felt the touch all the way to her toes.

The house was clutter-free and painted in shades of gray and earthy tones with white trim. Mark led them into a formal living room toward the front of the house. Hazel got the distinct impression that was no mistake, as though Annabel's father did not want to welcome them into their home.

Mark and Loretta stood on the opposite side of the entry, facing Callum and Hazel.

"First, I want to apologize for not coming to see you sooner," Callum said. "When you sent that invitation to the year memorial of her death, I should have at least called you."

"You vanish from our lives as though Annabel didn't matter one bit and you expect us to believe you? You discarded her like trash. Were you glad she was gone? That's how it seemed to us."

Callum shook his head emphatically. "I never meant to make you think that. I just… I just couldn't…"

Mark's brow creased in confusion. "You had nothing to do with her murder."

"I should have protected her. I could have."

"How?" Mark asked.

Callum pinched the bridge of his nose and then let his hand drop. "I should have known she would still be in danger after I finished protecting that witness."

"You did your job."

"You should have been with us during that time," Loretta said. "You abandoned us. You were all we had left of her."

"I'm sorry." Callum breathed out. "I'm here now. I'm here the soonest I could be, largely thanks to this woman here." He put his arm around Hazel. "She helped me see what I had been doing, which was burying extreme pain."

"What do you think we were going through?" Loretta asked. "We lost our daughter and our grandchild. When you vanished we lost a son-in-law."

Callum hadn't married Annabel, but they must have thought of him as part of the family.

"He didn't tell anyone in his family Annabel died," Hazel said.

"No one?" Loretta asked, incredulous.

"I couldn't."

Loretta stepped forward then. "Oh, you poor man." She touched his face. "You should have come to see us. You could have talked to us about it. We needed that with you."

"I know that now. I'm sorry."

"This doesn't make things all right with us," Mark said. "You caused our grief to be worse by not being with us."

Hazel thought that was a little over-the-top. Mark must not be a very forgiving man, but his wife was.

"I know it's taken me too long to come and see you. If there's anything you want to talk about, I'm here now."

Loretta stepped back. "There is something I have wondered all this time." She folded her arms. "Annabel told us about the baby the day after she found out, the day after you both found out. But I didn't get to talk to her much before she died. She came to see me once and we talked about how good things were going between you two. She didn't know at that time whether you were having a boy or a girl, but I know she had an ultrasound scheduled."

Hazel wished she could give the three some privacy. She felt this was a very personal moment.

"She was at twenty weeks," Callum said. "There was no sign of a penis and the doctor said we were having a girl."

Loretta covered her mouth with her hand as a sob wrenched her.

Hazel lowered her gaze, feeling she intruded too much.

"She was thrilled," Callum said. "So was I."

Hazel looked at him and became captivated by the light in his eyes, the slight curve of his lips the memory brought. That had been a magical moment for him. Hazel remembered when that day had come for her. *Magical* didn't come close to describing what seeing the miracle of life could do to a person.

As she realized the depth of his emotional injury, the weight of the risk to her heart settled in. His journey to healing wasn't over. And she had been instrumental in guiding him onto this path. She might be the rebound woman.

The image of Evie's gap-toothed smile pierced her. Her innocent eyes. Her tiny, soft-skinned fingers. The way she sometimes skipped instead of walking. When she talked to bumblebees and ladybugs. Not spiders. Although she did respect the aphid eaters… She didn't want to involve her child in a tenuous relationship with a hopeful father figure who had so much weight to bear. But the more time she spent with Callum, the more she felt like it was out of her control.

Chapter 12

Callum knew Hazel had suffered at least some tension during that visit.

He might be a brawny workingman, but he did have a sensitive side. He was grateful for her support despite how she must have felt like an intruder. And hearing about his and Annabel's special moment could not have been easy.

She had been quiet all the way to the hotel near the airport and now surfed channels on the television. Their flight back to Arizona was in the morning. Callum couldn't explain his need to make it up to her, to tell her that Annabel's memory didn't loom large as much as it used to. A voice said Hazel mattered more but that scared him, so he didn't give it any credence.

Going to the suite phone, he called room service and ordered champagne with strawberries and requested a delayed dinner of steak and crab. When he hung up and turned to Hazel, he saw her looking at him peculiarly.

"I figured we could use a nice dinner tonight," he said.

Her eyes narrowed.

"Okay, I figure I owe you at least that, if not more, for what you did for me today."

"Me? I didn't do anything."

"You were there for me." He walked over to where she sat on the sofa and took a seat right next to her. Taking the remote, he searched for a classical music station and found one playing a piano dominant tune.

After a few minutes, she said, "I know what you meant about seeing the sex of the baby for the first time."

"Were you alone when you saw it?" he asked.

"Yes. My family was in Colorado. But I sent them copies of the sonogram."

"That kind of thing bonds the parents together," he said.

"So I gathered." She inched away from him on the sofa. "You and Annabel had a special thing going."

He had brought up the bonding on purpose. He intended to lead into what he really needed to say.

"We did bond over the baby, but that didn't change the way either one of us felt about each other. I told you I would like to believe I loved her, but after all this time and much reflection, I know I didn't love her as much as I could love a woman." He wouldn't say how he knew that. He knew because he could love Hazel ten times more. "I loved her enough to marry her and have a family, but at some point, it would have become clear that she wasn't the one for me, and I would always have wondered who the right woman would have been."

"Would you have stayed in the marriage?"

"With children involved? Yes. Annabel was a good person. Honest, full of integrity. There would have been no good reason to leave her."

"Other than not being happy," Hazel said.

"I would have been happy enough with her. It's not like she made me miserable, nor do I think she ever would have." There were different degrees of happiness. People could find great joy even if they married someone they weren't madly in love with. As long as there was loyal companionship and friendship, marriage could work.

"I would have had plenty of good reasons to leave Ed, had he stayed and married me," Hazel said. "I'm not even sure I would have agreed to marry him."

Room service knocked and Callum let them in. The champagne was in an ice bucket and the strawberries in a bowl. The room service attendant put the tray on the coffee table. Callum tipped him and he left.

Going back to Hazel, he sat beside her. Leaning forward, he removed the bottle of champagne and easily and gently popped the cork, which didn't go flying. Setting that aside, he poured Hazel, then himself, some. Handing her a glass, he clinked his to hers.

"Here's to you being the amazing woman you are."

She smiled softly. "Thank you."

As she sipped, her golden-green eyes looked up at him suggestively, heatedly. When she lowered her glass, she said, "If you aren't careful, you might end up liking me too much to leave me when this is all over."

He'd rather not go there yet. "Maybe. I prefer to take it one day at a time."

"Me as well." She took a strawberry from the bowl and put it to his mouth.

He ate it and then took one for her, feeding her a strawberry.

"Mmm, there is something about strawberries and champagne," she said.

"It's the pairing of the sweetness in both." He sipped some champagne.

"What were you like before Annabel?" Hazel asked.

He wasn't sure what she wanted to know. "With women? The same."

"No, did you date a lot? My guess is you had girls crawling all over you in high school. After that you must have dated a lot."

He hadn't thought of that since Annabel was killed. He had been very different. "I did date a lot."

"Were you popular in high school?"

"I was a quarterback. I wouldn't say I was the most popular. I didn't get into school politics. That crowd seemed more popular."

She breathed a laugh, clearly disagreeing.

"What about you?" he asked.

"I was popular. I was a cheerleader and I dated the quarterback. He and I were king and queen at our senior prom."

"Do they still do that in school? Kings and queens." He grunted in humor. "Seems like another lifetime ago." He set aside his glass.

"Yes, and I'm only twenty-five."

More memories from that time came to him. He hadn't been popular with the good kids. He had run with a more rugged crowd.

"Back then I had more of a reputation as a bad boy," he said.

She nodded thoughtfully. "I can see that." She put her glass on the side table.

This conversation was far more interesting than sharing champagne and strawberries. "I started rebelling against my dad my sophomore year. That's when he began *prepping* me for joining the Colton Oil executives." He had not been executive material. Even as a kid he had always sought danger. Climbing trees. Riding motorcycles and mountain bikes. Rock climbing. Skiing. Anything exciting.

"I got into a lot of fights. Some of the other kids tried teasing me about being a Colton, a spoiled rich kid. Those kids usually got nosebleeds after I punched them. I almost was expelled. I think only my father's connections prevented that. He grounded me and tried reasoning with me, but I never listened. He never laid a hand on me but I bet he wanted to more than once."

"A bad boy. All because your dad wanted you to join Colton Oil?"

"Not just that. I aspired to a different existence. Something more earthy and adventurous."

"Hence the military and then personal protection."

Earthy and adventurous.

He had never conveyed his life journey to anyone in that way. He left his thoughts to look at her, this magnificent woman. "I loved the navy, but not the discipline. Being a bodyguard suits me perfectly."

Hazel sat back and sipped her champagne, crossing one slender leg over the other. In admittedly selfish pleasure, he covertly took in the shape of her knee and the lines of her fit thighs and the side view of the curves of her butt.

"Mr. Callum Colton," she said, turning her head with just the right angle to give her eyes a sultry slant. "You are one sexy, successful man."

Her relaxed pose and flirtatious words and tone threw him. "And…you are…" What could he say? She had already trumped him. *She* was one sexy, successful woman. Taking a chance, he moved in, touching her cheek and kissing her.

He would have encouraged her for more but she drew back, almost flinching.

Opening his eyes, he searched hers.

After several seconds, she asked, "Would you ever be able to try having a family again?"

Her catching, whispered question speared him.

This conflict would not go away. She had been abandoned, pregnant with Evie, and he had lost the mother of his unborn child, and with her a baby girl he would never know.

He and Hazel had issues that meant they might never be able to work together to form a healthy, new relationship. Everything felt so good with her. Everything felt right and safe. But was it?

Callum could never go through what he'd gone through with Annabel ever again. He had to be honest here. People died. Hazel could die. Something could happen to both her and Evie.

What if they had a child of their own? Something could happen to that child.

He imagined living with Hazel and Evie, having a blended family and living an everyday life together. Spending time in the evenings with them. Doing schoolwork. Going to bed every night with Hazel. He would fall in love with that life. He could already feel it to his core. And then, after growing more attached than he had ever been to Annabel, what if something tragic happened? Nothing and no one could predict life or what awaited everyone as time marched on.

"I don't know if I'm ready for that." Would he ever be?

His spirit plummeted as he saw Hazel's reaction. Her face hardened to disappointed stone and she lowered her eyes in sadness before getting up from the sofa.

"Good night," she said.

The urge to go after her nearly brought him to his feet. That urge, foreign in its powerful, primal need. *Go after her. Take her.* Never let her out of his bed. Ever.

But therein lay the problem.

He'd only just begun to confront the tragedy of his past. If not for Hazel, he would not have gone to see Annabel's parents. He had blocked all emotion where his ex-girlfriend was concerned. Nearly five years later he still wasn't over his loss. It was unfair to lead Hazel on, to let her believe he was ready for a future with her and Evie.

Evie.

Oh.

He could not, he *would* not, hurt that wonderful child—or her amazing mother.

Hazel hadn't liked Callum's answer yesterday, but there was little she could do about it. There was even less she could do about how she was beginning to feel about him. Conversation had been limited on the way back from San Francisco. Now they were back at the inn and Patsy arrived with another food delivery. With the help of two hotel staff members, the goods were unloaded on the kitchen island counter.

"Thank you, Patsy. You sure are indispensable for Executive Protection…and now me." She smiled.

Patsy gave a quick, "No problem," and turned to leave.

Odd, the woman seemed to be behaving differently than usual. She seemed awkward, as though something troubled her.

"Is everything all right, Patsy?"

"Yes, fine." She offered a half-hearted smile and left.

Hazel watched her go behind the hotel staffers and then turned to Callum, who sat at the dining room table in front of his laptop, digging up what he could on Nan, all the places she had lived, places she had worked, people she knew from her Facebook page and other social media sites.

"Patsy seems out of sorts today," she said.

He looked up. "How so?"

"I don't know. Does she have a happy home life?"

"As far as I know. She always seems happy to me."

"Hmm." She began putting food away, starting with the produce and perishables like milk. Next came the canned goods and other pantry items.

Lifting the jar of olive oil, her fingers came in contact with something grainy. Inspecting the jar, she saw traces of a white substance, a powdery film. And then she saw what appeared to be a fingerprint on the glass. Holding the jar closer to her eyes, she spotted undissolved white particles inside, floating in the olive oil. Twisting the cap, she found the seal had already been broken.

"Callum?"

He looked up again and then stood to come to her.

"This doesn't look good," she said.

He took the jar and placed it on the counter, then bent to examine it. "It looks like it might be poisonous."

Patsy's edgy demeanor came back to her. No. One of Callum's agency's assistants?

"You said Patsy was acting strange?" Callum asked.

"Yes."

"Someone could have paid her to try and poison us."

"Not me, my clients," she said. "I would have used this oil for recipes to be delivered."

His mouth flattened in consternation. "That doesn't sound like something the killer would do. He'd want *you* dead. You and Evie. Evie isn't here and he can't find her. While he must be getting impatient, I doubt he'd go after your clients."

Well, Hazel could think of only one other person who had a motive to see Hazel's clients die. Carolyn.

The next day Kerry reported the jar of olive oil had been tested. The liquid had been poisoned. Kerry also let them know she'd picked up Patsy and now had her in custody. Callum took Hazel to the police station. She entered the observation room with Callum and watched Kerry interrogate the nervous woman.

"This will go much easier for you if you cooperate," Kerry said. "Now, I'll ask you again. Why did you put poison in the olive oil that was delivered to Callum Colton and Hazel Hart's room at the Dales Inn?"

"I didn't put poison in it," Patsy said, wringing her hands.

"Then you must know who did, because you were the one who purchased the oil and helped deliver it."

"I don't."

Kerry sighed. "I know you do. I have enough to arrest you right now. We have a fingerprint on the jar. My guess is, it's yours. Do you really want to take that chance?"

"It's not mine," Patsy said. "I just made the delivery."

"How can you be so sure?"

Patsy continued to wring her hands and now added chewing her lower lip to her edgy movements.

"Whose fingerprint could it be?"

"If I tell you, are you going to arrest me?"

"I can't guarantee anything, but maybe I can ask our DA,

Karly Fitzpatrick, to see if we can work out a deal with you. We might be able to get you probation instead of prison time, especially since this is your first offense."

Chewing on her lip, Patsy flattened her hands on the table as she mulled over her options and the consequences of whatever decision she made.

"All right. It was Carolyn Johnson. She said she saw me make other deliveries to Hazel and offered to pay me to deliver the olive oil. She didn't say she was going to poison it, but I'd suspected she did something to it. I didn't think she'd actually try and murder anyone."

Hazel glanced at Callum. Surely Patsy would have known Carolyn had intended something terrible.

"How did she come in contact with you?"

"She saw me going in and out of the inn and approached me one day. She asked if I was close to Hazel and I said I didn't know her, I was an assistant, who brought them things they needed. She then asked if I could use a little extra cash to deliver something to her."

"How much did she pay you?" Kerry asked.

"Five hundred."

"Why did you do it?"

"I needed money. The agency doesn't pay me very much. They could afford to pay me more but they don't. I'm behind on my bills."

"I can't believe that," Callum said. "We pay all our employees top wages. What did you expect? Personal assistants don't make what executive bodyguards do."

"Desperate people do desperate things." Hazel was still reeling over her ex-boss trying to kill her clients. She must have intended for her to be accused of the murders. Revenge for causing her restaurant to fail? Since Carolyn had failed, Hazel should fail and her clients die?

"Is Kerry going to arrest Carolyn?" Hazel asked.

"If she can find her, I'm sure she will."

* * *

"You okay?" Callum held the station door for her as they walked to the rental.

She nodded. "Just shocked and disappointed."

She did seem pretty upset. Someone she had respected and might have even considered a friend or mentor had betrayed her in the worst possible way.

Today, they weren't in disguise, so extra precautions were in order. The emergency had prevented them from taking those precautions. He took care in looking around for potential threats.

No parked vehicles with anyone sitting inside.

No strangers walking dogs or sitting on benches—there were no benches.

Walkers didn't look their way. Drivers didn't either.

He escorted Hazel to the passenger side and then stepped up behind the wheel. He drove back toward the Dales Inn and thought again—as he had often since they talked—about whether or not he was ready for a serious relationship and even a family. With Hazel he would have one ready-made.

The more he considered that, the more the idea appealed to him, but he could not get past the fear of losing them in some horrible way. If he steered clear of ever having a family outside the one he already belonged to, he would spare himself nearly insurmountable anguish.

Just before they reached the inn, Callum saw a black SUV parked on a side road. The driver was bigger than the person in the gray SUV had been. This was not Carolyn. This was Nate's killer. He had waited there for them, most likely having seen them leave the inn and wisely not followed them as he had before.

Callum sped up, but the killer shot out one of Callum's tires. As he lost control of his vehicle, the right front tire caught on a pothole in the road. Callum could not correct the truck's path and they careened head-on into a tree. Momentarily dazed from the force of the airbag, he shoved the now deflating bag out of the way and saw Hazel doing the same.

"Are you all right?" He searched around for the killer and found him aiming a gun at him through the driver's side window.

He made a roll-the-window-down gesture.

Callum obliged.

"Where is the kid?" the man asked. He wore sunglasses and a beanie hat over longish brown hair. Around six feet tall and of average build, he had the appearance of a regular guy. No tattoos that Callum could see. Clean-shaven. Just as Evie had described to the sketch artist.

"I won't ask you again," the killer said. "Where is the kid?"

Callum had his hand on the door handle. He lifted his other, palm facing the man, more to distract him. "Just calm down."

At the same time that he opened the car door as fast and hard as he could, he karate chopped the man's wrist, knocking his aim off.

The gun fired into the air as the man fell backward.

Callum propelled himself out of the car as the other man rose to his feet. Swinging his foot, Callum kicked the gun from the man's grip, sending it flying into the road. He began to draw his pistol but the other man produced a second gun he had tucked into his boot. Callum ducked behind the open car door in time before bullets struck the side.

Callum fired back when he could, seeing the killer limping from the wound Kerry had inflicted toward the SUV. He shot and missed.

The killer raced off in his SUV, another failed attempt to shoot them.

Looking into the truck, he saw Hazel crouched low, eyes big and dark and round with fear.

"He asked where Evie was," she said.

Neither of them had to ask why. The killer wanted both Hazel and Evie dead. The little girl would be a witness to testify in a trial, if it ever came to that. A familiar wave of dread washed through him. What would become of Hazel and Evie?

Chapter 13

A few days later, Callum thought that Nancy Hersh should be back from her trip to Europe with her husband by now. Callum had told Hazel it would be good for them to be out of Mustang Valley. He was anxious to work more on finding out who shot his father and hopefully proving Ace didn't.

Once again, they stood at Nan's front door and this time she answered. Round faced with short hair dyed blond, she wore visible hearing aids.

"Nancy Hersh?" he asked.

"Yes?" She looked from him to Hazel and back to him. Then she snapped, "I have a No Soliciting sign on my door."

"We're not selling anything. We're trying to track down someone whose last known whereabouts was at Mustang Valley General Hospital forty years ago."

"My gosh, that's a long time ago."

"Did you go by the name Nan Gelman back then?"

He must want to be sure she was the maternity nurse who worked at the hospital the day of Ace's birth.

"Yes. Nan was a stupid nickname. I don't go by that anymore. People call me by my given name, Nancy. I haven't been Gelman in a very long time. Divorced twice before I met my now-husband."

"So you did work at the hospital?" Hazel asked.

"Yes. I did. I worked on the maternity ward."

"Did you work Christmas Day forty years ago?"

Nancy rolled her eyes irritably. "Yes. In fact, that day forty years ago sticks out like a sore thumb." She told them the year. "For one, a fire broke out that morning and destroyed the nursery records and nurses' station. Also, my rotten supervisor wouldn't give me the day off. I had to work Christmas Eve night and Christmas Day morning. I couldn't stand working for her. She had all the holidays off. Talk about narcissistic. I wanted to give her an award for loving herself more than anyone else I've ever known. She's the reason I left."

Her life had gotten better, at least financially, if she'd just gone on a long European vacation. Hazel wouldn't judge, but many people she had come into contact with who had gotten divorced more than one time had personal issues. She was no expert, though. She only had her few and far between observations.

"Do you remember the babies who were born on Christmas morning?" Callum asked.

"Everybody remembers the babies who are born each Christmas. I remember the ones who were born on New Year's Eve, too." She seemed exceedingly proud of her memory reserves.

"Do you remember a sick baby that day?" Callum asked.

Hazel heard the careful anticipation in his tone. He had high hopes this woman would have something for him.

Her eyebrows lifted. "Oh, yes. I haven't thought of that in such a long time, but the Colton baby boy needed special care. It was quite a memorable time. One of the nurses who worked there gave birth to a healthy baby that same day. Her name was…" The nurse stopped as she searched for a name.

Hazel saw Callum stiffen as though this was a huge piece of information.

"Luella something. I can't remember her last name. But I do remember she left the hospital later that day, the same day she gave birth. I thought that was odd. And the other reason that morning stands out is there was the fire. I'm sure you can imagine the chaos."

"I can," Hazel said. No wonder she remembered that day so vividly after forty years.

"All of the maternity records were destroyed. They were kept in those paper boxes back then." Nancy shook her head and made a *humph* sound.

"I can see why you remember that day so well," Callum said. "Are you sure you can't recall Luella's last name?"

Nancy thought for several seconds. "No, I'm sorry, I can't." Then she asked, "Who did you say you were?"

"Callum Colton and Hazel Hart," Callum said.

"Colton. That was one of the babies born that night." She at first seemed thrilled and then not so much. "Why are you asking about that night?"

"We really appreciate all of your help, Nancy." Callum took Hazel's hand and started to turn them away. "Have a good night."

In the rental, Callum seemed edgy and tense. Hazel waited a few seconds.

"What does all that mean?" she asked.

"We have a name," he said. "A first name, but it's more than my family has gotten on Ace's being switched at birth." He turned his head and twisted in the driver's seat as though looking for anything unusual. "We have to be very careful now. If whoever shot my dad knows we came here, we are a target of another killer. I have to get you somewhere safe and work with the police…or not."

As a SEAL? A human weapon? Hazel thought he was taking this to the extreme and she knew why.

"Callum, you don't have to hold yourself responsible for my safety. If the person who shot your father finds out what we learned today, then we are in this together. The same is true for the killer Evie saw. I'm glad you're our bodyguard but if the killer succeeds and Evie and I die, it won't be your fault. It will be the killer's."

He glanced at her sharply, as though he hadn't even realized where his reaction had come from—his penchant to bear all the weight of her well-being.

"I wouldn't want you to feel guilty if anything happens to me, and I'm pretty sure Annabel would have told you the same thing."

His cell phone rang, interrupting what Hazel had hoped would turn into a meaningful conversation.

"Hi, Marlowe," he said.

Hazel waited while he listened.

"All right. We'll stop by now." Then he said to her, "Marlowe asked if I'd stop by the office so she can talk to me."

"About what?"

"She said Payne's assistant found something that might be another clue." He called Kerry next, asking her to meet them at Colton Oil. Then he called Rafe and asked him to gather up everyone in the family and meet them in Marlowe's office.

He was quiet the rest of the way and Hazel wondered if what she had said occupied his mind.

Callum could think of nothing other than what Hazel had said just before Marlowe called. He hadn't even realized his fear was so great that he might not be able to keep Hazel safe. That meant he already felt at least as much for her as he had for Annabel. Even as that thought came, he had a terrible feeling that what he had with Hazel went far deeper. That only terrified him more.

Hazel was right. He couldn't blame himself if someone else

killed her. But he could blame himself if he didn't do his job and protect both her and Evie.

Arriving at Colton Oil, he was happy to have other things to keep him focused. They headed right for Marlowe's office.

"That didn't take you long," Marlowe said, standing.

"We weren't far." Callum pulled out one of the desk chairs for Hazel.

She took it and he sat beside her in the other one, facing Marlowe, who dressed like the CEO she was in a black fitted blazer and skirt outfit.

"Dee Walton rushed into my office about an hour ago," Marlowe said.

Dee was his father's assistant. She'd worked part-time since he had gone into the coma, helping Marlowe whenever needed.

"She was in Dad's office getting some files for me. When she dropped them and went to pick them up, she found a pin underneath the air conditioning unit. It's an Arizona State Sun Devils pin, the kind you can get at the university games."

That seemed odd. "Dad isn't an Arizona State Sun Devils fan."

"He does watch football," Marlowe said. "But he has no affiliation with that university."

"Do you think the person who shot him lost it there?" Callum asked.

"Dee thinks that's what happened."

Callum had to agree there was a strong possibility. But how would they ever know?

"This could be the first good clue other than the unhelpful camera footage," Callum said. "Do you agree with Dee?"

"I don't know. I haven't decided. She's been getting into a self-help organization called Affirmation Alliance Group. She can't praise the founder enough. Apparently, Micheline Anderson is gifted at boosting morale and giving healing talks to corporations and individuals. A while back, she asked if we could use them here at Colton Oil, to help people deal with what happened to Dad. She claims they helped her when her husband died last year. I don't know what that group is doing to her state of mind. I hope they're helping her but she may be distracted."

"Do you think they're legit?" Callum asked.

"I'm leery of anything with the word *group* in it. Makes it seem like a cult."

Callum smiled. "Some people go for that sort of thing. The self-help organizations."

Rafe stepped into the office with Ainsley. They both worked at the company, Rafe as CFO and Ainsley as a corporate attorney. Rafe had on an impeccable suit, Ainsley a flowing pantsuit.

"Grayson said he wasn't going to make it," Rafe said. "He also said Asher wouldn't either."

Owner of a first responder agency, Grayson didn't involve himself in Colton Oil matters. Neither did Asher, who was foreman at Rattlesnake Ridge Ranch.

"I'll make sure they know what we discussed today," Marlowe said. "Let's sit over here." She stood and moved everyone to the two sofas that faced each other across a long coffee table.

"Why did you want us all here, Callum?" Rafe asked.

Callum looked behind him and, through the window beside the office door, saw Kerry approaching.

"Ah. Just in time."

Marlowe's assistant, Karen, let the detective in. Her long auburn hair was up in a clip today and her blue eyes found Callum.

"What have you got? Something hot?" she asked, sitting beside him.

Yes, Hazel. Of course, he kept that unbidden thought in his head.

"I found the Mustang Valley General nurse who also gave birth at the hospital the same day as Ace was born," he said. "She quit the same day."

"What? That's huge, Callum," Marlowe said.

"Tell me you have more."

He told her about the nurse who had given birth that Christmas morning and who had left the hospital with the sickly Colton baby rather than her own.

"Her name is Luella," Callum said. "Nancy couldn't recall her last name."

Kerry finished writing on her notepad. "That makes it more difficult."

"But it's a name."

"More than we have so far," Marlowe said.

"Marlowe has some news, as well," Hazel said, joining in the conversation.

Marlowe explained about the pin. Rafe and Ainsley agreed there was a good chance it might have been accidentally left by their father's would-be killer.

"But aren't there Arizona State Sun Devils fans who work here?" Kerry asked, adding her detective insight.

"Yes," Marlowe said. "There are."

"Any one of them could have gone into Payne's office and lost their pin. We will run prints," Kerry said.

"True, but not very many workers other than janitors would have a reason to go in there," Marlowe said.

Not very good janitors, if they'd missed the pin.

"I agree. Finding a connection between the pin and the shooter isn't going to be easy," Callum said. "But it's something to go on."

"Definitely something that needs to be checked out," Kerry said. "Well, thank you for your help, Callum." Kerry nodded to Marlowe. In times like this, Callum was glad to have his family around him.

Back at the inn, Hazel noticed Callum was in a better mood after that meeting. Progress had been made on his father's case but they were still no closer to capturing the killer that Evie had witnessed bashing Nate Blurge over the head. She sensed Callum would be eager to work finding the threat to her and Evie, especially after she'd forced him to face his fear of loving another woman—especially one with a child.

Right now, she just wanted to enjoy a peaceful evening. She missed her daughter terribly. She had already prepared a delicious dinner. Cooking always relaxed her.

She found an action movie that was funny and not too violent and Callum sat beside her. Their talk over dinner had been about what he and his sister had uncovered about their father's shooting. He had also called the hospital to check on Payne. Still no change. Hazel had deliberately avoided any talk about his fears.

Toward the end of the movie, when the hero and heroine acknowledged their mutual attraction, Callum put his arm up and around her.

"Come here," he said.

Warmed that he must be enjoying this quiet evening with just the two of them, she moved closer and rested her head on his muscular chest, in the crook of his arm.

Because she was in her nightgown, only a soft, thin layer separated her bare breasts from his torso. Long, sleeveless and dark green, it covered her well enough and wasn't sexy by any stretch, but she still felt intimate this close to Callum.

Her phone rang. She had been waiting for Evie to call. Her brother had said they had plans to go to an amusement park for kids.

She sat forward and picked up her phone from the coffee table. "Hi, honey, how was your day?"

"Hi, Mommy," Evie said in a loud, excited voice. "I'm having a blast here. I like Uncle Owen and Aunt Jessica."

"That's great."

"We went to a park today. It had rides. I rode in a teacup with Jessica and a train and a roller coaster!"

"Wow, you did a lot. My brave girl." Hazel knew the roller coaster was a miniature version of those that adults rode.

"And we're having pizza!"

Her brother was going to have corrupted her daughter by the time she went to go get her. "That sounds good."

"I still like your food, Mommy. You're the best cook ever."

"Aw, thanks Evie."

"When are you coming to get me?"

Hazel wished she could say *right now, right this minute*. "I don't know yet. I'll call you as soon as I do, okay?"

"Okay." Evie's tone dimmed considerably.

Hazel felt both loved by her daughter and sad, which put a damper on her mood.

"What are you doing right now?" Evie asked.

"I was watching a movie with Callum."

"What movie?"

"None that you would like. An adult movie."

"Can we watch *Brave* when I get home?"

"Of course." She heard Owen say in the background that they had that movie there. Hazel was going to start to get jealous.

"Can I talk to Cal-em?" Evie asked.

Hazel was surprised by the request. Why did she want to talk to Callum?

"Sure." She put the phone on speaker—she wasn't about to miss a single second of this. "Evie wants to say hi," she said to Callum.

"Hi, Cal-em."

"Hi, Evie. You having fun?" He sounded as though he was a good sport but Hazel wondered if this would be difficult for him.

"Yes! I like my uncle and aunt's house. They're fun."

"That's good."

"Did you catch the bad guy yet?" she asked.

"I'm not a policeman. Kerry is the one who will catch him," Callum said.

"Did Mommy tell you I'm gonna be a police girl when I grow up?"

"No, she didn't. Why do you want to do that?"

"So I can get a badge and catch bad people," she said. "Why didn't you be a policeman?"

Callum looked at Hazel with a grin. Evie was full of questions today.

"I suppose I wanted to protect people instead of catch the ones who hurt them."

A few seconds passed as Evie absorbed that. "I want to protect people, too. That's what Kerry does."

"Yes, she's one of the good guys."

"She's a girl."

Callum chuckled. "Yes, she is."

A few more seconds passed and Hazel thought her daughter had run out of steam at last.

"Cal-em?"

"Yes?"

"Are you going to come with Mommy to pick me up?"

Callum glanced at Hazel. When the time came to go get Evie, all the danger would have passed. What would Callum do? Would he run?

"Of course, I'll be there," he said.

Hazel felt a surge of warmth and hope. Maybe there was a chance for them, after all.

Did she want that? It didn't take much thinking to know what her heart desired. Yes, she did. She wanted a chance to be a couple with him, maybe more.

"Are you going to come live with us?" Evie asked.

"I already have a place to live."

He lived in a mansion.

"But you like Mommy, don't you?"

"Yes, I do like her very much."

"And you like me?" she asked in a singsong voice.

"Yes, even more."

Evie laughed, a lighthearted giggle. "Nuh-uh. You like Mommy more."

Callum chuckled again, seeming to really enjoy the banter with the girl.

"I see you with her," Evie said. "You like her a lot."

"I said I did."

"Then you should come live with us, then."

Evie was so fond of him. Hazel would worry about her state of mind if he left them, but Evie was working her kid-charmed magic on him.

"Pizza's here," Hazel heard Owen say in the background.

"You better go get pizza while it's hot," Callum said.

"Okay. See you soon."

"See you soon."

Evie must have disconnected herself. Owen or Jessica didn't come back on. Hazel leaned back against the sofa with a sigh.

"I miss her so much," she said.

Callum put his arm back around her. "She is something else. Adorable."

She tipped her head up and over to see him. "Yes, she's a heart melter."

He smiled softly, meeting her eyes.

"She likes you a lot," Hazel said.

"How does a man who leaves a pregnant woman create such a gem?" he asked.

"That's easy. She got most of her good traits from me." Hazel smiled up teasingly.

"I'd say."

And there they went again, falling into this sexual energy. They looked into each other's eyes, which ended with him lowering his mouth to hers. Basking in the aftermath of his affectionate words, she grew hot all over.

She touched his face as the kiss deepened. When that didn't satisfy her raging desire, she climbed onto him.

"Uh." He grunted and then slid his hands to her rear to move her over his jean-clad erection.

She was lost at that point. All that mattered was him and how he made her feel.

He pulled up the hem of her long nightgown. She kept kissing him as his hands traveled slowly up her thighs to her bare butt.

Pulling back from the kiss, he met her eyes.

She smiled from pleasure in his heated response. Lifting his T-shirt to get it out of the way, she unbuttoned his jeans and then unzipped them as much as she could. He helped her by raising his hips, which incited her more because of the pressure. He pushed his jeans and underwear down.

Hazel resumed kissing him and moved back on top of him. His hands returned to her rear and their breathing became more ragged. She ran her hands along his hard chest, brushing her thumbs over his stiff nipples.

Callum lifted her nightgown and she raised her hands so he could take it off. He let it fall onto the sofa beside them. Then he gripped the back of her head and pressed an urgent kiss to her lips. She reciprocated with equal verve, moving over his erection.

With a gruff sound, he set her down over him. She was so wet and ready for him. Shivers of sensation numbed her to all else. She had to stay still for a moment, lest the pleasure end too soon.

She planted a kiss on his mouth. "I've never felt like this before." Her voice came out as a breathless whisper.

"Neither have I," he answered in kind.

That he'd confessed such a thing stimulated her passion even more. She kissed him long and deep, needing to soak every part of him into her.

He pumped his hips. Evidently his patience had run out. Bracing her hands on his shoulders, she did the same in rhythm with him. And just a few strokes later she came with such intensity she cried out.

He groaned his own release and she continued to move on him, not wanting this to end.

At last she put her forehead against his. He moved until he found her mouth for a gentle kiss. The tender, sweet action captured her heart. She was beyond backing off. She could not without suffering pain. Losing Callum would be the biggest heartbreak of her life.

Chapter 14

The next day, Callum stood in front of the bathroom mirror and admitted to himself that he would have difficulty leaving Hazel. But he would have more difficulty losing her permanently. At a loss for what to do, how to preserve himself if the worst happened, he fell into silent contemplation. Hazel had studied him more than once but never confronted him. That made him fall in love with her even more. She gave him the space he needed without judging.

Wait…

Had he just thought that he had fallen in love with her?

He finished getting into his biker disguise, wig and glasses in place. He left the bathroom to find Hazel waiting, way too sexy for his confused state. He would rather take all her clothes off and stay home.

"You ready?" They were headed to Joe's Bar to conduct another stakeout.

Her white-toothed smile and animated manner warmed a nonsexual part of him. This was Hazel. Positive. Loving. Strong in so many ways.

A mother…

"Yes."

He offered his hand, more of an obligatory gesture. He was so out of sorts.

She didn't take it. Instead, she studied him before saying, "Last night was beautiful."

Beautiful.

He had other words come to mind. Scorching hot. Heart-wrenching, in a really good way.

"I am happy with just that, Callum," she said. "Don't feel pressured. I know you have been through a lot. I'll be all right no matter what happens. Evie will be, too, because she has me."

The truth of what she said penetrated deep into him. Hazel would never push him. She wanted him for who he was and nothing less. She cared about him, his happiness above all else. He wanted to give that to her, as well. All of him. But he still felt so broken. So injured. A woman like her deserved the whole man.

He slid his hand behind her head, gently, then stepped close. Kissing her, he hoped she understood the unspoken message, how amazing and charitable she was.

When he drew back she put her forefinger over his lips as though sealing the kiss. "Let's go catch that bad guy."

"Hazel…"

"Shh." She lowered her hand. "None of that now. Let's go."

He took a moment to enjoy how beautiful she was and how sexy in that biker-woman disguise. "I must be a fool."

She put her pointer finger on his upper chest and ran it down to the waist of his pants. Then her striking eyes looked up at him. "You could never be a fool, Callum Colton. You just need to let go of past pain. I only hope I'm still in your life when you do."

She looked into his eyes, angling her head and assessing him. After she must have learned what she needed to from peering into his eyes, she turned and headed for the suite's entrance.

Rather than take a hired car, Callum called a cab. That would be less conspicuous. On the way, Callum phoned Kerry to let her know about their visit. She wasn't happy with their planning something like that on their own and on such short notice, but she said she'd assemble a team to wait in unmarked cars in the parking lot. She'd also send a plainclothes cop inside in case anything went wrong.

A short drive later, they reached the bar. Callum made sure no one saw them as they left the cab.

He guided Hazel into Joe's. After being seated they settled in to have an evening together, covertly surveying everyone there.

It was much the same as the last time they were there. Dim and dirty.

And the same biker crowd was at the pool table.

All appeared calm, until Callum noticed a redheaded waitress who kept looking behind her and all around the bar.

"Did you see that redhead last time we were here?" he asked Hazel.

She looked around the bar and zeroed in on the other woman. "No."

Hazel moved closer to him. "Might as well look the part."

"Careful."

"Of what?" She leaned in, her breast pressing against his side.

"Of more." He could have elaborated but he didn't.

"You should give in. You have no control over this. I realized that after last night."

She was sure being bold. Yes, last night had been earth-shattering. He couldn't face that right now.

"Let's get rid of this killer and then deal with that, okay?"

She smiled wide and bright. "Okay." Then she turned to survey the bar, covertly watching the redhead serve beers to a table of raucous men.

"She's wearing a wedding ring," Callum said. He looked at the other female workers. There were only two and neither wore a ring. If the killer had murdered Nate Blurge for flirting with his wife, he might have shown up tonight to keep an eye on her.

"The woman who served us last time didn't have one," Hazel said.

"And the redhead wasn't working that night, so if she is his wife, the killer probably wasn't here."

"Nope." She looked around the bar and he saw her stop short when she spotted a table with a lone man sitting there.

He was the same height and build as the man who kept showing up at the inn and following them and shooting at them. He had no hat on and no sunglasses. In a holey pair of faded jeans and a black *Deadwood* T-shirt, he had a day or two's worth of facial stubble. His longish brown hair convinced Callum he was their man.

"He's watching the redhead," Hazel said.

Yes, he was. And very intently. The killer's face turned stormy, his brows lowered. He had all the mannerisms of an insanely jealous man, a power tripper. He looked the type to need absolute control over his woman. He was so involved with policing the redhead that he didn't notice Callum and Hazel watching him.

Callum looked back at the waitress and saw her smiling at one of the men drinking at a table. The man didn't seem drunk. He was clean-cut and dressed in dark jeans with no holes in them and a nice polo. Callum watched him after the redhead left the table. He wasn't drinking fast and when the others ordered another round, he declined. He made the redhead smile and this time laugh as he talked with her.

"Oh boy," Hazel said.

Callum looked over at the killer. He had gotten up and marched across the bar toward the man at the table.

Standing up, Callum heard the killer say in a loud, angry tone, "Why are you flirting with my wife?"

Looking startled, the man looked up. "I didn't know she was married."

"She's wearing a ring, you idiot!"

"I didn't look, sorry, man. All I did was thank her for the beer and tell her she was too pretty to be working in a place like this."

"Why did she laugh like you said something funny?"

The other man stood. "Dude, calm down. Nothing happened. Just casual talk. You should be flattered I think you have a beautiful wife."

A woman who deserved better than a killer as a husband. Callum watched that man shove the other.

"Do you always hit on other men's wives?"

"Hey. What's your problem?" The man shoved him back.

The killer took a swing, hitting the other man. Callum stalked to them, planting his hand on the murderer's chest and getting between them.

"That's enough." Callum pushed the killer back, forcing him to step farther away from him and the clean-cut man.

The man behind him tried to get around Callum to go after the killer. Callum lost some balance and the killer took a swing at him and clipped his jaw. Callum's glasses went flying. The man behind him had grabbed hold of his wig, pulling it off his head. The man had meant to pull him out of the way but the wig stopped him.

Callum gave him a shove and growled, "Back off!"

"You!" the killer snarled, recognizing Callum.

Callum ducked as the killer made another swing at him and the punch caught the man behind him. Callum swiped his opponent's leg out from under him, sending him down. But the killer lunged for him, plowing into him and driving them both back into the table of drinking men. Callum landed on his back, spilling beer glasses and scattering the seated men.

Using his feet, Callum kicked the killer, sending him flying backward and sliding on his back through the broken and spilled glasses of beer. He bumped into another table.

Going toward him, he saw the killer get to his feet and look around, finding Hazel standing near their table. The other man sprinted toward her, causing an instant flash of fear in Callum.

He ran to Hazel as the killer drew a pistol and she pivoted and started to head for the exit. But the killer was on her too fast. He grabbed her, spun her around and put the pistol to her temple.

Callum stopped short, just a couple of feet from them. He looked at Hazel's terrified eyes. She must be thinking of her daughter. Callum had failed her.

He stood frozen for a few seconds, before anger took over. No way would he lose another woman like this!

With a lightning-fast gesture, he knocked the gun upward. It went off but the bullet shot toward the ceiling. Callum kicked the man and sent him back and away from Hazel. As Kerry and other officers, including the plainclothes cop, burst in, Hazel ran to the bar and huddled with some other people, and Callum drew his own gun and aimed it at the killer's head.

"I've got you now," Callum said to the man on the floor. Finally.

Kerry approached.

"That's him," Callum said. "That's the man Evie saw hit Nate Blurge over the head."

Kerry glanced at him sharply. "You're certain?"

"As certain as I can be. He's the same build and his hair is the same."

She nodded to two officers, who knelt down and searched the man, procuring a driver's license and handing it to Kerry.

"Billy Jansen," she said. "Run this by Motor Vehicle."

One of the officers left with the license.

Moments later the officer returned with the license and announced the plate number was a match.

"Take him to the station," Kerry said to the other officer.

The officer helped Billy to his feet and cuffed him, reading him his rights.

"The redhead over there is his wife," Callum said, pointing

to the woman next to Hazel who watched Billy with no small amount of apprehension.

"We'll need to talk to her."

"I'll tell her."

Callum walked over to Hazel and the redhead.

"Are you all right?" he asked Hazel.

"Yes, thanks to you." She rose up on her toes and kissed him, quick and grateful.

"You're welcome." Nothing felt better than that.

Facing the redhead, he said, "The police are going to want to talk to you."

"Why? They're doing me a favor taking him away."

"You're his wife. You can provide information they'll need to prosecute him and testify against him if you want to."

"How long will he be in jail?"

She was obviously worried he'd get out and come after her.

"If he gets convicted of murder, he'll be in prison for the rest of his life. What's your name?"

"Tina Jansen."

"What can you tell police about Nate Blurge's murder?"

"Plenty. He flirted with me the same way that nice man tonight did and ended up dead. Billy wasn't home when Nate was killed and Billy bragged about getting rid of him. He even threatened me that he'd kill every man I flirted with."

"Your testimony will only help. I can assure you he'll be put away for a long time." Callum couldn't believe that some killers talked about what they had done.

Tina smiled big. "Good riddance. I can finally divorce him without worrying he'll kill me, too."

Callum didn't doubt that. He was glad the man would be off the streets, but he still had one more problem to take care of before he could be assured of Hazel's safety.

Most of the police had gone and the bar had returned to its usual business. Hazel couldn't wait to get out of her disguise.

She went to the bathroom before she and Callum would go home. Finishing up, she washed her hands at the sink. They could retrieve Evie soon. When she lifted her head, she saw Carolyn's reflection in the mirror and she had a gun.

Seriously? Hazel's disbelief buffered the slight gasp of shock and fear.

The same night? "How did you know we were here?"

"Easy. I knew you were looking for that Blurge man's killer and Patsy told me you were going to be here one of these nights."

Damn that assistant.

"If you don't come quietly, I'll shoot you. It's what I've dreamed of doing ever since you left my restaurant. I knew I could never make it without a chef like you and I knew I'd have a hard time replacing you."

"Carolyn, you don't have to do this. I told you I was sorry. I never meant for any of that to happen."

"It's too late for all of that. I thought I could forgive you but I can't. Now get moving."

Hazel hesitated. If she went with this crazy woman, she would probably end up dead before morning. She had to find a way to alert Callum.

Callum.

What would this do to him? And what about Evie?

More determined than ever, Hazel started toward the bathroom exit. Carolyn jabbed her gun against Hazel's ribs, concealing the gun with the oversized sweatshirt she wore.

Would anyone find an oversized sweatshirt odd? Arizona was hot, but it was early spring and nighttime, when it got colder.

Outside the bathroom, Hazel stalled. Just as she suspected, Callum stood where he could see the bathroom. And he spotted her right away.

"Get going!" Carolyn jabbed her and forced her to hurry to the back door, which had been propped open to allow airflow.

They passed the kitchen entrance, where heat poured out

through the narrow doorway along with the sounds of frying food and workers having a lighthearted night.

Hazel dared not look back to see where Callum was. Carolyn forced her through the back door, and to Hazel's horror, she had her SUV parked right outside and the driver's side door was open. Carolyn had planned to make Hazel drive, presumably with a gun pointed at her in case she tried to escape or attract attention.

Did a dive bar like this have cameras? Not likely.

Hazel knew she had to do something. She could not get in that vehicle before Callum caught up to them.

Relying—desperately—on what she had heard about self-defense, she dropped all her weight straight down. Carolyn wasn't a big woman. Hazel felt her former boss stumble and rake at her clothes, to no avail. She stepped back to maintain her balance. It was enough for Hazel to scramble away, looking for cover.

She didn't have to panic long. Callum emerged from the back door, smacking Carolyn's head with the butt of his pistol, and she fell like a rag doll. He kicked her gun away and rushed over to Hazel.

"Are you all right?" He was breathless and his eyes were wild with fear.

She just grabbed his face with both hands and kissed him hard once. "Yes. I am, Callum. I love you." She kissed him hard again and then stopped herself.

What had she said? The words had tumbled out.

Heat hardened his eyes from frantic concern. Was the tension sexual—or maybe loving? But it appeared only for an instant.

"Go inside and get the police," he said.

She did as he asked. But as she ran into the bar and to the front, the glow of warmth she had seen in him crept into her in a different way. He'd caught the feeling and shut it off.

He wasn't ready for this, for her to have blurted out words of love.

Outside, she found the officers and told them about Carolyn.

They instructed her to wait. She'd have to give a statement and so would Callum.

She would rather call a cab and go get Evie, go home and forget any of this ever happened. She needed Evie more than ever. But she'd have to wait.

Chapter 15

Callum woke late the next morning. Having to give statements on two criminal incidents had taken time. He reached over to feel for Hazel and then remembered she had insisted on sleeping in her own room. He'd had a bad feeling about that the previous night, but the hour had been so late and both of them so tired he hadn't argued.

Now, with a clear head, he realized all of the adrenaline and his baggage with Annabel had taken their toll.

Hoping against hope, he flung the covers off and went across the hall. The room was immaculate. No trace of Hazel. The bed was made and all her things, and Evie's, were gone.

He ran his hand through his hair. He needed his sister.

After quickly showering, he raced to Marlowe's office, pacing outside until the worker she had a meeting with left. Then he went inside and closed the door.

"I heard you captured two criminals in one night. Nice going, brother."

"I need to tell you something." He could not believe he was going to do this.

He paced her office, one side to the other, three times.

"Okay, you're worrying me," Marlowe said.

He stopped and put his hands on the back of one of the chairs facing her desk and looked at her, still struggling with how to begin.

She angled her head. "This whole..." she twirled her pen a few times "...weak man thing isn't the twin I grew up with."

Callum lowered his head with a sigh. She had a way of reaching him he could never explain to anyone. He lifted his head. "There's something I haven't told almost anyone."

Marlowe lifted her eyebrows. "Go on. Don't stop now."

She knew him so well. He would have stopped, in this fragile state. Pushing off the chair, he straightened. "Annabel and I didn't break up."

Marlowe didn't move or blink. She just waited.

"She died."

His sister's mouth formed an O on an indrawn breath. "You lied?"

"I'm sorry." He opened his arms. "I'm so sorry."

"Stop being so weak. What happened?" she demanded.

Lowering his arms and taking a chair, he explained everything, the witness and Annabel's pregnancy—and her death.

"We knew all of that, Callum. What *happened*?"

"I was protecting a witness and was in court a lot. The drug cartel must have had me followed and the leader sent someone to assassinate her. I wasn't there to protect her."

Marlowe took several seconds to absorb that and, Callum knew, piece together what he hadn't said.

"Oh, Cal." She shook her head gently, full of empathy. And then she grew stern. "And you didn't tell *me*?"

"I didn't tell anyone. I couldn't." He had no way of explaining.

As it turned out, he didn't have to. His sister knew him like no other. "You blamed yourself but because you met Hazel, you can face it now."

Well, that he hadn't expected. His sister knew how to get to the point, but that was…he would have thought harsh but he checked himself. Her honesty, like Hazel's, showed him not only the brutality of the truth but also the healing power of facing it.

"Tell you what." Marlowe leaned back in her big leather executive chair. "I'll tell the family, and you go get this woman who's done you so much good."

Callum felt his insides twist with warning. "What? No. It's not like that."

Marlowe picked up a pen from the desk and dropped it in exasperation. "It's not? Look at you. Listen to yourself. You just told me that meeting Hazel has brought you here, confessing something huge that you kept from your own family."

He hadn't thought how his inability to deal with Annabel's death would affect his siblings. He hadn't cared about his parents all that much. They were always too involved with Colton Oil. And other than with Marlowe, he wasn't the type of brother to bleed out his soul to everyone. But Marlowe…

"I should have told you," he said. "You're right." He ran his fingers through his hair, disconcerted.

"Stop," Marlowe said. "Just stop."

He looked at her, not sure of her meaning.

"You should have told me, but I understand why you didn't. I know you like you know me. We are tough emotionally, and smart and strong. But we can be stubborn, Cal."

"I know, but—"

"What I want you to hear from me—and you better listen—is you have met a beautiful and wonderful woman who won't put up with your baggage if you can't handle it."

Nothing like putting it bluntly. He also liked the handling connotation. Baggage. Handles.

He laughed, deeply and from his core. "Marlowe, I love you."

"Go get that girl, you fool." She smiled and laughed softly in return. "There's no escaping it. Take it from one who knows."

She'd gotten involved with Bowie Robertson, the president

of Robertson Renewable Energy Company, Colton Oil's rival. She'd gotten pregnant and ended up falling in love. Callum still couldn't tell she was pregnant. She looked great.

Resigned to the fact that she was probably right, he stood from the chair.

"Hey," Marlowe said.

He met her teasing eyes.

"Do you love her?"

He recalled Hazel blurting she loved him and how that had made him feel. Confused. Scared. Weak, as his sister would say.

"Yes."

Both let down by Callum's brusque attitude and exceedingly excited to see Evie again, Hazel walked up to her brother's house. Owen opened the door before she got there and Evie bounded out.

"Mommy!"

Immense joy burst in Hazel. She crouched as Evie ran to her and took her into her arms. "Hi, Evie. I missed you so much."

"I missed you, too, Mommy."

Hazel kissed her cheek several times, making Evie laugh. Then she stood up.

Evie looked toward the street. "Where's Cal-em?"

"He couldn't make it." Seeing Evie's crestfallen face, Hazel felt a pang of guilt for not bringing Callum with her. She'd figured a clean break would be best for her daughter.

"But he said he would."

"I know, honey." She took her daughter's hand and walked to her brother.

"She's a great kid. Whatever you're doing, keep doing it."

She hugged Owen. "Where's Jessica?"

"She went to work. She said to tell you hello and thanks for convincing her to have kids. I'd like to thank you, too."

Hazel smiled, loving Evie's effect on them. "I didn't know you wanted them."

"I wasn't sure until now." He messed up the top of Evie's hair, which she wore down today. "You come back anytime, okay?"

"Okay!"

"Thank you so much, Owen. I owe you big for watching her."

"I'm just glad you caught that killer. We were scared for you. And your ex-boss." He shook his head with raised eyebrows. "That's so wild."

"Yeah. I still can't believe it. She was always so friendly."

"I guess everybody has their breaking point."

Even if Hazel ran into hard times like that, she didn't think she would ever break to the point of attempted murder. "I think I'd have to be on my deathbed before I broke."

"Yes, and normal people wouldn't murder anybody."

"No." She looked down at Evie. "Well, what do you think, kiddo? Should we go home?"

"Okay. Will Cal-em be there?"

"I don't think so."

Her brother eyed her in question. "I thought you two had something going."

She had to be careful what she said in front of Evie. She couldn't be sure what Callum would do, now that she was safe.

"It's still too early to tell."

"That's not how it looked to me," Owen said. "I've never seen you glow like you did with him nearby."

She'd been glowing? She had not been aware of that.

"Why didn't he come with you today?" Owen asked.

"I left early. I didn't wake him," she said neutrally. "We better get going. I've got a lot of meals to cook."

"Don't let a good man go because of what Ed did to you," Owen said. "And don't hold it against Callum for being rich. He isn't the same as Ed."

"I know, Owen." She might as well tell him all of it, Evie, too. "He has issues of his own. His pregnant girlfriend died in an accident. A drug dealer did it to get revenge on Callum for him protecting a witness during his trial. He hasn't gotten over her yet."

"All he needs is someone like you to know he has a soft place to land."

She was a soft place to land? Not if being with Evie all the time made him think of the baby he had lost. And not if he held back with Hazel and never let his feelings grow with her. She wanted more than that and Evie deserved more than that.

When Hazel arrived back at her little apartment above the bakery, she did not expect to see Callum's rental parked in the back.

"Cal-em's here!" Evie exclaimed.

Hazel parked and walked around to get Evie out of her car seat. She fidgeted and swung her tiny feet, anxious to get out of the SUV. Since she had been riding in Callum's vehicles, the Mercedes' mirror had been repaired.

She freed Evie, who climbed out of the SUV and ran toward the stairs. Hazel followed, wondering why Callum was here. She saw him get out of the truck as they approached. Evie veered away from the stairs.

"Evie!" Callum crouched and wrapped his arms around her as she crashed into him.

"You said you were gonna come get me," Evie said, small arms looping around his neck as she leaned back to look at his face.

"I'm sorry. That's why I'm here now." He looked at Hazel.

She saw pure adoration for Evie's sweet charm.

"And I also came to have a word with your mother."

Evie glanced back at Hazel.

"Let's go inside." Hazel walked to the stairs and Callum carried Evie up them. Inside, she felt she no longer belonged in this tiny place. She still wasn't sure she would be comfortable living in a mansion with all of Callum's family, or if she would get used to having so much money—that was, if he did love her.

He put Evie down and told her to go find them a good movie. She trotted to the living room.

Hazel faced Callum, prepared for anything. He was gentleman enough to make sure he talked to her personally about any decisions he had made.

He took her hands in his. "This last month with you has been more than eye-opening, Hazel."

"For me, as well."

"First I want to start off by saying I am nothing like Evie's father. I don't run from difficult situations or circumstances."

"I know that about you." He would face her and break things off ethically and with integrity.

"I'm rich like he was, probably richer, because of my family."

She nodded, lowering her eyes.

"But I have never lied to you, nor will I ever."

She returned her gaze to him. This was beginning to sound like he had no intention of breaking things off between them. Hope flared and her heart began to pound with responding emotion.

"You helped me through dealing with Annabel's death. And talking to my sister today made me realize that even though it's only been a month, I've fallen in love with you."

She couldn't believe her ears.

"That's why…" He got down on one knee and then let go of her hands to dig into his pocket.

No way. He wasn't…

He pulled out a ring box. "Now, I don't want you to feel rushed." He looked up at her and opened the box to reveal a sapphire and diamond ring. The sapphires were about a karat between them and surrounded by smaller diamonds. A man with his money could have gotten her something gaudy and blatantly expensive. But he knew her. He knew she wouldn't have appreciated anything like that.

"You pick the date, but will you marry me?"

Tears stung her eyes. This was the happiest day of her life! "When did you…"

"I stopped at the jewelry store on the way here. I knew you were going to get Evie so I had plenty of time. I guessed on the size."

She stared at the ring, loving it enormously.

"You haven't answered my question," he said.

She glanced at Evie, who was oblivious to this monumental moment. Hazel didn't have to worry she wouldn't approve. She was already treating Callum like her stepfather.

Then she looked at Callum. "Yes, I will marry you. I don't care when. It can be tomorrow or next spring. I'll still want to marry you as much as I do right now, because I have fallen in love with you, too."

Smiling, he stood and removed the ring from the box. She offered her hand and he slipped it on her finger. It fit perfectly.

Chapter 16

Marlowe had arranged for a family gathering at the mansion to allow Hazel to get to know everyone better. Over the last few days, he had relished in living with Hazel and Evie as a family. They had decided to stay at the inn a while longer to enjoy some downtime. Callum thought a get-together would be a perfect opportunity to show Hazel his home and let her decide if it was somewhere she wanted to live. They didn't have to live in the mansion. They could build something on the ranch. It was Sunday afternoon on a sunny, clear day.

"You all live here?" Hazel asked when the sprawling mansion appeared. Made of rock and wood to match the rugged landscape and the Mustang Valley Mountains in the distance, the multiple gables of the roofline and three stories of windows and balconies gave evidence to its size.

"Yes. My mom and dad live on the first floor in one wing. There are guest quarters in the other wing. Ace, Grayson and Ainsley have the three wings on the second floor, and Asher, Marlowe and I have the third floor wings. Then there are several spaces we share, like the living areas and the library."

He parked and got out, waiting for Hazel to get Evie out of the back. She had slept the whole way there. Now she groggily walked beside Hazel to the entrance. There were other cars here, but most were likely in the huge garage.

Inside the grand entry, Hazel took in the luxurious, floor-to-ceiling windows and exposed beam ceiling of the open living room. Callum saw most everyone was already here. The only ones missing were Grayson and Asher.

"Callum." Marlowe came to greet them, leaving Bowie standing with a glass of wine near the rock pillars at the entrance of the large dining room.

Kerry was there with Rafe, seated on the sofa with Ainsley.

"I sent someone to get Grayson and Asher. They should be here soon." She turned to Hazel. "So happy to see you. Looks like I talked some sense into my brother after all."

"Thanks for that." Hazel showed her the ring.

"Oh, that's beautiful!" Marlowe gaped at Callum. "Everybody, Callum is getting married!" She held Hazel's hand out for all to see.

"He's gonna be my new daddy," Evie said. Then, seeing the huge television, she meandered over. Ainsley changed the channel to a kid friendly show.

Hazel mouthed, *Thank you.*

Just then Grayson and Asher entered. All the siblings were together, a few of them attached to significant others.

Callum rarely saw Grayson. He doubted any of the others did, either.

"This is Hazel, Callum's fiancée." Marlowe introduced her to the two. "And her daughter, Evie."

Grayson reached over and shook her hand. "Fianceé?"

"Hey, it's about time."

"And that is Asher," Marlowe said. "He's Rattlesnake Ridge Ranch's foreman and a bit of a lone wolf."

"A pleasure to meet you both. You look like a real cowboy,

Asher," Hazel said. "With the longish hair and that face, you must make all the women swoon."

Grayson chuckled. "He's a lone wolf. He doesn't date."

Asher shook his head. "Thank you for the compliment, Hazel, and it's nice to meet you, too. Callum needs a good woman in his life. And a good daughter!"

"Thanks. What do you do, Grayson?"

"I run a first responder management agency."

"That sounds exciting. Do you like rescuing people?"

"He likes the adrenaline rush," Callum said.

"Yes," Grayson said to Hazel, "Helping people is the most rewarding part." Then he turned a disgruntled look to Callum.

"I've been trying to get a hold of both of you to update you on the whole situation with Dad," Marlowe said.

She hadn't told them yet?

"We found the woman who gave birth on the Christmas morning the babies were switched." Callum explained about the fire and the woman who'd left that same day with what everyone thought was her baby but must have been their biological brother.

"Her name is Luella. We don't have a last name yet," Marlowe said.

"Well, that's good news, I mean that you have at least a first name. Is she the one who switched Ace with our biological brother?" Asher asked.

"Yes, it is possible," Callum said.

"What kind of sicko does that?" Asher asked. "We need to catch her and find out, brother. Is he still alive?"

"I want to help," Grayson said. "What can I do?"

Callum found his brother's concern odd. He believed that Grayson did like helping people but this was different. "You haven't even gone to see Dad in the hospital. Why are you so gung-ho now to step up? You don't even hang out with your family. It's like putting a house fire out to get you to come to any of these."

"Somebody switched our oldest brother. That nurse has to pay. We have to get justice for Ace. He may not be our blood brother but he's still our sibling."

"Isn't that the truth," Ainsley said.

"We can't stop until we do find this Luella and bring her to justice," Rafe said from the sofa.

"I just want to know why you care all of a sudden," Callum said. The fact that he wasn't close to his brothers and sisters and never went to see their dad in the hospital didn't support Grayson's assertions.

"My relationship was always complicated with Dad. I'm sure you've had your ups and downs with him. I haven't resolved anything with him. I'm not sure he'd want to see me."

"Dad's in a coma. You should go for yourself, not him."

Grayson didn't respond right away. "It's not that simple, Callum."

"It can be. Just go see him. Talk to him. He might be in a coma but he can still hear."

"That's true," Marlowe said. "His brain will still hear you."

"You'd side with Callum anyway," Grayson said. "You're his twin."

Marlowe put her hands up. "I think it would be good for you to go see him. It has nothing to do with agreeing with Cal."

"Anyway, the real problem here is finding whoever switched Ace," Grayson said. "I want to find our real brother. He's out there somewhere and probably has no idea where he really came from."

"I feel so bad for Ace," Ainsley said. "Why isn't he here?"

"He's laying low for now," Callum said. "Until we can find out who shot Dad."

"Yeah, but he's all alone," Ainsley said. "And what he must be going through, dealing with the discovery that he isn't a Colton by blood. Does he think we all consider him an outsider?"

"I don't think so," Callum said. "At least, not everyone."

"Dad?" Marlowe put in. "Kicking him out of Colton Oil?"

"It's not enough to make Ace try to kill him," Grayson said.

"I think all of us want to believe that," Ainsley said.

"Yeah," Rafe said.

"Of course," Asher said. He walked into the kitchen, lone wolf that he was.

"Let's start with finding Luella," Callum said.

"Hey," Marlowe said. "Let's turn this into a celebration for Callum and Hazel—and Evie, too."

"Hear, hear." Ainsley lifted her glass.

Callum turned to Hazel and slipped his arm around her waist. "Hear, hear, for sure."

The siblings began talking of other things, leaving Callum and Hazel with a moment to themselves.

"Let me show you my wing," Callum said. "You can tell me what you think."

He took her to the third level. It took some time to get there, the home was so large. Then he arrived at a door and opened it. She stepped inside an expansive seating area with a high ceiling, a fireplace and a balcony. There was a bar, as well, and a dining table and kitchenette. That she didn't like. He showed her the master suite. It was magnificent, with a huge bathroom. No room for Evie.

"It doesn't seem suitable for a family," she said.

"I thought the same. I didn't expect you to want to live here. We can build a house here on the ranch or somewhere else."

She would probably like his family but living so close to them seemed too much for her. She preferred to have her privacy. They could come see his family as often as he liked.

"I'm not sure I want to wait that long to move into a house," she said.

"All right." He smiled. "We'll look somewhere in town." He kissed her and, as always, their chemistry heated. With a bed so close, taking this further was tempting, but with his siblings and her daughter downstairs, they should be getting back.

Hazel drew away and just looked at Callum, into his loving and incredible blue eyes. She had to be one of the luckiest women in the world.

Hazel and Callum opted for staying at the Dales Inn until they could find a house. They were headed there now, with Callum driving. But then she noticed he wasn't heading in the direction of town.

"Where are we going?"

"I have a surprise for you," he said with a wily grin.

"Callum Colton, what are you up to?"

"Yeah. Whatcha up to?" Evie asked from the back seat.

"You'll see. If I tell you it will ruin the surprise." He drove into a rural area outside Mustang Valley city limits, into an affluent neighborhood with large homes but not mansions. The houses were all stone with big windows and each measured about five thousand square feet.

She had a pretty good idea what his surprise was going to be. She turned to him.

"If you don't like it, we can look for another one," Callum said, having read her glance.

What was there not to like?

He pulled to a stop in front of a beautiful gray stone house with white trim. There was a veranda next to the front portico and a turret on the other side.

"My family already owns this house," Callum said. "It's technically a Colton family property but my mom, as my dad's representative, said she could transfer the title to us once we're married."

"It's beautiful." She helped Evie out of the truck and walked toward the front entrance. Inside, a two-story foyer soared above a spiral staircase going to the second level. The formal living room to the left had a fireplace and was open to the dining room, where double doors led to the veranda. A groin-vaulted ceiling over a short hallway opened to the living room and kitchen area.

The kitchen.

It was obviously professional grade, but without an overwhelming amount of stainless steel, with white walls and recessed lighting. The perimeter cabinets were white and the countertops soft green granite. The kitchen island drew her like a magnet. It had a green hood with a pan holder where several pots and pans already hung. There was a five-burner stove set in dark brown and tan granite that had a counter-mounted pot filler, which allowed a cook to fill big pots with water. The stainless steel refrigerator was twice the size of the one in her apartment. There were two ovens and a microwave was mounted into a cabinet. It was a dream kitchen.

"It was designed for hired cooks to entertain guests who stay here," Callum said.

Overwhelmed, Hazel turned in a circle and just admired it. She felt like she was in a dream. "I don't need to see the rest of the house."

"Can I pick out my room?" Evie asked.

Callum chuckled. "Sure." He showed them two master suites and two other bedrooms on the second level. There was also a theater room. He took them to a room done in pale blue, light gray and white that had a built-in oversized bunk bed, the top more like a mini balcony. There was a seating area, built-in bookshelf and an antique trunk.

"Wow!" Evie ran to the bunk bed and climbed up the white ladder to her tower, peering down at them with a big smile.

"There's toys in the trunk," Callum said. "Marlowe had it filled."

"Come on," he said to Hazel, "You need to pick out our room."

The two master suites were similar except one was decorated in darker colors and the one she fell in love with was more like a beach-house bedroom. The closet was big enough to be another bedroom.

"Oh, Callum. I can't believe this." She faced him. How could she have gotten so lucky?

"I take it you're willing to live here?" he asked.

"More than willing. This is wonderful."

"Good, then we'll get help bringing our things here in the morning."

"Oh, my…" She turned in another circle. "Are you sure?" Did he really want *her*?

He walked to her. "You deserve it." Sliding his hand around to her back, he pulled her to him.

"How will I ever match all this extravagance? I can never give you anything like this."

"You gave me your love, that's enough for me."

"But…"

"Shh. What is mine is yours. Never feel otherwise."

That would take some time. She'd have to get accustomed to having money. But she would never take it for granted. She appreciated him getting them a reasonably sized house. And for thinking of her profession. She would have to pinch herself every day to make sure it was real.

"I love you," she said.

"I love you, too." He kissed her.

"I want to have your baby." She kissed him.

"Let's get started right away."

She smiled against his lips. As soon as Evie was asleep, she'd like nothing more.

* * * * *

Colton First Responder

Linda O. Johnston

Linda O. Johnston loves to write. While honing her writing skills, she worked in advertising and public relations, then became a lawyer...and enjoyed writing contracts. Linda's first published fiction appeared in *Ellery Queen's Mystery Magazine* and won a Robert L. Fish Memorial Award for Best First Mystery Short Story of the Year. Linda now spends most of her time creating memorable tales of paranormal romance, romantic suspense and mystery. Visit her on the web at www.lindaojohnston.com.

Books by Linda O. Johnston

Harlequin Romantic Suspense

The Coltons of Mustang Valley

Colton First Responder

Colton 911

Colton 911: Caught in the Crossfire

K-9 Ranch Rescue

Second Chance Soldier
Trained to Protect

Undercover Soldier
Covert Attraction

Visit the Author Profile page at millsandboon.com.au for more titles.

Dear Reader,

Here is my second book in the wonderful, long-running Colton series.

Colton First Responder is book number four in the new twelve-book Coltons of Mustang Valley miniseries, which involves a large family in which a secret is brought to light.

Colton First Responder features Grayson Colton, the third child of patriarch Payne Colton; he chooses not to get too close to his family members. Instead of working for Colton Oil or spending much time at Rattlesnake Ridge Ranch, he began his own company of first responders who help in emergencies. When a major earthquake occurs in Cactus Creek, Grayson tries to find survivors—which is how he meets Savannah Oliver. The earthquake allowed her to escape from the van returning her to prison after a court appearance gone bad, since she's accused of murdering her husband. She asserts her innocence and Grayson believes her... but should he? Still, together, they search for the truth.

I hope you enjoy *Colton First Responder*. Please come visit me at my website, lindaojohnston.com, and at my weekly blog, killerhobbies.Blogspot.com. And, yes, I'm on Facebook, too.

Linda O. Johnston

Chapter 1

No.

The word kept reverberating through Savannah Oliver's mind, and not only now. It had done so for days. Even longer.

That wasn't surprising. This couldn't be happening.

But of course she knew it was.

She looked around the bland—yet terrifying—enclosed back area of the ugly transport van that was returning her to the Arizona Prison Complex in Phoenix. From where she sat strapped onto a bench—not particularly for her safety—with her back against the partition leading to the driver's area, she glanced up toward the high, wire-meshed rear windows of the van. No way could she get out of the vehicle through those and onto the rural road, in the middle of nowhere, that they now traversed. The windows were too small—and besides, cuffs kept her hands shackled together behind her.

She couldn't brush any of her hair away from her face. It was shoulder length and blond—and disheveled, she assumed, as it so often was these days. She couldn't even secure it with one of the pretty hair clips she loved.

She couldn't brush away any tears, either, but fortunately those had nearly stopped—though they threatened to begin again any moment.

Without meaning to, she looked down at her legs as she sat there—and nearly smiled in irony. At least she had been allowed to dress in brown slacks and a beige shirt for this outing, instead of the bright orange prison jumpsuit that was her usual attire these days. Her shoes were the same ones she wore every day now—casual black slip-ons.

She had just been in court. Not only had she been arraigned, but she had been denied bail. She would remain in prison—and not just the local jail because of the severity of her alleged crime—until her trial, and who knew when that would be?

But did it matter? Her lawyer, Ian Wright, had promised he'd try for bail, but he had warned her in advance that it was unlikely. She had already been labeled a flight risk, and the charges against her were serious. Very serious.

He had also told her that, notwithstanding the solid defense he would mount for her, she was likely to be convicted.

Now she sat on one of the few seats in this area of the van as it continued forward, attempting futilely once more to pull her hands out of the cuffs.

Wishing she had some way to get out of there, even if it involved somehow shoving open one of those windows and squeezing through. Better yet, if she could open one of the doors where the windows were located, and leap down onto the road.

Of course, she'd get badly injured, or worse.

But what could be worse than being incarcerated, possibly forever, for a crime she didn't commit?

A crime that might not have been committed at all, since no body had been found.

She was accused of murdering her ex-husband, Zane Oliver. Good old Zane.

Horrible, disgusting, appalling Zane.

His body hadn't been found, and she felt certain he wasn't really dead.

No, more likely he was hanging out somewhere, laughing at setting her up this way. He'd learn about this hearing, confirm that she wasn't permitted bail. And he'd smile and smile…

She needed to get her mind off this somehow. She needed a shoulder to cry on, but for the moment, at least, she was all alone.

Except for the driver in the cab of the van. He'd been the same one who'd driven her to court.

His name was Ari. They'd been introduced as she was led into the van at the prison and strapped in before heading to the courthouse. Not that he'd said a word to her then. He was young and skinny, with dark hair and a constant frown, dressed in a police uniform.

Of course they'd send a cop to ensure that vicious, murderous Savannah wouldn't harm anyone else.

She cringed at the irony her own mind presented.

Outside the courthouse, all Ari had done was to open the back door and unhook her when they'd arrived. Then he'd handed her over to another uniformed cop, who had led her inside to the courtroom where her attorney waited, as did the District Attorney, Karly Fitzpatrick. She'd been shown where to sit—as if that was a surprise. Right up front, facing the judge. The procedure had gone forward, with its terrible result, not even any bail, and she had been led back outside, handcuffed again and strapped once more into this van.

Ari had acknowledged her only with a nod of his head.

But now—well, she could at least try to get his attention. She turned as much as she could to face the closed window that led into the van's cab.

"Ari?" she called. "Ari, I know we're still a distance from the prison, and…well, I have a bit of an emergency back here."

She had many emergencies, but she was making up the one she would tell him about.

He didn't respond, or at least she didn't hear him.

"Ari, could we please stop at a gas station or something? I really need to use the restroom."

She concentrated to hear beyond the vehicle's rumble and the road noise beneath it in case Ari was mumbling, but she heard nothing.

Not that she was surprised. Even if she did have that kind of emergency, he probably wouldn't care. She'd either have to tough it out or just go—

Bam!

The van shook horribly at the same time Savannah experienced a shocking, deafening sound that lasted several seconds, maybe the loudest noise she had ever heard. She screamed, wishing yet again that her hands were free, this time so she could cover her ears.

Better yet, she wished she could use them to brace herself, since the van was careening from side to side. She hurtled back and forth despite being strapped in. She had to protect herself.

What had happened? What was that noise? Why hadn't the van stopped? Had it hit something? Had something hit it?

But no. The vehicle skidded and finally stopped with Savannah still attached to the seat, and even then the ground continued to shake beneath it.

Noises of other kinds abounded, too—as if trees were thudding to the ground. Savannah added to the noise, calling for help, unsure what to do.

She hadn't wanted to return to prison—but was she instead going to die?

She finally realized the likely source of the shaking, the bumping and the sounds.

An earthquake.

No time to think about it—though she'd been in a few smaller quakes and tremors here in Arizona. She hadn't had her life endangered then.

And now—what could she do?

Before any ideas came to her, the worst noise and movement of all occurred—a smashing metallic sound, abrupt. The van had hit something…hard. Or been hit. Something must have crashed down onto the front of the stopped van, behind where Savannah now lay sideways on the bench, her back sore from where it had hit the partition.

She screamed for help again. But she realized in a moment that one good thing—maybe—had come out of it. Her seat belt had loosened.

The van finally stopped moving. Whatever had happened, it remained upright. And Savannah tried to stand, wondering if the vehicle would begin shifting again.

Slowly, crouching, ignoring her soreness, which was fortunately not too bad, she made her way to the door. She had to go backward. The only way she had a chance of opening that door would be to use her hands, and they remained cuffed behind her.

At least the van wasn't moving any longer. She thought about calling out to Ari again but decided to wait, to try to get outside and find him, and maybe they could get to safety together.

Better yet, maybe she could somehow sneak away.

She wished she could see better. But the fact that the evening was already growing darker didn't help. Even so, she managed to find the door with her bound hands behind her, as well as the handle on one side that opened it. Was it locked from the outside? She hoped not.

She pushed down the handle—and the door opened! She felt like shouting in triumph, but this was only a small step in the right direction.

Speaking of steps, could she find the ones at the back of the van and get down without falling? She wouldn't be able to hold on with her hands behind her.

She shoved the door open as well as she could, still moving backward, then very slowly lowered her right leg till her foot touched a step. She glanced down but could see very little in the darkness. She carefully allowed her left foot to join the right one, and then remained on that step for a few seconds, half expecting the ground to roll again beneath her—or for Ari to show up and shove her back inside.

Neither happened. And after a short while she went down to the next step. The one below that was the ground, and she soon stood there, outside the van, breathing fast and allowing herself to smile, if only a little.

She had beaten one hurdle but there could be plenty more to follow.

She turned and looked at the road behind her. It was narrow, and there was some light shining on it from a few dim electric streetlights spaced long distances apart, probably put there for safety since the road was so rural.

Yikes. It seemed amazing that any of the light poles had survived. Most of the trees around there hadn't. Uprooted, they splayed onto the concrete, and one even blocked part of the road.

Had it been one of them that hit the van? Savannah assumed so, so she started walking carefully around the vehicle on the driver's side.

Sure enough, a large tree had obliterated that part of the cab, crushing the car from the hood all the way to the passenger area. Savannah swallowed hard as she drew closer, looking at the smashed area where Ari had sat to drive.

How amazing that the tree had only crushed the front of the van, and not where she had been sitting. Despite all that had been happening to her, she had actually experienced a little bit of luck.

But what about Ari? Had he been hit by the tree?

She hoped he'd had time to slide over to the other side, assuming it was less destroyed.

As she got closer, she even called out his name. "Ari? Ari, are you okay?"

She heard nothing—and as she got to the huge tree branch that stuck out past the crumpled van door, she managed to look inside.

And backed up fast.

Ari was there…what was left of him. She couldn't see everything with those branches there, but she did see part of his body. What she could make out was covered with blood.

She gasped. "Ari?" she said again. No response. No movement. Since the window was broken, she made herself turn and carefully reach inside, her hands still behind her, and managed to touch Ari's neck. No indication of a pulse—and considering what he looked like, she knew he was dead.

She felt tears stream down her face. Okay, she hadn't liked the guy, and he clearly had felt no compassion toward her. It wasn't his job to give a damn about her. But no matter who he was, she didn't wish this on anyone.

She moved away—but what could she do now? She had only the slightest idea where they were, since she really didn't know the route from the courthouse to the prison, and this was way off in the middle of nowhere.

And even if she wasn't hit by a falling tree, how long could she survive out here in the elements, after an awful earthquake—and unable to free or use her hands?

Ari had secured her in the back of the van, remembering to check her handcuffs before they'd left. Was there any possibility he'd kept the keys?

Surely so. He'd need to unlock the cuffs when they reached the prison. Of course there might be a separate set there, but just in case he had one, she moved toward the passenger side of the van's front cab, going around the back of the truck since the tree blocked her from the front.

As she walked, she listened. No more loud sounds like those caused by the quake but there were plenty of calls of animals and birds in the surrounding area. No sound of other vehicles—or people—that she could hear.

Nothing else suggesting further tremors—or worse. At least not at the moment.

Reaching the passenger door, she turned around and used her bound hands to try to open it.

Success!

And amazingly, there was a key ring attached to the console between the two seats. Not only that, but there was a small leather suitcase on the floor—and it had her name on it. She'd seen it before. It contained some of her personal possessions that the cops had seized upon her arrest and kept at the prison—and would have been given back to her in the event she was released from court that day.

Well, that hadn't happened, but those were still her things.

She tried not to look at Ari any more than she had to as she entered the van—although she did see his bleeding arm and grasped his wrist, again hoping for some sign of life, but there was none. She then turned so she could grab the keys. She got out and laid the keys on the seat. Contorting with a lot of effort, she tried to unlock the cuffs.

No luck, damn it. Not at first, at least. But somehow she managed to succeed after five minutes of trying over and over.

There! She shook her hands free and dropped the cuffs on the ground. She wouldn't need them and didn't want to see them ever again. Next, she grabbed her bag from the floor.

She couldn't help glancing once more at Ari. He hadn't moved. No surprise.

"I'm so sorry, Ari," she said, meaning it. He'd just been doing his job—and that probably included ignoring requests and pleas from suspects he was transporting.

She looked around at what she could see of the road, the surrounding forest, the downed trees and more. She still had no idea where she was—but she nevertheless got moving, running for her life.

She was free! At least for now. And somehow, she needed to use this opportunity to clear her name, though she'd no idea how yet.

She only knew she had to find her rat of an ex. Unless he'd

actually stayed around this area and had been killed in the quake.

Under other circumstances, she would cheer at that idea—but she had to find him, to make him confess to his lies, so she would be able to show the world that she was no murderer, no matter how much she detested the creep.

So now she ran into the vaguely illuminated night, carrying her bag, having no idea where she was going—but hoping she would find some kind of shelter…and somehow survive.

After the initial earthquake more than an hour ago, Grayson Colton had foreseen that the drive along this rural yet usually well-traveled road leading out of Mustang Valley, Arizona, would be a battle against nature. But after his initial assistance and communications, he had chosen this part of town and beyond to search for people who needed help after the highly disturbing tremors the area had experienced.

And was still experiencing to some extent, since the ground continued to rock now and then with aftershocks.

Grayson slowly drove his specially equipped company SUV along what was left of the road as well as he could, avoiding, where possible, the cracks and cavities in the formerly well-paved surface—as well as some downed trees. It was dark out, so his headlights helped him see what he was coming up against. So did the few but helpful lights on remaining poles along the roadside.

That moderate quake, reported so far as 5.9 in magnitude, had been centered around here, so he had taken it upon himself to head this way. He knew what he was doing—although his staff members did, too, or they wouldn't be working for him.

Right now, he had to traverse what was left of this minor highway as best he could. It was who he was, his responsibility, his calling.

And more. He had founded, and continued to run, First Hand First Responders. His small but significant agency employed dedicated first responders who assisted official responders in the police and fire departments, hospitals and other formal emergency organizations in Mustang Valley. And FHFR members helped out often, since the authorized organizations were understaffed in this area.

Grayson had been at his company headquarters when the quake struck that evening. Not much damage had been done to the three-story building he owned in town, fortunately, although the walls had swayed around him and some items on top of desks and shelves had been thrown to the floor.

Calls and police radio communications had immediately started coming in to the office from the Mustang Valley Police Department, including its primary 911 dispatcher and other agencies.

Apparently the structures housing the police and fire departments and even the local hospital hadn't been damaged significantly, a good thing. Same thing with local schools, from what he'd heard. But quite a few buildings in town had suffered damage, sometimes significant, particularly in older areas. As had a bunch of homes,

And who knew what people were out and about and might be in danger?

That took first responders to find out. And the authorities who called had requested their help—extensively and immediately.

Grayson's staff included an emergency medical technician, EMT—Norah Fellini—as well as Pedro Perez, a former firefighter, and Chad Eilbert, a former K-9 cop. Eilbert also had an emergency responder background, and just happened to still have his well-trained search and rescue dog Winchell as his partner.

They'd all been in the FHFR offices, too, when the help requests had started coming in. He'd given them their assignments based on what he'd heard from the official departments' representatives regarding suspicions of where injuries, missing persons and fires were most threatening, primarily in city areas that were not close to downtown, and therefore most in need of attention from extra first responders.

They had all driven off in their vehicles similar to his, containing special equipment such as defibrillators to help to save people's lives. Pedro had a portable fire hose with a pump system in his vehicle. And Chad also had special safety equipment for Winchell.

Then Grayson had made some calls himself. Fortunately, the exclusive, upscale Colton property, Rattlesnake Ridge Ranch—where he still lived most of the time with his large family, including parents and siblings—had been spared any damage.

He'd thrown on his bright neon green first responder vest over his long-sleeved T-shirt and heavily pocketed black pants.

Then he had dashed out, entered his vehicle and spent some time checking on some of the hardest hit areas outside downtown, where he had helped several people out of buildings destroyed by the quake. Fortunately, other firefighters had also shown up there.

That allowed him to head briefly toward one of his favorite spots, an abandoned bunker he had adopted as his own when he was a kid trying to find some privacy from his family. It wasn't far from the family ranch, and like many similar places in this area, it was also an abandoned mineshaft. No one else seemed to know about it, and he'd been able to fix it up over time to be less of a mine and more of a livable hideout. He had headed there now because it was important to him and he wanted to check on its condition. And fortunately, it had completely survived the quake.

Next, he had chosen to head to this area far out of town. He'd begun his career as a wilderness guide. He would be much more skilled in locating and helping people injured out here by the quake than the rest of his staff.

So here he was in his vehicle, glad he'd continued throughout his life to work out intensely and often. With all the potential for disasters way out here, he might need even more strength today to follow his chosen path.

Leaving town along the main streets of Mustang Valley had been interesting. Lots of people out on the sidewalks. Lots of damage visible to some downtown buildings, though, fortunately, none seemed to have been destroyed. The pavement there appeared more wrecked than anything else. No deaths around there, fortunately, and no fires in this area, either.

Grayson had stopped once to help a mother holding her young child cross a damaged street to EMTs and an ambulance. He stopped another time to help a teen catch his fleeing dog.

After that, Grayson kept going out of town, avoiding cracks in the road as best he could.

So far, on this rural road, he hadn't seen much of interest except many downed trees, which sometimes meant he had to ignore what was left of the pavement and drive on the leaf-strewn ground as well as he could. He had seen no recent indication of anyone, either on the road or the roadside, requiring a first responder's assistance.

He decided to proceed for another ten minutes, and if no situation he needed to deal with materialized, he'd check in then with his employees to determine where he should go next to be of the most help.

The road turned to the right a bit, so he did, too. And then he saw what he'd been after but had hoped not to see: a van crushed by a large tree that had fallen on its front. At least that was what it appeared to be as he approached it from behind. In fact, the road was effectively blocked by the black van and the felled tree.

"Okay, what's happened here?" Grayson said out loud, pulling his SUV to the side and parking. He got out quickly, grabbing the medical bag he kept on the floor. He had earned his EMT certification, so he knew how to conduct more than the basics of on-site medical care that could be necessary to save a life.

He also grabbed his large flashlight and used it first to check the ground as he approached the driver's door of the van. He saw, as he got close, that the vehicle's markings labeled it as belonging to the Arizona State Department of Corrections, the kind of van used to transport prisoners from one place to another.

If so—well, first things first. He needed to make sure everyone had gotten out of the vehicle's cab safely.

Only…that wasn't the case. In the bright glow of his flashlight, he immediately saw a man in what was left of the driver's seat, covered in blood.

Grayson's EMT training immediately kicked into gear. He opened the door carefully and checked to see if he could remove the injured person from where he lay after disconnecting his seat belt, without having to get the tree off the van.

Fortunately, he was able to.

Unfortunately, after he gently laid the victim on the ground and began checking for vital signs, he found none. He nevertheless ran into his van and got the defibrillator, but still no response.

Even so, he yanked his phone from his pocket.

"911," said a female voice nearly immediately. "What's your emergency?"

Grayson identified himself and quickly explained the situation, including the fact that he believed the person he'd found to be dead.

"But in case I'm wrong—"

"We'll get someone there as fast as we can under the circumstances, Grayson," the operator, Betty, said. "I promise."

"Fast" turned out to be about half an hour. Grayson couldn't complain, particularly given the fact that there were likely to be a huge number of 911 calls that evening. Meanwhile, he attempted further CPR on the van driver—to no avail.

An ambulance eventually appeared. The EMTs in it—two guys he'd met before—took over for Grayson, but their conclusion was the same as his.

"We'll take him to Mustang Valley General," Sid said, while the other guy, Kurt, hooked the victim up to an IV. Necessary? Grayson doubted it, but hoped the man really was still alive.

"Thanks," Grayson said. "Keep me informed about how things go." Or not. Did he really want to hear that he was right, that the falling tree had killed the man?

Might as well, he figured.

He took a few photos on his phone of the fallen tree and ruined van. And as the ambulance took off, he looked around further.

He had already checked out the back of the van earlier, as he waited. The door was open, and there was no one inside.

Did the open door mean someone had been incarcerated inside? Maybe.

He'd walked around before the ambulance arrived and hadn't seen any sign of someone else injured—or worse. But he felt obligated to check a bit farther now, just in case.

At least he knew that ambulances were currently available, if necessary. But had there been someone inside the van's rear area? Someone this now-deceased driver had been transporting? If so, was he or she okay?

Grayson was not a cop. If whoever it was needed to be captured again, that wasn't his job, although he could notify the Mustang Valley PD if he found him or her—most likely his sort-of best buddy there, Detective PJ Doherty; his brother Rafe's fiancée, Detective Kerry Wilder; or even his cousin, Sergeant Spencer Colton. Though all were undoubtedly swamped right now.

But if anyone had been inside the van and was now hurt and out there somewhere in the forest, injured and needing help—well, that was something Grayson intended to find out. He would remain careful, though. Anyone who had been in the back of that van was most likely a criminal and could be dangerous.

Chapter 2

Sitting on a wooden kitchen chair in the remote and damaged cabin she had somehow found here in the middle of nowhere, Savannah breathed slowly, carefully—pensively, for that was what she was doing: thinking, while staring at her hands clasped in her lap.

Her unshackled hands.

Where was she? She didn't know. For the moment, at least, it didn't matter.

So far, the earthquake had somehow brought her good luck. There'd been a couple of aftershocks from the quake, but they'd been mild.

Oh, she certainly hadn't wished Ari the kind of harm he had suffered, notwithstanding the way he'd essentially ignored her. But at least she was free, for now and hopefully forever.

Especially if she could find her louse of an ex and prove she hadn't murdered him.

But first things first. Tonight, she had at least located someplace to sleep, to bide her time till she decided what to do next. To ponder how to fulfill her promise to herself: find Zane, reveal his lies and treachery to the world, and return to as normal a life as she could.

A cabin. She'd never have imagined there could be one way out here in the woods. She had hardly been able to see anything once she'd left the place where the van had been smashed. Frightened, yet determined to survive, she'd needed to figure out what came next.

She'd heard a lot of animal noises around her and had nearly stumbled into a nearby lake before she'd found the cabin.

Eventually, the moon—only a half moon—had appeared overhead and provided at least a small amount of light.

And somehow, miraculously, it had helped her find this cabin. Lots of miracles, in fact, despite the fact that a portion of the cabin had crumbled because of the earthquake. But what was left seemed at least somewhat habitable.

In the undamaged area, the door was locked, but she had pushed open a window and climbed inside. None of the switches turned on any light, so she found herself in near total darkness, with no electricity, evidently. That was thanks to the quake, or thanks to the owner's turning it off before leaving. But she had nevertheless located a flashlight someone had left on one of the counters.

Who and where was the owner? Were they coming back soon? That appeared unlikely, considering the location and the earthquake, but who knew?

Fortunately, she had at least found no indication that anyone was living here now. Looking around with the flashlight's illumination, she had seen some dust here and there, but some of it could have been caused by the quake.

However, it seemed a nice enough cabin. There was even some furniture—a kitchen table surrounded by other chairs like the one she now sat on. A bed at the far side of the room with sheets on it. If she removed the sheets and turned them over, they should be clean enough for her to sleep on.

Assuming she found herself eventually calm enough to fall

sleep. Exhaustion wouldn't help her accomplish what she needed to do tomorrow.

But she also couldn't forget that she was a fugitive. Once the van was found without her, she had no doubt that the authorities would be searching for her. She would have to remain careful.

For a better idea of her current environment, she unlocked the door and walked outside, using the flashlight to look around. She aimed it carefully, mostly toward the ground, although she had no reason to believe any other people were close enough to see the light. A narrow dirt road that ended at this house hadn't been affected by the caving in of part of the cabin.

Where did it lead? Maybe she would find out tomorrow.

She also looked at the area at the back of the house that was crumbled. Fortunately, it still provided a wall of sorts, a barrier, so no person or wild animal would be able to enter that way.

For now, she went back inside. One thing she had to do was to find some water and food. Was there anything like that in this deserted cabin? If she found anything, would she dare to eat or drink it, or might it make her sick?

Well, first things first. She would at least look around a bit more. She stood up again and, using the flashlight, walked along the wooden floor, making as little noise as possible—not that she anticipated anyone was close enough to hear her footsteps. She first looked at the inside of the partially caved-in wall and the part of the cabin that had suffered some damage. She wasn't certain what had been there—a storage area, maybe. But the rest of the place seemed fairly livable.

Next, she headed toward a kitchen with a sink and cabinets.

The door of the first cabinet creaked a bit as she opened it. All that was inside were some light green plastic plates and bowls.

She closed that door and tried another. A little better. There were some cans in it, of soup and corn and black beans. Yeah! Assuming she could find a can opener, she might be able to get both sustenance and a bit of liquid in her from one of those. She pulled out the vegetable soup, figuring it would potentially be the most nutritious. Since beggars couldn't be choosers, she considered not even checking the expiration date stamped on the bottom of the can—but it probably would be better for her to know, if it was out of date, by how much.

Making herself ill after her escape wouldn't be a good idea.

Still standing there by the cabinet above the sink, she moved the flashlight to examine the bottom of the can more closely.

And smiled. It had plenty of time left before its expiration date. That suggested people had used this cabin recently, but she remained glad they weren't there now.

Okay. Now she needed to find that can opener, plus a spoon. She aimed the flashlight toward the areas on both sides of the sink, seeing drawers there.

The first drawer she opened had some gadgets in it, including a spatula, whisk—and, yes, a can opener and scissors.

Scissors. One of the things she could do to change her appearance was to cut her hair, make it a lot shorter than its current shoulder length. People who didn't know her might not recognize her—since she was now on the run.

She had already gone inside the bathroom after her arrival and had noticed a mirror over the sink there. Now, scissors in hand, she hurried back across the wooden floor in that direction.

Was this too impulsive, especially in the darkness? The flashlight helped, but it wasn't very bright. Sure, it might be a dumb thing to do, but achieving anything to alter her appearance even a little couldn't hurt.

And so, after regarding herself and her current hairstyle in the mirror, she started snipping. Then snipped some more, creating short bangs, cutting her hair everywhere she could see, everywhere she could reach.

When she was done a few minutes later, she shook her head and laughed, just a little. Who was that waif with a chin-length haircut staring at her in the mirror?

Surely that couldn't be Savannah Oliver, right?

And actually, she wasn't an Oliver anymore. Zane and she

were recently divorced, but, partly thanks to his disappearance and its consequences, she hadn't yet legally returned to using her maiden name, Murphy. First on her list of places to go would be the DMV, where she could get a new driver's license.

Someday.

For now, she used her hands to gather as much of her hair from the sink and floor as she could and placed it in a small pile on the floor near the wall. Once it was light out again, she would need to find a plastic bag or wastebasket to dump it in and hide it. No need to leave evidence of her changed looks if anyone searching for her found this place.

Okay, now she was finally ready to eat, and to drink what she could from the can she chose. She exited the bathroom and returned to the kitchen.

Before opening the soup, though, she went looking for bottled water. The refrigerator was turned off, but she found a few bottles of water inside.

Yes! Savannah took one out and closed the door.

She opened the can of soup while standing near the sink, pulled a spoon out of another drawer after looking around again and sat down at the kitchen table.

Even cold, the vegetable soup tasted good. She ate it slowly, savoring it, continuing to see in the near darkness thanks to the glow of the flashlight, and keeping the scissors with her, too, in case she felt compelled to cut even more hair off. She'd check in the mirror again once daylight arrived, to see if additional trimming was necessary to even it out.

And as much as she hated to think about it, the scissors could also become a weapon if she was attacked by anyone looking for her, or even a looter or wild animal, out here in the middle of nowhere.

As she ate, she felt exhaustion closing in. And no wonder. It had been one heck of a difficult yet promising day. She'd go to sleep after this. What would tomorrow bring?

She finished soon and stood, waving the flashlight again toward where she presumed the garbage can would be. And—

What was that? A sound from outside—a scraping, maybe, from the front yard.

Had she imagined it? It could just be something moving after the quake....

She moved slightly to face a window near the front door—and saw light. Not moonlight, but a glow that could have come from a flashlight, only more heavy-duty than hers, since the light was really bright.

Had the cabin owners come back here now, in the middle of the night after an earthquake?

Or—might the van have been found, and any authorities sent out to find her?

Savannah looked hurriedly around, attempting to find something to use as cover but wound up staying where she was.

Had she locked the door behind her when she had ventured outside? Damn. She didn't believe she had, since she had intended to peek out again.

She clasped the handle of the scissors tightly. If necessary, she could—and would—defend herself.

His search had actually led to someone.

Grayson hadn't really believed he would find anyone out here in the middle of the night and this far out from town. It was his mission to continue to seek people in trouble after the earthquake, including whoever had left the back of the van, if anyone. Whether or not a criminal, any person in that position could have been injured.

Still, if someone had been inside that vehicle and gotten out—well, it was a van from the prison department, so Grayson did not forget his promise to himself to be careful. He didn't want to lose his own life attempting to save someone else, especially someone who was dangerous and didn't want to be found.

After the EMTs had taken away the deceased driver, he'd

continued to look, finding no one else on the road or in the woods on his way here. He had reached a cabin, one of his last potential locations to scout before heading home. He had figured this cabin or another one nearby would be a logical place for anyone in trouble to seek out. It was a fishing cabin owned by one of the families in Mustang Valley. There was a small lake nearby, fed by a stream.

At first glance there seemed to be no one present, but he'd stopped to check. Especially when he thought he had seen a moving light through a window.

Using his own bright light to look around, he noticed that one side of the cabin, maybe a quarter of the whole structure, looked nearly destroyed. Would anyone really have gone inside?

Maybe, if they were injured or desperate. He had to find out.

Slowly, carefully, still using his own light to be sure he saw anything, he approached.

First, though, he knocked on the front door before testing to see if it was unlocked. It was. He pushed it and called as he walked inside, "Hello, anyone here?"

"Yes, I'm here." He heard the voice at the same time he saw a woman standing there, facing the door he had just entered, holding a pair of scissors threateningly. "But you can go now."

He aimed the light toward her eyes, hoping to blind her enough to stop menacing him. And then he blinked at the same time she did—but for a different reason.

He recognized her.

At least he thought he did. She was Savannah Oliver—but if so, this Savannah didn't look exactly like the woman he'd seen at the various parties and fund-raisers he'd been dragged to by his Colton siblings, silently kicking and screaming, though he'd gone along anyway because...well, they were his brothers and sisters.

And now he had a good idea who had disappeared from the

back of the prison van: she stood before him, still aiming scissor blades toward him.

Her hair was a lot shorter than he'd seen it before. Even so, or maybe even because of it, she was one beautiful, sexy woman.

A woman he'd avoided feeling attracted to. After all, she was married—no, she had been married—to one of the biggest investment bankers in Arizona, Zane Oliver.

The husband she'd recently been accused of murdering.

"Hello, Savannah," he said calmly. He wasn't armed, had no weapon with him—and wouldn't have used it on her even if he had.

For one thing, he had heard about her arrest, the charges against her, in the news. But he hadn't believed them.

"Hello, Grayson," she said without moving the scissors—except that her slender arm, in its long-sleeved beige shirt, was trembling a bit. "What are you doing here?"

"I could ask you the same thing, although I can guess. You're running away, right?"

She didn't answer directly but said, "And I assume you're doing your first responder thing out here after the quake. Well, if you're looking for people to help, you don't need to worry about me."

"That's good, but—"

"But what? Should I make you stay here?" She waved the scissors toward him, but the expression on her face appeared more desperate than threatening.

Under other circumstances, he might have liked the idea of staying overnight in a deserted cabin with a woman as lovely as Savannah. But she was a fugitive, accused of murdering her ex-husband. And at the moment, another earthquake could hit at any time.

"No thanks," he said.

"But—I don't think I'd better let you leave. I mean, well—you own that first responder company, right?"

"First Hand First Responders," he said. "That's right."

"So if I let you leave here—you'll just go tell your cop friends or associates that you found me. Or—you're not going to try to bring me with you now, are you?" She suddenly appeared panicked.

And why not? She didn't know, no matter what he'd said, that he wasn't carrying a gun or other weapon.

He glanced around what he could see of the cabin in the light he carried. It looked like—well, a regular fishing cabin, except for the area destroyed by the earthquake.

And Savannah? She wasn't in any kind of jail garb, but everyday clothes of a light-colored shirt over darker slacks. Maybe he was wrong about her.

And maybe not.

"Look, Savannah," he said. "If what I've heard about you is true, then I can understand why you feel threatened by my being here."

"I assume you heard the worst about me," she said. "And—well, I didn't kill my ex-husband." Looking at him for a reaction, she raised her hand with the scissors even more. He just stayed calm, nodding his head. "I can't let you arrest me."

Grayson shook his head. "Let me tell you right now that I'm only the kind of first responder who tries to help people in trouble, both medically and otherwise. I don't attempt to arrest anyone, or anything like that."

"But you can get in touch with those who do," she retorted.

"But I won't," he said. "Look, why don't we sit down over there." He gestured toward the kitchen table across the room where she had apparently been sitting and eating. "I'll tell you what I've heard about you—and how much of it I believe. Which isn't much."

"Really?" Her eyes widened. And even in the light he carried, he could see their lovely greenness glowing, even as her blond eyebrows narrowed in apparent disbelief.

Yeah, she was definitely good-looking—and he'd better be careful. He didn't want to get too interested in her.

He might not intend to turn her in, but neither did he intend to try helping an accused murderer escape justice.

Did he?

"Really," he said. But she still didn't appear convinced. And why should she? "Hey, I see you have a bottle of water over there. I assume a place like this doesn't have anything stronger, so is there any more?"

"Yes, in the refrigerator, though it's not cold." She still looked and sounded wary.

"That's fine. I'll go get a bottle for me, then sit down over there." He gestured toward the table. "Then we'll talk, okay?"

"Do I have a choice?" Her voice sounded hoarse and he wished he could say something more to reassure her.

But what?

"Not really," he said with a grin. "Only, I'm really not such a bad guy. Honest."

"Honest?" she repeated. "Hah." But when he looked at her, still standing not far from him, her posture seemed at least a little more relaxed. "Okay, let's give this a try," she said.

"Great. I'll go get my water." And Grayson headed to the refrigerator.

Oh, yes, he intended to talk with her. Maybe get her side of the story, since she had asserted her innocence.

And he didn't think it was just their unusual circumstances at the moment that made him want to believe in her.

Chapter 3

Savannah lowered the scissors as she watched Grayson get water from the refrigerator, then sit down. He placed the bottle in front of him beside his large flashlight.

What should she do? What could she do? She hoped he was telling the truth, that even as a first responder he wasn't here to arrest her again, or call those in authority at the police station who'd bring her in. But even if he lied, she wasn't really going to stab him. The best she could do would be to run out the door when he wasn't looking, then continue running—in the near darkness. But where?

For now she would just remain alert and wary and hold a conversation. If he'd been telling the truth before, maybe it would be okay to talk with him.

But even then, when he was ready to go—well, would she be able to trust him not to turn her in, no matter what he said?

She would just have to see how things went.

Not that she could control them anyway. At least not entirely.

"So tell me what happened," Grayson said as she sat down facing him, gently placing the scissors on the table before her but within reach. "Tell me how the van was struck and how you got out of it. I assume you're aware the driver was killed."

Savannah nodded solemnly. "Yes. His name was Ari. I… I didn't know him well, but I did check on him when I finally got out of the van and…and…well, I'm not an expert like a first responder, but I tried to help him and didn't see any sign of life." She felt herself tear up. Well, she truly was sad about the situation.

Grayson. She had seen him at parties and social events now and then. They were from similar backgrounds, since their families were both among the Mustang Valley elite. She had enjoyed those kinds of festivities, even after she married Zane.

But Savannah hadn't paid much attention to Grayson—except to notice his good looks. His body tall and slim, yet muscular, beneath the high-end clothing he generally wore at parties, his well-styled dark brown hair and gorgeous blue eyes. He wore his current outfit well, too—a long-sleeved black T-shirt with a neon emergency vest over it. His stubble was trimmed short and added to his sexiness. Of course, she hadn't been interested in how attractive a man he might have been when she believed she had most recently seen him, although she couldn't recall exactly when it had been. But she believed now that she had still been married, and though her marriage was ending she certainly wasn't interested in flirting with someone else. And with Grayson—well, she had gotten the impression he wasn't thrilled about being at most of those parties, that his family had twisted his arm to come. She knew he wasn't part of the family business, Colton Oil.

"I assume you found Ari's… Ari," she continued, choosing not to use the term "body."

He nodded. "I wasn't able to get a response, though, and neither did the EMTs that Mustang Valley General Hospital sent after my 911 call."

"I'm sorry," Savannah said.

"You were in the back of his van, right? Was he moving you from the state prison somewhere?"

She felt her eyes grow huge as she reached slowly for her bottle of water and stared at it—but she shouldn't have been surprised at Grayson's spot-on guess. She'd been in the news, as much as she hated that. As much as she hated all of this.

"Yes," she said quietly. That was close enough. Ari had been moving her from court back to prison, but she didn't choose to elaborate.

"So you were able to escape unharmed," Grayson stated. He took a swig from his bottle, but his eyes didn't leave hers. "That's a good thing, especially since you already told me you didn't kill your husband. And I assume that's the truth."

"It is." She kept her voice low but wanted to scream it out—the truth. Instead, she glanced toward the door. Should she run now?

Would Grayson grab her?

But when she looked back toward him, he hadn't moved. He was watching her, though, with an expression on that handsome face of his that suggested amusement.

Amusement? When her entire life had been turned upside down, and he now was in a position to possibly ruin her tiny, precarious opportunity for freedom that resulted from an unpredicted earthquake?

"Got it," he said. "Now, want to tell me about it?"

Grayson was used to finding people in difficult positions and not only helping them physically but mentally, too. To doing all he could to assure their survival in all ways.

This beautiful woman he had met several times before appeared totally fragile now—and frightened. Of him.

Which he understood. But he didn't like it. And he wanted to help her in all ways.

And there was something he'd recalled about her, how well she had treated someone at one of the parties they'd both attended, that told him she was the kind of person who helped people, too—and didn't kill them. In fact, she had helped to save the life of a woman who had just been extremely nasty to her.

"I really don't like talking about the situation with Zane," she said now. "And there's really not much to tell. What's out there is all lies."

Well, she could be lying, too, of course. But he wanted to hear her side of it, since the media often liked to take things out of context and exaggerate them, even stress the nastiest facts—anything for a good story, although they also did base it on truth most of the time. Or so he believed.

So even though Grayson could in fact bring Savannah back to the appropriate authorities, no matter what he'd told her, or could just leave her here to do whatever she wanted, he still would rather hear her side of the story before deciding.

"Convince me," he said with a smile he hoped she would interpret as friendly.

For now, at least, it was.

"Okay. Let's start with the fact I don't believe Zane is dead."

That startled him a bit. With all the news and hype, he'd considered that a given. "Really?"

"Really," she replied. "My ex is missing. I'll admit that's true. But I didn't kill him and hide his body somewhere, and don't believe anyone else did, either. We'd stopped caring about each other quite a while ago but our divorce was only final about a month ago. He blamed it on me, made some pretty nasty allegations that were totally untrue, that I'd been unfaithful when he was the one having affairs…and he was furious with me for wanting a divorce. And—well, I can't prove it yet, but I believe he even got one of his friends to help him and frame me, while he's off somewhere, maybe even someplace as remote as Bali. He used to talk about going there someday. Wherever he is, I'm sure he's checking what's going on from his computer and otherwise—and laughing his head off. He's undoubtedly considering his revenge against me sweet. And this way, he might even be able to keep my part of the divorce settlement."

She really appeared steamed now, looking down toward the table and shaking her head so her short hair rubbed at her shirt collar.

He couldn't help it. He needed to know more about this allegation that her ex wasn't even dead, let alone murdered—and Zane might have plotted the entire thing. He put his elbows on the table and leaned toward her.

"So Zane is really alive? Do you have any proof?"

"No, but there's no real proof he's dead, either. He's missing, yes. He and I argued, privately and in public. And when he went missing, the cops found a knife in the guesthouse on his property, where I was living temporarily till I decided where to move. They found it in my closet, of all places. There was blood on it—Zane's, according to the official analysis. There were no fingerprints on the knife, though, and his body wasn't found."

"But—"

"Sure, that doesn't look good for me. The district attorney apparently took it seriously, though my lawyer assured me all the evidence was circumstantial, clearly not proof that I did anything." She was clutching her water bottle as if it was the DA's throat and she wanted to strangle her. Or maybe Grayson was just imagining that from the anger and frustration on her face. "I admit it looks pretty bad that the bloody knife was in my closet. But someone clearly sneaked in and hid it there—Zane himself, probably."

"I understand," Grayson said. "Not sure if I know all the claims or evidence supposedly against you, but I did hear a lot a week or so ago, when they said you'd just been arrested."

He'd been surprised to learn that this woman he knew remotely and met occasionally, a mere acquaintance who'd seemed nice enough, was a murder suspect. But what had been blared out on TV, newspapers, online and radio news was that Zane

Oliver had disappeared and was believed dead, partly thanks to that bloody knife.

Suspicions had immediately landed on his ex-wife. They'd divorced not long ago, and the media more than hinted that the reason for it was that Zane's wife, Savannah, had been having a torrid affair with a local real estate developer.

"I can't tell you how thrilled I am to be the main, maybe only, suspect when Zane disappeared that way," Savannah went on, her tone dripping with sarcasm. "Oh, and you want to hear more of that circumstantial evidence that's all false?" She didn't wait for his reply before continuing. "There were—are—some horrible false rumors about me. It seems I was having a hot and heavy romance during the end of my marriage to Zane with Schuyler Wells, of all people." She glared at Grayson as if daring him to say something.

Which he did, though nothing accusatory. "Right. I read about that."

"Didn't you hear his interviews in the media? Zane must have paid him well, since he claimed we had something and planned to run away together as soon as my divorce from Zane was final. Not!" She practically screamed the last word and stood, grabbing the scissors as if she was going to use them on him—or someone. Fortunately, she quickly realized what she was doing and, tears running down her lovely cheeks, collapsed back into the chair, gently pushing the scissors, handle first, toward him. "Here."

He pulled them closer on the table but didn't hide them, as if showing he believed her.

"And," she continued, her voice rasping, "what a surprise. Schuyler has a solid, impeccable alibi, on a business trip during the crucial time of the supposed murder, with people who don't even work for him vouching for him. But, gee, he does admit to having had a really steamy affair with me." Her head shook back and forth in utter denial. "No way. I've met the guy, even got some real estate advice from him, but I never liked him.

And as I said, one of the reasons Zane and I got divorced was because he was having affairs. I wasn't."

"I get it." Grayson reached across the table and grasped Savannah's hand, where it now rested beside her water bottle. And he did get it. He didn't believe she'd made her side of it up.

Besides, what he'd recalled before gave him a clue as to Savannah's underlying personality, someone who helped to save lives rather than taking them. That situation had occurred at a fund-raiser his siblings had thrown for First Hand First Responders when he was just starting up the business. As he recalled, Savannah was not only there, but she was arguing with another socialite type who seemed very malicious. As a few other attendees started hollering at them to be quiet, they'd gone out onto the balcony of the two-story, swanky restaurant in downtown Mustang Valley.

Grayson, somewhat amused at the time, had watched through a window near one of his family's tables as they continued to argue. He'd been shocked when the other woman took a swing at Savannah and missed her—but the woman had been close enough to the railing that the movement made her nearly fall over it.

And Savannah, acting fast, had leaned over the balcony to grab that woman's wrists, hanging partly over the side herself for a while till a couple of guys ran out and pulled them both safely and completely onto the balcony.

Though he barely knew her then, Grayson had been impressed that Savannah had immediately endangered her own life to help someone who'd just been mean to her. That was distinctly not the behavior of a cold-blooded killer.

And no matter how difficult her relationship with her ex had turned out, he just couldn't see her as a murderer.

He didn't mention that to Savannah. But he did say, "I assume you won't be going back to town tonight, maybe not for a long time. In case you're wondering, this place is a fishing cabin, and the owners never come here until late in the spring—and this is only April. You can hang out here for now, if you'd like."

"Oh yes, I'd like that." She sounded relieved and her expression as she looked at him across the table seemed—well, grateful.

There was nothing she needed to be grateful to him for. Not yet, at least, if ever. Did he really want to put his own freedom into jeopardy by helping her? Maybe. He would have to think about it.

What about bringing her back to town, then attempting to help her by finding her ex?

He doubted she would go along with that, and he wasn't about to take any steps to get her back into custody. Not now, at least.

Well, he figured this place was a good potential hideout for her, at least temporarily. Despite being a walkable distance from the destroyed van, it wasn't that close to where she had escaped from it, although the cops might wind up looking around here.

In any case, he wasn't about to help her find someplace else. But he figured he would help her a bit by bringing her some supplies, since he doubted this place held much in the way of food and other necessities at this time of the year.

He would have to be careful, though. He was buying into her story, but was it true? Was she innocent?

He would assume so…for now. But he would also stay alert for anything that told him otherwise.

"Let's take a look at the damaged part of the cabin, though," he said, waving toward the far side where the wooden walls were somewhat smashed.

They both stood and walked in that direction. Grayson had an urge to take Savannah's hand and hold it encouragingly, but he decided that would be a bad idea.

They stopped beside each other and looked at the damaged wall from this angle. Some panels had even fallen down and left gaps, and the windows at that part of the room no longer existed.

But fortunately, most of the broken glass and wooden boards, insulation, shelves and other building materials must have landed outside, and somehow the remaining walls had fallen into a sideways slant so there wasn't even much in the way of an opening.

The rest of the place certainly looked habitable.

"It's not so bad," Savannah, at his side, whispered.

"I agree," Grayson said more loudly. "I've got a couple of phone calls to make now to ensure that my team doesn't head this way looking for me or for any injured people, then I'll head downtown. I'll bring you some supplies tomorrow, okay?"

"Definitely okay," she said, smiling at him. He couldn't help smiling back. "And—"

She stopped, so he prodded, "And what?"

"Well, I no longer have my phone, as you can imagine. Is there some way you could get one for me? I'll be glad to repay you for all this whenever…whenever it's all over and I get my life and my money back."

He laughed. "Sure thing," he said. "I know where I can get you a burner phone with internet access, so you'll be able to stay in touch with what's going on."

"Thanks."

He moved away then and called Norah Fellini, the EMT on his team.

"Hi, Grayson," she said immediately. "Where are you? Is everything okay? Do you need help with any other victims?" Of course she knew about his finding the van driver who didn't make it, since he kept his team apprised.

"No, I don't need any help now, thanks. That deceased driver was picked up by an ambulance, and then I headed toward some of the fishing cabins just to make sure no one was hurt or trapped inside. So far, I've checked the cabin on Rural Route 2 and haven't found anything I need to deal with, so I'm going to the next one that's about five miles away before driving back to town. I'd appreciate it if you'd let the rest of our team know, okay?"

"Sure," she said. She filled him in on what she and the other two team members had been up to. They'd had to find a couple of missing kids and give medical attention to them and a few other people, but they hadn't dealt with any major emergencies. "We did report in to our local PD and other contacts and all, so we should get paid—although that's not the main thing, of course."

"Of course. Just glad no one appeared badly hurt. See you tomorrow." He said good-night and hung up.

He walked to the table once more since Savannah sat there, looking exhausted. Well, he was, too, but he'd do as he had told Norah, then head back to town. At least he should be able to drive there, although it would take a while since he had left his vehicle near the crushed van.

"I'll be back tomorrow with some supplies," he told Savannah as he got ready to go.

"That's so nice of you." She stood up again. "Oh—and, well, maybe I shouldn't mention it, but I wanted to let you know I'd heard that someone shot your dad. I'm so sorry. How is he?"

Grayson's father was Payne Colton, chairman of the board of Colton Oil and owner of Rattlesnake Ridge Ranch—where Grayson lived with his siblings.

He felt himself cringe at Savannah's question. His dad wasn't doing well at all. Recently shot by an unknown person, Payne had gone into a coma—and hadn't come out of it yet.

There were more family things going on, too. They had just recently learned, thanks to a strange email, that his oldest brother, Ace, might have been switched at birth with another baby.

But to Savannah he simply said, "We think he's improving. Thanks for asking." He reached out to take Savannah's hand, but she pulled him closer, giving him a brief hug.

A hug that somehow made him want to get even closer, though he didn't. "Glad to hear that. So—see you tomorrow?"

"Yes," he said. "See you tomorrow."

He hoped. Oh, yes, he would return. But would she still be here? Would she be okay?

He would find out when he got here.

Chapter 4

Savannah held open the cabin's door and watched Grayson walk away along the uneven ground and through the trees in the glow of his large flashlight, heading essentially the direction from which she had come. Soon, she didn't see any more signs of him.

She had a sudden urge to dive back inside, grab the small flashlight she'd found and leave this cabin, too.

To dash after Grayson? Only if she could feel certain he was genuine, that he was as nice as he'd seemed—and that he really believed in her innocence.

She had no reason to doubt him, except that this situation was so horrendous that she simply couldn't—and didn't—trust anyone.

Sure, he could have dragged her along with him now, called authorities who could take her into custody and been done with the situation, but he hadn't.

That didn't mean she didn't need to worry about what came next. Would he really just turn up here tomorrow with supplies and a phone for her? Allow her to remain loose while the cops looked for her, potentially gathering more false evidence of her guilt? Assuming, of course, that an escaped fugitive remained high on their radar at the moment, despite the earthquake.

In any case, would Grayson help her as he'd promised?

She wasn't stupid, though her marriage to Zane didn't exactly show her to be a good judge of character—notwithstanding the fact that she'd had impetus from her dad, who had been impressed with Zane's wealth, to be in that relationship. Partly thanks to him, she had convinced herself that she loved Zane, but in retrospect she wasn't sure how much she had really cared.

But what was her best alternative for staying here? Running from the cabin and going the opposite direction to Grayson? With that small flashlight being nearly her only illumination, and damage to the ground and any other buildings she might come across, plus the possibility of more aftershocks? There'd be a lot of potential danger in that, at least if she didn't wait till daylight.

"Okay," she finally whispered to herself, backing into the cabin once more and closing the door. Locking it this time, at least—so maybe she would hear if someone showed up and attempted to get inside.

Meanwhile, she felt exhausted. She decided to go lie down on that inviting bed, allow herself to sleep—and hope that her subconscious would awaken her if anything happened or someone else showed up.

And tomorrow? Well, she really wanted to believe in Grayson and his honesty. He was one heck of a guy, sure, but she'd had enough of men. She genuinely believed that Zane had set up his supposed murder to ruin the rest of her life.

But Grayson? He was a first responder, so he at least cared about people, even strangers, on some level.

Turning, she picked up the flashlight, walked to the bed and sat down.

Grayson. Would she decide in the morning to wait here for him, see if he was as kind as he appeared to be? Whether he responded to her needs rather than the reality of who and what she currently was—an escaped prison inmate?

She would see how she felt. She hadn't harmed anyone to allow herself to escape, though she was certainly happy for her freedom.

But what would she do next? How could she possibly look for Zane or any clues that would prove she was right, that he'd framed her and that he was still alive?

It might help if she had that burner phone Grayson and she had discussed.

And if he did turn up here tomorrow with the supplies he'd promised, including that phone, she would feel a lot more comfortable trusting him.

For now? She didn't want to wear out the flashlight batteries, so after she turned the sheets over and lay down on the bed—not particularly comfortable, but at least it had a pillow with a case she turned inside out—she shut the light off, then closed her eyes.

"Good night, Grayson," she whispered with a small smile, recognizing the irony in her words and current attitude. "I'll see you tomorrow, when all my worrying about your truthfulness will be over."

She hoped.

The next morning, Grayson awoke at the family ranch.

Now he sat at his wing's kitchen table, more decorative and undoubtedly more expensive than the plain wood one at the cabin last night. He grabbed toast and coffee for breakfast, getting ready to meet the new day and learn more about how his employees had done yesterday. From what he'd grasped when he spoke with Norah, everyone had been out there helping people successfully. But he hadn't spoken with any of them again afterward. He wanted confirmation today, as well as more details.

He also planned to check out what downtown Mustang Valley looked like after the quake, and do a shopping expedition there, as well.

Then—well, then, he would have the pleasure of going to see Savannah again. Lovely Savannah, who claimed she had been set up by her ex and falsely accused of murder. Very falsely.

He had thought about Savannah a lot last night after leaving her. Maybe he should just stay out of the whole thing, neither help her nor rat on her to the authorities. But—well, he liked her.

And he hated the idea that she was being framed by her ex, if that was true.

He'd gotten out of a bad relationship recently, too. But they'd both just walked away. His ex hadn't plotted any revenge against him, and he hadn't against her, either. That sounded so absurd in Savannah's situation. But it could of course, be true.

Hell, he was a first responder. He helped people who needed it. Who deserved it. And he truly believed, at least for now, that included Savannah.

He would find out soon, he figured, if he had been duped by her, and she actually was a killer.

He took a sip of coffee from his mug with the FHFR logo and phone number on it.

That mind of his unsurprisingly kept going back to yesterday and the quake and its aftermath.

Once he'd left Savannah the previous night, he had returned to the place where he'd earlier found the damaged van and its dead occupant. All was gone now—except his own useful SUV.

Then he carefully drove along a couple of the mangled dirt roads to check out other fishing cabins besides the one Savannah was occupying, but they were empty, a good thing. And he'd seen no other evidence of people needing help, though quake damage was still evident.

He had considered stopping again on his way home to check on Savannah but had decided against it, since he was sure she was asleep by then. He doubted anyone else knew she was out here, and he intended to see her tomorrow anyway, while bringing the supplies he had promised her.

And tomorrow had arrived. Now that he was awake and preparing to start his day, he kept thinking about her. A fugitive. One he couldn't get out of his mind. Was he nuts?

Maybe.

"Okay," he muttered. Today was going to be undoubtedly interesting. He stood and put his empty plate in the metal kitchen sink but carried his remaining half mug of coffee.

He headed down the stairs after closing the door of his bedroom behind him and locking it.

He drove to the First Hand office.

When he arrived in the greeting area, he rapped once on each of their doors in order from the bottom of the steps—Pedro's first, then Norah's and Chad's. He heard a low woof after that last knock and just smiled. Winchell, Chad's K-9 companion, knew better than to bark here, even when on duty, but he was always alert.

In moments, the gang had joined him in the reception area. They were all present here at the office, so apparently no additional calls had come in after the ones he had heard about last night, and they'd already accomplished the searches they had needed to do immediately after the earthquake, depending on their individual expertise.

His employees greeted him with handshakes and pats on his back, as he did with them. "Good to see you all," he said. "And I'm looking forward to your reports."

"We want to hear yours, too, boss," Pedro said.

There was a reception desk for greeting people who walked in off the street seeking help, against the far wall from the entry door. Plate glass windows circled the room—all intact, fortunately, after the quake, Grayson had noticed last night. The floor was laminate, and the walls beige drywall decorated with photos of successful rescue operations and waving people they had saved. Half a dozen blue upholstered Parsons chairs were arranged with their backs toward the windows, so the room's occupants, if they spent any time there, could see one another.

And there were a couple of extra doors to offices that could be allocated to additional staff.

Grayson waved his bunch to the chairs so they could start their discussion. Once they were seated, he glanced beyond them to his view of the street. All seemed fine outside.

His mind returned to the damaged cabin where he had left Savannah. Hopefully she remained okay—and there.

"Okay, who's first?" Grayson asked, putting that behind him for now and looking at Norah.

"You, chief," she said.

"Nope. I'm last. So tell me your experiences with the quake and after."

Norah didn't argue but leaned forward in her chair. Before joining First Hand, she had worked for the City of Phoenix as an EMT but always crowed about how she'd run right to Mustang Valley when she heard of Grayson's start-up of a private first responder company a while back. She was well trained and a certified expert in emergency medical techniques, and was doing a great job with FH. She was thin yet very strong, and she kept her light brown hair in a style that framed her face.

Most important? With her ongoing and always increasing EMT skills, she was excellent at helping to save lives.

"I was right here when the quake hit." She motioned toward her office door.

Since not too much around there was damaged, she had hurriedly driven to Mustang Valley General Hospital. The staff there had immediately assigned her to ride in one of the ambulances, to assist the drivers and hospital EMTs.

"Six different locations, and we helped over a dozen people, although their injuries were of different severities. Some weren't too bad off, but there were maybe four that probably wouldn't have survived if we weren't there." Her grin totally lighted up her slender face, and Grayson smiled back.

"Great job," he said, then turned toward Pedro. "Any fires?"

Pedro Perez had been a firefighter in Las Vegas—but he'd informed Grayson when he'd hired him that he was excited about the opportunity to come to Mustang Valley and be the premier firefighter for FHFR. Pedro was dark-haired, large and muscular.

"About five, across town. Only one was really bad, though. I heard about it in the news before heading there and helped the local fire department get it under control. They know me, of course, so they asked me to help with the rest. And after we got those out, I hung out with the gang at the station for a couple more hours just in case. I gathered that all the fires were electrical fires because the wiring in those buildings was badly damaged by the quake and aftershocks. And I remain on call now, too, with the department in case they learn of any other blazes."

"Excellent," Grayson said. They all then turned toward Chad and Winchell, his German shepherd. "So—what's your story, both of you?"

Chad had been a K-9 cop with Tucson PD before coming to work for First Hand. He'd brought along his assistant Winchell, who was a certified search and rescue dog as well as a police K-9. He was moderate height and wore glasses, and always asked if Winch and he could do more.

"There were a few reports of break-ins across town in the area where the quake hit worst—you know, the shopping area where stores are plentiful but not especially elite. I got a call from one of the dispatchers at the police department, and Winch and I headed there. We actually nabbed a couple of guys who dared to try to loot some damaged stores—those SOBs. Fortunately, they were scared of Winch, so we were able to turn them over to the PD."

Grayson intended to visit just such a shopping center soon, where he wouldn't be recognized as a Colton by store owners and other shoppers. There he could hopefully find all the supplies and the cell phone he had promised Savannah.

For now, he stood and approached each of his employees, reaching out his hand to shake theirs. "You know, when I went into this, opening a private first responders' outfit, I wondered not only if I could succeed, but if I would be able to find assistants who were okay working in the private sector but do as well, or better than, first responders working for the official departments. Well, damn it, I did great in choosing every one of you."

"And we did great choosing you as our boss," Norah responded.

Both of the guys vocally agreed.

"But we're not done here," Norah continued. "What did you find, Grayson?"

Grayson trusted these people with his life. And with other lives, those they worked so hard to save.

But did he dare mention he'd found Savannah?

Maybe eventually, especially if he wound up needing their help. Plus, if he was found out and there were any legal ramifications against him, his staff could be affected, too.

For now, he decided to be cautious. He sat back down and described finding the van and its deceased driver.

"Was there anyone in the back?" Chad asked—not surprising from a former cop.

"Apparently there had been at least one person there," Grayson said, looking Chad in the other man's dark brown eyes, which kind of resembled his dog's. "But no one was in it when I got there, and though I looked around for a while to make sure no one was injured or otherwise needed my help, I didn't discover anything or anyone that had to be taken care of or reported." He'd phrased that in a way that remained sort of true, at least.

"Sad," Pedro said, "but I gather there weren't a whole lot of injuries or deaths due to the quake. A lot of property damage in some locations, though."

"Like the older parts of town," Grayson said, nodding. "I'm going to go take a walk around there soon and size up the damage—assuming no new information comes in requiring us to do any first responding right now. Meantime, I'd like each of you to contact the officials in your areas of expertise again just to confirm that all's well for now, and to offer your services if needed, of course."

FHFR received most of its funding from the public departments they assisted, being paid a general retainer and getting more each time they helped out.

And when needed, Grayson supplemented his company's finances with his own money received as a Colton.

He always made sure to pay his excellent employees well.

"Yes, sir," Chad said, rising and saluting as if Grayson was his superior officer—which he was, in a way. Grayson, grinning, saluted back, and his smile grew even wider as Winchell held out his paw for a shake.

Grayson wanted to make a couple of calls, too, to his major local contacts—in case he or his people were needed now, so he walked up the stairs to the second floor to where his own office was.

But he looked forward to heading soon to the other side of town.

First, though, he decided to check the news on his computer. He wanted to see what the local media said about the quake and the havoc it had caused.

And anything about the destroyed van and its driver…and the passenger who had disappeared.

Sure enough, although most of the news was about the quake itself, the crushed van and the death of Ari, its driver, was out there, too.

Grayson turned on the sound on his computer and listened to a couple of those reports.

They all ended with the fact that the female prisoner being transported from court back to the local prison had apparently escaped.

The authorities suspected that the passenger, Savannah Oliver, had killed the driver so she could flee. Her handcuffs had been found beside the destroyed van, after all.

Oh boy, Grayson thought. The idea hadn't crossed his mind, since he had seen Ari and the van and the tree that had caused the driver's death. But not everyone had. And the photos on his phone wouldn't necessarily do away with the suspicion.

What would Savannah think of these additional accusations against her?

He felt certain he would soon find out.

Chapter 5

Savannah had previously looked around the cabin for a TV or radio or anything else that would allow her to learn what was happening in the outside world, but she'd found nothing.

The tall, unsteady-looking set of wooden bookshelves along one of the walls held quite a few volumes about the area and fish and traveling, but nothing that would provide her with the kind of knowledge she now sought.

And until Grayson returned with the phone he'd promised, she was on her own here.

Was that a good reason simply to leave in order to learn what she could about how the earthquake and aftershocks had affected Mustang Valley?

No, she intended to stay here, at least for today, and see if Grayson really did return. But she would of course remain alert and conscious—in case he wasn't the one to arrive first, or at all.

The cops, if they weren't overwhelmed with quake stuff, were probably looking for her.

And if she could figure out an inconspicuous way to do it, she wanted to be out there soon, somewhere, somehow, looking for Zane, or talking to any people she thought of as his co-conspirators, like Schuyler Wells. As if she'd had any interest in him, social or professional.

Although, at the moment, she was definitely interested in finding—and talking to—Schuyler, too, since unlike Zane, he was still out and about. However, he was also the kind of person likely to call the cops to pick her up right away if he had any knowledge of where she was.

She had pondered why Zane would fake his own death, and figured that, if nothing else, it would be to spite her. To hurt her for dumping him. And maybe his finances weren't as good as he let on to the world, so he'd wanted to find a way to hide. She wasn't sure. All she knew was that he was a horrible person who lied and cheated and she should never have married him.

And, it seemed, Schuyler had become his coconspirator. For money? If so, Zane must still have some.

"I'll figure it out," she muttered to herself, again sitting at the table that had become a sort of refuge in this remote cabin, drinking another bottle of water—and hoping that Grayson brought some more when he got there.

If he got there.

But she couldn't stay here for long—certainly not after she came up with a viable plan to track down the people who had done this to her, and somehow extract the truth.

Now all she needed to do was determine how.

Unsurprisingly, downtown Mustang Valley was a mess.

Oh, in the nicer area where Grayson's office building and other newer, well-constructed ones were located, the earthquake damage was visible but not extensive. The cracks didn't appear too deep in some of the walls, although there were fractures in the streets and debris had fallen on the streets from the structures. Maintenance crews were already out there working on repairs, though Grayson assumed there would be more in upcoming days.

The sidewalks were at least mostly passable, so he walked toward the other area of town that had been around longer without upgrades. He'd assumed the damage would be more obvious there, and it was: deeper gouges in the streets often turning them from two-lane to one—or less. There were also larger portions of the buildings that were ruined, reminding him a bit of the cabin where Savannah was.

Savannah. She remained on his mind a lot, largely because of his promise to buy her supplies…but not entirely. He kept wondering how she was doing, if she trusted him to keep his word and was waiting for him to return. Whether anyone official had been looking in that area for her—or had found her there.

He figured he would hear about that if it happened. Her disappearance might be a result of the earthquake, but it had newsworthiness of its own, particularly under the circumstances of the driver's death. Grayson understood that. He'd be a lot more dubious about her innocence, too, if he hadn't talked to her. Believe her? Maybe. He hadn't liked, hadn't trusted her ex Zane, so maybe she wasn't making anything up.

As he continued walking, he thought about his siblings. He had only ducked into his wing at the ranch late last night and out of it fast this morning so he hadn't seen any of them, but he had called most of them as he left that day. He might not be close with them, but he wanted reassurance that none was hurt. Fortunately, he heard only good news.

He'd even spoken with Ace. He still considered him his brother, even though Ace had taken a DNA test after the email that the Colton Oil board received. It confirmed that he was not a biological Colton. Grayson might not be good buddies with all his family members, but he didn't dislike Ace.

Now he noticed he was far from alone here. There were more pedestrians than automobile traffic, but the few cars there proceeded slowly, causing traffic jams. No one looked at him, and he paid no attention to anyone else.

He did, however, notice a kid playing in some rubble near

a damaged building. The kid wore an Arizona State Sun Devils T-shirt, which reminded Grayson of the Arizona State Sun Devils pin that had been found in his father's office after his dad was shot. Payne remained in a coma—and no one knew yet who'd done it. The pin might be a clue to the shooter's identity.

Grayson suddenly found himself uncharacteristically overwhelmed by concern for his father. He wasn't particularly close to him, but still, Payne Colton was his dad, and he had been shot.

Maybe his emotions were brought on by the earthquake and knowing people had been injured, sometimes killed, and parts of the town had been wrecked…

Well, despite never really feeling close to his family, or particularly fond of Colton Oil, right now Grayson felt even more isolated from his siblings than usual.

And why didn't he feel close? Because of nearly everyone's obsession with Colton Oil. Sure, it made a lot of money for the family, but he hadn't like the pressure he had felt while growing up to get involved with the business. In fact, he had wound up ignoring it, starting out in the military, then becoming a wilderness guide and ultimately a first responder instead. Which hadn't sat well with his dad or some of his siblings. Well, too bad.

Drawing his gaze away from the kid and attempting to shrug off those thoughts, he continued walking. He frequently looked down streets leading off the main road. Some homes appeared okay, at least from this angle. Others seemed damaged—and a few were destroyed.

What a shame, he thought.

He passed one chain discount store that looked closed, damaged, possibly ruined. Then there was an open pharmacy but he wasn't sure he could find all he wanted there.

Interestingly, he saw several tables arranged along what remained of the sidewalk, staffed by people he didn't recognize. The signs indicated they were members of a small self-help group he had heard of: the Affirmation Alliance Group. They seemed to greet everyone who walked by, although Grayson didn't stop. Some even called out to passersby that they were there to help them. They claimed to have a place for people to stay who couldn't go back home now, right at their own very special guest ranch. How had they gotten things set up so fast after the quake? Of course, from what Grayson had heard about them, they were supposed to be all about teaching others how to help themselves, so maybe they had procedures developed for all kinds of situations or disasters, including earthquakes.

He'd heard a lot about the good work the group and its founder, Micheline Anderson, did, including holding self-help seminars at that ranch, but something about them made him a bit uneasy.

Good thing he didn't need someplace else to live. In any event, if that group truly helped people in need around here, more power to them.

There. He had reached another chain discount store where he should be able to find all the supplies he intended to buy. It appeared fine, and open. He went inside and grabbed a cart, glad he didn't see anyone he knew as he started picking up a lot of basic stuff that most people, especially the Coltons, were likely to already have around their houses.

If anyone asked, he would claim that the earthquake was his rationale, since, although he knew his family ranch was fine, who knew when all the basic supplies would be available around here again?

So…he tossed into his cart cleaning supplies, paper towels, batteries, a couple of additional flashlights—the size of his and not Savannah's—and a lot more.

However, he'd thought this place also carried basic food items like bread, but it didn't.

When he got into the checkout line, one of half a dozen in a row, all with signs indicating they were open, he thought he recognized the clerk, darn it. And even if the man hadn't recognized him, Grayson had stuck a credit card in the reader, so of course his name appeared.

"Oh, hello, Mr. Colton," the guy, a senior with white hair and a beard, said. "Did you find everything you were looking for?" He looked curious yet friendly.

Grayson decided not to mention the food. There was a store he would pass later that would be better for those kinds of provisions anyway.

Instead, he offered a bland explanation of sorts. "We're probably just fine, but I wanted to make sure we've got the basics at the ranch—especially since I'd imagine your headquarters' ability to deliver more to this store could have been affected by the quake."

"Could be, but I think we're fine. Anyway, come back anytime if you need anything else. We'll do all we can to accommodate you, of course."

"Thanks," Grayson said, not surprised by the guy's attitude. Grayson was a Colton, even if he maintained a distance from his family. But strangers wouldn't know that. And it might not matter anyway. The Coltons had power.

And they, and even he, had money, thanks to Colton Oil.

The clerk stuffed everything into three large plastic bags.

Fortunately, the store that was his next goal was only another block away. He just hoped it was undamaged and open, too.

Which it was. It sold tech, including computers and telephones—and of course the latter was Grayson's target. He was able to purchase a disposable one—a burner phone—without anyone asking questions. Although the woman who waited on him commented he wasn't the only person seeking this kind of phone today, since so many people had apparently lost their phones and technical connections in the quake that they'd come here to buy temporary phones till they figured out what to do next.

He simply nodded and put on a sad face, telling her, "That sounds familiar." He had enough cash with him so he did not have to provide a credit card here. He was glad he so seldom came to this part of town that no one in this store, at least, recognized him. Plus, he bought a battery-operated charger and extra batteries. He wanted to make certain the phone had plenty of time and power connected to it so Savannah would be able to use it for a while anonymously.

And when she couldn't use it any longer? Well, it wasn't really his concern, but he *was* concerned. He would just have to see where things stood then—and whether he would feel committed to acquire another of these important devices for her.

He walked back to his office building as quickly as he could, again relieved that he didn't see anyone he knew. When he arrived, he immediately went around back to the parking lot to place his purchases in the trunk before going back inside to check in with his staff again.

"I'm just going to do some looking around to see if there are any others, government agencies or otherwise, who need our help today," he told Pedro, the first of his gang that he saw in the reception area.

Then he got into his car and drove first to the nearby grocery store, where he would stock up even more on basics, then head toward the fishing cabin where he had last seen Savannah. Would she still be there?

As she'd anticipated, Savannah had spent the morning pondering what she could, what she should, do to get her out of this fix and find the men she needed to resolve it.

She focused on her need to find Zane and turn him over to the police. The real question, then, remained how she would be able to do that. Surely his anger at her wanting to be rid of him because of his lies and infidelities wouldn't keep him away from his former, normal life forever. Though his faking his death with the idea of getting her thrown permanently in prison...well, she didn't know how he intended to return and deal with that.

Or could he get people to continue to run his business for him here and give him access to its proceeds?

She eventually stood up, figuring she wasn't getting anywhere just sitting at the table. Now she was walking around outside the house for the second time.

Looking into the surrounding woods, enjoying occasional views of birds and the tree branches waving in the wind, inhaling the scent of the outdoors, and paying attention to her footing, hoping there wouldn't be any further earth movement that day.

Most important, she was thinking and trying to come up with different methods, different angles to get out of the mess she was in.

Attempting to dive into Zane's mind, despite his not being here, despite his being out of her life—at least as her husband.

Zane had run an investment bank and liked using social media and tech in many aspects of his life. He'd surrounded them with various security devices in their home, which at that time had helped to make her feel protected.

Yeah, from everyone but Zane.

Despite not being a techie, she believed she had a reasonably sharp mind. Sure, she was considered a socialite and didn't have a genuine, well-paying career, but thanks to her family resources, and, more recently, Zane's, she had spent her time learning about various charitable enterprises and participating in events where money was collected to help people in need.

Unlike her.

Before she'd been accused of murdering her husband, at least.

What would come next for her? Freedom, she hoped. And plenty of time to determine what else she wanted to do with her future now that Zane would be out of her life—hopefully in prison instead of her, for his chilling attempt to scam the authorities and frame her.

More charitable functions? Maybe, but if so she would get more involved, maybe even find a way to help manage one or more of them. She was unsure what her financial situation would be, of course, but it should be okay thanks to the money she had inherited from her grandparents that had supported her before, as well as her divorce settlement from Zane. She would deal with it, no matter what.

And—well, oddly enough, she was very impressed with Grayson and what he did. Would she want to learn to become a first responder, too?

She would definitely like to be able to save lives. She had always enjoyed helping people when she was helping to run charitable enterprises before. And now, she wished she'd been able to help Ari, no matter how indifferent he had been to her. And even if she hadn't been shackled inside the van, she doubted if she could have done much more for him.

Still…

"Okay, time to go back inside," she finally muttered to herself, watching a crow in the air above her spread its wings and soar off, uttering a caw as if agreeing with her.

She entered the cabin again and locked the door behind her.

Though she had hand-bathed several times, she really, really wanted a shower. She had already begun using a clean towel that she had found in the bathroom, and recognized she could make even better use of it. Plus, she had peeked into the shower stall and seen a substantial bar of soap on a small shelf inside it.

Now was a good time to start her new life, whatever it might wind up being. And she'd just as soon do it clean.

At least, thanks to the bag she'd brought here, she had a change of clothes. So far, she hadn't changed, but she looked forward to wearing something different from the outfit she still had on that now reminded her of her latest courthouse appearance—and all that had happened afterward.

Of course, the other outfit looked very much like this one. And the shirt and slacks were a good reminder of her current freedom, which she hoped would now last forever.

She went into the bathroom and rinsed off the bar of soap, although it already appeared clean enough to use.

Then she stepped into the shower.

Not for long, though. She only wanted a short shower. And she knew full well that, despite the water working, the power wasn't turned on here, so it wasn't a big surprise that the water never warmed up. The April Arizona air around here wasn't extremely cold, but it wasn't particularly comfortable. She soon turned off the water and dried herself.

That was when she thought she heard a noise from somewhere inside the cabin.

Oh, great. She hoped she was imagining it. And if she wasn't—well, her next hope was that Grayson had returned.

But what if it wasn't him? She had figured out how to get inside through the window, and other people besides Grayson could undoubtedly do it, too—especially if they were looking for her and had reason to believe she was here.

She needed to get out of there. Protect herself, no matter who it was.

But here she only had a towel to keep herself covered.

Had she been foolish again? Maybe she shouldn't have showered. Or maybe she had just imagined the noise…and maybe not.

What was she going to do?

Well, she could at least confirm that someone was there—and that it was the person she had anticipated. Hoped for.

Grayson.

Wrapping the towel around herself, tucking the edges so it would stay wrapped—and also holding it—she opened the door just a crack.

"Who's there?" she called out. She still hoped her imagination was on overdrive and no one was there, but—

"It's me, Savannah. Grayson. I'm back."

Relief swept through her. "Since I know I locked the door, I assume you crawled through the window," she said, feeling amused and embarrassed, too.

"Yep. I'm getting to know my way around this place."

Savannah had opened the bathroom door wider at the confirmation of who was there—and her easy recognition of his deep voice. Sure enough, there he was, standing by that dratted table again, his back toward her clothes on the chair. He no longer wore the neon vest, and his long-sleeved T-shirt today was dark blue, the same shade as his jeans.

He looked in her direction. Scanned her, with her towel, head to toe.

She barely knew the guy, but somehow his warm, interested expression turned her on.

That, combined with her happiness at realizing her visitor was the man she'd wanted to see again, caused her to dash toward him, smiling, arms open wide. "Welcome to my refuge—again—Grayson."

She threw her arms around him, and at the same time he grasped her and pulled her close.

Good thing she had done a reasonable job of securing the towel around her beforehand.

"Thanks, Savannah," he responded. "Good to see you again, too."

And before she could stop herself, she reached up, brought his head down to hers, and gave him one hot, sexy kiss.

Chapter 6

What the heck was he doing?

Kissing Savannah, of course. Or responding to her kissing him. And it felt wonderful. All over.

Sure, Savannah looked damned beautiful in only a towel framing her slender body that nevertheless suggested lots of curves, which were confirmed by the feel of her in his arms.

And, okay, she hadn't been the only one wanting a hug. Or more. From the instant he had seen her that way, wrapped only in that towel, smiling welcomingly at him, her shorter blond hair wet and forming a halo around her gorgeous face, he certainly hadn't objected to her grabbing him. And he had definitely grabbed her back. And joined in that amazing kiss.

But right now, he ended it. Let his arms drop. Then he backed slightly away.

She smiled but seemed to blush a little as she, too, stepped back and stood there looking at him. Or around him.

Oh yeah. He'd seen some clothes stacked on one of the chairs he now stood in front of.

"Hey," he said, moving sideways, farther from the clothes.

"Wait till you see all the supplies I brought for you. Maybe that kiss will be the first of many." He was teasing, of course.

But he pictured her pulling that towel away altogether. And then imagined what happened between them…

Okay, he felt a real attraction to her. One that made a certain part of his body stand at attention, although his jeans were loose enough that he didn't believe that was obvious.

Or at least he hoped not.

But that attraction was highly inappropriate. She was a woman in trouble. He was a man whose main purpose was to help people in trouble—not add to their problems.

No matter how strong his urge to touch her beneath that damned towel.

And besides…well, he had no intention of getting involved with her other than to help clear her name. He had no intention of getting involved with any woman, possibly ever again. Not after the miserable way his last romantic relationship had ended.

"Thanks so much," Savannah said, and he knew she referred to his comments about the supplies he'd brought, not his simmering thoughts about her. "Let me get dressed now, and we can go out to your car and bring it all in." She walked a step toward the pile of clothes, then stopped. "Did you drive all the way here this time?"

"Yeah," he said. "No closures or major impairments along the way despite the destruction in other areas. Not to mention all the downed trees and poles. Of course the dirt road that ends right here had some lumps and moderate rises that were probably the result of the quake."

"But your car is here," she said. She looked a bit pensive—another attractive expression on her pretty face.

Was she thinking about where to ask him to drive her?

But where could she go and remain safe, not grabbed by the law?

And he definitely didn't want to be seen helping her.

He decided instead to tease her about it. "So, do you want to drive my car off somewhere? If I let you, I'd have to say it was stolen. And everyone would guess who stole it, probably, considering the fact that you're the most likely flight risk around here at the moment."

"You're right." Her tone was so sad that he wondered if she was about to cry.

"Hey, I was kidding. Sort of. No, right now I think you're safer just hanging out here until we come up with some kind of plan to get you out of this mess." He purposely stressed the "we" a bit, so she wouldn't think that by bringing up her difficult situation, he was abandoning her.

At least she couldn't think he'd turned her over to the cops, since here he was, on his own, with stuff in his car to give to her.

And as a first responder used to helping people in distress, that felt damned good with this woman who, right or wrong, he still believed to be innocent. Maybe it was because he hadn't known anything particularly good about her husband, and couldn't ignore her claim that Zane was still alive, framing her. Not until there was more evidence either way, at least.

"I agree." Her tone was strong now, her expression somehow fearless—and he wanted to take a few steps toward her on the cabin's dingy wood floor and give her another hug.

He didn't.

"I'll go get dressed," she said. She maneuvered her way around him—almost, but not quite, touching his back with her own—and tugged her clothes off the chair.

He hadn't noticed before, but he saw some underwear peeking from beneath her shirt and slacks. It didn't look particularly sexy. Whatever she had here now was probably the same thing she had worn in prison, utilitarian and bland.

But just the hint of seeing it made him wonder what she would look like in something tiny, or without it…

Enough of this, he told himself, turning his back toward the bathroom door after she disappeared behind it.

He opened the cabin door and stepped outside. He stood there looking around and listening for a moment, just to be safe. He'd no reason to believe he was followed here, nor had he seen anyone else driving or walking around who might wind up here. But he wanted to remain safe—to have Savannah remain safe—so he needed to stay alert and cautious.

He heard and saw nothing to warn him of any problems, so he continued to the rear of his SUV and opened it. He pulled out the nearest bags, paper ones filled with the food he had purchased at his third store before returning here.

He had managed to find what he hoped would be enough to keep Savannah fed and healthy. Bread, yes, which had been his first thought, plus several different kinds of fruits and vegetables, which wouldn't last forever unrefrigerated, but she surely would be eating some of it fairly fast since it was the only food she would have here. He had additionally brought some canned meat—Spam and tuna—as well as wrapped and sliced meat, so she could make sandwiches. Plus, he'd bought some more bottles of water for her...and a little wine, just to make their meal more enjoyable, perhaps, if he ate here with her at all. And the food was in addition to some other essentials, such as a first-aid kit, paper products and some cleaning supplies, although he hadn't brought much of those this time.

Still alert for sounds, he heard his own footsteps crunch a bit on the loose dirt and leaves on the path back to the front door. A couple of crows cawed, but he heard no other birds or wildlife making any sounds. No breeze, either; the trees were still and soundless.

He soon was inside the house—and staring slightly down at Savannah, who'd been about to come out the door. She was fully dressed now, even wearing the black slip-on shoes he had seen her in previously. She was equally attractive with her clothes on, and Grayson was glad, for his own peace of mind, that she'd gotten rid of the towel.

She looked down at the bags he held. "What do we have here?"

"Groceries," he said. "I left water and other supplies in the car."

"I'll go get some," she said.

"No, show me where you want these and we'll get the rest together." He didn't want her alone out there, even while he was around.

But his protective instinct was controlling him, and he needed to use it for her as long as they were together.

"Okay," she said, fortunately not disputing him, although she did give him a quizzical look. And after he'd put the bags on the kitchen counter where she indicated, she said, "Is everything okay outside?"

"As far as I know," he said, realizing that probably didn't give her a lot of reassurance.

Even so, she was with him on their next couple of trips outside to bring in the rest. "Wow," she said as they both put down the bags they'd been carrying. "Why didn't you get some more?"

Of course she was attempting a touch of humor. He responded in kind. "Oh, I figured this was enough to hold you through tomorrow morning. I can bring more then."

"That's good," she said. Then she grew more serious. "I'd really like to have some sense of how long I'll need to stay here—and what I can do to figure out what happened to Zane. As fast as possible, of course."

"Of course," he acknowledged. "I don't know what to tell you, other than we need to discuss more of your sense of what happened, and its timing. Then maybe we'll come up with some ideas."

"Not just maybe," she contradicted. "We have to figure it out. Or at least I do."

"We," he said again. "I intend to help."

He went back outside again, this time to retrieve the phone. Savannah was in the kitchen area, standing on tiptoes in her black sneakers, placing packages of paper towels, paper plates, napkins and more into a floor-to-ceiling wooden cabinet.

"As soon as you're done there, I have something else to show you."

"What's that?"

"You'll see."

She seemed to speed up the pace of stuffing the still-sealed packages onto the shelves, stretching to thrust some into the areas above her, then kneeling to also use the lower ledges. He enjoyed watching her lithe form as she maneuvered. Not a good idea, he told himself, but observed her anyway.

Finishing in about two minutes, she strode over to him. "I can put the food in another cabinet and in the fridge soon. Even knowing nothing will get chilled there, it'll make a good storage area. But first—what else do you have to show me? I'll warn you, though. I have an idea what it is."

"Of course you do." He pulled the phone from his pocket. "Let's go to our favorite place here and I'll turn it on, then we'll make sure you know how to use it."

In moments, she sat at her usual spot watching him—and, amusingly, batting her eyelashes. She seemed to have a natural beauty that was entirely her own.

"What's taking you so long?" she asked.

He pulled out his chair and sat down beside her. "Here we are."

The phone resembled major manufacturers' equipment—black and rectangular, with a screen in front. He also pulled the new battery-operated charger from his pocket.

"Okay, here's how you turn it on. Nothing crazy or unique." He pushed a button along the narrow side of the phone. "I assume that doesn't look unusual, though I don't know what kind of phone you had."

"Not much different from that one," Savannah confirmed.

She held out her hand, and he placed the phone in her palm as the screen came to life. The wallpaper on that screen showed a blue sky with white cumulus clouds. When he swiped at the screen, a bunch of apps suddenly appeared. One was the play store from which more apps could be downloaded. Another was a camera. Then there were the standard ones for making calls on the phone, getting to the internet, and sending and receiving text messages. And though Grayson didn't know what internet connection there was at the cabin, there must have been something because everything appeared to work.

"Looks nice and familiar," she said again. "Can I get its phone number from you?"

"Of course." He pulled his own phone from his pocket and checked his list of contacts. He had added Savannah's new number at the tech store where he'd bought it.

Of course he didn't use her name in his contacts list. Not that he anticipated anyone would be checking his phone for it, but no sense taking any chances.

No, she was listed there under the name of a girl he'd been buddies with in college, Charlene Farmer. Not a girlfriend, but a girl who was a friend. That number had an area code for Arizona, but there wasn't anything else that should reveal its owner's location any more than her name.

After he explained all that to Savannah, she said, "Please give me a call. That way, I can save your number. I assume it's okay to use your real name as my contact."

"Absolutely. But I assume I don't have to tell you to be careful and not make calls to anyone you know without thinking it through first. They may not recognize your number or your name on the phone, but—"

"I understand. No way will I call anyone I don't trust. You can be sure I'll be cautious."

"Good," Grayson said, then he did as she had requested and called her from his phone.

She answered it. "This is Charlene. And who am I talking to?"

"Some weird guy who wants to know exactly where you are so I can come and hassle you."

"Okay, weird guy. I've got your number." And Savannah pressed the button to end the call.

"I think I'm in trouble." Grayson made a mock-nervous face and aimed a grin toward Savannah.

But what was next? He could leave now, but the kind of help he had provided that day wasn't all she needed.

To provide an excuse to stay longer, he said, "I think we deserve a late lunch now, don't you?"

"I certainly do," she said, rising. "And since you brought all the food and other stuff we need, I'll make us a salad and sandwiches. That okay with you?"

"Definitely," he replied.

It was an excuse, of course. Savannah was perfectly happy using the things Grayson had brought to prepare as nice a lunch as possible for them.

But mostly she didn't want him just to drop things off, show her how to use that critical phone—and then leave her here, alone and unsure what to do next.

Besides...well, she enjoyed having him around.

Especially after that kiss.

Of course, even if he stayed for a while, that moment when he left would come. He couldn't, shouldn't, stay here much longer. Yet she hated the idea of hanging out here alone again. Although, now that she had a phone she could use, it wouldn't hurt to try to do some research on Zane and what was being said about him on the internet. Would she find any answers? Well, she definitely wouldn't if she didn't try.

Without another word to Grayson, she went to the kitchen. She used the cleaning materials he had brought to scrub the sink, then washed some of the utensils she had found in the kitchen drawers.

She cut the head of lettuce Grayson had brought, along with a tomato, placing them into a clean bowl. Then she made sandwiches from the cold cuts and kept everything on paper plates.

While she was doing all this, she glanced at him now and then. Which wasn't a chore. Grayson's gleaming blue eyes seemed to sparkle when he looked at her, and particularly when he teased her and helped to keep her mood from becoming completely depressed despite her questionable freedom.

Plus, he was a first responder. Could he use his skills and help her figure out what really happened to Zane?

Plus, Savannah couldn't help thinking about before, when he had first arrived that day.

When she'd had no clothes on, only a towel around her, and had impulsively hugged, and kissed, him.

She had an urge to do it again now. In thanks for what he had brought.

In thanks for appearing to believe in her. For helping her. For bringing her food, and hanging out to share a meal with her. Unlike Zane. Oh, they sometimes shared meals, but that had become a lot less frequent before they separated.

During part of the time she prepared their lunch, Grayson seemed to be texting someone, maybe more than one. His staff?

He eventually stood and crossed to the far side of the room, where he conducted some phone conversations, too. Though he was talking to whoever was on the other end, he kept his voice low so she couldn't hear more than a few words of what he said.

At least his staying here didn't seem to prevent him from communicating with people he needed to.

And her? Who would she dare to communicate with using her new phone?

She might need to ponder that for a while.

For now, though…

She saw Grayson pull his phone away from his ear and cross the small cabin. He wasn't smiling.

Was something wrong?

But as he reached her, he said, "Okay, I'm free for a while. Talked to everyone I needed to. So when do we eat?"

Savannah waved toward the food she had clustered, still on

the counter near the sink. “Right now,” she said. “Take a plate and sit down.”

She was so glad he was staying. She really enjoyed his company.

Not to mention the idea that he was the kind of person who just might try to help her prove her innocence.

Chapter 7

Grayson sat down to a pretty tasty lunch on a thick paper plate. Of course, it consisted of the stuff he'd bought, nothing even hinting at gourmet. Even so, Savannah had put it together in a way that looked appealing.

And that was what he told her. "This all looks really good," he said as he placed a second half sandwich onto his plate.

"It looks like what you brought here," she said dismissively, although he caught the smile on her face as she scooped up some salad.

"Ah, but your serving skills added a lot."

She laughed as she aimed her green eyes at him in an expression that seemed both amused and appreciative. "Taste it first," she said.

He finished filling his plate and went to sit down at the table. He savored the food, such as it was, partly to keep her amused—and because he wanted to hang out here a while longer. He intended to discuss her situation and what he could do to help her not only survive, but end what was happening to her—and how he could help her uncover the truth about Zane.

She was most likely being hunted now by the cops. In their phone call yesterday, Chad had indicated that was in fact the case. Chad had heard that the cops, including the few who had K-9 partners, were mostly occupied with checking out damage, though a warning had been issued for people to be careful not only of potential looters, but also of a murderer who might be loose among them.

He also assumed from what Chad said that there hadn't been time to look for her…yet.

Now he took a significant bite of sandwich, watching Savannah watch him as he did so. It actually tasted pretty good, probably because he was hungry.

"So what's your favorite food when you aren't in the middle of nowhere helping an innocent prison escapee?" Savannah asked him. Although the tone of her sweetly feminine voice was light, the expression on her pretty face remained wry.

"Oh, I like sandwiches, though I'm fondest of really good, thick burgers. Roast beef sandwiches, too. Steaks and—"

"I get it," Savannah said, interrupting him with a laugh. "Beef and you are buddies."

"You don't like my faves?" He tried to sound as though his feelings were hurt, and he squeezed his mouth into a pout. He liked the idea of keeping this conversation light. For now. But soon they'd have to start discussing what was really on their minds.

"In moderation," she responded. "Along with good, healthy food, like salads and other veggies. Fish and chicken, too."

"You sound like a health nut," he said, shaking his head.

"Guess what, I prefer healthy."

"Well, I actually like sides along with my meats, and that can include the salads and veggies you mentioned. Good fruit, too."

"Then maybe your family did bring you up right," Savannah said. "Even though from what I've heard you can afford to eat anything, anywhere, that you want." Her turn to put down the plastic salad fork and take a bite of sandwich.

"That's what I gather about you and your family, too," Grayson said, and as she stopped chewing and looked down, he knew he'd made a mistake even mentioning them. Even though she had brought up his.

He had understood, meeting her at elite parties before, that her family had money, too. She was essentially a socialite, he believed, although he knew she helped to raise money for organizations that helped people who were less fortunate.

But his bringing up her family now wouldn't call into mind charitable events, or even just her parents and siblings, difficult or not, but also a particularly nasty, wealthy ex who was now apparently framing her for murder.

Family. Grayson, at age thirty-six, was the youngest of three from Payne's first marriage to Tessa. He had an older brother, Ace—the one to whom it now appeared he might not be biologically related—and an older sister, Ainsley, plus adopted brother Rafe.

Ace was still a Colton, genetically or not.

Then there were three more siblings from his dad's third marriage, to his stepmother, Genevieve: twins Marlowe and Callum, and Asher. In between his late mother, Tessa, and Genevieve, Payne was married to the sinister Selina Barnes Colton. Although they had been divorced for years, Selina still remained in a prominent position at Colton Oil, leading the siblings to wonder what she held over their father.

Grayson's second phone call earlier had been with Callum.

Callum had confirmed to Grayson that Payne remained in a coma. They still didn't know who'd shot him. And couldn't Grayson get a little more involved with helping to figure that out, or working with the authorities more, since he knew them better and interacted with them as a first responder?

That wasn't the first time Callum had suggested it. Or had prodded Grayson to get more involved emotionally, too—though he didn't phrase it that way. Callum had recently uncovered the nurse who might have swapped her own newborn son with a sickly Colton baby forty years ago. That woman, Luella Smith, might be Ace's biological mother. Callum had also fallen in love with a charming single mom, Hazel Hart, and adored her daughter, Evie.

But although Grayson was okay with the fact he was a Colton, he wasn't really close to the family and didn't intend to change that even now, partly for fear they would try to twist his arm to get involved with Colton Oil.

Although, close or not, he was really concerned about his father and how he was doing—and whether he would survive.

With his mind off on that tangent, Grayson had been looking more at his nearly empty paper plate than at Savannah, even though he had last mentioned her and her family.

While his family and their father's situation might be important, they weren't why he was here.

Or involved with what he wanted to do here.

He tore his gaze from the boring plate he'd not really noticed as his thoughts flew around. He looked up at Savannah.

She, too, appeared to be studying her empty plate. Her face was pale, her expression pensive but leaning toward sorrowful. Maybe even distraught.

"Are you okay?" he asked.

She looked up at him. "Of course. It's just that you mentioned my family. They're a good group, my mother and brother. And yes, we have some money. But my father's gone now."

The thought clearly, and understandably, made her sad. It was time to put this lunch behind them and do something else. Something that hopefully would be productive—in improving Savannah's mood, if nothing else.

Better yet, they could discuss a bit of the past and hurl it into what they could do in the near future to change things drastically for the better for his lunch companion.

"Hey, Savannah," he said. "You ready to take a walk outside? We need to take a bit of a hike to work off some of the calories from this enormous, filling lunch."

* * *

Her family.

Ignoring the fact that it recently had included—been usurped by—that jerk Zane, Savannah briefly let her mind wander further as she stood up and cleared the table, tossing their plates into the plastic bag she was now using for trash. She also picked up the bottle of water she had been drinking from and placed it beside, though not in, the refrigerator. Why bother?

She wondered what her mother and younger brother, Randy, were thinking now. Her dad was gone, and of course she was sad about that—but he'd been a major reason she had wound up marrying Zane.

Oh, she'd had an elite upbringing, despite there being no private schools good enough around Mustang Valley for the Murphy children. Her parents, Randolph Senior and Eleanor, had imported live-in tutors to work with them while they also attended those public institutions, like the local high school, part-time, to ensure they learned everything privileged children of their ages should learn. And their mansion at the fringes of town had plenty of room for live-in help. That had been largely due to her father's income as chief executive officer of a highly profitable manufacturing company, as well as his inheritance.

Her dad was gone now, but Savannah had not worried about her mother and brother after the earthquake. Neither would have been affected. Randy had moved to Phoenix to join a highly successful stock brokerage firm. Her mom was on an extended trip to Europe with some friends.

Savannah had lived in the family mansion until she married Zane, partying and enjoying her life, including getting involved with all the charitable events she could. She'd continued to help throw fund-raising events, which wasn't much of a career, she realized, but she'd enjoyed it.

And she didn't give a damn about what, if anything, was now left of the other mansion she'd lived in, her ex's. While, apparently, he was enjoying multiple affairs.

Well, she wasn't going to talk about any of those things as she took her walk with Grayson.

Still, she appreciated his company. And his apparent intention of helping her get through this and finding the truth so she would be exonerated. She didn't know what she'd do with her life then, but she would definitely be out of prison.

Or so she hoped.

Since they had eaten everything she had prepared as their small lunch, she just checked to ensure that she had encased the remaining meat and salad fixings as well as possible in the plastic wrap Grayson had brought. She put them back with the rest of the food, knowing they wouldn't last long with no power in the refrigerator, then turned back to him—only to find him right behind her.

Or maybe she wasn't so surprised after all. He certainly hadn't startled her.

"Are we ready to go?" she asked.

"Absolutely." He held out his right elbow, as if inviting her to latch onto it with her own arm, which she did—for the few seconds it took them to reach the front door.

She opened it, but Grayson stepped in front of her. "Me first," he said. Which she appreciated, especially when he began looking around, his head raised as if he was listening, too.

He was undoubtedly checking for intruders to the area.

"Okay," he said after a few seconds. "No obvious problems, but we'll stay alert."

"Of course," she agreed. Without even thinking about it, she, too, stopped for a moment to listen for anything that didn't belong there. But other than the breeze flowing through the leaves and branches of the fir trees around them, she heard nothing except for an occasional bird call, mostly crows.

Nothing that sounded like people stalking her. No cops on her trail…but she knew she had better expect the worst eventually.

Still, she also might as well enjoy her freedom for the moment and attempt to figure out a way to guarantee it in the future.

Grayson didn't offer to take her arm again as he walked slowly around the cabin on the narrow, uneven path. "Have you walked around this way before?" he asked.

She nodded, staying at his side as they strolled along. "Yes, partly just to get out of the cabin, partly for a touch of exercise—and mostly just to think as I walked."

"I can guess what you were thinking about. Did you reach any conclusions?"

She sucked in her lips as she considered the circumstances—as if she wasn't thinking about them all the time anyway. "I want to get out of here. But as much as I'd like to find a way to flee the area, what would I do then? I'd need a new identity, and I'd always be looking over my shoulder for someone to recognize me and drag me back here to stand trial."

"Not if you could prove that the only crime committed was your ex framing you for his murder."

Savannah stopped abruptly and looked at Grayson. He'd described what she really wanted. And of course he knew that, since she hadn't exactly kept it to herself.

But his mentioning it here and now felt—well, as if he had somehow handed her a key to the future she really craved.

Not that he'd offered any guidance about finding that proof.

Still, she had an urge to hug him for his understanding.

Heck, she had an urge to hug this kind man again for more than that.

This amazingly handsome, sexy man who could have just obeyed the law and turned her over to the authorities.

And as she looked straight into his intense blue eyes, even more striking beneath his thick, sculpted brows, she had an urge to do even more with him—like drag him back into the cabin and seduce him.

Possibly the last passionate encounter she would ever experience if she was, in fact, recaptured and thrown back into prison.

Instead, she turned and restarted their walk. She inhaled the fresh, April-cool air of the woodlands. "Yes, that's the current goal of my life. I really want to dig up the truth. Find my ex and show the world what a horrible man he is. And find out for sure why he decided to frame me, although I think it's just because I refused to stay married to him while he did what he wanted, like seeing other women."

"Okay, let's start trying to figure out how to do that."

"How?" Savannah blurted. Since escaping and hiding in this place, she had been racking her brain for ideas—and hadn't come up with any good ones.

"Good question." This time Grayson stopped, and Savannah immediately halted again, too. He looked down at her with an expression that suggested he was attempting to see into her mind.

To judge whether she was actually innocent?

She wasn't about to ask.

"I want to hear it all," he said. "From the moment your ex disappeared and the world started to believe he was dead—but you didn't. What happened? Maybe, if we brainstorm after we discuss it, we can come up with an idea or two."

Or hundreds, Savannah thought, since it might take that many to clear her. But she appreciated this man's concept.

She appreciated him.

And if—when—she did get out of this, she would do what she could to repay him.

At the moment, though, as they exited the path to walk farther into the woods, onto hard ground covered with clumps of leaves—and fortunately no visibly big cracks after the earthquake—she again tamped down any idea she still retained about having sex with him.

That could lead to…well, caring.

And she didn't intend to care for any man again for a long time, if ever. Not even one as kind as this guy.

"Okay," she said. "Although if I get choked up—well, it's a pretty emotional tale for me. And it's one I've had to repeat multiple times after I was arrested. I told it to the cops, to my attorney and to nearly anyone who asked, but if anyone believed me it still didn't help me get released."

"I get it." And damned if, as they continued forward, Grayson didn't reach over and take her hand—possibly for stability in their walking and possibly for emotional support.

Tightening her grip slightly, Savannah forced herself not to let her eyes tear up—at least not much.

"It was like this," she said. She explained that the night Zane had disappeared, she had been out in the evening at a friend's place near the Rattlesnake Ridge Ranch to talk about a fundraiser for the Mustang Valley General Hospital's children's wing. "Nothing was decided that night, but the group I get together with for that kind of thing has put together that scale of an event before, so we were just touching base and getting the idea started for a new bash."

"Yeah, I think a couple of my sisters get involved now and then."

Savannah saw a thick tree limb lying on the ground in front of them, as did Grayson, who still held her hand. "Let's go this way, rather than climbing over," he said, and they turned to their right. "Okay," Grayson said in a minute. "Please continue."

And Savannah did, hating to relive that night and the next day as she yet again described what had happened.

"We had just finalized our divorce," she told Grayson. "I didn't want to move back in with my family, nor did I want to stay anywhere near Zane, but I hadn't yet figured out where to move. So I was living in a separate guesthouse on the grounds at the back of his house—our house—though he got it back as part of our divorce settlement. I avoided Zane for the most part, and he kept encouraging me to move out as soon as possible, which was fine with me. In fact, I already had someone helping me to look for a new place. Only in retrospect that turned out to be a mistake."

Savannah almost stumbled as she thought about that particular mistake, and what it had added to the horror of her situation.

"Why was that a mistake?" Grayson prompted beside her.

"The real estate guy's name is Schuyler Wells," she said. She tried to concentrate on the crunchy sounds of leaves beneath their shoes to distance herself from the anger and frustration of what came next.

"I've heard of him," said Grayson. "He's a big-deal developer around here, right?"

"Right. He had ideas and connections and—well, as things went south I was accused of having a long-term affair with him. He even hinted to the cops that we had planned to run away together once my divorce was final, that we'd decided to even before…before Zane disappeared."

"And you weren't?" Grayson asked.

Again Savannah stopped, this time just long enough to stomp her foot on the ground. "No way." She remained quiet until they continued forward again. She hated the way this aspect of the horror etched its way through her mind.

"Go on, please," Grayson finally said.

Savannah explained how, living in that small back house, she hadn't kept track of Zane's comings and goings, so of course she wasn't aware of whether he'd been home at all the night he supposedly disappeared.

Not that his absence would be a surprise. Even when they were married, he often wouldn't come home at night, and Savannah assumed he was having an affair or several, although he'd always explained his absence the next day as somehow related to his business. Savannah had never bought that. Why would the owner of a highly successful investment bank need to conduct an all-night meeting? No, she'd heard rumors of his affairs and even caught him once, just before she filed for divorce, with another woman.

Still, as their relationship had deteriorated, Savannah didn't mind his absences. She'd been irritated, though, when he'd claimed she had been going out, as well—which she recognized afterward was probably his way of boosting the allegations of her affair with Schuyler. And of course Schuyler later claimed they spent a lot of time together looking for someplace for Savannah to move, but he implied there were other, sexier, reasons, too.

"But then—well, that night was one Zane didn't come home. The next day, late in the morning, I got a call from his office. He hadn't shown up there, either—and that was unusual. Nor did he show up later that night or the next day. Not that I cared about him that way anymore, but I became concerned, and apparently his staff did, too. Someone called the cops, who showed up and began questioning me about what I knew about Zane and his disappearance, and why was I still living there, and what had our relationship been like recently. And then—and then—"

She had to continue. She recognized that. And if Grayson was aware at all about Zane's alleged murder, he'd probably heard it.

"And then what?" he said.

"And then—the cops found a knife in my closet, hidden under a box. It was bloody. Of course they grabbed it and took it in and had it tested."

"I assume the blood had Zane's DNA in it," Grayson said, stopping and turning to face Savannah, who also stopped but refused to look him in the face.

"You assume right," she answered with a sob.

Chapter 8

Grayson wanted yet again to take Savannah into his arms, to hold her tightly against him as she cried.

Too bad the cops didn't see this. Surely she wouldn't be crying that way if she'd killed the SOB.

On the other hand, she'd probably told this story before, and might have cried then, too. They hadn't released her.

And they could interpret this as her being sorry about getting caught, not about her ex's apparent murder.

Instead of hugging Savannah, Grayson took her hand, pulling her closer on the dirt beneath them. "Let's go back inside," he said, attempting to keep his tone light. "Did you notice? I brought you some wine, and I think this would be a good time for a sip or two."

Savannah, now facing him, swallowed and appeared to attempt a smile. "I saw that. A nice, not-too-expensive brand that no one would particularly notice when you bought it."

"Exactly." He held onto her hand as she started leading them back to the cabin.

Once they got inside, Grayson made sure the door was locked

as Savannah picked up the wine from the back of the counter beside the refrigerator. And yes, it wasn't especially expensive or high quality. It came in a screw-top bottle, since he'd doubted there was an opener here in the cabin and didn't want to search for one to buy when he was on that outing. There were a few glasses without stems that the owner of the cabin had left in a cupboard, so they didn't need to drink out of the bottle.

Grayson offered a toast. "Here's to getting all of this resolved quickly and well."

"I'll drink to that," Savannah said solemnly, clinking his glass with her own.

Grayson gestured toward the table. "Let's sit down and—"

"And talk about you for a change," Savannah asserted. "I'm sure I'll be the topic again soon, but I'd like to hear about you, Grayson. How did you happen to become a first responder in the first place, then start your own company?"

The explanation had its good and bad points. In any case, Grayson didn't want to talk about it now.

But sitting across the table from Savannah as she sipped her wine and regarded him with an expectant expression on her face that was beautiful despite the redness around her eyes from crying, he didn't want to tell her to mind her own business. She deserved answers, too. And he could keep things as light as possible.

"Well," he began, "I started out after high school in the military—the army. Did my duty but decided I didn't want to make it my long-term career." But it had been a good way to get out of town briefly and begin his own life, away from his clinging Colton family.

"Wow," Savannah said, taking another sip. Her short blond hair fell forward as she tipped her head to drink, and he resisted the urge to reach across the table and push it back. "I'm impressed. A Colton soldier."

"Exactly. Did my stint as a private in basic training and a bit more. I left, though, as soon as my enlistment ended and came back here. Then I became a wilderness guide, but only for a short while." Though he had stayed in close touch with some fellow soldiers with whom he'd become good friends.

One such pal had been Philip Prokol, formerly of Tucson, who'd been sent overseas to Iraq, where he was wounded in the military and had come back with PTSD. That hadn't killed him directly, but his attempt to flee everything he had known before, including his hometown and family, had caused him to be out in the wilderness in northern Arizona in a major rainstorm. He'd died from being washed away in a flood.

Could he have been saved? Apparently there hadn't been enough first responders to deal with that disaster and the many people swept into the water.

Hearing about it, first on the news and then from Phil's family, had almost destroyed Grayson inside. He should have done more to help his friend. He'd already ended his own brief career as a wilderness guider and started college. He should have been with Phil when he'd run off to try to find himself again.

Saved him.

And remembering Phil's fate in the wilderness during a disaster was one reason Grayson had headed out of town after the quake…to save people who might be in similar situations.

"Are you okay, Grayson?" Savannah interrupted his thoughts, a good thing. It was probably better that he not dwell on why and how he had decided to become a first responder.

"Sure," he responded brightly. "Just thinking of what I did when I returned to the States. I'd decided first to become a wilderness guide, then ended that to go to college and major in business."

And when he'd dropped out, his family, especially his father, hadn't been happy, and Payne had made that very clear. But Grayson had done what he wanted.

"Sounds good. So did you get a corporate job when you got your degree?"

He laughed. "What degree? I dumped it all when I decided

to become a first responder. I left the university for a smaller school where I could learn what I needed to get my emergency medical technician credentials, and I learned more than enough to get my official certification, and there I was."

Savannah's wine glass was nearly empty, and so was Grayson's. He picked up the bottle from the table and poured them each a little more.

"Thanks," Savannah said. She'd furrowed her brow, which didn't detract in the least from how pretty she was. "But why did you want to become an EMT? A first responder?"

"I just did." He had no desire to talk any more about it. "And you? Did you get a college degree?" From what he knew about Savannah, she didn't have an official job, although her charitable efforts were admirable.

"Yes, I had the fun of moving to Los Angeles for a few years to major in English at UCLA. I loved to read then, and still do, so that worked out well."

He wanted to ask her how she used her degree now, if she did, without a job. But before he decided how to phrase it, she said, "And in case you're wondering, I never really got a job where I could use my degree, but I do go to the elementary schools in and around Mustang Valley a lot to work with kids who are reading challenged. It's really a kick to see them improve and know I at least had a little to do with it."

So the wealthy socialite who was Savannah might not earn money to cover her own expenses now, but she certainly earned kudos by helping others.

"That sounds great." And it did, to Grayson. This woman had made good use of her time and family's money—and her ex's—to help other people.

Not a first responder, but definitely someone who gave a damn and attempted to do something about it.

To prevent her from asking more about him and why he was who he was, he decided to press her some more and get her to describe some of the kids she'd helped with their reading. Then he urged her to talk more about her favorite charities that she helped now, like the hospital children's ward.

She apparently liked kids. Maybe she'd intended to have some with Zane. Well, that clearly wasn't going to happen now, nor would it even if Zane wasn't ostensibly dead, since they'd already divorced. That could have been a motive for her to kill him, Grayson supposed, or the district attorney might approach it that way: anger that he hadn't given her kids.

Nah, too ridiculous.

Grayson didn't know what the terms of the divorce settlement were. Had it been fair, or had Zane's lawyers cut her out of everything?

He had a thought then. "Any idea what your lawyer might be thinking now that you've disappeared?"

Like was he—or she—now upset because Savannah wasn't currently racking up any fees? Or was he looking bad because his client had flown? Grayson assumed that, married or not, the socialite in front of him had money of her own to pay her counsel before and after her arrest.

"Who? Ian? I don't know. He'd warned me that the evidence against me looked grim, but he'd seemed to be completely on my side, eager to at least try to get me off."

"But he didn't think you were innocent?" Grayson shook his head, eyeing the bottle of wine again but deciding he'd had enough for now.

"I thought he did, although he kept enumerating all the evidence that could keep me from even having any bail set for me, let alone getting off at trial. He reassured me a lot, though, that he would do everything in his power to get me cleared."

Yeah, like spend a lot of time—and her money—to try to prove her innocent. Well, Grayson didn't know any attorneys named Ian, but he did know others, and even the good ones appeared to be money-grubbing. "What's his name?" he asked. "Ian what?"

"Ian Wright," Savannah said, "but please don't contact him."

She sounded alarmed. "He's an officer of the court, like all lawyers, he told me, which means he might have to turn me in if he found out where I was. He asked me if I'd killed Zane, said it was okay for me to admit it to him. Because of attorney-client privilege, he wouldn't reveal it to anyone else. But of course I didn't admit anything, since I'm innocent. I trust him. I like him as a lawyer. But I don't want anyone, even him, to know where I am. Not now, at least. Or that you've seen me."

Grayson didn't like the sound of that. Not that he'd tell that Ian Wright anything. But even though Savannah trusted him, Grayson trusted no one on her behalf. Not now. Not until he'd learned a lot more about her situation.

"Got it," he said. "With your phone now, you can contact him if you decide to and not give your location away"

Savannah nodded and smiled at him, her expression more relaxed—and trusting. Damn. She shouldn't trust anyone right now, even him.

Still… Evening was approaching now. He needed to leave, get back to the office for a while before going home.

"Sorry," he told Savannah, drinking his last few drops of wine. "I'd better get on my way."

He was about to tell her he'd be back again soon, though he didn't think it would be tomorrow. He'd brought her enough sustenance for a few days, anyway. And wine.

"I understand," she said, nodding slightly. If he read her expression correctly, she probably understood but felt bad about his leaving. "That's fine. I appreciate our discussions today and think I might have an idea of what to do next, but I want to think about it more, so being here on my own will be fine. Only—"

"Only what?" he asked when she hesitated.

"I don't suppose you have a pen and paper in your car that you could give me so I can make some notes, do you?"

He laughed. He'd expected something a lot more significant than that, given the change in her expression to uncertainty, maybe fear—or worse.

She needed to jot something down, apparently. And he always kept a notebook or two in his SUV in case he got a call and needed to jot down quickly where to go and why.

"Sure," he said. "I'll bring them in right now—before I leave."

Grayson had left an hour or more ago, but Savannah had tried not to think about him as she sat at the same old table once more, making notes.

And realizing she needed to get out of there soon. In some ways, the cabin was as much a prison as her cell.

Not just because she felt lonely with her only current contact, Grayson, gone. She recognized that she missed him not only because he was attempting to help her but because…well, she liked the guy. Felt attracted to him, despite herself.

But she also recognized that was a mistake. He was a good man, dedicating his life to helping people, and at the moment that included her.

It didn't mean he liked her as anything more than someone who needed him.

Despite the hugs and the kiss they'd shared, which to Savannah had suggested more. A lot more.

But that wouldn't happen.

Savannah rose again to turn on the lanterns to avoid being left in the dark. She checked to make sure the door was locked and the windows fully closed. She had no intention of going outside again that night.

And tomorrow? Maybe. Hanging out inside here alone could drive her nuts—even nuttier than she already felt. But what else could she do?

She would ponder that tonight where she could go, what she could do, to locate Zane and show the world what a horrible person he was. A living person. But how?

And what would she do if she didn't ever see Grayson again? After handing her the notebook and pen, he had said he might not be back tomorrow but promised she would see him again soon.

But *soon* could mean anything from another day to a week or more. And his saying he'd return didn't mean it would come about. Even when the food he so kindly supplied her with was gone.

So…now what?

She was a murder suspect who'd fled and was most likely being chased, or would be once the authorities finished with disaster relief.

If she left here, she would have to walk through these woods and beyond, in an area she didn't know at all—unless she found her way back to town, a horrible idea if she couldn't remain hidden somehow. She'd be recognized and arrested again, probably immediately.

But what was the alternative?

She had an idea, but it depended on Grayson's returning. More than once.

Which meant, yes, she relied on him. A lot.

She trusted him, sure. Because she had to. She needed him to help her hang on to the last shred of sanity she still had.

And if he didn't come back here even once?

Well, she could stay here until her remaining food ran out and then see what happened.

And in the meantime?

She decided to try to keep her sanity a bit by working out details for that idea she had.

She placed the notebook Grayson had given her on the table in front of her. Then she hurried into the bathroom and examined herself again in the mirror. At least she liked her new hairstyle—sort of.

Returning to the main room, she set a water bottle on the table and poured herself a small amount of wine before opening the notebook.

She began sketching on the first page.

Chapter 9

Grayson's mind remained on Savannah and what to do next to help her, as he headed his SUV back toward his office. He knew where he'd start once he sat down at his computer.

He was worried about her, unsure what she'd do without him hanging around and encouraging her to stay put while they worked out a plan. But even if no one paid attention to where he was going and he therefore didn't endanger Savannah further, he couldn't keep visiting there as much as he had without his company suffering.

But he didn't want her to suffer, either.

Would she run before he showed up again? It wasn't really his business, yet he felt like it was. He'd promised to help her get through this. And as long as he believed she was innocent, he intended to assist her.

But did he fully trust her? Maybe not, but until he found some reason not to, he'd act as if he did.

And help her. After all, that was his calling in life: helping people.

Plus, something about Savannah Oliver made him want to

pull out all stops to clear her name. Her resigned yet hopeful attitude and this miserable situation were what did it, he told himself.

He could handle the unwanted attraction he felt for her. He had to.

Still, better that he do things quickly to try to clear her—like what he intended to do that evening and tomorrow.

He answered a few phone calls as he drove, mostly business-related but also concerning his family—darn it. Of course he was worried about his father, but at least Ainsley let him know that Payne was holding his own at the moment. And then there was the Ace situation. No matter what, the guy was their brother, even though not by blood.

He drove even more slowly once he reached downtown Mustang Valley. The earthquake damage wasn't what kept his speed low, or not entirely. The cracked streets he traversed had already been at least temporarily fixed, or detours designated. The sidewalks around them had been improved a bit, too. The buildings not so much, at least not yet.

But what particularly kept Grayson from driving at a normal speed was amazement at how many tables along those sidewalks he now saw that had Affirmation Alliance Group signs on them—even more than before. He still liked the idea that they were out there trying to help people who'd suffered damages from the quake. But though he couldn't quite put a finger on why, he still didn't trust them.

His curiosity about them inflated even more after he reached his office building—and saw one of those tables on the sidewalk on the next block. The sign there was even larger than the rest—and it invited people to come and meet the group's founder, Micheline Anderson.

Grayson had heard of Micheline—all pretty good stuff. Maybe his opinion of the group going overboard would change if he actually met her.

And so, after parking his SUV behind his office building, he walked around to the front and crossed the street.

The table here was larger than the others he'd seen. There were lots of flyers on it, and several people sat or stood behind it.

One had an identification card folded in front of her: Micheline Anderson.

The woman behind it appeared to be a really attractive senior. She had long blond hair, dangling earrings with pearls at the ends and a face that resembled a movie star's. She wore a blue shirtwaist dress and stood behind the table.

Beside her ID card was a larger sign. It said Be Your Best You! Grayson had heard that before. It was her organization's slogan.

He approached her. Several other people dressed nicely, yet less formally than Micheline, stood around her, and a couple were talking to others lined up across the table, apparently handing out flyers and discussing the group with them.

"Hello," Grayson said to Micheline. She'd watched him as he approached, a large smile on her face. Did she recognize him? If so, how and why?

"Hello," she said, drawing out the word as if she was happy to see him. "Welcome to the Affirmation Alliance Group. I'm Micheline Anderson." As if he couldn't tell, despite the others hanging around the long table with her. "And you are...?"

"I'm Grayson Colton." He watched both her eyes and smile widen even more as he said his last name. Evidently, whether or not she thought she knew him, she was aware of the prominence of the Colton family—as who wasn't around here? But not many people actually knew him...and his not-so-thrilled attitude toward most of his relations.

Although, on his way here, one of the calls he'd received was from his half brother, Callum. And after a bunch of arm-twisting, not easy over the phone, Grayson had agreed to join his relatives for dinner at the ranch house that night. The others intended to discuss some family matters and really wanted him there.

Which had also added to his concern about when he'd next be able to visit Savannah and help keep her motivated to stay where she was.

"How do you do, Grayson Colton?" Micheline held her hand out for a shake. "Thanks for coming to say hi. I assume you don't need a place to stay after the quake, since, from what I've heard, the Rattlesnake Ridge Ranch survived just fine. That's one of the reasons we're out here, you know—to let everyone know we have a place people can stay, if they need it. But can I convince you to come visit us anyway and participate in one of our seminars? We give them often, on a variety of subjects to help people achieve our goal to 'be your best you.' There's a charge, of course, since we use the money to help others."

She smiled as if expecting him to compliment her for that, but he just smiled slightly in return.

"And you—" she continued, "I know you're a first responder and like to help people too, right?"

Grayson realized it had been a mistake to come to this table, despite how curious he was. The woman might have good intentions—or not. But what she definitely had was an open hand in which she wanted money deposited, no matter what she intended to use it for.

His passing thought earlier, that meeting her might help him accept her and her group more, had been only that—a passing thought that definitely wasn't coming true.

He needed to leave here right now, but without causing any kind of scene. He assumed Micheline would stop at nothing to achieve one of her goals, so he figured he'd need to do this as politely as he could.

"That's great that you know who I am," he lied, looking into her blue eyes, which he'd have found attractive on a younger and more trustworthy woman. "And I appreciate your invitation. I'll definitely consider it." Like hell he would. "But for right now I'm still working hard on helping people affected by the quake, as you are, so I can't commit to doing anything else."

"I understand." Micheline's smile seemed to drop a bit and her eyes showed irritation. "But here." She picked up a bunch of flyers from the table and handed them to him. "Call anytime you're able to set something up. And I hope it's soon."

"Thanks." He accepted the paperwork, figuring he'd dump it into a recycle bin in his office as soon as possible. "And good luck to you in helping as many folks in need as you can."

He strode away, across the street and into his building. Only then did he feel as if he could breathe naturally again.

He stood in the large, empty lobby, not yet approaching any of his staff. Okay, Affirmation Alliance Group could be everything Micheline claimed. Maybe more. But it sounded too good to be true. Plus, he didn't trust people easily, partly because of ways his own family had tried to guilt him into giving up his own company and join Colton Oil.

Anyway, he didn't need to stay in touch with their leader or any of them. And he hadn't lied to her. He and his gang were still working hard on helping people affected by the quake. For him, that included the fugitive Savannah, and after he caught up on what he needed to do that day, he'd take another approach to helping her—and proving her innocence.

He hadn't thought in advance about which of his staff he'd drop in on first now that he was on the floor where their offices were, but as often happened, Winchell decided that for him. Winch was well enough trained that Chad didn't generally keep him leashed in the office, although his door was often closed. As it had been—till now. It opened, and Winch ran out toward Grayson.

As Grayson bent to pat Winch, Chad joined them. "Hey," he said. "Good timing. Winch and I just ended our assignment for the day from the MVPD. And guess what?"

Grayson had a pretty good idea, considering the big grin on

the retired cop's face that moved his glasses up a notch on his cheeks. But he let Chad inform him. "What?"

"This excellent K-9 of mine found a survivor who'd been buried in rubble from an apartment building just outside town."

"Good boy!" Now Grayson knelt on the floor and gave the dog a big hug. "Tell me more." He stood again and faced Chad, as Pedro came out of his office, too. "I assume you've already heard the story," Grayson said to Pedro.

"Not all of it," the former firefighter said. "I want to hear more. Fortunately, though I helped to get rid of several fires, there weren't any casualties—survivors or otherwise."

"Let's sit down here, then." Grayson gestured toward the seats in the reception area. "Is Norah here, too?"

"No, I gather she's back at the hospital, since the EMTs needed more help today," Chad said.

His hand still on Winch's head, Grayson listened to the story of the old and not particularly well-maintained apartment building in the part of town worst hit by the quake. And yes, it had been a couple of days, but the authorities were aware, thanks to info from others in that building, that at least one resident had remained missing. A couple of others, too, though they likely were out of town.

"The victim was elderly," Chad said, "but word was that she exercised a lot and was in fairly good shape for her age. And nearly as soon as the neighbors pointed us in the general direction of what was left of her unit, Winch began reacting—though a small distance away, which was probably why the woman hadn't been located before. Some firefighters and city staff were there digging, and in a short while they located her. She'd fortunately had an air pocket and had been able to breathe."

"So Winchell's a search and rescue hero," Grayson said with a grin, still petting the dog.

"You've got it," said his owner and handler. "Media folks were there, too, so I made sure to let them know Winchell and I were part of First Hand First Responders."

"Then you're our hero, too." Grayson stood again and held out his hand for Chad to shake it.

After making a fuss over Winch some more, Grayson excused himself, letting his staff know he'd be in his office for a while. He had a lot of work to do there.

First, he sat down at his desk and faced his computer. He researched the location of the buried senior and saw exactly what Chad had described, including some videos of Winchell at work—and Chad's mention of First Hand. Grayson virtually applauded.

The woman they'd saved, Susan Black, had suffered some significant injuries and was still in the hospital, but she was expected to make a full recovery.

Good. Grayson was glad the woman would be okay. He was also glad to see positive publicity for First Hand.

He next plowed through his emails, answering a lot of questions in them about what his company of first responders had done during and after the quake.

He was also glad to see that a few were from contacts from police and fire departments they'd worked with outside but not far away from Mustang Valley. But some were strangers, inquiring into what his first responders could and couldn't do in emergencies. Fortunately, Grayson kept his billing amounts within reason.

Finally, he got to what he had intended to do all along: research the people involved in the case against Savannah.

First, he searched Zane Oliver online. No surprises there. From all Grayson found, the guy had disappeared and was presumed dead, murdered by his ex-wife. A knife had been found in her home with his DNA on it.

Grayson tried a little further digging. It appeared that Zane's investment bank was still alive and profitable even without his presence. If so, Zane probably hadn't been trying to run from a career gone bad.

It was a shame, though, that Grayson couldn't instantly find information about Zane's personal finances.

Maybe Savannah's ex had invested his money back into accounts in the company to keep incurring further profits, still growing on behalf of his heirs, whoever they were, now that he was divorced.

That was something Grayson would have to look into, too. But not right now.

Next he researched that real estate developer Schuyler Wells, with whom Savannah had been accused of having an affair during her marriage. The guy was featured on a lot of websites mentioning construction and property sales, primarily around Mustang Valley. His picture was included in several of them, as were videos in which he described what wonderful homes and apartments and office buildings he'd been involved with planning and constructing—and now selling, undoubtedly for a nice profit, Grayson assumed. From what Grayson could see in the photos the middle-aged guy looked earnest and dedicated, with eyes staring straight into the camera, a tenor voice, and a hint of a knowing smile on his long face. His hair appeared short and impeccably groomed. He appeared to be of moderate height and mostly wore suits. A real real estate agent.

But Grayson began getting bored with all the hype, finding nothing particularly exciting about Wells. Grayson figured it was nearly time to go on to his next subject—

Only, oddly, he found something on one of the sites he next checked. Or not so oddly. Real estate moguls, with lots of construction and sales to their names, undoubtedly needed good attorneys to handle issues with buyers who found flaws or were otherwise unhappy with their purchases.

Therefore it wasn't a huge surprise to learn of a lawsuit that had been filed against Schuyler Wells Real Estate—or that his defense attorney in the tort action had been none other than Savannah's criminal lawyer, Ian Wright.

So the two of them knew each other. That didn't necessarily mean they discussed Savannah.

But of course they could have. And the impression Grayson had gathered was that Schuyler Wells had lied about an affair with Savannah to make her appear to have a stronger motive to kill her ex—although that didn't make complete sense, since they were already divorced. Even if Zane had heard about a supposed affair and used that as a reason to divorce Savannah, once they were no longer a married couple, there'd be no reason for Savannah to murder Zane. He would have had more of a motive to murder her.

Although of course Grayson didn't know what the settlement of their assets involved. Even so, it was unlikely Savannah would become better off with Zane dead. She wouldn't inherit anything since they were divorced, and it might be even harder for her to obtain whatever their divorce settlement was, if she hadn't received all of it yet.

Anyway, Grayson compiled the information that he had found on researching all three men. He'd show it to Savannah tomorrow.

And then? Well, Grayson thought he might pay a visit to at least the lawyer, Ian Wright. Maybe just indicate that, since he'd found the van that had been transporting Savannah, he'd become interested in the murder case against her—and where would Ian go with it now if and when Savannah was found. What were his thoughts about that bloody knife that had become so vital in the case against Savannah? What else would he do to prove her innocent?

Of course the guy would undoubtedly rant about attorney-client privilege. But even so…well, maybe he'd say something that would give Grayson a better idea of whether it would make sense for Savannah to turn herself in—or to run far, far away.

Only then would Grayson let her know what he'd found out from Ian.

And he wouldn't be at all surprised if that lovely, determined woman who definitely thought for herself would listen to what he hoped would be his sound advice.

It was late afternoon. Savannah sat in her usual spot, reading an article on the Mustang Valley city government website about the history of the town. She already knew most of it, but at least it occupied a fragment of her mind. She'd used the battery-operated charger to make sure her new phone continued to have power.

So far, no new ideas about chasing down Zane. And she hadn't admitted it to herself, but she'd hoped that Grayson would come visit her sometime that day.

That was just because she now had something else to ask him. Or so she told herself—even without believing it.

Added to that was that she was lonesome, of course, with no one else around to talk to, no one she could trust enough to call even just to say hi.

And—well, she refused to admit to herself that she really enjoyed Grayson and his company. His obvious determination to help her.

His appealing looks that she could speculate about for the future...

Not.

Okay. Enough of this. She exited the website and pushed the button to make the phone's screen go black, saving at least a little power.

She glanced down at the notebook on the table beside her. Oh yes, she'd been making notes.

Notes about things she would ask Grayson to do to help prove her innocence, though those remained sparse, and she couldn't be sure he would do them anyway. More of her notes contained items she would ask Grayson to purchase for her—and of course she would reimburse him. Eventually. As a Colton, he undoubtedly had enough money to buy it in the first place.

But he shouldn't buy it anywhere in Mustang Valley or in a

town near here, because she had listed a lot of things she needed to disguise herself so she could at least escape this cabin. Maybe go into town and eavesdrop or snoop around to find evidence against Zane. Even ask questions without being recognized. Or so she hoped.

She grabbed the notebook and returned to the bathroom, where she again looked in the mirror.

Good thing she'd been a thespian in a local high school, though she hadn't followed up afterward. She'd acted in a couple of different plays, even starred in one during her senior year.

The English teachers had been in charge and they'd taught the actors—including Savannah—how to put on makeup that helped them resemble their characters.

Savannah's favorite role had been as a grandmother to a bunch of kids in a comedy. That meant she'd learned how to apply makeup to look older, which she intended to take advantage of now.

She usually wore makeup to enhance her appearance, which she considered attractive enough.

Now she would only ask Grayson to buy certain shades of foundation, eye shadow and hair dye, of course, since she planned a new haircut that would help disguise her even more. And she would be less recognizable if she wasn't a blonde.

She could always return to her original coloring in the future, when this was all behind her.

As she had before, she studied her face and imagined what it would be like once she added lines to make her appear older, though her eyes would remain green, which could be a problem. But she didn't want to suddenly start wearing contact lenses and possibly damage her vision.

She looked at herself, then down at her list, and up into the mirror again.

Okay, the list seemed good enough. Particularly because it also included the kind of clothes she would generally only wear while cleaning or on a hike or something—ratty T-shirts and jeans that already had holes in them, or whatever else was available at a discount shop.

And as embarrassing as it was, she would also have to request more underwear. She hated to provide her size, but what else could she do? They should not be the luxury kind she usually wore, though no one but Grayson would know that.

And yes, a new pair of athletic shoes, again not expensive but different from what she had now, the ones she had worn leaving the prison.

Now all she had to do was wait until Grayson showed up again. Sometime.

Surely he would. He'd promised.

And she could request then that he leave town and go buy her all she needed.

She only hoped he didn't get caught. For her sake, sure. But also for his well-being, which was becoming more and more important to her.

Chapter 10

Grayson sat on the swanky beige coverlet on the antique bed in his room at Rattlesnake Ridge Ranch. Sort of. He had his own small wing on the second floor of this mansion, and so did each of his full siblings Ace and Ainsley.

He'd seen Callum on his arrival, but no one else so far, since he'd kind of edged his way in via a side door as he mostly did. That was a good thing.

But soon it would be time for dinner, the main reason he had come here at this time. After Callum's coercion.

Those who were here would discuss not only their dad's dire medical condition but more about the current status of the family mystery: the true background of their oldest brother, Ace—and what had happened to his parents' biological firstborn, for whom Ace had allegedly been swapped at birth.

It had been a common topic of conversation among the group, ever since someone had sent those allegations to the Colton Oil board, which had shocked them all. But were they true? Even Grayson, despite his intentional distance from the family most of the time, wanted to know.

He was curious.

For now, he sat on the bed and surveyed the masculine headboard of pale wood, matched by the nightstand and the dresser with a mirror. He had picked these out when he was a lot younger, before he had even joined the military. He still liked them. And even if members of his hot-stuff wealthy family weren't thrilled with them, they hadn't gotten rid of them.

After all, at least some of those family members still encouraged Grayson to actually live here full-time.

His cell phone rang, and he pulled it out of the pocket of his dressy gray slacks. He'd been dressed fine for work before but here, at the Colton digs, he always felt he needed to shine.

It was Callum again. "Everyone's starting to arrive. Come on down to the dining room."

"Right," Grayson said and hung up.

He took a deep breath. Would all of his siblings be here? He'd soon find out.

He considered checking how he looked again in the full-length mirror in the bathroom—and ruled that out. Heck, even the change of clothes was more than he should have done. He was here, and that was all his family should care about.

He strode out the door leading to the rest of the house. Before he reached the stairway that led down to the first floor—where the dining room was—he saw Ainsley approach from her wing, next to his. Ace's wing was on this floor, too. All three of them had the same mother, the late Tessa Ainsley Colton.

Maybe. That remained a question as to Ace.

"Hi, Grayson," Ainsley called, clearly hurrying to catch up. Ainsley was slightly older than Grayson, thirty-seven to his thirty-six. Their only other full sibling was Ace—or so everyone had thought before questions arose.

"Hi, Ainsley."

Grayson waited till she reached him. She was much more involved with their relatives than he was—particularly as an attorney for Colton Oil. In fact, Grayson found her maybe a bit too devoted to the family, but that was just him. Ainsley was a pretty lady, well groomed even when not dressed in attorney clothes, like her current long-sleeved floral T-shirt and slacks. She was shorter than Grayson, with light eyes and hair an attractive chestnut shade.

"So you did come." Ainsley continued to walk toward the stairway as she patted him on the shoulder. "Callum said you would. I hoped so, especially because all of these horrible questions about Ace and whether he shot our father. Or not."

"I gather someone has more information, and that's the reason we're meeting up, right?" Grayson asked. He figured that if anyone knew anything around here, the smart and involved Ainsley would be it.

"Yes, but—"

"Hi, you two," Callum called from the bottom of the steps. Younger than Ainsley and Grayson, he was a product of their dad's relationship with his current wife, Genevieve. Callum was a big guy and a former Navy SEAL, and currently a bodyguard.

And he was definitely a Colton.

"Good evening, Callum," Ainsley called, and Grayson just waved since they'd already seen each other since his arrival.

"Hurry up," Callum said. "Dinner is about to be served."

They walked through the amazingly decorated living room. Its wooden floor matched the trim on the walls. In the middle was an ornate table surrounded by upholstered chairs. It had a fireplace and an attractive vaulted ceiling, and a wide window overlooking one of the ranch's pastures.

The dining room connected with it via a rounded wall. It had an impressively carved table in its center, with upholstered chairs for diners, and splendid chandeliers above.

Grayson headed there, with Ainsley and Callum behind him. Their other siblings were already seated.

Grayson greeted Marlowe, Callum's twin, and their older brother Asher, who was also Genevieve's child. Genevieve wasn't there, though. Was she at the hospital with their dad?

Selina wasn't there, either, but that was no surprise. Even though she was a big wheel at Colton Oil, their father's second wife hadn't had any children and wasn't that close with Payne's actual offspring. She did have her own house on this property, though.

Grayson sat down beside Ace, slightly surprised he was there. But heck, no matter what his actual DNA might be, Ace had been brought up as a Colton, their oldest brother, and that was who he still was, at least in Grayson's mind.

Still, on hearing about the discrepancy, which was proven by a DNA test, their dad had immediately fired Ace as chief executive officer of Colton Oil, due to company bylaws.

Even worse, because of their ensuing argument, Ace was also a suspect in their father's shooting—probably another false allegation, like the accusation leveled at Savannah of her ex's murder.

Ace hadn't been arrested, at least not yet, so Grayson supposed he could do whatever he wanted, at least for now. Although he had also heard that Ace had been told not to leave town by the MVPD, including Kerry.

Would any of that be brought up this evening? Most likely, or why was Callum so insistent he join his siblings tonight?

What did they all want to talk about?

"Hey, bro." Ace gave Grayson a high five. "Long time no see." Ace's light brown hair was more unruly than Grayson was used to seeing it. Of course, when he'd represented Colton Oil, he had to maintain a professional look. He studied Grayson with his closely set dark eyes, as if trying to figure out what was on Grayson's mind.

"Lots going on as a first responder after the quake," Grayson said, figuring that was a good enough excuse—though he'd been avoiding seeing people at the ranch even before that.

He considered asking Ace more about how he was doing, and what he was doing now that he no longer ran the company.

But as interested as he was in his brother's answer, he decided to hold off for now.

Water glasses had already been left by each place setting—all antique crystal, as far as Grayson could tell. Now a member of the kitchen staff whom Grayson hadn't met previously placed salads arranged on fine china out in front of them.

This was definitely a formal dinner.

Grayson appreciated sitting between Ace and Ainsley, to whom he was closest, since they shared a mom.

They had become even closer after their mother died, especially when their father began remarrying. Grayson had never become close with either of his stepmothers, though he had made himself get along with them. But the additional marriages, and siblings, had also contributed to his distance from the family, along with the urging by many of them for him to get more involved with Colton Oil.

Now, the family members who were here all dug into their salads, conversing with the others around them. For a while. For a frustrating while to Grayson. And so he was the first to speak up.

"It's good to see all of you," he lied, looking around. Well, maybe it wasn't a total lie. He didn't enjoy much camaraderie with his family members, but it was okay to see them now and then. "And I know something is going on around here, which is why I'm here. But first thing—I'd really like to know how Dad is doing."

There. That should get them talking. Grayson glanced first toward Ace, who stared at him as if he'd been slugged.

"He's still alive, at least," Ainsley said from between them. She clutched her salad fork, then placed it on her plate. "But he remains in a coma."

At least their father still held his own, Grayson thought. That was a good thing. He wanted to ask about the investigation into the shooting but, for Ace's sake, hesitated.

Ace spoke up, though. "And in case any of you still wonders

if I was the one to shoot him, the answer is no. But I don't know where the cops stand on their investigation, other than to make assumptions about me because I'd argued with him."

"An understatement," laughed Callum. "Oh, I'm not accusing you, bro, but you certainly weren't pleased when he fired you from Colton Oil."

"Can you blame me?" Ace countered loudly.

Their adopted brother Rafe, son of the ranch's old foreman, got into the conversation. "I don't imagine the cops believe you're the source of that Arizona State University pin," he said to Ace. "That's got to be something in your favor." The pin, found near their father when he was shot, was considered a possible clue.

"Certainly nothing I had anything to do with, either," Ace said.

"Besides," Callum broke in. "So what if Ace wasn't a Colton by blood? The bylaws should be changed. And one of the reasons I wanted to get you all together was to give an update on our investigation into who actually was the baby Ace was swapped with."

For nearly the rest of the meal, Grayson listened to the discussion going on.

Callum had narrowed in on Luella, a nurse at the hospital, who had also given birth to a baby on the night of Ace's birth forty years ago. She had left quickly, allegedly to find better medical care for her baby, since that infant had major medical issues.

No one had yet been able to find Luella to learn any more. One good thing, though, was that the nurse who'd first identified Luella had recently let Callum know she'd finally remembered Luella's last name: Smith. Of course that wasn't great news because the name was too common. But Callum hadn't given up.

The conclusion at the end of dinner that night? The search continued. Callum told them he'd tracked every Luella Smith in Arizona and bordering states. Three had seemed like possibilities because of their ages. But none had panned out.

"The last time Luella Smith seemed to have existed was on Christmas Day forty years ago," Callum said, "and then she vanished off the face of the earth. There's no birth record of her son, since those records were destroyed in the hospital fire. And since she apparently switched babies and took one that wasn't hers, she must have forged a birth certificate for him."

"She must have taken on a fake name, don't you think?" Grayson asked.

"Yes, that's what we think," Ainsley replied. "And we'll find her one day, somehow, someway. Turning over rocks always reveals something."

Grayson's siblings had also begun trying to track down the other babies born locally on Christmas morning forty years ago by checking through newspaper microfiches and doing online searches. Maybe one of them was the real, missing Ace Colton.

Well, Callum had said that one reason why this dinner had been called was to let them all know the status of the search. And it was an interesting update, kind of.

Fortunately, the meal included some great-tasting steaks. When Grayson finished eating, he tried to excuse himself.

He wanted to return to his office and do a bit more research.

His intention was to hurry to see Savannah in the morning, let her know what he had already found and discuss with her what to do next—although he figured he knew.

But before they let him go, Callum said to him, "You can't leave yet. We all want to hear more about how our first responder brother did after the earthquake—and the man you found dead."

Grayson remained seated and refrained from rolling his eyes. A lot of this had already appeared in the media.

But this was his family, so he described how he had found the crushed transport van with the dead driver.

"But the back was empty inside, right?" Ainsley asked.

"That's right," Grayson agreed.

"But they said there'd been someone inside being transported," Ainsley pressed. "Savannah Oliver, right? She'd been arrested for murdering her husband and was on her way back to prison from the courthouse."

"That's what I understand." Grayson tried not to grit his teeth.

"That whole situation is sad," Marlowe said. "I've known Savannah for a long time—Savannah Murphy. Some of you have, too, right?" She looked at Ainsley, who nodded. "She's a nice person. I find it really hard to believe she's a murderer."

An accused murderer, Grayson wanted to say but kept quiet. He didn't want them to figure out he even knew Savannah, let alone that he was attempting to help her.

"People snap and do terrible things sometimes," Ainsley said. "But I have to agree with you, Marlowe. I find it hard to believe that Savannah's a killer."

That, at least, was good, Grayson thought. And fortunately the topic of conversation moved to how Colton Oil was doing now that their dad Payne wasn't in charge of even his executive staff. Marlowe was now CEO. And Rafe was CFO.

Which was of some interest to Grayson, but not much. Especially since all seemed to be going relatively well.

"No dessert for me," he said a little while later as the staff began clearing plates and bringing out sweets. "I've got to get on the move." He ignored the irritation on his siblings' faces as he left. "See you again soon," he said—lying somewhat again.

He was interested in what they might eventually discover about their missing oldest sibling, so he might meet up with one or more of them again soon about that.

And he wanted to stay informed about how their father was doing.

But otherwise—well, he wasn't hanging out in the dining room here. He was going back to his wing to spend the night.

So he could get up early the next morning—and head for a certain fisherman's cabin.

Savannah's eyes popped open. What time was it? Daylight poured into the cabin through its multiple windows, illuminating its shabby but utilitarian contents that she had come to know too well.

She thrust the sheet off and sat up in bed. She had actually slept last night, at least for a while. Amazing!

She wore a long T-shirt, the one that had been in the bag she had rescued. It felt good to get out of the other clothes she'd been wearing pretty much all the time since her flight from the van—and before.

And with luck, she would be able to convince Grayson to buy her the things she had listed to help turn her into someone who appeared quite different from the fugitive Savannah Oliver. That would include utilitarian nightwear of her own.

Before leaving the bed, she sat there listening for any sound that could have awakened her. There were a few birds tweeting outside, but nothing suggested she was about to have any human visitors.

Unfortunately, not even Grayson. But he'd already told her not to expect him that day.

And if he did turn up tomorrow or the next day? Should she really just continue to stay in this cabin waiting for him—and imagining that no one else could find her here?

On that miserable thought, she finally stood and headed toward the bathroom, where she stepped into the shower. She had left her clothes on the bed, and when she was done washing she dried herself and opened the bathroom door again.

Yesterday, Grayson had been there, and she'd kissed him. She listened once more, just in case, but heard nothing. Saw nothing. And so she got dressed.

She wasn't especially hungry, but she'd seen some cereal bars with fruit filling that Grayson had brought, and so she took one out of its small box in one of the kitchen cabinets and brought it to the table, along with—what else? A bottle of water. She wished she had caffeine, but with no power here, let alone any kind of coffee maker, she was out of luck.

One of these days, though…especially if she accomplished what she wanted to and started looking like someone who wasn't her at all. Could she then work directly with Grayson and somehow investigate what had happened to Zane? If not, she would still ask for his advice on how to prove her innocence.

As she was eating, she considered what she would do that day—assuming she didn't just go crazy and flee this place. But if she did, where would she go?

No, it made more sense to hang out here one more day and see if Grayson did show up tomorrow. Then she could make her request for disguise material, and if he agreed and got what she asked for, that would be the time to leave.

If he showed up.

After all, the men in her life such as Zane, and even Schuyler, had betrayed her. Could she believe that Grayson wouldn't do so, too?

For now—well, she noticed that her burner phone was fully charged, fortunately. She quickly added more batteries to the list she'd been making, though. She had no idea how long these would last.

Then she decided to take a walk around the cabin for a modicum of exercise before starting whatever research she could come up with on the phone.

She put the phone in her pocket, just in case she needed it, then headed to the door. She opened it, and gasped. Grayson.

Chapter 11

Savannah reached out, grabbed Grayson's hand and pulled him into the house.

She closed the door behind him and did what she'd vowed never to do again. She hugged him. Tightly. And looked up into his wonderful blue eyes. Which also looked down at her, but only for an instant, until he bent his head…and they kissed.

Oh, what a kiss. Savannah felt Grayson's hard body against her, his heat surrounding her, his slight beard scratching her face just a little, his—well, she definitely knew that he was as aroused as she.

Bad idea. Bad idea. The words started circulating through her brain even as she pulled him even more tightly against her, her mouth absorbing every heated moment of that kiss.

But this couldn't go on forever. And that it had happened at all felt foolish.

And amazing…

She gave him one more kiss against that hot mouth of his, the slightest, most wonderful of pressures, then pulled away.

"Wow," he said, looking at her once more.

"Well, that's what you get when you show up when you're not supposed to," she said, then realized how absurd that sounded. "I mean—"

"I get it," he said. "And I'll remember it. Maybe what I should do is tell you each time I come here that you won't see me again for a while, and then come anyway the next day."

She made herself scowl at him, though it wasn't real and he undoubtedly knew it. "I don't like being lied to—even when the results are…are…well, good ones." She stepped back even further. "Anyway, why are you here today? I had the impression you had a lot of things to take care of at your office, or whatever."

"Well, I got quite a bit done after I left here yesterday. And part of it made me want more answers that maybe you can give."

"Oh," Savannah said. "What are the questions?"

"We'll discuss them in a minute," he said. "For now—well, I'm not sure if you like coffee, but I brewed some in my apartment and brought it in two insulated travel mugs so it's still hot. And none of my family was around when I left, so no one saw me carrying two, so don't worry about that. But if you don't want any, I'll—"

"I'd love some coffee," Savannah said, feeling herself smile as if he'd offered her a bag of diamonds.

Diamonds. They made her think of commitments—although she of course no longer wore the one Zane had given her when they'd gotten engaged. She'd kept the ring with the big, expensive jewel, though. It served him right for being such a jerk while they were married.

And that was also part of their negotiated divorce settlement.

Not that it would do her any good now, especially since she had it locked in a safe deposit box at her local bank. She couldn't just show up there and claim it, even if she got access again to the code to let her in.

Divorce. Relationships. She never wanted another one again, after Zane and his nastiness and infidelities. Not even with a man who looked and kissed like Grayson, who seemed so nice, who was helping her…

Enough.

She looked at Grayson. "Hey, can I come out to your car and help you carry the coffee in?"

"No thanks, but in case you didn't eat breakfast, or even if you did, I also brought a half dozen doughnuts."

When things normalized a bit, Savannah figured she'd be able to eat more sensibly, more healthfully. But considering everything, including her mood and lack of much appetite, she doubted she would gain much weight right now.

"Sounds good," she said, then watched him head back out the door.

She returned to the bathroom again to see what she looked like. She'd used her fingers to comb her hair, as was her norm right now. But even with no makeup, she figured she didn't look too bad.

Maybe she would look a lot better soon. Or at least a lot different.

Grayson was gone only a few minutes before coming in with two metallic coffee mugs with caps, as well as a plastic bag containing the doughnuts he had mentioned.

They both sat down at their now-regular places at the table. Savannah immediately took a nice, long sip from the mug Grayson placed in front of her. It tasted good, not too strong or too light, and it had maintained a sufficient amount of heat. She closed her eyes for a moment to savor it.

"I gather you don't mind drinking coffee," Grayson said.

"Not at all." But after taking a glazed doughnut from the bag, along with a napkin, Savannah said, "So what brought you here today? What questions do you have?"

"Well, out of curiosity, how did you happen to hire Ian Wright as your lawyer? Did you already have a professional relationship with him?"

"No. I…well, I did have a local lawyer, John Morton, representing me in my divorce. When I recognized that I needed a criminal attorney when…when it appeared that Zane had been killed, I asked him for a referral. He suggested a couple but said that Ian, whose office was also in his building, had experience in different legal areas but had recently successfully defended a client in a murder case in a nearby town. I looked that up on the internet, thought he sounded good, so I called him and he came to see me at my home before the cops came for me, and I hired him."

"Got it," Grayson said.

"Why did you ask that?" Savannah felt a bit puzzled.

"Well, I spent some time on the computer yesterday checking into Mr. Wright's background, as well as Schuyler Wells's. And funny thing."

Both curiosity and anticipated dismay rocketed through Savannah. "What?"

"It turned out that your supposed buddy, Schuyler the real estate mogul, had a lawsuit filed against his company a few years ago. Nothing criminal, but a civil suit. And guess who his attorney was?"

"Ian." Savannah knew better than to turn that into a question—not with the way Grayson was staring at her with both inquisitiveness and compassion. "But…but Ian never mentioned that, despite all the lies about my supposedly having an affair with Schuyler leading me to murder Zane."

"My initial reaction is to assume they were in collusion over this," Grayson said. He reached across the table and grasped Savannah's hand with empathy. "Maybe with Zane, too, if he really is alive, though I didn't find anything specific to make that more than a possibility."

"So Ian had a reason to not represent me fairly? He was somehow in cahoots at least with Schuyler, and possibly Zane, too? But why? Though that would explain why he wasn't able to get me out on bail…"

Savannah felt like putting her head down on the table and

crying. What was she going to do now? How could she ever prove her attorney was a phony? Especially when she didn't dare contact the authorities for any reason, at least not at the moment.

"I… I don't know what to do about that," she finally said to Grayson.

"I have some thoughts," he said. "No one is aware that I know where you are, but since I found the van you were in I can certainly express professional curiosity as a first responder. In fact, I have an idea how to introduce myself to your lawyer to see his reaction. I can lie a little and tell Mr. Wright I've been hired by local authorities to try to help find you since I did discover the van you were in, plus, thanks to my background, I know the area pretty well. We'll see what his reaction is to that. But I won't do it without your okay."

"You've certainly got my okay," Savannah said, feeling shocked by this new twist on her situation. "I'll be eager to hear his reaction."

"I'll let you know how it goes as soon as I can," Grayson said.

"I… Things keep getting crazier and crazier." Savannah shook her head, partly to keep the tears welling in her eyes from falling. "I just don't know how I'm going to get out of this."

"We'll figure it out." Grayson captured her gaze with his own.

"I wish I could be there when you question my wonderful lawyer. Maybe he really is as good as he tells me, and the fact he once knew Schuyler is irrelevant."

"Well, I'll tell you what he says when I can."

"Right," Savannah said. "And ask him who he thinks the most likely suspects are in Zane's murder, excluding me, of course." Savannah had already expressed some of her ideas to Ian, including members of Zane's bank staff, since she'd gotten the sense from some things her ex had said, that he might have played games with the company's income and blamed it on them, or maybe some of the women he'd had affairs with, but she had nothing that even barely resembled evidence.

And even if she got all the things she was going to request Grayson to get for her, it wouldn't make sense for her, whoever she became, to accompany him.

But she would broach the subject of his obtaining a good disguise for her before he left.

That greeting. Grayson had been only partially kidding when he'd told Savannah that from now on he'd say he wasn't coming, then show up. Both times he'd visited her now, they'd wound up kissing.

He took a long swig of coffee as he remained at the table with her, half wishing it was alcohol, even at this hour of the morning.

He wanted to hang out here a lot longer, but he needed to leave now to get started on his upgraded research for Savannah. Also, he had to spend a few hours in his office getting in touch with some of his police and fire contacts to make sure they were happy with First Hand's response after the quake, and to seek more assignments.

Besides, he wanted to make some suggestions regarding official preparations for any future quakes. After all, he wanted, needed, to keep a good relationship with all of them.

So, as much as he regretted leaving Savannah, he said, "I'd better get on my way now. I can see you're doing okay, and I'm glad you consented to my talking to your lawyer the way we discussed—although he's likely to claim attorney-client privilege and all that if I ask him some of the pertinent questions I have in mind."

"About his knowing Schuyler, the liar who convinced the cops I killed my ex? Good old Schuyler—and good old Ian. I'll definitely be eager to hear what Ian says. But—well, I have something to ask you before you go."

Her expression after she said that appeared both eager and apprehensive. What was she going to ask?

"I appreciate all you've been doing for me, Grayson," she

began, picking up the pad of paper he had given her previously and fiddling with it somewhat nervously. He could tell that she had written notes on it. "And that you're continuing to help me. But I'm sure you can imagine that I'm going nuts hanging out alone here, knowing that if I go anywhere else I'm likely to be spotted and taken back into custody."

"Yes, I'm sure that's difficult," he said, wondering where she was heading with this. And he did sympathize with her. Even with her ability now to look things up on the phone he'd brought her, watch videos on it, read free magazines on it and whatever, she remained alone out here in the middle of nowhere.

"And I hate to ask you to spend more money on me now."

He began to react, since that wasn't a concern to him and she knew it.

"But," she continued, "as I said before I'll repay you when I'm able to. The thing is, I don't want to be me any longer. Or at least I don't want to be recognizable in any way."

"What do you mean?"

She immediately jumped in to explain, showing him the list of items she wanted him to purchase for her—and suggesting he not shop anywhere near Mustang Valley, where he could be seen, and where people would know he didn't have a significant other to buy all of this for.

And those people could become suspicious.

She jumped up from her seat then and motioned for him to follow her into the bathroom, where she looked in the mirror and gave a better explanation of what she intended to do with the makeup and all, pointing out what changes she would make.

He had to hand it to Savannah. Of course, as a former debutante and someone who had apparently been featured in a few high school acting roles, she'd come up with a lot of good ideas for disguising herself.

"So, if I'm able to find all this stuff, I gather that your nose will look longer." He reached over and touched her nose softly with his index finger. "Your hair will be deep brown instead of blond—and in this style that no one but me has seen you in anyway." He gently touched the side of her hair. "Your eyes will appear larger, with dark lashes and brows over them that match your hair." He touched those brows, too.

As he was doing this, he realized how ridiculous it was—and yet how sexually stimulated he was becoming. And Savannah's eyes widened as she met his gaze in that mirror.

It was as if he was getting emotionally attached to her. In some ways, maybe he was. But he knew only too well that he didn't want to get involved with any woman.

This one had particularly gotten under his skin with her sad situation. Well, he didn't need any kind of relationship with her except as her helper. Anything else would be way out of bounds.

He still believed she was innocent, believed it enough to continue to help her.

Bu what if he was wrong? What if she actually was guilty of killing her husband?

Nah…although he hoped that confronting her attorney and learning more about her that way would convince him even more of her innocence.

It had better. He didn't want to get caught abetting a genuine murderer.

And touching her here and now? He had to stop. And so he did. He took a step back though he continued to look at her in the mirror.

"Sounds like a good idea," he said. "But once you look that different, what do you intend to do about it? Run away? Unless you have someplace specific in mind and means to get there, it's a bad idea."

"Even so, I really can't just stay here forever." Her usually sweet voice had turned into a bit of a wail, and he couldn't help putting an arm around her.

But she wasn't having any of that, at least not now. She pulled away and returned to the table, where she sat back down and put her hand on that notepad.

"So what do you suggest?" she demanded, her tone harsher.

"Well, here's what I think we should do." He purposely emphasized the "we." He had already dived into this situation on her side, and she certainly should recognize that—and listen to him.

But would she?

"What's that?" she prompted.

"I'm going to go see your buddy Ian first, assuming he'll grant me an audience. I'll go get the things you've asked for, but only after that discussion and some business I need to conduct, when I have some time to get away from the office without anyone questioning where I am. That means I'll have to get a few things done first. Until then, you need to stay here. Okay?" That, of course, was important.

"Sure, as long as you call me when you can to let me know what Ian says, or tell me if you didn't get to see him."

"Sounds fair." But now he was going to impose a condition she probably wouldn't like at all—even though it was for her own sake. "The other thing I want you to promise is that, even after I buy the things you want, and you change your looks, I'll want to give you the once-over before you leave here, to confirm that you really do look like someone else."

"Fine, as long as you get here quickly after I notify you. I'll just send you a text message that says 'Done.'"

"Okay," Grayson said. "That was the first condition. The second is that you don't leave until I agree it's the right time, and then only after you've told me where you're going and how long you'll be there—and I will also have to agree with that. Might even come with you." He stared at her hard across the table. He recognized that was being pretty restrictive, but as a professional first responder he had a better sense of where she should or shouldn't go.

"You're awfully controlling, aren't you?" Those amazingly attractive green eyes were hard and she was clearly irritated.

"Yes," he said in as jovial a tone as he could muster. "When it makes sense." He hunkered down then, leaning across the table toward her. "And you can be sure that in this case it does. Do we have a deal?"

Savannah sucked in her lips and closed her eyes for an instant, obviously reining in her emotions and most likely her inclination to say no. She finally opened her eyes and took a deep breath before continuing. "Do I have a choice?"

"No," Grayson said.

"Well, under the circumstances, then I guess we have a deal." She put her hand up, and he noticed the shortness of her plain fingernails, probably required while she was in prison. Did she usually wear polish?

"Good," he said, standing and reaching for her hand to give it a businesslike shake. "I'll get on my way now and let you know as soon as I can what happens with Ian—and also go on your shopping expedition as fast as I'm able."

Her hand grasped his a bit more tightly than he'd anticipated, and didn't let go immediately. "Thank you, Grayson," she said in a soft voice. "I might not always agree with you, but you do seem to have my best interests in mind."

"Yeah," he said, pulled her closer around the table and gave her a quick hug before he left.

And as he walked out the door, now locked behind him and headed to his car, he wished he could do something to reassure Savannah that everything would be okay for her, and soon.

But first, he needed to do whatever was necessary to start believing that himself.

Chapter 12

Okay, now what? Savannah trusted Grayson. She had to.

But she had also trusted Ian Wright—and she'd had to do that, too.

She was outside the cabin now, walking around it in the open air as she had done with Grayson because she had to do something. Physically, at least. She didn't want to just wait inside, playing with her phone like a kid.

Not at this moment.

Soon, Grayson and Ian would meet. Savannah had no doubt that Grayson would convince the attorney to see him—especially because of his plan to tell Ian he needed his guidance in tracking Savannah down.

If Ian was the horrible person she now feared he was, a cohort of Zane's and Schuyler's, he'd undoubtedly open his office door wide and invite Grayson in so they could discuss where in the world Savannah was likely to be now. He would be keen to find her, professionally or worse.

And Ian might use his lawyerly arguments to state why Savannah should turn herself in so she could go through the legal system as she should.

With Ian still representing her, of course.

Not.

In fact, what would she do now if she were caught again? Would the courts let her fire her current attorney? Probably. But then, who could she hire in his place who might actually help her?

She realized her pace had increased. She was now stomping her way around, possibly noisily, to help calm her inner thoughts—but she was instead igniting them further. If there was any wildlife around, any birds, she had to be scaring them off, even though a sighting of them might help to calm her. They represented ongoing life.

She looked around at the trees surrounding her, through their branches where she could, toward the blue April sky.

She was free now, despite the kinks in her ability to go places. She had to remain free.

Would Grayson actually bring her the disguise items she'd requested?

If so, would they work at all?

Okay, enough of this. She had to go back inside and—

And what?

Survive. Think.

Maybe plan what she could, and would, do once she donned a disguise and left this place.

And determine what Grayson might approve. No, she didn't need his approval, but she trusted him.

Could that turn into more?

Definitely not, especially when all of this was behind her and she could finally connect again with other people—in a friendly way.

But even then—well, at least for the moment, she hoped Grayson would remain in her life.

She sighed as she turned the corner again from one side to

the front of the cabin. Time to go inside again. Get her mind off all of this—or at least try to.

Would she ever be able to?

Not likely until this was all worked out and her innocence was no longer in question.

And she could only hope that would occur very soon.

Grayson drove a longer route back to his office. Not that he thought anyone was following him, but since he kept coming into the area where the cabins were, he didn't want to take any more chances of being noticed than necessary.

He checked often into his rearview mirror and saw nothing unusual.

Of course, taking a longer route also meant more streets within Mustang Valley, many of which were easily drivable now despite the quake just a couple of days ago. That also meant some additional views of tables and signs from that Affirmation Alliance Group. Oh, well. He didn't stop to talk to anyone and didn't see Micheline Anderson. Maybe she was out assisting more people today. He had done a little additional research on her group and noted that they had a reputation for doing all sorts of useful things, including helping out in other natural disasters besides earthquakes, even heat waves, handing out water and supplies and generally trying to make things at least a little better in whatever situation they found themselves.

Sounded quite good—and yet, especially now that he had met Micheline, he felt glad he didn't need to deal with them—or her—again.

He parked his car as usual behind his office and walked around to the front door.

As he looked through the windows, he saw Norah sitting at the reception desk against the far wall. Not a surprise. Even though all his employees knew to act as greeters if anyone came in off the street, Norah seemed to like it best. She spent at least part of each day staffing that desk, unless she was off on an assignment as an EMT and not around to help.

They were getting busy enough now, and not just because of the earthquake, that Grayson was considering hiring a receptionist.

"Hi," Grayson called after pushing open the front door and walking into the large room. "Anyone out on a job?" When he was around, he always had all assignments run by him. But in urgent situations, he never required that anyone wait for his approval when a job came in.

"Yep." Norah leaned forward. Her light brown hair was pulled up in a bun on top of her head, and she wore a First Hand First Responders T-shirt in red today. "We got a call from the MV Fire Department about an accident on a nearby freeway, possibly caused by quake damage. A big rig and a couple of cars caught fire. There's a bigger blaze downtown they're working on, so they asked for Pedro's help at the accident." Like the Mustang Valley police, the local fire department knew how well Pedro could help them in a difficult situation.

"I hope no lives are lost," Grayson said automatically, but meaning it. "Are Chad and Winch here?" He sat down in one of the blue chairs nearest the reception desk.

"No, they were called out, too—this time a sad follow-up from the earthquake. An eighteen-year-old kid is apparently still missing from one of those less affluent areas that had the worst damage. His parents think he probably fled into the desert since he was out on a hike by himself around when the quake hit. They've been looking for him and so have some of the official PD first responders, including one of their K-9 cops, but everyone's getting worried and desperate and asked Chad and Winch to get involved."

"I hope they find the kid," Grayson said.

"Alive and okay," added Norah, and Grayson nodded.

They talked a little longer about how things were going around here—and what Grayson had been up to. Only he didn't tell even his probably most discreet and reliable employee the whole truth. "I've been in touch with the police to see how things stand in their investigation of the death of the truck driver I found." That part, at least, was true. Maybe because the local media kept prodding the cops for answers about the missing passenger. "Not much new so far."

"Do you think they'll ask us to bring Chad and Winch in on that, too?"

"Could be." Grayson didn't want to talk about it anymore with Norah. She was too smart, too insightful. No way would he encourage her to find out what was really going on with Savannah. "Anyway, I've got a few things I need to take care of, so I'll see you later."

He raised one hand in a wave as he headed for the stairway.

Once inside his office, he closed the door. He got on the computer for a few minutes to look up where his staff members were assigned.

He then searched for news about the crushed transport vehicle. There didn't appear to be any new information, at least not as reported by the local newspaper or other media—which of course didn't mean things weren't happening that were being kept confidential.

He also looked up the website of the office of Ian Wright. He studied the photo of the man before he prepared to call him.

Wright was an older fellow whose hairline had receded, but who still had enough graying hair to provide a nice frame to his face. He stood there in a suit, arms crossed, clean-shaven, staring with intense eyes beneath stern brows into the camera. Grayson continued to look at that picture as he pressed the law office number onto his phone.

As he anticipated, a receptionist answered. Grayson identified himself as the CEO of First Hand First Responders—and also the person who had located the destroyed vehicle that had apparently been transferring Mr. Wright's client from the court back to prison. He wanted to speak with Mr. Wright about that and ask him some questions.

The woman got off the phone for a minute, then returned. "Mr. Wright is about to start a meeting here that will last for most of the afternoon. Can he call you back later?"

"Sure," Grayson said, then left his number and said goodbye. And smiled. It appeared that Wright was in his office, after all.

Well, Grayson wouldn't know for sure until he got there. Wright might call him back soon, if he thought the first responder who found Savannah missing could be of any help getting her back, assuming the lawyer was attempting to help Zane and Schuyler. In any case, Grayson prepared to go to Wright's office as soon as he finished some other calls. First, he sent a few follow-up messages to professional contacts in nearby towns, reminding them that First Hand could help them if they needed any assistance now, particularly after the earthquake.

That was the kind of email message he sent often, though he'd never needed to mention something like a quake prior to the last couple of days. But he always remained in contact as closely as possible with the various local groups who might—and did—use their highly qualified and well-certified services.

In a little while, he closed down his computer and headed downstairs to the reception area.

"I'm about to leave for a meeting," he told Norah, quickly averting any questions she might have about that meeting. "And—well, I'd love to check in with Chad and Winch later. Do you know where they are?"

"Kind of." Norah described the desert area northwest of town where the young man was thought to have disappeared. She also showed Grayson a report she had found on her phone about the missing guy.

"Please text that link to me," Grayson told her. "If I get a chance, I may even head there after my meeting."

The area was on its way toward Mountain Valley, a nearby

town whose police and fire departments sometimes requested their help.

It was also someplace Grayson wouldn't be recognized, so he could at least start acquiring the disguise materials Savannah had requested.

But Wright's office? It was right in downtown Mustang Valley, not far from Grayson's own building. And as Grayson had already figured, Ian Wright was apparently in his office right now, unless he'd instructed his receptionist to lie.

Which was entirely possible.

Grayson decided to drive there anyway, despite its proximity.

He pulled his SUV out of the parking lot behind his building and drove the few blocks to the ornate yet professional-looking structure that housed the law firm of Wright & Jessup. It had a parking lot behind it, too, and Grayson easily found a spot there.

He went around to enter the front of the building, where he checked out the list of businesses it contained that was hung by the elevator. No receptionists here, just a few glass doors with signage beside them describing the offices they opened into.

He saw that the building housed a couple of other law firms, as well as a local office for a tech company based in Phoenix, and a few other groups Grayson didn't recognize.

Ian Wright's firm was listed as being on the top couple of floors.

Grayson pushed the button and the elevator door opened. He touched the number for the lowest floor of Wright's offices. The elevator was slow but not especially noisy.

When it arrived and the door opened, Grayson got out and looked around. Sure enough, the door to the law firm's offices was straight ahead, and that was where Grayson headed. He opened it and walked in.

A large black laminate desk took up most of the front room. Behind it sat a fiftyish lady with clearly bleached golden hair. She looked up, regarding Grayson from behind her blue-rimmed glasses. A sign on the top of the desk read Connie Glasser. She was probably the person he had talked to when he had called Ian Wright earlier.

"Hello," she said, greeting Grayson. "May I help you?"

"I'm Grayson Colton. I assume you're the person I spoke with before."

"That's right," she said. "And—"

"Well, after we talked, I called Mr. Wright directly, and he told me to come right in. I assume his meeting is over, right?"

Even if it wasn't, Grayson intended to slip through the door behind the reception desk. And he didn't have Wright's direct line, but Connie didn't need to know that.

"Well, yes, but he didn't mention—"

"Oh, that's okay. Thanks." He figured he might as well be polite as he walked around the desk and behind Connie Glasser, even though there wasn't anything to thank her for.

Fortunately, the large, paneled wooden door with Ian Wright's name on it wasn't locked, and Grayson slipped right in.

There sat Wright behind a large and angled mahogany desk. He had a phone pressed to his ear and held a file that matched the many piled on the desk.

Of course Grayson recognized the man from his website—sort of. Sure, he looked like the same handsome, professional older man depicted online. But this version looked even older, his face lined and pale, the divots in his cheeks deeper, his blue eyes narrowed and dipping down at the corners.

"Hi," Grayson called to get his attention.

That happened immediately. Wright looked up, straight toward Grayson, and appeared to blanch even more as he hung up his phone. "Who are you? How did you get in here?"

"Just walked in," Grayson said, answering the second question first. "I'm Grayson Colton. Did your secretary let you know I called earlier? I need to talk to you about your client, Savannah Oliver."

"If you know anything about the legal system, you know I can't talk to you. Attorney-client privilege applies, and—"

"I haven't said what I want to discuss with you. It won't involve anything covered by attorney-client privilege." With no invitation, Grayson walked farther into the room and planted himself on one of the upholstered leather chairs facing Wright's desk.

"But—"

"Here's the thing. You might know that I'm the person who discovered the ruined transport that was supposed to be moving Ms. Oliver from the courthouse back to prison. It was way out on a road that was affected by the earthquake. I also found the driver dead, and no one in the back, where presumably Ms. Oliver had been secured. She's apparently escaped, and— Well, you may not know but I'm the owner of First Hand First Responders, a private first response company, and the local authorities know it. They've hired me to try to find Ms. Oliver, since I also know that wilderness area pretty well."

"I see. But I can't help you." Ian Wright stood and clearly glanced toward the door behind Grayson.

Interesting. Grayson figured that Wright would want Savannah found, or at least would give that impression in public. But, then, he already figured the lawyer was hiding things for Zane.

"Oh, I'm sure you can. You see, what I need you to tell me is the location of the rendezvous places where Savannah Oliver met up with her lover, Schuyler Wells—all the places you know about. She might have returned there because those spots were familiar. I at least need to check them out."

Would Wright's knowledge of any such place be privileged? Grayson didn't know but he'd take the position they weren't. And he hated suggesting Wells was Savannah's lover, but taking any other angle now might affect this conversation.

Wright looked even more uneasy now, a nervous wreck, maybe. He was sweating. "I wouldn't know the answer to that. Ms. Oliver and I talked a lot, of course, but not about where she might have seen Mr. Wells. And that assumes she did see him."

"Ah, then you question that, too? I understand from what I

saw in the media that Ms. Oliver denied the affair, denied anything unseemly with Mr. Wells."

"Sorry, but we're getting too close to attorney-client privilege with that."

Which could give the impression that Savannah had admitted the supposed affair to her attorney. Clever guy for suggesting it. Grayson continued, "Oh, but I assumed you also spoke to Schuyler Wells for information that could help in her defense, right?"

Wright grew even paler, Grayson thought, if that was possible. "Well, I did talk to him a little, but he wasn't much help. He admitted to knowing Savannah and—well, that they'd had an affair and had even considered marrying after Savannah's divorce became final. He also said he was acting as her real estate agent to help her find a new home. But he never mentioned when and where they might have met up, even at sites he was showing her, and neither did Savannah."

Wright seemed to be bouncing back and forth regarding what could be privileged information. What was he trying to do—convince Grayson that Savannah was guilty without getting into anything she might have discussed directly with him?

"Then please tell me all you know about Schuyler Wells. Since you've spoken with him, maybe he told you, or hinted about, some of the places he and Savannah allegedly got together."

"I don't know anything!" Wright was standing now, and seemed to be shaking. He appeared more than nervous.

Was he hiding what he knew, not only about the nonexistence of Savannah's affair with Wells—but also about whether Zane remained alive?

Was he representing his client adequately? Even if he was on Zane's side, could Zane or Wells be blackmailing him into making things worse? Could Wright even be withholding evidence he knew that would get his client off? Failing to file motions that could help her? Anything else?

Hell, Grayson knew his imagination was running wild—maybe because he was searching for ways to get Savannah vindicated fast and completely.

But he doubted he would learn any more right now.

"Okay," Grayson said. "I'll leave now. Here's my card." He reached into his pocket and drew one out, handing it to Wright, who acted as if it was covered with fatal bacteria. "Please contact me anytime you think of somewhere I should look to locate Ms. Oliver. Surely that's to your benefit, too, and hers. If you do your job well, you might even get her found innocent, but it'll be harder if she's spent a lot of time on the run. Even if she is innocent, she could look guiltier that way."

"Exactly." Wright let his breath out in a sigh. "And I understand you're just doing your job, too. For her benefit, I'll let you know if I think of anyplace she might have gone, though as I said, I don't know of any possible rendezvous points."

"Then maybe I should talk to Mr. Wells directly to see if he will give me that information. I'll let him know that I have spoken with you and that you suggested I contact him."

"Oh no. Don't do that." Wright's tone seemed almost frantic, but then he seemed to force himself to calm down. "I think it would be better if you just let him know why you're trying to find Ms. Oliver, since they were apparently at least close friends. And now, I hate to chase you out, but I am expecting an important phone call on another case and need to prepare for it."

Sure, he hates to chase me out, Grayson thought. But he said his goodbyes, said he would be in touch again—and watched Wright's face grow stony—then left.

Chapter 13

Grayson fought the urge to call Savannah as he got into his car. After meeting that awful attorney, he felt even more worried about her.

Sure, he could rush right out to the cabin and visit her, but what good would that do now? No, he had to act normally—or as normally as possible.

Since the quake, and the dinner with his siblings, he had been meaning to go to the hospital to visit his father. He'd received plenty of text messages from his siblings reminding him but no updates on Payne's condition.

Why not go now? He wouldn't stay long. And so Grayson drove to the Mustang Valley General Hospital, which wasn't far from the law office. He parked in the lot at the back and walked around the large, well-respected hospital to the front entrance.

And was surprised, and unhappy, to see Selina Barnes Colton there, walking toward the outside door in the wide hospital lobby.

Selina had been his father's second wife, disliked by all of Payne's kids and his current wife, Genevieve. She was on the board of directors of Colton Oil, nonetheless, and also its VP and PR director. From what Grayson understood, that was because his former stepmother was holding something over his father, but he didn't know what.

Grayson had an urge to leave. Or at least enter the hospital another way.

Selina saw him, approached the door where he stood, and came outside. He drew in his breath as he stood there.

Selina was a pretty woman, with long brown hair and blue eyes that always seemed to be amused. She had perfect cheekbones and a lovely chin, all touched up by attractive makeup, and her left ear and its earring were often exposed by her hairstyle.

Too bad her personality didn't match her looks.

"Well, Grayson, what a surprise. When was the last time you've been to the hospital to see your dad? He was shot in January, and now it's April."

He thought about making excuses, but why do that with her? "Not everything is done with the purpose of being recorded for posterity or on cameras, security or otherwise. I may not be viewed as a perfect son who visits often, but I think of my dad often and privately send him all my best thoughts." Or at least some. He might not adore his dad, but he certainly didn't want him to die.

Selina laughed. "How adorable. That sounds like hokum from that Affirmation Alliance Group. Those do-gooders are all over town spouting their positivity—and that makes me want to barf." She gestured across the street from the hospital. Sure enough, Grayson saw one of those Affirmation Alliance tables there, where two members sat. In front of them was a banner that said Displaced From The Earthquake and Need Assistance? Let Affirmation Alliance Group Help! There was even a line of three people waiting to talk to the men behind the table.

But Selina had started talking to him again. "Enough of that. And your being here? You know, Grayson, your dad figured before that you think he's a corrupt jerk, so why be fake and sit at his bedside and pretend to feel something you don't?"

He'd come here to see his dad, damn it, no matter what this woman said. He wanted to push past Selina and do what he'd set out to.

But he also recognized that Selina was right. He was being fake by coming here, and he'd be fake if he visited Payne and spouted platitudes his father probably couldn't hear.

It wasn't that he really hated his father. But he did hate how Payne had tried to make Grayson obey him even as an adult, rather than live his own life. Maybe things would be different if his mother had lived...but why even contemplate that now?

Without saying another word to her, he stalked away to return to his car—hating that Selina had won.

Once inside his car, he pondered what to do. Something to improve his state of mind, certainly.

As a result, he headed his SUV out of town toward the desert outside Mustang Valley, where Norah had said Chad brought Winch to look for the missing young man. Had they found him yet? Could Grayson help? Even just trying would make him feel better.

And help him forget this fiasco of an attempt to see his father.

As he drove along the main road that wound through the area, Grayson figured that without more information, he was unlikely to locate any of the searchers, let alone his employees. Of course, this was also the direction toward the town of Mountain Valley, and if he couldn't find the search group, he could at least spend a little time there looking for the items on Savannah's list.

Which would give him a better excuse to go visit her later than just to tell her what a jerk her lawyer seemed to be.

It didn't take long to get outside Mustang Valley and onto the road through the desert. Grayson became more determined to meet up with his first responder employee who was out there and see how things were going. He called Chad on his car phone system.

"Hey, Grayson." Chad answered immediately. "Can't talk. Looking for a young guy missing since the quake, and Winch just alerted on a scent."

"The kid's?"

"Yeah. His family thought he went in this direction, and some locals saw some footprints in this area earlier today, though they didn't lead to the kid."

"How do I find you?" Grayson quickly told Chad where he was and got directions—about ten miles ahead of him. "Thanks," he said but realized Chad had already hung up.

Grayson saw no additional cars out here—not until he reached the general area Chad had described. Several cop cars and an ambulance were parked there. Grayson parked, too, and got out.

He introduced himself to an officer standing beside his vehicle, staring into the distance. The area was mostly covered with sand and light patches of dirt, with quite a few cactus plants rising toward the blue sky that way, in the direction Grayson assumed Chad and Winch had gone.

Which turned out correct, according to that cop. And so, after putting on his sunglasses, Grayson rushed ahead.

In a few minutes he saw a small crowd ahead, some in uniform. He sped up to join them, then hurried to the front of that line.

Which was where Winch, at the end of the leash attached to the back of his K-9 vest, pulled Chad along behind him. Chad was holding a T-shirt, presumably one worn by the missing kid and provided by his family. One of K-9 Winch's skills was following a scent.

Chad saw Grayson then and motioned for him to catch up. "Looks good," he shouted.

In seconds, Winch found the missing kid he'd alerted on. Grayson couldn't believe his good luck—he'd happened to be there just at the right moment. The teen was sitting on the ground in the shadow of a cactus.

Seeing the dog, the young guy screamed and rose and stumbled toward Winch, throwing his arms around the dog's neck as he began crying. "Thank you, thank you," he managed between sobs. Thin and pale, he wore jeans and athletic shoes and a gray T-shirt, all of which appeared filthy and in bad condition—and no wonder. He'd apparently been wearing them for around three days out here with no food or water or shelter.

"You're Marty?" Chad asked.

"Yes. Yes, I am. I want to go home."

"Absolutely," Chad said, and Grayson noticed that a lot of the people who'd been back around the vehicles had now joined them, including an EMT who began examining the young man. Then there were a few people filming what was going on. Were they live on social media or just recording everything?

In any case, it didn't hurt to give First Hand a little publicity. They'd earned it, thanks to Chad and Winch. And since Chad was being kept away from Marty by those tending to his health, Grayson approached and held out his hand to his employee. "Great job, Chad. And Winchell." Grayson bent to pat the sitting, panting dog on the head between his pointed ears. He was glad Chad was wearing a First Hand shirt—a blue one—and he gestured toward it. "Our company, First Hand First Responders, is really proud of you." And Grayson was bold enough to smile at the cameras.

Chad laughed. "That's a bit over the top, boss—but you know we're both proud to be private first responders for your company. Aren't we, Winch?"

At his name, the dog looked up at him and gave a quick bark, causing nearly everyone around there to laugh as Chad stroked Winch's back.

Grayson had an urge to pat his human employee on the back and to let Chad know he'd get a bonus for this. He didn't do either…yet. But he would.

Grayson told Chad, "Go ahead and hang out here for a while in case more help or information is needed. I've got to run—but I can't tell you how glad I am that I saw Winch and you in action and doing so successfully."

"I can guess, boss." Chad aimed a salute his way, and Grayson, saluting back, turned to head toward his car.

Well, something, at least, had gone well that day. And now it was time for Grayson to start picking up those supplies for Savannah.

Savannah. If only he could help her reach as successful a conclusion as this.

But how? Getting her inept attorney into the media the way this had been picked up?

He just wished he had more answers—and could get them quickly.

Okay, Savannah thought. Patience. She needed patience.

She also needed to hear from Grayson.

It was late afternoon. Had he seen Ian Wright yet? If so, what did he think now about her lawyer?

When would she hear about it?

When would she see Grayson?

She was inside the cabin, going crazy as she usually did these days. Was Grayson at least getting her the disguise items she needed?

If not, she still had to get out of here, soon. Sitting at that darned table nibbling on apple chips that Grayson had brought wasn't doing her any good.

Neither was thinking about Zane, and why he was so angry with her that he'd decided to fake his own death so he could frame her for murder. They could have found a way to get along as time went on after their divorce, couldn't they?

Zane clearly didn't think so. And though Savannah thought he could have disappeared to someplace as far away as Bali, she wondered if he was instead hanging out around here to laugh at her.

Okay. There was one thing Grayson had brought that could at least get her mind occupied so she wouldn't feel so nuts.

Maybe.

She pulled the burner phone off its charger. Again. She was doing that a lot. She certainly hoped that Grayson continued to keep her well supplied with batteries for the charger.

What she needed to do now was figure out where to go from here and how to get there—notwithstanding whether Grayson actually came through with her disguise.

Too bad she couldn't just place an online order for what she needed. She preferred actually shopping in person, enjoying the outing, but she had used the internet for acquiring plenty of things before.

But even if she wanted to shop online, where could she have anything sent?

She needed to decide at last where to go.

Maybe to Phoenix—still in Arizona and not extremely far away.

Or Los Angeles—so big and crowded she could surely get lost there.

Or Mexico. It was just across the border from Arizona, after all. But just being in another country wouldn't solve her problems, especially since she didn't really know its language. And she didn't have the ID she would need to leave the United States.

Or—where else? New York City? Washington, DC? But how would she get there…or anywhere? And how could she live there on her own, with no money since she didn't dare to try to access any of her ample accounts? They had probably been frozen anyway, considering that she was accused of committing a murder and had even been denied bail.

No job. No identity she could use.

She sighed. Maybe looking at the news or some feature stories would help. Would she be able to learn how other fugitives got away—successfully?

She started her search this time at the local level. On her phone, she found a link to stream the news on the local affiliate of a national station. She turned up the sound on the phone and started looking.

And she immediately gasped aloud.

The story that came up wasn't at all what she was expecting. It couldn't be true. And yet, how could it not be?

With a photo in the background that seemed much too real, too familiar, and a banner at the bottom that said "Breaking News," the female newscaster with the solemn face was saying, "The police are not giving details yet, but the body of attorney Ian Wright was just discovered by his secretary inside his office building. More details to come. Ian Wright was representing murder suspect Savannah Oliver, now a fugitive. Although police have not publicly commented on potential suspects, we understand Oliver might be a suspect in this murder, as well."

Savannah sobbed as she closed the browser. She pushed the buttons on her phone to call Grayson, whether that was smart or not.

He answered right away. "Hell. You heard?"

"Yes," she managed to say. "Had you met…had you seen Ian?"

"Yeah, I did. I'll tell you about it later. Right now—well, stay where you are. I'll see you soon."

And then he was gone—when she perhaps needed to talk to him most.

He'd seen Ian. Talked with him.

Murdered him? Surely not. Why would he?

But the only thing Savannah could be sure of was that she hadn't been the one to kill Ian.

Damn.

He had just stopped making calls and turned on the car radio, driving along one of the nicer, four-lane downtown streets in Mountain Valley, from a discount store to a more posh one a couple of blocks away. Grayson had earlier bought some of the disguise makeup that Savannah had asked for, as well as a few other supplies like batteries. When he heard about Ian Wright on the radio, he nearly drove into a car parked along the curb.

Which was when Savannah had called. He pulled over and answered immediately, wishing he was with her to comfort her.

What the hell had happened? When he had left Ian, the attorney looked nervous yet had definitely been in lawyer mode. He'd done whatever he had to do to get Grayson out of his presence.

But he had definitely been breathing. And Grayson might have been the last person to see Ian alive. Except for his murderer.

Apparently the SOB had been shot—but who had done it?

Savannah had sounded scared on the phone, and no wonder. The media probably didn't know all the details yet but the reports indicated that Wright's cause of death was gunshot wounds. Whether or not the cops had suspects in mind, the media had taken no time to latch onto Savannah as their prime suspect. Even though she presumably had an alibi—being at the cabin—for this period of time, which they wouldn't know.

That was logical. Grayson admitted it to himself. Savannah theoretically could be mad at her lawyer for not getting her out on bail or clearing her name.

Grayson had wanted to keep talking with Savannah now but knew that wasn't a good idea. Instead, after ending their call, he continued to listen to the news as he drove toward the fishing cabin.

Even though no one was likely to be aware he had any connection to Savannah or Ian other than having found the van and visited Ian, Grayson recognized he could be under some kind of official surveillance regardless, as a result of those events. Or unofficial surveillance by Zane or his cronies attempting to frame Savannah.

And so, again he took a circuitous route to the cabin, keeping an eye out for anyone behind him. He even looked up to see if someone might be overhead in a helicopter or following him with a drone, since the authorities might be even more inclined now to be conducting a search for Savannah.

It might make them look bad if they didn't.

But Grayson had to continue to act normal, or at least appear that way.

Through the city streets he drove, going the speed limit while wanting to race. Into the suburbs, then along a road circling the town and back toward Mustang Valley. But instead of heading into town he aimed his car to the back roads that had been affected by the quake—out toward the fishing area and the cabins abutting parts of it.

All the time watching out for anyone following.

He shut off the news and called Chad, again congratulating Winch and him. Then he called Pedro to hear about the vehicle fire he had helped to put out, the drivers and passengers he had helped to save, along with the town firefighters and EMTs.

Finally he called Norah at the office and calmly discussed with her the successes of the others that day—and thanked her for being the backup in charge.

"I guess no one's in big trouble today," she said, "or I'd have been called out as an EMT, too, to help save a life or two."

He heard the humor in her voice and said, "Or three or four. Well, wait for it. You're always on call, you know, like the rest of us. And you always do your job well."

"Like you, boss," she countered.

He hoped so. But if the world knew what he was up to right now, who he was trying to help—well, his company would be in big trouble

He soon hung up from that call, too, and continued driving slowly, carefully, along the narrow and uneven road into the wilderness that had come to mean a lot more to him these days than it had when it simply contained old fishing cabins, trees and wildlife.

Now, it contained a woman on whom he had bet his life, his ongoing existence, in a way. And despite how absurd, how dangerous, it might be, he was glad.

He had come to really believe in Savannah. To care for her. To cherish those kisses they'd shared and hope for more. A lot more.

Well, hell. All he had to do was figure out the best way to exonerate her from all accusations against her. Clear her of two murders—one of which might not even have occurred, according to her.

And the other?

The sky was growing darker along this remote road; he occasionally saw another car going the other direction. He was nearing the cabin. He would soon see Savannah—and prove to himself that she was indeed there and could not have buzzed, carless, into town, murdered her attorney and returned to eventually cry on his shoulder.

Right?

What was he doing? Why was he risking so much to help this woman? Why did he believe in her and her innocence, despite there apparently being plenty of evidence against her?

Well, heck. He hated to admit, even to himself, that he was attracted to her...despite himself. For now. But he would slough that off soon, when he no longer needed to do things for her.

There. He had reached the turnoff to the cabin. He slowed to make sure he saw no one nearby, then drove in that direction.

He soon parked beside the cabin. He didn't see Savannah outside, at least. Was she inside? Was she hiding?

Was she okay?

He realized he needed to stay calm and act certain that all would be well, or he would just make things worse for her. She must be freaked out, justifiably so.

Well, as far as he was concerned, another glitch had occurred that they would need to deal with, but life would just go on and they would find a way to fix things for Savannah.

He had to. His mind leapt to why he had become a first responder in the first place, how he hadn't been able to help his friend Philip Prokol, who'd come home from military service with PTSD, which had killed him.

Well, nothing like that would happen to Savannah. Grayson would help her. Somehow.

He got out of his car and pulled out from the trunk a couple of bags of things he had bought for her.

Then he went to the cabin's front door. It was locked—a good thing. He knocked.

"Yes?" called a familiar voice from inside. Or was it familiar? He had heard Savannah in distress before, but the quiver in her tone and higher pitch suggested she truly felt tormented now.

"It's your deliveryman Grayson, Savannah," he called out, keeping his tone light.

The door opened immediately. Savannah appeared as anxious as he had imagined, her face ashen, her lips straight and tight. "Come in," she managed to say, and as soon as he was inside she closed the door behind him and locked it.

He looked down at her in the light from the lanterns, holding out a few bags.

She didn't reach for them. Instead, she headed for that same old table and sat down.

And put her face in her hands. "What am I going to do, Grayson?" Her voice was a wail—although a sweet, despairing one.

He wished he had an answer for her. A good answer.

For now, he placed the bags on the table in front of her and reached down, encouraging her to stand again.

Which she did. And again looked up at him. Her eyes sought his. Her mouth opened slightly—as she reached out at the same time he reached for her.

Their kiss was soft at first, as he attempted to use the contact to reassure her physically.

But then it began heating up, their contact growing fiercer. He felt her arms pull him closer as his did the same. He allowed his hands to range along her back, touching her buttocks, then released her slightly so he could reach between them and feel her wonderfully firm breasts.

He grew harder, even as Savannah pushed her body against his even more. She clasped him tightly to her, then moved enough so she could first grasp his butt, too, then move her hand forward to touch his erection as their kiss became hot and all-encompassing. He couldn't think of anything else but her.

Except—

"Please, Grayson," Savannah said, stepping back only enough to start unbuttoning his shirt.

So what could he do but do the same with hers, while leading her toward the cabin's bed?

Chapter 14

This was such a bad idea. A stupid idea. And yet Savannah wanted it, wanted Grayson, more than anything else at this moment.

No, it wouldn't last long, but for now all she needed to think about was how being near him this way set her body ablaze with desire. Concentrating on what was here and now and not happening anyplace else, whether or not it concerned her.

She had tamped down her interest in him from the moment he had arrived at this cabin. It had seemed so inappropriate. It didn't matter that he was the only person she could communicate with in her current, small world. That wasn't the sole reason she found him attractive.

She had forced herself before to ignore any interest in him, or at least keep it deep inside.

No longer.

"Are you sure, Savannah?" Grayson's voice was raspy, totally sexy in tone and it stoked her desire even more, even as she considered her answer to him.

"Yes," she said with no hesitation.

Would this wind up being the last good memory she had of freedom before she was caught again?

Would it be the beginning of something new and wonderful?

Or would it be a huge mistake? After all she had gone through, she still had no intention of getting involved in the long term with Grayson or any other man, no matter what the circumstances were now…or later.

But she needed this.

She needed him and what he could do for her at this moment.

And she would do all she could to reciprocate.

They were sitting on the bed now, on top of the sheets. As soon as she pulled his shirt off, he did the same with hers. At the same time she gazed at his muscular chest, she rejoiced in his hot stare on her breasts and wished she wasn't wearing a bra.

That wish immediately came true as he reached around her, hugging her close but only for an instant as he unhooked her bra and drew it off.

She trembled in anticipation as he drew in his breath, looking at her as she felt her nipples grow taut—until he reached for her, bringing her close to him once more as he dipped his head to kiss and suckle those sensitive tips.

They weren't the only part of her that reacted to him now, but she wanted to see him, feel him, before she bared the rest of herself. She reached toward his pants, intending to maneuver him as he sat facing her and pull his clothes down, but instead connected with his erection again. She rubbed at the fabric outside it with the heel of her palm, then grasped at it—as Grayson pulled back.

"Oh," Savannah said.

But the delay was only for an instant as Grayson used it to pull down his dark slacks and the shorts beneath them.

His thick, enticing shaft was revealed, causing Savannah to reach for her own pants. She had help as she pulled them down and pushed them away.

"Grayson," she gasped aloud as he began stroking her, moving from her breasts slowly downward as he again kissed her mouth.

His fingers were hot, probing, magnetic, exciting her even more—especially when he reached her hottest, most female area and explored it with his touch, his grasp. Those fingers were long and thick and utterly engaging, and when Savannah felt one, then two, inside her, she began to writhe, to beg internally for more.

For everything from him.

For that amazing erection of his inside her, pumping and—

Suddenly he pulled away again, farther this time, and she felt like crying—and demanding more at the same time.

Was that it? Would he be the one to regain sanity and call this off?

"What—" she began, and heard him give a short chuckle that was somehow also sexy.

"Hey," he said softly, rolling over and reaching for his pants, which were now on the floor at the side of the bed. "I'm a first responder. I come prepared."

In moments Savannah understood. He had pulled his wallet from a pocket and removed a condom from inside it.

Her turn to laugh. "I should have expected that from you." This man anticipated everything.

Maybe.

Before he could unwrap the package, she pushed him back on the bed until he lay there, fully exposed. She bent over until she could take him, still unsheathed, into her mouth—and enjoy his heated groan. She continued playing him, but not for long.

This time, he was the one to roll her over, positioning her on the bed till she lay beneath him—and he had the freedom now to wrap himself in that condom, then press the head of his erection exactly where it belonged.

Savannah drew in her breath as he entered her. It stung just a little until her body stretched to take him in, since he was so large and she hadn't engaged in this kind of experience for a long time. But the discomfort faded quickly. She wanted him. Now. She moved her hips to encourage him, and in moments he was pumping inside her and she was matching his eager motions with her own.

Please let this last, she begged silently, even as she knew it couldn't. For now, she would enjoy and appreciate every moment of it.

This was what she wanted.

This was here and now.

And it was all she could and would think about.

But much too soon she reached the critical, wonderful climax, even as Grayson, too, moaned and stopped moving. She managed to open her eyes enough to see that his remained closed, but that gorgeous body of his had risen somewhat and she could see the tension in it as he, too, came.

"Wow," he said as he gently lay down partly on her and partly beside her.

"Wow," she agreed, reaching to hold him tightly against her.

Wishing this moment could stay just like this—forever.

This had not been the reason Grayson rushed to the cabin this evening. In fact, it hadn't even been on his mind when he had headed here. Or at least as nothing more than a whimsy at the back of his mind that he'd never thought would come true.

But it had happened. He had helped to initiate it, had kept it going, and now they were lying in bed together.

Did he regret it? No way. Savannah was quite a woman. She had impressed him before with her attitude in a situation that appeared no-win for her—at least not without his help.

And so far, he hadn't really helped her.

But he still believed in her. Although he couldn't allow a miraculous bout of sex to swing his beliefs beyond what was logical as reality.

Still…

Bad idea, maybe, but he certainly had enjoyed it.

Wanted more, though not right now.

He would need to be careful, though. Sex could lead to long-term relationships if one wasn't careful.

Long-term relationships could lead to nothing but trouble. He'd seen that in so many other people that he had minimized getting too involved with anyone. His own recent failed relationship had been short-term. He was a first responder, but that didn't mean responding too deeply, too long, to a woman who attracted him.

Now Savannah was breathing deeply beside him, her head pressed against his chest.

Neither had donned any clothes, although they now were under the sheet. It was growing a little cooler—but he hardly recognized that, thanks to their combined body heat.

It was late now, dark outside.

He moved slightly, though his intention was to stay the night. Not for more sex, but to try to be there for Savannah during this difficult time.

Okay, he had come to care for her. Maybe too much.

On the other hand, it would probably be better for both of them if he left and pursued further leads.

And maybe got the rest of the disguises he had promised Savannah.

What else could he do to help her?

What—

"Grayson? Are you awake?" Savannah was moving now beside him, though she still remained close against him.

Which caused a certain part of him to react, despite how busy it had already been that evening.

"Yes," he said in response to her question.

"I—as much as I've enjoyed our time together, I'm worried again. Still. I—I can't just stay here and wait and maybe be found this time. Did you get any of the things we discussed?"

"Some, but—well, I heard about what happened to Wright while I was shopping and just headed here. I figured you might need the company." And he needed to see her, too, out of his caring for her, his concern for her.

"Thank you." Her voice sounded low. Humble, even. He turned to pull her tightly into his arms as they remained lying there. Her body heat, and the feel of her flesh against him once more, turned him on again.

But what they had done before, as wonderful as it was, had been somewhat inappropriate. He realized that adding to it now would only be more so—and they needed to focus on her case, not their chemistry.

"Hey," he said. "Let's get up and have some of that wonderful food I brought tonight and I'll show you what disguise stuff I've already bought. And then—well, we can talk about what comes next."

Grayson had some ideas about what should come next—but wished he could just whisk Savannah out of this place and…

Hey. He did know of someplace he could potentially move her if necessary.

More to think about, more to discuss, he thought.

"Sounds good," was Savannah's reply. Sadly, but not unexpectedly, she moved away from him and got out of bed on the other side.

And started pulling her clothes on. So of course he did the same.

After leaving the bed, they ate dinner. It consisted mostly of a couple of sandwiches already put together and purchased in town by Grayson—roast beef, pretty good. She enjoyed hers.

She enjoyed the company even more.

Her mind kept hopping back into bed with him, though they had put that behind them, at least for now.

And every time her thoughts started back on what had happened that day in town, what the possible consequences to her might be, she forced them back on the good things that had happened today instead.

Or at least she tried to.

Once they'd finished their meal, Grayson went back out to his car for some additional bags, which he handed her. "Sorry, not everything is there since I didn't have time to get it," he said, "but you can start working on your disguise with this stuff. I'll try to find the rest tomorrow."

Which meant he would leave tonight, of course. She would be alone again—with her thoughts.

She could handle it. She had to.

Forcing herself not to think about that, she looked inside the bags, took some contents out and laid them on the table. They included a lot of the eye makeup she had asked for but not all of it. Nor were the cream and foundation there.

"I think I'll wait right now to see if you are able to get the rest before I start experimenting," she told Grayson, although if this was all she acquired, she would make the best of it.

"I want to get some of the clothes you mentioned, too—the droopy, casual kind of things that you've likely never worn before—but no one you know is likely to recognize you in."

"Right," she said. "After all, I'm a society girl and always looked that way." She shrugged. That was the truth, after all. She figured her casual clothing generally cost more than a lot of women's dressiest stuff did. She'd sometimes wondered if she should start dressing "normally" but was glad now she hadn't.

Not when she didn't want anyone to know who she was. Except Grayson.

Grayson. Was she trusting him too much? She certainly was relying on him a lot. But what else could she do—at least for now?

After she went through the things he had brought, they jokingly discussed it, trading ideas on how she could change her appearance the way actors were changed—into zombies or superheroes or gorillas or anything other than who they were.

Their discussion morphed into the kinds of TV shows and

movies they were fondest of. "So what do you think I like best on television?" she asked him.

"Sitcoms," he said decisively, and he was right—but that wasn't all.

"Add news specials to that," she said. "And some talk shows, depending on the host."

"Got it."

She told him more. In theaters, her favorites were romantic comedies, even though she knew they were all fiction, especially the ones where the main characters fell in love and anticipated, at the end, a happily-ever-after.

A happy few minutes, maybe, or a few days. Or even a year. But she'd married a guy she believed she loved, and who claimed to love her. And what had she gotten? A torment-ever-after, as long as they were together. Once they were divorced, she had assumed that would be the end of thinking about Zane and his infidelity and everything else about him.

And it was, for a brief time. Until he'd framed her for his murder, probably just to get even with her for divorcing him.

But she didn't want to think about that now.

As Grayson probed for her likes and dislikes, she turned the tables on him. She wasn't surprised that he liked cop shows and superheroes, and he didn't even mention shows with romance in them.

Which was as she'd anticipated. Sex was one thing. Staying together? That wasn't on his agenda either, she felt certain. All the more reason to just enjoy his company—and maybe his body, too, again sometime. Meanwhile, she would hope he continued to help her as long as she was unable to help herself.

And expect he would soon be gone from her life one way or another. With luck, by then she would be free and exonerated.

But until she could find out how to clear herself, the burden of potentially being convicted of Zane's murder—and now Ian's—was hanging over her head.

Their conversation wound down. Savannah tried to figure out something else to talk about, but she was actually getting tired.

Not that she would mention that to Grayson.

She didn't want to encourage him to leave. She liked his company too much.

She needed his company, someone to talk to and to help her feel a good ending to all of this could—would—occur.

Not that they were discussing any of that. Not now.

But she wasn't surprised when Grayson stood up. "It's getting late," he said.

All she could do at first was nod and look in his direction without meeting his gaze. "Yes, it is," she finally agreed.

"I think we need some sleep, don't you?"

"Yes," she said again, feeling a bit puzzled. Why hadn't he said he was about to head home?

He must have seen something in her expression that concerned him, for he sat back down again. "I mean, let's head to bed here, okay? Together—and I'm not talking about having fun to keep us awake again. Not now. But I can sleep here, stay till tomorrow morning. I'll go back to town then, to my office, and get some work done. And find out how other things are going in town, too."

"Like the investigation into the latest murder," Savannah said, not making it a question. He—they—could find out more tonight, she realized, on their phones.

Not that they were likely to learn that way the motive for someone to have killed Ian. She assumed it had been Zane or Schuyler, but why?

And maybe they should, or at least she should, learn all she could to make sure that potential number one suspect—her—hadn't been discovered here in this cabin.

Although if she had been, there'd be some activity outside, and probably inside, too.

"That's right," Grayson agreed. "I'll determine what else

we need to do, then head to another town to finish picking up your disguise materials. And come back here with it. Okay?"

"Sounds good," she responded as casually as she could, but her insides almost melted in relief. Although she recognized she couldn't, shouldn't, count on anything, not even his return as promised, until it happened.

But oh, how she hoped he was serious. Because her latest problem was that she was becoming much too serious about him.

"So, let's go to bed now, shall we?"

"Yes," she said, "Let's."

Grayson joined her in bed soon after, and drew close enough to her to put his arm around her.

She turned, snuggling against him.

They shared a wonderful good-night kiss, and although Savannah felt her body churn a bit in lust again, she didn't pursue it. Sleep sounded like a good idea.

Tomorrow could be a big day—even if she remained stuck here for all or part of the day.

"Good night, Grayson," she whispered against him.

"Good night." She felt him kiss the top of her head.

And hoped that wouldn't be the last time, either tonight or on future nights together.

Though she knew better than to count on that to count on anything,

Even regarding the wonderful Grayson.

Chapter 15

Grayson didn't fall asleep for a long time, and judging by her breathing, neither did Savannah. But it felt good, really good, to hold her like this with no current worries menacing them.

Wouldn't it be great if this was the beginning of some real time together? A future they shared.

Yeah, right. He recognized that he was beginning to care for her too much. Once the danger to her was over, so would any chance of a relationship between them. Which was for the best.

And that danger? When he had gone into the bathroom earlier to prepare for bed, he had brought his cell phone and checked for updates on Ian Wright's murder.

The media seemed to be having great fun with the idea that it was a follow-up to Zane Oliver's murder. They suggested that since the poor, hard-working, by-the-book attorney had failed to get his client out on bail for that killing, Savannah would have wanted revenge on him, too. Or so the various stories mostly asserted.

Grayson had seen that kind of hype and accusation before, of course. He would look into it more tomorrow when he was no longer here—and would also do further checking into the status of the murder investigation with his professional contacts.

And now…

Now, finally, he felt his body relaxing enough to let him drift into sleep. He concentrated on the feel of Savannah against him once more before he allowed himself to drop off.

"Sorry I don't have anything more exciting for breakfast than an English muffin and jam," Savannah said to Grayson the next morning. He was going to leave soon. She knew it.

And he would also be back. He had told her so. He had been reliable—and more—so far, so she believed him. Or at least wanted to. But how long could he help her without someone noticing his trips to the cabin?

She knew better than to assume that them being together in such a special manner last night would happen again.

But, oh, how she had enjoyed it.

And couldn't recall ever feeling that close to Zane.

"Sorry I didn't bring anything more exciting for breakfast than English muffins and jam," Grayson countered, and they both laughed.

What would she do today after he left, Savannah wondered.

For now—

For now, she ate slowly, not being especially hungry but knowing she needed to get something down. She mostly watched Grayson, who wolfed down his muffin enthusiastically—also watching her as he did so, as if attempting to set an example so she would eat more, too.

She didn't, though she appreciated his apparent concern. She simply wasn't hungry. Especially knowing he would be leaving soon. And would he be back to stay with her that night? She certainly couldn't count on it.

"Hey," he finally said. "The sooner I leave here, the sooner I can get back with the rest of the things you asked for."

"Right," she said, attempting to sound pleased. The sooner

he left, the sooner she would once more be alone here with her thoughts, and for how long?

They would undoubtedly be worse now. She'd assumed the cops were looking for her when she'd fled the destroyed van, but then they also had things to do regarding the earthquake. But now, if they actually believed she had killed Ian, they might focus more on finding her.

"Hey," Grayson said. "I have an idea. I already brought more batteries, although I probably should get even more to make sure your phone charger remains usable."

"Right," Savannah said, not sure where this was going.

"I'll leave you some additional paper, too, that I have in the car. I'll find you a small but powerful tablet computer, too, if it looks like you'll be here much longer. Although—" He hesitated, and Savannah figured he was weighing the pros and cons of her remaining in the cabin while the authorities might ramp up their search for her. He clearly was aware of that possibility, too. "Anyway, taking notes on paper should work okay for now. Here's what I'd like you to do."

It turned out that he wanted to start a website chronicling first responders' achievements, both his employees' and others'. Their actions would be described in detail so other members of the public could learn more. He wanted to explain what they did, why they were important and what went into the certification process.

"I don't want accolades for myself or my company, but I want to inform the public so they'll know who to call and when, and what to expect. And maybe contribute money to the public emergency departments to help them increase their first responder involvement. But I haven't had time to even start researching what would need to go into this kind of project," he finished. "You have some time, at least for now. I would really appreciate it if you'd start it for me."

Savannah liked the idea. A lot.

Spending her time compiling achievements by first responders, how they jumped in and saved endangered lives, put out fires, and more?

Oh yes.

Including him, but he'd said he didn't want to applaud First Hand.

She hadn't thought much about first responders until the earthquake—and meeting Grayson. Now, she was highly impressed by them, by him, and would love to learn more. And help him.

And have something to do besides sit here and stew over what her life had become—and what would happen to it in the future.

"Yes!" she exclaimed. "I'd love to start your research." She didn't bother reminding him that it might be a pipe dream she would never be able to accomplish, thanks to what was going on with her.

She had to remain optimistic. She *would* remain optimistic. And a lot of that was because of Grayson, and all he was doing for her. At least she could pay him back just a little this way. Plus, maybe she could come up with additional ideas for helping first responders achieve even more.

"Excellent." He pulled his phone out of his pocket and looked at it. "Time for me to go. But I'll see you later."

He rose and approached Savannah rather than heading straight to the door. She stood, too, and quickly found herself in his arms.

Their kiss was quick but hot and seemed to promise more. Or at least she hoped so.

But she knew better than to count on anything right now.

Even Grayson.

She would wait here for him, though. At least for today.

First things first. Grayson took a long detour, all the way to Tucson, fifty miles away from Mustang Valley. But it was early and traffic wasn't bad—and no one there knew him.

He checked his surroundings a lot, though, in case he was

being followed, unlikely as that was. Still, his paranoia wasn't a bad thing since he was aiding an escaped prisoner. And he had a lot of experience and knowledge about how to spot anyone who oughtn't be there.

He used his car phone system to check in at the office. He told Norah, who answered his call, that he was engaged in some promotional work in nearby towns. She sounded happy because she had an assignment that day working with some high school kids who wanted to learn more about being first responders. The school system had hired First Hand to present a program to a club for teens who were interested in future medical careers at Mustang Valley General Hospital. Chad and Winch would come along for a short while, too, and Pedro would most likely stay in the office attending to calls and whatever else needed to be done—unless a call came in. Or more aftershocks occurred.

"Thanks," Grayson said to Norah before hanging up, meaning it. He loved owning the company, being in charge—and having such skilled and dedicated employees at his back. And what Norah was doing would be a great addition to the website he planned to work on with Savannah.

Finally reaching Tucson, he visited several shops, high-end makeup, low-end clothing and more, just to be sure he was getting the right stuff and not forgetting anything. This time, he would bring everything else Savannah had asked for, plus several versions of some things like items of clothing and slightly different colors and quality of makeup.

He also found a tablet computer for Savannah, assuming she remained interested and hung out at the cabin enough to work on his project. He needed help, she needed something to do. It all seemed perfect for the moment, assuming Savannah remained free.

When he was finished, he secured it all in the back of his SUV in a crate installed there for carrying any equipment needed on the job. No one would be able to see its contents.

He'd been pondering how to look into the investigation into

Ian Wright's murder and decided to visit the Mustang Valley police station when he returned to town. He'd been seen in Wright's office, after all, so it shouldn't be too over the top for him to express interest in what happened.

He hoped that his usual primary contact, Senior Detective PJ Doherty, was there. Grayson felt more comfortable asking PJ questions than any of the other cops, even his distant cousin Spencer, although Grayson knew most of the pros respected him there. He decided to call PJ to check on his availability and was glad when his friend answered.

"Yeah, I'm here, and unless something comes up I should be around when you get here," PJ said. "No first responder stuff going on at the moment that I know of, but I suspect I know what you want to talk about."

"I suspect you do, too," Grayson said. Of course PJ knew he'd found the destroyed vehicle and dead driver, and therefore might have a continuing interest in the escaped prisoner who was being transported. That same escapee who was in the news once more.

It took Grayson longer to get back to Mustang Valley than it had been to drive to Tucson, thanks to midday traffic, but he soon parked in a lot near the police station. No problem walking to the one-story brick building on Mustang Boulevard. Cops in dark blue uniforms filled the lobby area, a few talking to visiting citizens. Grayson stepped up to the front desk and asked the officer there to let PJ know he was there. "He's expecting me."

The cop got on the desk phone and in moments PJ came out, dressed in uniform. "Let's go out for some coffee," he told Grayson. A chain coffee shop was within easy walking distance, and they headed that way along the sidewalk.

PJ was tall, a few years younger than Grayson. He had blond hair and blue eyes and kept glancing toward Grayson almost impishly, as if he was trying to read his mind. They'd talked a few times since the earthquake but this was the first time they'd gotten together.

"Okay, what do you want?" PJ finally asked after they entered the shop. They sat down at a small round table near the door after getting their drinks.

"All that stuff in the news about the murder of Ian Wright. Has anyone mentioned I went to see the guy yesterday?"

"Yeah, we heard about that. What did you talk about?" PJ's eyes narrowed a bit as if he was working even harder at mind reading.

Grayson knew he would need to be careful. "Well, I understood the guy represented Savannah Oliver, that prisoner who escaped from the van I found after the earthquake. I don't have any professional reason to be interested."

Despite what he had told Wright, PJ would definitely know that Grayson hadn't been hired by the police department to help find the woman.

Grayson continued. "But I feel a connection anyway. I talked to him about his representing her, what he could tell me that wasn't attorney-client privileged, which wasn't much. I still got the impression he thought his client could be guilty. And now I've heard on the news that Savannah Oliver is a suspect in his murder, too. Logical, I guess—but is that true?"

"You know we don't talk publicly about ongoing investigations for a while, till we believe we have sufficient evidence for a conviction and all, and we don't talk about that evidence much, either. And we certainly don't have need for a first responder in this situation. But hell, I can understand your interest, even though it's remote. You could have found that woman in the van. Even been attacked by her if she'd been there. And now you do have a sort-of connection with her next victim."

Grayson forced himself not to object to PJ's assumption, but the detective must have seen some kind of reaction on his face and held up his hand.

"Okay, she's only an alleged killer in both cases. But…look, my friend, can I trust you to keep a secret about the evidence we found?"

"Of course." Grayson forced himself to stay calm and not push PJ to talk more and faster. What secret?

"We haven't revealed much to the media, but in case you're interested, Mr. Wright was found with two gunshot wounds to the head, definitely not self-inflicted. Not sure why others in his building didn't hear it, but the walls at his upstairs office were soundproofed. The weapon wasn't left there, either. But something else was."

Grayson wanted to shake it out of PJ, whose tone and teasing expression suggested that was what he wanted Grayson to do.

"You going to tell me, or do I have to wait till I see it on TV eventually?" Grayson kept his tone cool and calm as he grinned as wryly as he could toward his friend. "So why do you think she put those gunshot wounds into her lawyer's head?"

"Because," PJ chortled triumphantly, "he didn't get her off the charges against her right away, didn't succeed in even getting her bail. I've seen photos of her." Not anymore, Grayson thought, but didn't say so. "And we know she kept her long hair pulled back into those decorative clips some women wear. Because—" he said again.

"Because?" Grayson prompted.

"Because it must have fallen out of her hair at the latest crime scene. Maybe Wright and she fought for a while before she shot him, or maybe she was just careless. But one of those clips was found under Wright's desk, a pretty thing made of what I was told is called tortoiseshell plastic—and it had initials on it."

"Let me guess," Grayson said, his hopes falling. It was a setup, sure. But it seemed to be working. "Were those initials SO?"

"SMO," PJ contradicted. "Including her maiden name."

Grayson's head was spinning. Savannah was being framed—again. Her ex? Probably. But since he couldn't show up in town there had to be someone else. Wells? That was more likely.

What could Grayson do to protect her? To put the cops on the right trail?

He didn't know.

"Very interesting," he said to PJ, trying to sound somewhat excited. "So you really do have a viable suspect." Should he suggest that the clip could have been planted?

No. That might give away whose side he was on.

"Yep, we do," PJ said. "Still don't know where she is, though. But we're putting together a bigger task force to search for her. Maybe she's still hiding out in the woods near where the van went down. Meanwhile, we're out there. Expanding our search. And we'll find her."

That was what Grayson was afraid of.

"And good thing we're together now," PJ said. "We'd intended to contact you to interview you about your meeting with Wright. Can you come to the station when we're done here? From what we have found so far, you were one of the last people to see him alive."

"Sure," Grayson said, his heart sinking. Well, he wouldn't have anything helpful to say. "And after we're done, I'd appreciate it if you would keep me informed about your investigation as much as you can. I'm interested, especially since Wright was killed so soon after I saw him. And if you need a first responder or two or three in your investigation, be sure to let me know."

Chapter 16

"What do you mean, we're leaving?" Savannah demanded.

It was late afternoon. Grayson had just returned to the cabin and said he'd brought everything else she'd requested, and more.

But he was acting strange. His expression was worried. Very worried.

And that worried Savannah.

Of course she was more than emotionally ready to leave this place. But practically?

Where could she go?

She hadn't changed her appearance yet, so she would most likely be too identifiable to go nearly anywhere.

Even so, since he was pushing this, Grayson had to have someplace in mind.

"Look, everything's probably fine," he said, "but I do know they're looking for you in earnest right now."

Savannah felt herself both stiffen and shudder, looking at Grayson's face. Its features were the same, utterly handsome and appealing—except for the unnatural frown.

"Who is looking?" But of course she knew.

"The police. I'll explain shortly. But right now, go ahead and change into one of the new outfits, including the shoes I brought."

He'd shown her some athletic shoes that looked pretty inexpensive, unlike anything she would have chosen for herself before.

He had also brought her some cheap-looking T-shirts and other tops and jeans, nothing anyone who knew her would expect her to wear, which was perfect.

He had just brought her some hair dye, too, but she hadn't had time to use it.

But how did he know the police were after her right now? Not that it should be a big surprise.

And if they were, did she dare leave here? Or were they more likely to find her here than someplace else?

Grayson seemed to have taken charge—again. Was he truly on her side? He still appeared to be, but how could she be certain?

Well, she didn't have much choice if he believed the cops might come looking for her here.

And at least she might get an opportunity to run.

She closed herself in the bathroom and did as he directed. She changed clothes and modified her makeup, adding eye shadow, eyeliner and mascara, although she didn't try aging herself. She also practiced slumping, especially her shoulders, since most women she'd associated with from successful families walked and talked like models, with gentle waves of their hands.

Not that she felt certain how people of a lesser public status held themselves, but she would give it a try. In addition, she forced herself to practice walking in a way that stuck her stomach out more than usual. She felt highly uncomfortable, not so much physically as mentally. This wasn't her—yet it was, for now.

In a short while, she exited the bathroom with her new clothes and less prideful demeanor. She tilted her head slightly and looked up sadly and uncomfortably toward Grayson.

"Hello, Mr. Colton," she said, making her voice rasp. "Do you know who I am?"

He smiled at her. "If I didn't know, I definitely wouldn't recognize you now. Great job, Savannah! Now let's go."

Though Grayson doubted anyone would recognize Savannah the way she looked now, he couldn't be sure. As a result, after they quickly cleaned the cabin to make it look as close as possible to how it had when Savannah moved in, leaving no extra food but replenishing the water bottles, he had her lie down on the back seat of his car.

He hadn't bought her a hat, though maybe he should have for when—if—they were out somewhere with other people around. Later. But he did have a baseball cap in the back of his car—fortunately not one branded with the First Hand logo, but a gray one that just said Mustang Valley. He handed it to her to put on eventually and at least partially shield her face.

He explained their destination to Savannah as he drove as far as he could beyond the lake area where the cabin was, twisting his way through the forest in the direction of his family ranch. He'd decided that, first and foremost, he needed to get her out of there. If the cops did a better job of fanning out from the location where the van had been destroyed, they could easily wind up near the lake—and its nearby cabins.

He drove toward the bunker he had found ages ago as a kid and used as his refuge, to hide from the family when he could. Even when he was younger, he'd needed time and a place away from his sometimes overbearing and controlling family.

And now, he had visited the bunker briefly after the earthquake to ensure that it remained undamaged and no one had been caught there.

"Here's what's going on," he said to Savannah. He told her first about his conversation with his buddy Detective Doherty.

"The cops have what they believe is good evidence—a concrete reason to put you at the top of their suspect list, Savannah."

"What?" she demanded, her voice muffled from the back seat.

Grayson wished he could watch her as he spoke, hold her in his arms to comfort her as much as possible. He could imagine the frightened expression on her beautiful face anyway. But he'd been a bit spooked and his mind had gone in many ugly directions while he drove back to the cabin.

The bunker should be a safer hideout. Even though a lot of people knew about the many abandoned mineshafts in the area, no one else to his knowledge was ever aware he'd used that one.

"I'll tell you soon," he said. He wanted to soothe her as he told her the situation as he knew it—and his further fears about it. He wanted to hold her tight, and not just to protect her, although that was most important at the moment. But later? He could imagine their making use of the bunker to engage in more of the wonderful sex they had already experienced. He didn't know how things would be in the future, but he definitely craved keeping Savannah in his life.

A few cars passed on the remote street until he turned off and headed down a dirt road beyond the Rattlesnake Ridge Ranch, between it and other ranches. He drove as far as he could into a grove of trees near the side of a fair-sized hill and parked behind bushes that obscured his vehicle.

He got out of the car and looked around, listening.

"Okay," he finally said, opening a back door. "Time for you to visit the next exciting mansion where you'll hang out for a while."

"I'm not sure I like your sarcasm, Grayson," she said, stepping out of the car and pivoting to look around them into the woods.

He noted that she retained her disguise, slouching and frowning and sticking her gut out to appear heavier than the lovely, slender woman she was.

She'd have made a great actress, he figured. But he didn't tell her that. Not now, at least. Not until they'd put all this behind them and she could return to her life as an heiress with contacts and charitable instincts—and then decide if there was anything else she wanted to do. He could only hope it would still involve him.

"So where are we going?" she asked in a moment.

"This way," he said and took her hand.

It still felt the same to him—warm and sweet and sexy as she held onto his while they began walking.

You're doing this because you're a first responder who does all he can to help people, he reminded himself. And this woman needed help.

Eventually, no matter what he wished for, they might both go their own ways, and he could only hope, at this point, that hers didn't involve prison.

His either, since if anyone caught him he could be charged with abetting a fugitive.

He reminded himself that he shouldn't care for her beyond someone who desperately needed his help, but recognized that was no longer entirely true.

Ignoring the calls of birds and the sound of twigs cracking beneath their feet, the only noises out here, he led Savannah around the rise at the base of the hill—and beyond some bushes he pushed aside to reveal the opening into the bunker. At first it was like walking inside a cave, and Grayson still held Savannah's hand as they entered, using the flashlight function on his phone in the other. But at the back was another opening, and it led farther inside to the area Grayson had made his own.

It had no windows, of course, or other openings to the outside, but over time he had brought in folding chairs and a cot and shelves where he stacked foods and chips and things that didn't go stale fast, and of course bottles of water.

Not to mention a whole variety of battery-operated lanterns, better than the ones he had brought to the cabin.

Over time, he'd also brought in ornate draperies to hide the stone walls, and vinyl tiles resembling wood to cover most of the floor. He had walled off the end that led to the actual mineshaft. And he'd spent enough time here that he had brought in a tall bookcase that was now loaded with books he had read—even though now he used an e-reader more.

He had even worked out an area that could be used as an off-the-grid compost bathroom retreat, with another drape as a doorway.

It was his haven as a kid and occasionally now, too.

And it was about to become Savannah's.

"What is this place?" she asked.

He explained his childhood retreat. Yes, he was a Colton and lived at the Triple R with the rest of his siblings and his father and stepmother, but he'd needed to get away, too.

"I was never particularly close to any of them," he said. "I'm still not, though I can't explain it entirely. I knew I didn't like taking orders from them and would eventually have my own life, and so I did—but this former mineshaft became my refuge when I needed it as a kid. I call it my bunker."

"It's amazing," Savannah said, looking around. She turned back to him. "And I appreciate your sharing such an important place in your life with me."

"Any time," he said, meaning it. He figured she might have wanted a refuge like this when her relationship with Zane began to deteriorate, but he didn't ask.

"So now I want to hear what you learned in town that made you decide I couldn't stay in the cabin anymore."

"It may be fine," he responded. "But...well, maybe we'll go back there depending on how things work out over the next day or so. But here's the thing."

They sat in folding chairs across from each other, and Grayson told Savannah about his conversation with PJ—and the hair clip that had been found beside Ian Wright's murdered body.

"Oh no!" Savannah looked frightened and reached for what

was left of her hair. "That does sound like one of mine I had monogrammed. Obviously, it was planted there. I'm being framed again."

"So I figured." Grayson reached toward her and took her hands in his once more. "I was pondering that on my drive to the cabin. If you're being framed, it has to be whoever framed you for the first murder—most likely your ex, if you're correct about his still being alive. He'd have been recognized going into Wright's law office, but then so might Schuyler"

"I agree," Savannah said, nodding. "Do you think it could be both Zane and Schuyler working together?"

"Exactly," Grayson agreed, "since it appears they were co-conspirators before and that relationship most likely continues. Now all we have to do is figure out a way to point the cops in that direction rather than at you. My suspicion is that it was Schuyler who murdered Ian since he's more likely to be out in public than Zane, though it's not clear how anyone sneaked into the law office and got past the receptionist without being seen. I guess that will come to light when the case is finally solved. I just wish we knew of a way to show the cops the way to go with some genuine evidence."

Savannah sat back, letting go of his hands, her expression thoughtful. "You know, I may not have mentioned before, but dear old Zane liked to think of himself as a techie genius. He hid security devices on his computer and phones, mostly to protect the security of his investment banking interests, though he only used one main camera in the house since he didn't want to be photographed. He recorded conversations on the phone and in various rooms and all, but I didn't know what happened to it all after we divorced. I didn't particularly like it when we were married, and as things went downhill I figured he was recording me. I confronted him to try to protect my privacy, but he mostly ignored me. I assumed the equipment was still there but once I wasn't living in the house I didn't care. But right now—well, it may be a stretch, but if my disguise is good enough I'd like to sneak into his place and find out if there's anything there of his conversations with Ian and Schuyler about his disappearing or me or anything."

"Didn't the police check for stuff like that?"

"I don't know. I heard in court that they did conduct some investigation at Zane's house, but any particularly valuable stuff might have been well hidden. I got the impression from Ian that it wouldn't be a good idea to mention it since Zane could have said things about me that would implicate me even more, so I kept quiet about it. And now that I know Ian wasn't really on my side… Well, since I've been sitting around thinking so much, I've come up with some ideas where those kinds of things could be. They may lead to nothing, of course, but I'd feel so much better if I could at least try." She looked at him with a hopeful grin on her face, which looked so different with the makeup. "Could you imagine that? Finding proof to exonerate me?"

"Sounds like a great idea."

"So…later today or tomorrow, I want to go to town, disguised even more thoroughly than I am now. I need to figure out a fake name in case someone asks, but I want to go to a store or fast-food place or something near where I used to hang out and see if anyone recognizes me. I know it could be a mistake, but I don't think so. Once I feel secure in my disguise, I can go places and do a whole lot more to try to locate Zane and find evidence that he and his friends framed me."

Grayson stood as adrenaline spiked and mental alarms went off inside him. "I don't know—"

"I do," she said. "Just for a short while, and I don't want you anywhere near me after you drop me off someplace secluded, so no one will know I was in your car. But now that I look at least a little different, I'm finally feeling some hope, despite all the awful things going on and what you told me about the cops… I need this, Grayson. To give it a try. Please."

Her appeal was echoed in her pleading expression. "Well—" He felt himself giving in.

"Please, please," she repeated. "Pretty please with lots of sugar on it, or first responder good stuff or whatever. I promise that, no matter what, I won't mention you or how you've helped me if I do get caught. I need to take the chance. I just need to do something at last."

He could understand what she was saying.

He also knew he wouldn't just drop and desert her. He would act as the first responder he was: he would help her.

Because she would need help, he told himself. Not because there was anything other than friendship—and lust—between them.

"Well, okay," he finally said. "But I'll be there, too, in the background at least. We have to agree on when and how you should contact me so I can get you out of there if it becomes necessary. And—"

"Of course," she interrupted. "Thank you, Grayson, for this and everything else."

He was surprised when Savannah stood and moved to put her arms around him. "Hey," she said. "You have a cot over there." She gestured toward that part of the room. "Wouldn't you like to enjoy this new person? I'd like to see what it's like to make love in this new persona of mine."

Grayson laughed. "I liked your previous self, too, but I'm always interested in variety." Not exactly true—he liked her in every incarnation—but that fit the moment. He stood, too, and took her into his arms.

Their kiss was long and hot—like the others they had shared when she was just Savannah. Not *just* Savannah. She was a lovely person, no matter what her face looked like, no matter how she held her body.

Savannah eventually pulled back and looked up at him. Despite the bit of makeup she had used so far, her eyes remained the sharp, sweet, sexy green he had come to know. "So what do you think about this new me?"

"I still have a lot to learn about you," he said and, taking her hand, led her to that cot she had pointed to.

A while later, Savannah wriggled her naked body against Grayson's, feeling his waning hardness, feeling his heat. They were quite close together, since the cot wasn't very large, but they hadn't needed a lot of room.

He wriggled back and pulled her closer, his arms still around her body.

Who knew? Before the events of the last few days, she wouldn't have imagined herself making love so soon after her divorce, if ever again. And with a man she hardly knew? Grayson was not one of the men she would have anticipated getting physical with. Though he and his family had money, she believed he had only appeared occasionally at her social functions. He, unlike Zane, hadn't seemed to be excited about appearing in public at events held for the town's elite. But who cared?

He was a first responder, and he definitely had responded to her in many ways.

"So," he said to her. "That was a first for my bunker, and it certainly was memorable."

"Good. I'm glad to have helped you make history here." But her mind was zooming. "Even so, there's still some daylight outside, or at least I think so. None apparently penetrates this place."

"Nope. But are you suggesting you're already prepared to get out there and test your disguise, like you mentioned before?"

"I am, but—"

He read her mind. Or maybe it was obvious. "But do I think it's time, and do I think you look different enough to give that a try? Yes, I do, if we're careful. And we will be. Both of us."

"That's good." There wasn't much she could say to that except, "I agree. And believe you, Grayson. Thank you so much for everything."

He again pulled her close, and she loved how her body reacted to his naked presence, from her nipples to the warmth of her most sensual parts below.

Well, heck. It was late in the day. She figured waiting till tomorrow to start checking on Zane would be the better plan.

Plus, this way she could practice putting on her disguise again in the morning.

Tonight she could attempt to seduce Grayson again.

And so she did.

Chapter 17

This had to work and provide her with the information and optimism she needed, Savannah hoped the next morning as she again slid into the back seat of Grayson's car, being careful not to rub her glasses along the surface as she lay down. If all went well, if she had done a good job with her makeup and clothing and all and looked as different as she hoped, she might be able to go out in public and learn all she needed to fix her life now and prove she was innocent of all accusations against her.

If not…well, she didn't want to think about that.

She did want to think about last night, though. It had been wonderful spending it in the small bed with Grayson, even between their fantastic bouts of sex. Grayson had been fine with hanging out with her that way. In fact, he had seemed happy about waiting until they had a whole new day before beginning their latest plan. They had eaten a brief breakfast of things he'd brought to the bunker, and Savannah had gotten into her disguise once more before they left.

Grayson hadn't initially mentioned it, but he had also bought her two pairs of glasses—one, sunglasses, and the other, regular glasses with a dark, wide frame but with no prescription

She had checked out her appearance again before coming out to the car. Grayson's bunker also had a large mirror in its bathroom, and thanks to the lantern in there, she was able to see herself well enough to confirm that she looked quite different from the usual Savannah Oliver.

Which wasn't her name right now, nor was Savannah Murphy. She'd chosen a new name out of thin air in case she wound up talking to someone and needed to identify herself: Chloe Michaels.

Savannah had done a quick search on her phone for the name and saw quite a few faces come up, which was a good thing. The more, the merrier. That way, she was unlikely to be confused with any other person, or so she hoped.

It was time to get started. That hopefully would include sneaking into Zane's house and looking for...well, whatever she could find that might tell her who her ex recently communicated with, and how and what they'd said. She at least had some ideas about what types of high-tech gadgets he had used.

Fortunately, she knew more than he'd realized

Those he talked to could, and probably would, involve at least Schuyler and, most likely, Ian.

If so—well, she could hope there was enough there to turn over to the police as evidence of her own innocence. Would anything show that Zane wasn't in as excellent financial condition as he'd let on to the world? Would there be any evidence of plane tickets he had booked or hotel reservations he had made?

Savannah had already informed Grayson about what she intended to seek, and he sounded happy to help. Grayson had started driving. "Are you okay back there?"

"I sure am," she responded.

They had already discussed where they would go first. Savannah had an urge to visit one of the stores she had once frequented, where she hoped the sales staff and patrons wouldn't recognize her.

Grayson had talked her out of that. "Let's start small," he said, convincing her to go to a convenience store she sometimes visited for things she needed at the last minute, where maybe someone could recognize her usual appearance but they didn't know her well.

Savannah had agreed to do things Grayson's way. After all, he was the first responder. He knew a lot more about police investigations.

Besides, if all went well at the convenience store, they could follow it up by doing things Savannah's way—

Before she did as she intended, whether Grayson agreed to it or not. She would sneak into Zane's house, her former home, and do the search she had been thinking about, which could help her get out of this mess. Maybe. At least she had a plan that shouldn't call attention to someone entering the house.

As they had discussed, Grayson pulled into a parking structure at the edge of town, on one of the middle levels. He got out first without locking the door.

Savannah—Chloe—had her burner phone with her, sound turned off. About five minutes after Grayson left, he called her, and her phone vibrated. "I'm at the stairway and don't see anyone else around," he said. "You can get out now."

She stuck the cap Grayson had given her over her head above the glasses. She also pulled on a bulky, old-looking jacket he'd given her over her T-shirt. Keeping her phone in her pocket with her hand over it, in case she needed to yank it out and call Grayson again, she did her best to sneak out of the car from her prone position on the back seat. They had decided she could take the elevator downstairs—her first experiment with being seen and, possibly, recognized.

Which she wasn't. A woman rode with her in the elevator, and she didn't seem to know, or pay any attention, to Savannah.

Step number one—a success!

The convenience store that was Savannah's target was a couple of blocks away, and she headed there at a good, strong pace without, she hoped, appearing too fast or too slow. In a few minutes, she arrived and pulled open the glass door at the front.

The first person she saw was Grayson. They ignored each other. But Savannah liked the way he looked. Today he had on a long-sleeved blue T-shirt he must have kept at the bunker.

Savannah walked around and picked up supplies like water, wheat bread and cheese slices. Normal stuff. Nothing to call attention to her. Grayson had given her cash to pay for it, which she did.

"Did you find everything you were looking for, ma'am?" the young guy at the checkout stand asked. He looked familiar and looked at her as he spoke but didn't react in any way.

"Yes, thanks." She tried to keep her voice from shaking. The kid was just being polite by talking to her, as sales clerks were supposed to do. If she remained cool and just acted like a regular patron, everything should be fine.

"Good." He handed her the plastic bag containing her purchases, and some change. "Have a nice day."

"You, too."

There. That interaction was normal. He undoubtedly asked the same question of all the customers and wished them each a good day.

Everything still was going fine.

Until she walked outside.

She'd met Grayson's eye where he stood near the door. He was thumbing through a local newspaper, but she had seen him glancing at her now and then.

She had ignored him as if he was a total stranger. Which he was, to Chloe.

Now, as she moved onto the sidewalk, a police car drove slowly by. She tried to keep her gasp inside and keep walking.

Were the cops inside it looking at her? Did they know who she was? Had someone in the store called them?

Well, she knew she didn't look like the Savannah they might be looking for. She made sure she used the relaxed posture she'd been practicing. Her hair was different. Her face, too.

She wore those glasses.

Still, she had an urge to run. To call out to Grayson—assuming he was within hearing distance. But what could he do anyway?

Instead, she kept walking. She glanced curiously in the direction of the police car. Normal people would do that, after all. The officer on the passenger side was looking in her direction, but the car continued on.

It didn't stop. Surely, everything was fine.

She'd fooled them!

Maybe. She couldn't allow herself to get too excited, too confident. They could just have been headed to get more backup, then come after her.

Savannah remembered only too well what it felt like to be taken into police custody. To be swept off to jail. To be questioned and—

She forced herself to put as many of those thoughts aside as she could. She walked at a normal pace, glancing into a clothing store as she passed it, then a furniture store—like any normal pedestrian.

No cop car drove by again. No one showed up to confront her.

Maybe this had worked out. She felt jubilant—but quickly tamped that down again.

She soon made it to the parking lot, where she took the elevator back up to the floor where Grayson had parked. No one was around, so she called him.

He answered at once. "I'm already in the car and don't see anyone around. Come on over and get in."

Which she did, opening the unlocked door, putting her package on the floor, and again lying down on the back seat.

"How did it go?" Grayson asked as he started driving.

"Fine, though I was worried when the police car drove by. Did you see it?"

"I did, but I figured your disguise, including your posture, wouldn't let them recognize you. You're quite an actress."

"Me? Not exactly the career I'd choose if I decided to really work for a living." Which actually sounded good now. She could make more choices for herself that way—assuming she was ever exonerated of these murders.

Which was definitely what she intended.

And so, she told Grayson, "Since I don't resemble myself and I'm such a great actress, here's where I want to go right now."

She gave him Zane's address, which he apparently already knew.

"It's a big house in a neighborhood of big houses but not many people. This car looks enough like a delivery vehicle that I doubt any neighbors will pay attention if you pull onto the street a little distance away and we get out there. I'll pretend to be a new cleaning lady if anyone pays attention to us, and you can bring a bag or something to deliver. The house is on a middle lot and we can get through the gate and inside in a way I know. Zane isn't that friendly with anyone on the street anyway."

"Okay, Chloe," Grayson said. "I understand this is important to you, and why. I just hope we find what you're looking for."

"Me, too," Savannah-Chloe responded.

And she was very glad he had said "we."

Grayson had agreed to do as Savannah wished, despite a whole lot of reservations. But he understood why she wanted it.

And it truly did make sense, if they could actually find something to prove the guilt of Schuyler Wells—or even Zane Oliver himself. Even though Savannah's access to the property as a resident of the guest house was now most likely limited since she was a fugitive.

He only wished he could somehow do this on his own, keep her fully out of danger as he cleared her name. But that couldn't happen. She was the one who knew the house and where Zane might have hidden anything that might absolve her or indicate that Zane had faked his own death.

But if things went wrong…

Well, they couldn't. But in any case, he would keep his distance, mentally at least.

He would also help her as much as he could. But he'd additionally have to convince himself that she was just one more person he helped as a first responder, no matter how much time they had spent together in the past few days.

No matter how much he enjoyed her presence, and in so many ways.

After all, he wouldn't develop an ongoing relationship with this woman, even if things worked out as he hoped. She might not want to be with him anyway, since he might remind her in the future of all that was happening now.

This time, he had her ride in the front seat with him as he followed her directions to the house. It wasn't in an area he visited a lot. He wasn't likely to be recognized. Hopefully, neither would Savannah in her Chloe disguise.

He drove to one of the most upscale residential areas of Mustang Valley. It didn't include ranches, but it did include large estates that fronted on a well-maintained road, Vista Lane. Not even a sign of earthquake damage here. Along the road were large homes including mansions, most set back behind fences. Grayson knew where Zane Oliver had lived, but though he'd looked up the address again, he mostly counted on Savannah—no, Chloe. He had to start thinking of her that way.

They had already decided they would park some distance away, maybe a quarter of a mile, for unobtrusiveness. There was also an alley behind the homes that paralleled the main road. Savannah would walk that way back toward the house, while Grayson would carry a box he had stashed in the back of his SUV to make it appear he was delivering something, if he was approached.

As they drove by the huge gray stone house, Savannah

pointed out where she would enter the yard, through a gate at the side where she would be less noticeable.

Grayson would go that way, too, since the neighbors would undoubtedly know that Zane had allegedly died and no one would be at home to open the front door for packages.

Looking at the place made Grayson remember who Savannah Oliver was, notwithstanding her being a murder suspect and fugitive. She came from wealth and had married into it, too.

Not that Grayson, a Colton, was unfamiliar with having a lot of assets.

But seeing where she had lived exemplified her background, and he could hardly imagine what it had felt for her to be in police custody, incarcerated with a lot of people who were undoubtedly guilty of the crimes they were charged with.

He had an urge to take her into his arms again at that thought. Good thing he was driving.

"How about there?" Savannah pointed toward a road veering to the right. It was a short distance from Zane's home, and there were other vehicles parked along it, too. The cars varied from relatively new ones like Grayson's SUV to older ones, and he figured some household help, or maybe handymen, parked here.

Good. His car wouldn't be obvious, even though it was in better condition than most.

He made the turn, then parked in the first available space.

"Okay," he said. "Here we are. You go your way first, and then I'll come down the street beside the house and you can let me into the yard, too."

"Sounds good." She tossed him a smile behind the sunglasses and disguising makeup she now wore.

She might not look as beautiful as before, but he knew who was beneath that disguise. He pulled her toward him and gave her a quick kiss, then moved away.

"See you soon," he said.

Chapter 18

The walk along the back alley to Zane's house—and her guest-house—seemed to take forever in the Arizona heat. Savannah kept her pace fairly fast along the even cement in her new clunky shoes, while holding the kind of posture she had assumed along with the rest of her disguise. The wind had suddenly grown strong so the jacket she wore, and even her jeans, seemed to blow and flutter around her, making her feel even more uncomfortable. At least the cap on her head, which was part of her camouflage, along with her glasses, stayed on. Hopefully she looked different enough that even if she was seen, no one would associate her with Savannah Oliver.

Fortunately, no one else was around. But if someone did appear, if anyone saw her or talked to her, she could let them know that she was a maid by profession and Mr. Oliver's family had asked her, Chloe Michaels, to do some housecleaning and to come in this way.

Zane had often had workers arrive through the side gate, after all, and when he knew they were coming he would leave it temporarily unlocked and without enabling the security alarm.

But who in his family now would ask for help that way? Good question. Big-time investment banker Zane had staff as well as executives at his company whom he must've trained well enough to keep the place going. When he'd discussed traveling with Savannah, long before their divorce, he had indicated he wanted that kind of professional support in place.

That had never happened. And now that he was "dead," perhaps living in one of the far-off areas he'd thought they might visit someday, his allies were undoubtedly keeping the company successful for what they believed to be their own benefit, as well as Zane's heirs.

Oh, he still had parents and a sister. They were most likely his official heirs now, as long as people believed him to be dead. Savannah certainly wasn't one, and might not have been even if they were still married as a result of Zane's ungenerous attitude. In fact, her allegedly wanting to get her hands on more of his assets, despite her own wealth, was one of the motives the authorities had ascribed to her for his murder, as well as revenge for his affairs. They'd never put an estate plan together, even though she'd suggested it, thanks to her father.

Arizona was a community property state, so she had been entitled to at least some of what Zane earned while they were together, but she'd gotten some money from him when they divorced that was supposed to satisfy the law. She assumed it still sat in the bank where she had deposited it.

Thoughts of her dad brought to mind why she had married Zane in the first place. It had largely been her father's idea. He had advised Savannah to marry soon and marry well, and when Zane Oliver had shown some interest, her dad had jumped right on it, urging her to go out with him. A lot. And marry him? Oh yeah!

Oh, she had thought she loved Zane, but she hadn't felt the kind of passion she'd anticipated having for the man she married and intended to spend the rest of her life with.

Grayson's face suddenly popped into her mind.

Ridiculous. She was grateful to him. She enjoyed sex with him. And rightly or not, she trusted him.

But she didn't love him. Couldn't, either now or later. He didn't seem to want a relationship, and she certainly didn't want one on the heels of what had happened with her terrible marriage and afterward. She needed time and space…and trust, which would be really difficult for her now.

She turned the corner into the narrow outdoor passageway between Zane's property and the one next door, both lined with fences. That was where she would open a gate and get inside. She knew where Zane put the key to that door, so even if he had changed locks, there should be no problem, assuming he hadn't changed hiding places or the code for the security alarm.

She hoped.

She glanced toward the neighbors' side and was glad to see the row of cacti still there. They apparently didn't use their gate here, and hopefully didn't stare at the plants along the fence.

And she wouldn't even glance toward the guesthouse.

Fortunately Grayson had brought them both gloves to don to avoid leaving fingerprints. Savannah pulled hers on, then quickly searched for the key to the fence lock. There. It was where she'd anticipated, in a small box buried to the right of a fence post. This had been intended to be an emergency way to get on and off the property—and it worked right now.

The main house's front door? It was much more likely that neighbors would see her there, even if they didn't recognize her. Plus, she didn't have the front door key any longer. And the house's main security camera was aimed there.

As Savannah stepped inside the fence, in the shadow of the vast and lovely mansion she had called home for a couple of years, she saw Grayson approach from the direction of the main street. She waited for him. He, too, wore gloves.

"So far so good," he said as he reached her side.

"Yes. And—well, I never told Zane, of course, but I kept a key to the side door of the main house hidden on the grounds, too. I didn't think I'd have any need to use it, but it just—it made me feel a little better, a bit more in control. And I never disposed of it when we got divorced."

As they talked, they approached the side of the house. A key pad was attached to the wall near the door, and Savannah pulled it open and pressed in some numbers—and waited.

"Good," she said. "He mustn't have changed the alarm code, either, or we'd hear a buzz to indicate we needed to try again."

"Really? Then we wouldn't have been able to get in the house, even if you know where the key is." Grayson sounded unhappy.

"From what Zane told me when I moved in, that code hadn't been changed in decades, so I wasn't too worried." There was a garden area off to the side, with a hopbush hedge nearly against the house. Savannah walked five steps with one foot in front of the other, then bent and dug a small hole in the sandy dirt. Sure enough, she found the key in a small box and stood up. Waving it toward Grayson, she said, "Let's go inside."

She used the key in a side door, and soon walked into the kitchen—an appropriate entrance for the help, the way she wanted to appear at the moment, she thought.

This was a swanky kitchen, with ornate and imported tile on the floor, and ebony wooden cabinets surrounding the most expensive major appliances, all in gleaming metal.

"We're in," she said, knowing her grin was huge. Grayson smiled back, then grew serious again.

"Okay, now that we're in here, what are we looking for that might have evidence of Zane's collusion with Schuyler Wells and even Ian Wright?"

Savannah felt her face drop. "Well, I have a couple of ideas, but— Look, here are the possibilities I thought of." She proceeded to tell him about Zane's security camera, which was always aimed at the front door, as well as his proclivity for recording all phone calls—or so he'd told her. He'd never let her listen to any. But he did maintain a landline in his home office, so it was worth looking for it and grabbing anything that could have recorded calls. "He probably recorded some or all of his cell calls, too, but I've no idea where that phone is. I assume the police have it—or he still does."

Grayson looked at her. "So first thing, we need to go check out what's recorded on the security camera at the front door."

"Maybe," she said. "But we need to be really careful. The way it's hanging high up on the wall, I don't know if we can get to it without having our photos taken, too."

"Not good. Well, if we do, we'll just have to bring the whole thing with us so no one else will see us."

She nodded, though she said, "I'm not sure that's possible. Getting to it, even with a ladder, isn't easy. Besides, I think that the recordings of landline calls will be the most likely to include any conversations he had here with Schuyler and Ian. They might not have come to the house at all."

"Got it. Now, where's the front door?"

Savannah led Grayson out of the kitchen and through the wide hallway decorated on both sides with modern artwork. They soon were near the front of the house, but she stopped before taking him into the large, open entry area. She pointed toward the wall to indicate where the camera was mounted, though they couldn't see the device from here.

He got it. "Do you have any ladders?"

"Yes, in the basement. Let's just go up the back stairway to Zane's office for now. Maybe we can find what we're looking for there."

She thought that was a better idea, especially since past conversations she'd had with Zane were now tiptoeing into her head—where he talked about phone calls he'd had with friends or business associates while he was working here in his office. He'd laughed and said he figured they'd all feel screwed if they knew, because he got them talking about things they would never admit if they thought anyone else had the possibility of hearing them.

In other words, he'd recorded them. But he hadn't mentioned how, or where he kept the audio files.

Still, when they got up the stairway and Savannah led Grayson to the closed, ornate wooden door into Zane's home office, she said, "I assume you're more techie than I am. I'm not sure what to look for, but we can check to see if there's any kind of recording device." She hesitated. "Although—well, Zane never seemed to trust anyone."

She was glad when Grayson preceded her into the office and began looking everywhere, starting around where the phone sat on Zane's huge but far from ornate wooden desk. Nothing there, nor inside the drawers. Or on any of the shelves behind the desk, or under the comfortable-looking desk chair or any of the other furniture in the room.

Grayson sat at Zane's desk, pulling some of the drawers out beside him. He extracted files and laid them on top of the desk, going through them and checking out the now empty drawers.

Then Grayson looked toward Savannah. "I gather you're not sure Zane had any kind of recorder here, though he implied it." As Savannah nodded, Grayson shrugged and shook his head. "Unfortunately, I don't see anything here that would do what you hoped for."

He somehow looked cute in his frustration Cute? Why was she even thinking in that way?

To pull herself out of this situation, out of here? Out of her own frustration at not finding what they needed—something to clear her, right away?

That was ridiculous.

"We should probably look other places, though, just in case," Grayson continued. "If he was trying to hide something, his office would probably be too obvious, after all. Where else did he spend time?"

"He liked to watch the big-screen TV in the den," Savannah said after realizing that Grayson was right and pondering an answer to his question. "We were kind of separated for a while inside the house, both emotionally and physically, even before we got divorced. He had his own bedroom then, before I moved into the guesthouse, so that's another possibility."

"A potentially good one," Grayson said. "Let's start there and check it out, okay?"

"Sure." Savannah felt a bit embarrassed taking Grayson to her ex-husband's bedroom, although she hadn't been there for ages, and the last time she was there was probably well before Zane and she unofficially split up.

But that might make it a perfect place for him to hide something, right? Not that it would have mattered after she moved out. He could even have hidden the recorder in the room she had last used inside this house, the master bedroom.

She showed Grayson where Zane had slept while staying far away from her at night. They went up the wide wooden stairway, turned left at the end of the upstairs hallway and walked along the hall that was covered with imported Persian carpets laid end to end.

It felt so odd to Savannah to be here, seeing some of the things she still loved about this place. Her emotions roiled, but she ignored them. She was here to think, not to feel.

The white wooden door was closed but not locked. Inside, the place looked as Savannah remembered it, with a king-size bed beneath a woven, imported coverlet embroidered in gold and silver threads. Zane had a very tall and wide chest of drawers on one side and an ornate, full-length mirror beside it. He always liked to admire how he looked.

The place still smelled like him—not that "dead" Zane was likely to have visited recently. But he had used an aftershave with a lime citrus scent, and that aroma remained in the air.

The large dresser had two sides, each with separate drawers, with a bottom cabinet area with two separate doors. Savannah began searching through the drawers on the right side. Not that she appreciated thumbing through Zane's expensive underwear, but she had to find that recorder—unless Grayson did.

Nothing in the first drawer, and as she turned she noticed that Grayson was on his side on the floor, looking under the bed. Then he rose a little and began prodding the area between the mattress and the box spring.

Savannah turned back and closed the top right drawer, opening the next one—and almost gagged. It contained mostly socks of different styles and colors, no big deal there. But it also held a moderate-sized box with a colorful exterior that was labeled with a manufacturer's name and the word "Condoms" written decoratively in the middle.

She knew full well how much Zane engaged in sex with other women, and this suggested he had continued to have a lot of fun in that way before his "death." Before their divorce? She'd known he had but never found a good way to prove it.

She started slamming the drawer shut, too—but before she could, Grayson's arm reached out to stop her, startling Savannah. "Just a sec," he said.

Why? Did he want to take some of those condoms along with him? Even having him see them in Zane's drawer embarrassed Savannah. She had wanted out of that horrible relationship, but this could give the impression not only that her ex was a sex fiend, but that Savannah hadn't satisfied him in that department.

Sure enough, Grayson pulled that box out of the drawer. Feeling mortified, justifiably or not, Savannah started to walk away. But then Grayson opened the box and crowed, "Here we are! I figured that might be a place to hide something without nosy people getting into it—except for us."

He pulled a black technological gadget out of the box. It was not very large but had a screen in front with buttons below and auxiliary ports. It was maybe an inch thick at the widest spot but tapered toward the bottom. With it were a couple of long wires with plugs at both ends.

"What is it?" Savannah asked in a hushed voice.

"Not my area of expertise, but I'd guess it's a landline phone call recorder. I just hope the memory card has lots of helpful recordings on it. Now we can continue looking for something else, too, but—"

A loud noise sounded from downstairs. "Police!" yelled a loud voice. "Is anyone here?" Savannah noticed what looked like some bright lights through the door from that direction. It was late morning, but even so maybe the cops were using inside searchlights before barging inside.

"Damn!" Grayson muttered softly. "Could the alarm have gone off after all?"

"Zane might have modified it," Savannah said nervously. He had talked about hiring a security company to improve the system someday, but he hadn't done that while she was living here.

"Anywhere we can hide?" Grayson whispered.

She felt her face light up, if only a little. "Yes. Zane was always secretive." She, too, kept her voice low. Raising a finger, she beckoned Grayson to follow her. She hurried as quietly as she could back to the same dresser, where she pulled open the wooden door on the bottom left. The open area there was surprisingly vast and even extended into the wall. Savannah had wondered what Zane planned to hide there someday. Cash stolen from his job? She wouldn't have been surprised—but if he had, he'd fortunately taken the money with him. That left an area large enough to hide both Grayson and her.

They both got down on the floor and crawled inside, and Grayson, holding the recorder, pulled the door closed behind them.

They waited. Savannah felt terrified, but it helped that Grayson snuggled against her as they both sat on the base of the cabinet and bent forward at the waist. He even put an arm around her. He was warm and comforting—and Savannah hoped that the cops didn't find them here and now.

It apparently took a while for the police to conduct their search of the place, and eventually Savannah heard footsteps in the hallway, then voices as the cops came inside Zane's bedroom. She glanced at Grayson, who was hardly visible in the darkness of the cabinet. He hugged her slightly harder as if in reassurance, then eased up. And stared at the cabinet door as if ready to leap out and attack the intruders.

But it didn't sound as if they would remain there long. They seemed to be grumbling about being there, talking about how the damned wind might have blown a door open and set off the alarm at the security company, which had notified the police station. From what Savannah could tell, they just walked through Zane's bedroom, circling it for maybe a minute as they talked, then started out again—or so she hoped.

Savannah was a bit startled when Grayson pushed the door open just a little and looked out.

And appeared a bit startled, too. He closed it quietly and quickly, then held Savannah's arm to keep her motionless for a short while that felt like forever.

He seemed to be listening. Concentrating.

And in a while he whispered to her, "Let's go."

Chapter 19

Grayson extracted himself from the bottom of the cabinet first and stood. He stretched, listening, and heard nothing. No one.

Not even his cousin Spencer.

Grayson had thought he recognized Spencer's voice when the cops were in the room talking. That was why he had carefully peeked out. And confirmed who it was. And fortunately hadn't been noticed.

If the other cops hadn't been there too, would Grayson have let Spencer know of his presence and Savannah's?

No. He couldn't do that to either Savannah or Spencer. Spencer would have had to arrest fugitive Savannah, even if Grayson made a good case for her innocence.

Which he certainly believed he could.

Even so, to do his job right, Spencer would probably have felt compelled to take Grayson into custody for abetting her.

Maybe even Grayson's brother Rafe's fiancée, Detective Kerry Wilder, would feel the same way.

Grayson hadn't thought he would have to hide anything from his family members, but that was before Savannah.

Grayson waited another few minutes in case he heard more from the cops, then said quietly to Savannah, "Okay, I think they've left. Time for us to get out of here."

He helped her to her feet, noticing the pinkness to her face beneath her makeup. That jacket had to be making her feel awfully warm. But it did help in her disguise, so he didn't suggest she take it off, at least not yet.

In fact, in case someone saw them, he handed her the recorder and its wires, and asked her to hide them beneath the jacket, since it wouldn't fit in her small purse nor in his pockets. The base of the jacket was secured by a cord belt, so the recorder should easily remain there.

"Okay," she said. "Do you think it's all right for us to go out the same way we came in?"

"Better than the front," Grayson responded. "And I gathered that the neighbors at that side don't use that entrance to their place, or so I figured from the amount of cactus around their gate. They probably won't notice us. So, yes."

Grayson insisted on preceding Savannah slowly along the hallway and down the stairs to the kitchen, continuing to remain alert the entire way. But fortunately, he still believed he was correct in assuming the police had left.

Finally, they reached the door they had come in. Again, he insisted on going first and opened the door just a little to ensure he didn't see or hear anyone outside before they exited.

In a few minutes, they had gone out that door and through the gate. He held Savannah's hand as they inched their way along the fence to the alley.

Soon, they were making their way along that alley. A breeze was still blowing, but it didn't affect them now. In fact, Grayson was glad for that wind. It had sounded like the cops had accepted it as the reason the house's front door had opened and set off the remote.

Did anyone look this way from their homes backing onto this

alley or otherwise? Grayson didn't think so, or at least he hoped not. They walked quickly to his car and got inside.

Grayson felt relieved. "Let's listen to those recordings back at the bunker," he told Savannah as soon as he drove away in that direction.

"Fine with me," she said, "although do you have enough batteries to power the recorder along with the lights? We may be listening to it for a while and using up its juice."

"I've got something better," he told her. "A generator. As I mentioned, I used to spend a lot of time at my bunker."

He hoped, though, that they'd be able to work things out so Savannah didn't have to spend much time there. It was partially underground, after all, an even more stressful place for her to hang out than the fishing cabin, or so he believed. Still, although it was a former mine, since he'd closed off the shafts years ago he didn't consider it dangerous.

Besides, now that they'd begun testing her disguise, maybe she would be able to get out and about, at least a little.

Better yet, prepare to move somewhere else altogether and let Grayson ultimately figure out how to clear her name around here. But his ability to do that might depend on what was on that recorder that was now on the center console between them.

"That bunker of yours is amazing," Savannah said. "You've got the place furnished quite nicely for what is pretty much a cave. You must have really liked it while you were growing up."

"I did," he said, "though now I have even better ways of staying away from my family when I choose to. And I never let them control my life."

"You're fortunate," Savannah said, surprising him a little. "My dad's gone now, but I married Zane largely because of his urging me to. I miss my father, but I certainly don't miss his pushiness."

Interesting. "My dad's on the pushy side, too," he said. "Or he was, before." He knew Savannah was aware of how Payne Colton had been shot and remained in a coma. Even though he still resented some of his father's attempts to control him in the past, Grayson felt awful about what had happened.

Another thought struck him about his family, something he really ought to let Savannah know about. "By the way, I should tell you one of the reasons I acted a bit stupid while we were hidden and peered out toward the cops. I thought I recognized a voice, and I was right. My cousin Spencer Colton was one of them."

He heard Savannah draw in her breath. "Oh, that could have been terrible. If he'd found you, I mean. I'm so sorry that I've been putting you into that kind of position, where even your family members might turn against you."

"Oh, I doubt that would be the case with Spencer." Grayson tried to keep his tone light, though he appreciated that this woman was smart enough to recognize problems like that without his suggesting them.

And it wasn't only Savannah's intelligence that he appreciated about her. He enjoyed her company, her warmth and caring, her body, and, well, nearly everything about her. Would there be any possibility of their developing a relationship after Savannah was cleared? He was beginning to hope so. A lot.

But none of that mattered now, while he still had to figure out how best to help her. Hopefully, that would get resolved when they listened to the recordings.

And the things he admired about her might not matter after this was all over.

They might wind up going their own ways…

But he certainly hoped not.

Meanwhile, now, he continued to drive around town as he had become used to doing, avoiding potholes and ruts still there after the earthquake, looking in the rearview mirror often to see what vehicles might be behind them, turning off onto smaller streets to ensure they weren't being followed, then veering off again to keep checking all was well.

He knew the cops were smart, too, especially Spencer. It was possible his cousin had seen him in Zane's house, or saw him after they left the house, and was now stealthily following them.

He had to be sure that wasn't the case before they finally headed to his bunker. It was not someplace he had ever told Spencer—or anyone—about.

It was still late morning, so no chance of hiding easily if anyone happened to be following them. But Grayson was being careful. He pulled into the parking lot of a small chain grocery store. "We need some supplies for tonight," he said. "And probably tomorrow, too."

Like breakfast, he thought. Would he stay the night again?

Quite possibly. If he could.

"Wait here," he told her, but she got out of the car at the same time he did. She drew closer to him on the sidewalk in front of the entrance. There were other people around, so he didn't want to scold her.

Especially when she got close enough to kiss him on the cheek—just pretending they were an item, he figured. She also used the opportunity to whisper to him, "Just checking my disguise again."

"Be careful," he instructed, and shook his head as she stuck out her tongue and preceded him inside.

He looked around the parking lot but didn't see anything that made him suspicious, so he followed.

The stuff they picked up after quickly strolling the narrow aisles of the store was the usual—a few sandwiches, more water, some chips and dip, and sweet rolls for the morning. Not a lot of the latter, but enough that they both would have an adequate amount if he did wind up staying the night, and Grayson was sure Savannah recognized that. But neither of them mentioned it.

He paid, of course. The young woman at the cash register didn't pay much attention to them, a good thing. Then, with Grayson holding the paper bag, they returned to the car and he began driving again.

On the route back, he did a few more twists and turns just in case but still saw no indication of anyone following or otherwise showing any interest in them. He finally headed his SUV toward his bunker.

"So everything's okay?" Savannah asked from beside him. Of course she would have noticed his weaving around local roads even after their small shopping expedition and understood why—smart lady that she was.

He aimed a smile at her before turning onto the street that would take him to the dirt road toward the bunker. "Yep, but we can't be too careful, can we?"

"No," she said, then added, "I'm learning so much from you, Grayson. And I'll never be able to thank you enough for all you're doing for me."

"Sure you can," he said teasingly. "I'll always be glad to hear it. First responders always are."

Once more he glanced at her—and wished he could just pull over and put his arms around the woman who was smiling so sadly at him. A pretty woman despite her disguise, including those silly glasses.

A sexy woman—and he definitely knew that about her, thanks to experience. Not that he dared to anticipate much more, if any.

But he had to keep his eyes on the semblance of a road through the forest beyond his family ranch, so he turned back to look out the windshield. Soon, they got to the area where he always parked and he put his car in its secluded spot.

She waited for him to go first as they approached the opening to the former mineshaft, though. Inside the cave, he again used the light from his phone to illuminate their path, and they quickly reached the rear part and entered the bunker area.

He lit the lanterns, then walked quickly to where he had stored the generator in an area off to the side and picked up the large container of gasoline he always left there, poured it into the machine, then turned it on.

Savannah had apparently been watching. "That's so cool," she said. "This place could turn into quite a home if you ever wanted to live here."

"That was the point," Grayson responded.

He couldn't resist. The last time they were there, the previous night, he hadn't been able to keep his hands off her, and he wanted to touch her now. Which he did. But he limited himself to giving her a quick kiss. For now. And was delighted that she returned it.

Then he plugged the recorder into the generator while Savannah went into the bathroom to change back to looking like Savannah. They soon sat down on two folding chairs in the middle of the room and used a third to hold the recorder. Grayson looked the machine over, then pushed the buttons he thought would get the audio started, hopefully from the beginning.

It took a little more effort, though, since what they heard at first included some static and telephone sounds like a busy signal. But soon Grayson had it working just fine.

And from what he could tell, they were initially listening to telephone conversations Zane Oliver had had some time ago, maybe a few months. Most seemed to be with business associates, though not all of them.

Grayson was sometimes captivated, sometimes amused, by the conversations they heard, though nothing was particularly helpful when Zane talked with, chided, and even threatened people who apparently were mostly customers of his. Grayson was disappointed that he heard nothing from Zane admitting anything incriminating. Even the threats were fairly inconsequential.

Grayson only hoped there would be some other, more helpful conversations to come.

It felt so weird to Savannah to be listening to these phone conversations. Listening to Zane being Zane, encouraging business associates to invest lots and lots of money in his bank.

Before sitting down, she had removed her disguise. That felt better, but it also felt good to know her trick had worked.

The folding chairs Grayson had in this attractively decorated cave were surprisingly comfortable, with cushioning on the seats and back, a good thing because Grayson and she might be there for quite a while hearing the recorded conversations. Grayson had given Savannah yet another pad of paper to write on, this time so she could make notes about whose voices they heard, if she recognized them or figured out who they were from what they or Zane said.

Savannah was able to identify quite a few people, even those who didn't live in Mustang Valley. Zane had had a lot of contacts all over; at parties and other occasions many people attempted to get to know him better, impress him, so he would not only do business with them but would also provide information and support for them and their companies.

Some of the names she heard included Rex Affler, owner of a local brewery, and Miranda Borden, from a national clothing manufacturer. All businesspeople who undoubtedly had appreciated having a contact at a successful investment bank like Zane's.

All people who apparently wanted something from him.

Which Zane clearly knew, sometimes stringing them along, sometimes telling them to call back the next day when he was at work. Sometimes insulting them. Sometimes insinuating threats if they didn't invest money through his bank's services. And sometimes even telling them he was sorry, but he couldn't help them.

But Savannah knew Zane and his voice well enough to be sure he wasn't sorry at all, at least in most cases.

Plus, after some of those calls, the next conversations would be with one or another of his own employees at the bank, with Zane often making fun of those business associates he'd just spoken with.

At least none of them were with his lovers, thank heavens. Not then, at least.

Grayson and she listened for an hour without hearing anything that could be helpful to her.

No, what she wanted was to reach out and grab Zane by the throat—not to kill him as she allegedly had, but demand when he would actually say something helpful.

Assuming he ever would.

"Are you okay?" Grayson asked. She must have made some kind of movement or otherwise indicated her frustration, since he was looking directly at her.

"Fine," she grumped, then repeated "Fine" in a tone that she hoped was closer to sounding fine.

"Hey, I'm going to bring our lunch over here," Grayson said.

"Good idea." But Savannah didn't let him do it on his own. She rose and began helping him—and when their arms touched, she looked up at him…and she wanted so much to drag him over to that bed.

Not then, though. The recording was still droning on, and it was vital that they heard all of it as quickly as possible.

Surely sometime, it would contain the voices of at least Ian Wright and Schuyler Wells—along with Zane.

And when it did, would they be conspiring to frame her for Zane's eventual imaginary death?

Now, though, Zane held a conversation with one of his employees. How did he ever decide which calls, or other work, to take care of at home rather than at his office? Savannah had no idea.

Grayson and she each chose a sandwich. They turned to sit back down and bumped into each other.

"Sorry," she said.

"I'm not." Still holding his own sandwich, roast beef, Grayson bent down to kiss Savannah right on the mouth. "Mmmm," he said. "Potato chips and dip. I can't wait to taste you again after you've eaten your sandwich."

Savannah laughed, and the thought of dragging him over to the cot once more permeated her mind.

Not going to happen, but her windows of opportunity to get him to bed again were dwindling.

But after another hour of listening and nibbling on their sandwiches, they still had nothing useful.

Savannah was beginning to give up hope.

"What should we do if there's nothing here?" she finally asked Grayson. At that moment, Zane was talking to someone whose name or voice Savannah didn't recognize. From the conversation she had learned that the other speaker was apparently not only a female executive of a local consumer electronics company, but someone he'd slept with—or was trying to seduce.

Not a surprise, but Savannah was disgusted anyway. She was happy when that call ended.

And the next one? Hearing the second voice caused her to stand up in excitement.

Zane was talking to Ian Wright! So he had known the attorney, as she'd come to believe.

"Hey," Grayson said softly. "That's good news." Then he put one long finger over his own mouth as if to shush himself and listen.

Savannah kind of wished it was her finger there—but instead concentrated on the conversation.

Ian was apparently returning a call from Zane about possible representation on a legal matter for the investment bank.

Nothing about Savannah. Nothing conspiratorial about framing her for Zane's murder.

But at least this proved they'd known one another.

And it gave Savannah hope there would be more later on. And ended at least some of her frustration at all the unhelpful calls before.

She couldn't rely on what she heard now between Zane and Ian being of much use, though. She needed the reality of more conversations, discussions that finally made it clear that those two had done more than discuss banking and legal issues.

With Schuyler, too.

Grayson had also finished his sandwich. He must have seen the conflicting encouragement and discouragement on Savannah's face that she felt inside. He moved his chair closer and put his arm around her as they continued to listen.

For another hour. Savannah, who put her head down on Grayson's shoulder, appreciated his nearness, even if they wouldn't, couldn't, do anything about it.

She appreciated him. Still. More.

Realized she had come to hope for a future that included him.

But—

She closed her eyes, figuring it wouldn't hurt to go to sleep—and then, there it was.

Zane was not only talking to Ian, but to Schuyler, too. Was it a three-way phone conversation? Were Ian and Schuyler together?

No matter. The main thing was what they were saying.

"So, Schuyler," Zane said. "You know my divorce is final, but unfortunately that's not the end of things. Did Ian explain what I want both of you to help with?"

"Hey, yeah," said Schuyler Wells. Savannah recognized his voice. Of course. Wasn't she supposed to have been having an affair with him at the time of this conversation?

She would have laughed—but she needed to be completely quiet to hear this.

"I gather," Schuyler said, "that you're about to be murdered, right? By your wonderful ex—and I'm going to get to know her better. Way better. You'll disappear, and the cops will just happen to find some damning evidence against dear Savannah. But without your body around—well, there should be arguments that you're okay, that your ex is innocent. And our buddy Ian there is going to take her case to prove it."

"Or not," Ian said, and all three men laughed.

The conversation continued a little longer. Savannah was staring straight at Grayson, knowing her eyes were wide and she was smiling. She had proof now. She didn't kill Zane, and the world—and the authorities—would know it. She would be exonerated in court at last. She wanted to shout, to hug Grayson, to laugh and laugh and engage in nice, celebratory kisses with him.

And when those men hung up, Grayson said, "We've got it!"

Chapter 20

And that call wasn't the last of it. Grayson chortled as, still sitting there with his arm around an excited Savannah, they heard a couple more conversations—and the final one on this subject contained verbal confirmation of everything they would need to demonstrate to the police that Zane was still alive, and Savannah was not guilty of killing him.

It should also let the authorities know there were a couple of better suspects in the murder of Ian Wright—one of his coconspirators in framing Savannah.

"This is so amazing," Savannah said, looking at him with a huge grin after one of those calls finished. "I don't know why my ex was stupid enough to record those calls, since they're proof of so much against him. But I'm so glad he did!"

"He might have wanted some kind of reminder of what was said in case he needed to use it against his coconspirators," Grayson told her. "Or maybe he just wanted to save them as proof that he hadn't been alone in this, if the truth ever did come out. As it will now."

One of those last calls was certainly the best. In it, the men had all agreed to do what was needed to frame Savannah as Zane's revenge against her. He promised to be generous in his payments to the others, and the amounts he mentioned seemed a lot more than that.

And the very last call? It described how Zane would cut himself with the knife and hide the bloody thing in her closet. He would disappear then.

Too bad he didn't mention where he would disappear to.

Grayson's mind began spinning. What should they do next? But his thoughts were interrupted when Savannah rose and pulled him up to stand, too. In moments, they were kissing, sweetly and happily at first, and then more heatedly.

Grayson felt his body reacting. He wanted more, much more, as part of their celebration. But this definitely wasn't the time. They had to act on this and get Savannah cleared before anything else.

And after? Well, maybe they could get together again, to celebrate or whatever. And determine if that would be their happy ending, or if there could be more...

There had to be more. He hadn't planned on it, but he had fallen hard for this vulnerable, yet smart and sexy, woman. She had stood up in the face of adversity and was about to win. They had to have a future together.

But this wasn't the time to think about that.

He finally broke away from Savannah, as much as he hated to. He looked down at her ecstatic face.

"Here's what I want to do now. I intend to take this recording to the police, of course, but first I want to get a copy of it. I know enough cops I can trust, including Spencer and my brother Rafe's fiancée, Kerry. But I want to make sure this doesn't get misplaced, intentionally or otherwise."

"Great idea," Savannah said, still smiling but a bit less so. "Where will you get it copied? Do you have any equipment that'll do it in your office, or do you know someone you trust enough to do it?"

He nodded. "I may not adore all my family members, but most of us do care enough to help each other whenever possible. My brother Callum is a bodyguard, and you wouldn't think someone like him would have technological equipment as part of his profession, but Callum does. I'll call him from my car and head to his office. I don't know if he's working at the moment, but unless there's something going on right now, he'll meet me there and we'll get this copied right away."

"Sounds good." But Savannah's tone didn't sound as enthused as before.

"It is," he said. "I want you to stay here, where it will be safer. Even if you get your disguise on, I don't want the cops to see you until I turn the recording over to them and they have a chance to listen to it. I'll come get you then, okay?"

"Sure." Savannah looked up at him again. "But make it fast. Please. I can't wait till I'm cleared and this is all behind me."

"Me, too." Grayson unplugged the recorder.

He took Savannah into his arms then and gave her a long, deep, celebratory kiss.

"Hey, girl," he said when the kiss ended and he had stepped back just a little, looking down into her gorgeous green eyes. "In case you can't guess, I've fallen for you. Hard. See you soon."

"And I've fallen for you, too," she said, making him smile.

Then he left.

Savannah paced the inside of the bunker after Grayson left. She wanted to clap, to cheer, to run outside and restart her life. With Grayson in it. Forever.

But she knew it was too soon.

After Grayson got everything handled, took a copy of the recording to the police and made sure they listened to the right part, he would return here for her. He'd promised.

In the meantime, she simply had to wait.

Not so simply, though. She at last had more than hope. This horrible time would soon be over.

For now, she just needed to be patient.

Right.

Grayson hadn't been gone long, and Savannah needed to occupy her mind as she waited. She spent a few minutes sitting on one of those folding chairs and checking things on her burner phone but nothing captured her interest. She put the phone down on the chair beside her.

Work on Grayson's first responder website idea? She wouldn't be able to concentrate.

She wasn't hungry, so she didn't try eating another of those sandwiches.

Looking around, she spotted the tall, thick bookcase that didn't look as it if belonged out here in this former mineshaft. The shelving looked potentially unstable and likely to collapse on this uneven floor and spew the many kinds of books on it onto the vinyl tiles. It seemed surprising that it hadn't toppled in the earthquake a few days ago, but maybe the shaking hadn't been too bad right here.

Who knew when Grayson had brought the bookcase to this bunker? It had probably been when he was a kid, and she gathered that it hadn't fallen over yet. Or at least he hadn't mentioned it, and she saw no damaged parts.

In any case, she approached it for the first time and looked more closely at the books on it. They ranged from thrillers to biographies and travel guides to all sorts of countries.

To her own surprise, she picked out a fiction book that was apparently about a first responder. She was fascinated not only by Grayson himself, but also what he did.

She would need a new life after this was all over. Would she be able to become a first responder and have him hire her?

After all, she enjoyed helping people. Had learned a bit from Grayson about all that first responders do. Enjoyed the idea of becoming one herself.

And that way, they would definitely remain in each other's lives—even if only professionally.

As she sat there starting to thumb through the book, she realized she hoped they would remain in each other's lives for additional reasons, too.

It might be too soon for her to embark on a real relationship with another man. But if she ever did, Grayson was one man she was certain she could trust.

And love.

Unlike that horrible former husband of hers, who had tried so hard to ruin her life.

A noise sounded from the entryway. This was much too soon for Grayson to return after having a copy of the recording made and taking it to the police. He'd hardly left. Did he forget something?

She stood and put the book down on the chair. Surely it could only have been Grayson she'd heard, though—right?

Unless some animal also called this bunker home sometimes.

Or—

Oh no!

"Hello, Savannah," Zane Oliver said with a smirk, walking through the opening.

He was a man of moderate height, with dark hair but a receding hairline. He was a few years older than Savannah's thirty-one, but his sagging jawline made him look a lot older. He'd been relatively good-looking when they had met, but not any longer. Or maybe that was just because Savannah had come to despise him.

How had he found her here? This place was Grayson's. It pained Savannah even to see this miserable person in a location she had come to value so much, thanks to the wonderful man who had brought her here.

Like her, Zane was wearing a completely casual outfit—a light yellow T-shirt and black shorts—that wasn't at all like his usually professional attire.

"Hello, Zane," she said back, forcing her tone to remain calm, even though she wanted to scream and race out of there.

She couldn't, though. Zane, blocking the exit, held a gun in his hand and was pointing it toward her. "Interesting refuge you've got here. I'd never have thought someone like you would wind up living in a former mine. On the other hand, I never thought someone like you would wind up escaping from the cops and eluding them for so long."

"How…how did you find me?"

"Oh, that wonderful phone recorder I rely on so much has other functions, too. There's a GPS transmitter on it. I followed it, and here I am."

Savannah felt herself shaking. But something about that didn't make sense. "It's not here," she told him. Grayson had it with him wherever he'd driven to, but she wasn't going to say anything to her horrible ex about that.

"I know that. Your new buddy—he's a first responder guy, right? Anyway, we saw him drive off a little while ago, and the dot showing the location of my recorder went in that direction. But we could see he was the only one in the car, so I followed what the dot showed before, and here I am." His smile seemed to grow even more evil, if that was possible.

"Who's *we*?" Savannah had to ask.

"None of your business, but I want to take care of both of you and get my recorder back."

Which meant Grayson could be in danger, too. But at the moment, there was nothing Savannah could do about it. She had to save her own life first, before she could try calling Grayson.

Under the circumstances, she had to assume that the other person was Schuyler Wells. There could be others she didn't know about, of course. But right now it didn't matter who it was.

"Okay, Zane, let's talk about this." Savannah spoke in as reasonable a tone as she could. "I'm a bit surprised to see you in this area. Don't you think someone will recognize you?"

"Like someone recognized you? Hey, I'm not going into town. This is far enough out that I'm not too worried. But I do have one concern."

He paused, so Savannah did as she figured she was supposed to and asked, "What's that?" She was still standing near her chair, from which she'd risen before. Zane, however, was walking around the room, glancing around as if looking for something.

"I'm debating whether just to shoot you here or take you somewhere else. This isn't a bad place, since when your buddy is gone I gather not many people, if anyone, would think of looking for you here."

Then they were planning on killing her, and maybe Grayson, too. She had to warn him somehow.

"The thing is," Zane continued, "I want this to look like a suicide. After all, you did murder me and your lawyer. It's only natural you'd feel some sense of guilt." Another of those evil smiles.

That was enough. He wanted her to be afraid. And she was. But after everything she had gone through, she wasn't simply going to submit to whatever he intended to do with her.

Thinking quickly, she said, "Oh, I do. I feel terribly guilty that I didn't dump you sooner. And I'm sure you're the one who killed your friend Ian."

He didn't deny it. "Could be," he said, still smiling.

"But why did you do all this?" she couldn't help asking. "Why pretend to be dead and frame me? Are you low on money and needing to hide? Or do you just hate me enough to want to ruin my life? Or—"

"All of the above," he said with a laugh. "It was so nice to have you around as a scapegoat, dear wifey, though I'm sure I'll be able to pop back eventually from where I recovered after you 'killed' me and bring my business back from its current mediocre status to its former huge success. I'll just tell everyone you scared me enough when you tried to kill me that I pretended at first to be dead. When I survived, I couldn't bring myself to return for a long while, so I hid in another town. But hell, you divorced me. That was the best reason for me to do all this. I'm in charge. I always was. And when you did something I didn't choose so you could change my life, I had to do something to pay you back. And now, when you're found dead, I'll pretend to give a damn. Pretend."

That was enough. Savannah a bit scared but even more determined, turned briefly and grabbed the chair, using it as a shield as she approached Zane.

Would she survive to see Grayson again? She had to.

Zane shot at her, but she darted sideways, still holding the chair. Zane went the same way, keeping his aim steady as she dashed to one side of the room.

She leaped forward and hit him with the chair, hoping she'd knock him out or at least distract him enough that she could run away.

That didn't happen. Instead, Zane moved sideways again, not aiming at her for the moment as he regained his equilibrium—

That was when Savannah got the idea of how to stop him.

Not looking to her side, she nevertheless moved that way, dropping the chair and grabbing that tall, unstable bookcase she'd been examining before and yanking it sideways so it toppled. Onto Zane.

Knocking him to the floor. One of the large, thick wooden side panels hit him in the head, as books tumbled all around him.

Knocking him out.

Savannah grabbed his gun, smiled as evilly as she could at the unconscious body of the man she hated, snatched her phone from the chair that had been beside her—

And fled the bunker.

As soon as she got to the opening and figured she would have a good signal, she called Grayson.

He answered right away. "What's up, Savannah? I haven't gotten very far, and—"

"It's Zane! He found me. I knocked him out and I'm running

away, but he said someone is after you in your car, too. Watch out, Grayson. Please be careful."

She didn't hear another word from him.

But she did hear what sounded like a car crash.

"No!" she screamed and began running along the dirt road.

Damn. His head had hit the side window before the airbags deployed. And now it hurt like crazy.

But at least Grayson was still awake. And mad at himself. Never mind he was here in the middle of nowhere. He should have remained careful, watching around him.

Seeing that car that hit him before it could run him off the road.

And now?

Pain shot through his head. But he knew better than to move.

Zane was with Savannah? Damn. Grayson should be there with her, protecting her. But he wasn't. Although it sounded like she'd handled the situation well, at least for now.

She was okay. She had to be. He wanted to grab her and shield her and care for her forever.

But they both had to survive for a forever to happen.

What about him?

Well, if Zane was with Savannah, someone else had run Grayson off the road. Chances were that it was Schuyler Wells. But who it was didn't matter, at least not much.

How Grayson handled this did. He had to get back to the bunker fast. To Savannah.

He heard a nearby car door slam shut. If whoever it was thought Grayson was unconscious, all the better. Grayson allowed himself to continue slumping against the inside of his door.

Sure enough, that door was pulled open. Not a great thing, but Grayson allowed himself to slide out onto the ground, fortunately hitting his shoulder before his head came to rest on the forest floor. Pain nevertheless shot through him yet again, but at least he remained conscious.

"Okay, first responder guy," he heard a voice say and recognized it as Schuyler's. He didn't dare open his eyes yet. "Where's that damned recorder? Zane should have known better. I didn't know he was taping his conversations. He just told me about it."

The guy was talking as if he was holding a conversation with Grayson, but since he didn't do anything to hurt Grayson further he had to believe his target here was unconscious. Good.

Feeling a movement against his side, Grayson fought not to moan or move. But he did open his right eye just a little, in time to see one leg hoisted over him as Schuyler—yes, it was the man he'd seen on those real estate websites—stepped partway into the car, apparently trying to find the recorder.

Also good. Grayson remained lying there for another few seconds until Schuyler bent forward even more. Then Grayson roared to life, pulling the guy from between his legs and onto the ground, pummeling him in the face.

Schuyler screamed and attempted to fend Grayson off—unsuccessfully. Ignoring his own pain, Grayson rolled the other man over till his face was on the ground and pulled his arms behind him. Too bad he didn't have cuffs with him. Holding Schuyler down by kneeling on his back and arms, Grayson pulled his fortunately long-sleeved T-shirt over his head and rolled it until it became rope-like. He used it to tie Schuyler's arms together.

"Hold still, jerk," Grayson said to the man squirming beneath him. "It's over."

Only it wasn't. Not completely.

Grayson was worried about Savannah, where she was—and how long Zane would stay immobilized.

He felt a little chilly in the shade of the forest without his shirt, but at least it was springtime in Arizona.

He stepped over Schuyler and leaned into the car, extracting the oh-so valuable recorder from the floor on the passenger's side and tucking it into his belt. He also found his phone on the floor and retrieved it. Then he opened the glove compartment, extracting a small but definitely lethal gun. Backing out again, he pointed the gun at Schuyler.

"Okay," he said. "Here's how it's going to be. Your buddy Zane has been subdued, too, but we're going back to the bunker and make sure both of you are sufficiently secured. Stay there a sec, then you'll stand up."

First, though, Grayson wanted to call Savannah. He took a few steps backward, still facing Schuyler, still pointing the gun at him. He didn't particularly want Wells to hear his conversation, but he wasn't going far enough away from his captive to ensure he didn't.

He pushed the button on his phone to call Savannah. She answered immediately.

"Grayson? Are you okay? What happened?"

"I'm fine, and I'll explain it all in a few minutes, when I see you. I'm not far away. But are you outside the bunker?"

"Yes, but I'm near it, hiding behind some bushes, watching the opening to make sure Zane doesn't come out."

"Perfect! Stay there. If he does come out, try to figure out his direction but don't get close, okay?"

"Okay." She paused, then added, "I'm so glad you're okay, Grayson. I was so worried."

That sent a zing of pleasure through him that he had to ignore for now.

"Don't worry," he said. "And I think this'll all be over with very soon."

Chapter 21

Savannah continued to crouch on the dirt behind the bushes. The best part was that they were thick and concealing. There were uneven rows of them in this area. A good place to hide.

She was so glad Grayson was okay. The sounds she had heard after calling him had been scary. Had the person who'd been after him, presumably Schuyler, hit his car?

She wished he had told her more, but he'd promised to do so soon. And she had come to believe Grayson's promises. She would see him in a little while. He'd said so.

And she couldn't wait. Wisely or not, she had come to really care for him.

To love him.

It was late in the day now, but fortunately there was still enough light for her to see the bunker's opening.

She had certainly intended to hurt Zane, and the fact she had knocked him out was a good thing, even though she couldn't have been certain of that outcome. She just hoped she hadn't killed him. Wouldn't that be ironic under the circumstances?

The good thing was that she would have proof he had remained alive, at least until now. And that he had conspired to frame her for his murder.

Time seemed to pass so slowly as she waited there. No indication that Zane was leaving, at least, unless he had found some exit she didn't know about. Through the mine somehow? And what direction would Grayson come from?

How long would it take him to get here—

There! She saw movement from the edges of the dirt road. Two people, walking.

Fortunately, one of them—the one walking behind—was Grayson, not wearing a shirt. Savannah couldn't help staring at his sexy body, even in these stressful circumstances. But she quickly brought herself back to reality.

The man in front was Schuyler Wells, the guy who'd claimed to be Savannah's lover as part of the attempt to frame her. As she'd believed, he must have been the one who'd gone after Grayson and the recorder.

The one who'd apparently caused Grayson to be in an accident. At least Grayson appeared okay. He walked normally, and she saw no blood on him.

She just observed his gorgeous, carved chest…

And Schuyler appeared to have his hands tied behind his back as he moved slowly forward, prodded by Grayson.

She wanted to scream out in happiness and relief and run toward them, but she didn't. She would wait until they had entered the bunker, keeping watch out here in case Zane had somehow escaped another way, but then join them inside.

And so she waited—and good thing that she did. Sure enough, Zane appeared at the opening to the bunker. As far as she knew, she had his only weapon.

Grayson apparently saw him too, and stopped. "Hey, Zane. Good to see you," he called.

"Not good to see you," Zane called back. His voice sounded a bit fuzzy, and he wasn't moving fast, either—possibly as a result of his injuries from the bookcase.

Or, possibly, he was faking it to put Grayson off guard as he approached.

In case it was the latter, Savannah moved away from her hiding place and out into the open—holding Zane's gun and aiming it at him.

"Hi, Grayson," Savannah said, glancing in his direction but looking back immediately. "Should we go inside the bunker now, or somewhere else?"

"The bunker will do. I've got some rope there and you can help me tie both these guys up. I've got Schuyler secured, but that would work better."

"Damn you," Zane cried. "I'm not going back in there. And you're not going to tie me up like some stupid animal you've captured."

"Oh, is that what you are?" Savannah couldn't help asking. She basked for a few seconds in Grayson's smile. "Anyway, that's exactly what I'm going to do. And if Grayson wants you inside the bunker, that's where we'll go."

"Actually," Grayson said, "we can hang out in the entry area." He had his gun in his hand, and now he aimed it at Zane, too. "Looks like our buddy Zane is the bigger flight risk at the moment, and I've got control over Schuyler. Let's go into the entryway, then I'll tell you when to go inside for the rope, Savannah, and where it is."

Which made her feel wonderful. She'd started to fear that maybe things weren't over after all.

But now she had reason again to believe they were. Or could be.

And she could only hope that the future became as wonderful for her, with Grayson, as she now desired to have.

Oh, yes. She desired it. And him.

They were sitting on the stone floor of the entry cave to the bunker—Zane and Schuyler, both secured with good ropes, and Grayson certainly knew how to bind them well. But just in case, he still held his gun and encouraged Savannah to hold hers, as well.

Savannah. She looked so happy now, so radiant.

And he loved her smile.

He also loved the fact that she would soon be cleared of all wrongdoing, particularly of murdering her ex.

Would she want to put it all behind her now, including him?

If so, he would have to convince her otherwise. And not just on a cot in a bunker.

Grayson had put his shirt back on. Now, his phone rang. He looked at the caller ID and smiled. Sergeant Spencer Colton of the Mustang Valley PD.

His cousin. The cop he had called after he and Savannah had tied up the two men. He'd given Spencer a fairly detailed explanation of what had occurred in as few words as possible, and told him where he could come to pick up the criminals in this situation. His cousin had said yes, he and some colleagues would come to take the real bad guys into custody.

This time, Grayson would be glad to see him. "Hi, cuz," he said, answering the phone.

"Okay, we're here. Give me better directions. Where the hell are you?"

Talking to him a bit more, Grayson learned that Spencer had passed the area of his car wreck and continued down the dirt road. "You're probably right outside," he said. "I'll send Savannah out to greet you when you get here."

Fortunately, although it was getting later, there was still some daylight left, so Spencer and his fellow cops should be able to see her fairly easily.

"You okay with that?" he asked Savannah.

"If the other choice is staying here with those two—" she gestured with her gun hand in their direction "—then I'm definitely okay with it."

She looked so good that way. So natural. Would she have any interest in becoming a first responder, too? That would be one way they could work together, though he wouldn't want that to be the only way.

"Good."

She exited through the opening.

"Look, Colton," Zane said. "You really don't have to do this. I may be 'dead.' To most of the world, but I still have resources. Financial resources even you wouldn't believe. If you just work with me, tell your cronies that everything was set up by Schuyler, here, I can pay you—"

Grayson laughed. "Oh, you're really a hoot, aren't you, Oliver? Even if I needed your money, assuming you still have any after disappearing that way, no way would I take it."

And on the ground near Zane, Schuyler was shouting, "You SOB," and clearly attempting to get closer to him by edging along on the stone base.

Grayson didn't need to stop him. Three cops were suddenly at the entrance to the bunker, followed by Savannah. None of them appeared to be taking her into custody, fortunately.

As the two other uniformed officers, probably the same ones Grayson had glimpsed at Zane's house, took Zane and Schuyler into custody, cuffing them and reciting their rights, Spencer came over to Grayson, who now stood near one of the rough stone walls.

Spencer looked a lot younger than he really was—but he had a good reputation as a cop. He had sandy blond hair and blue eyes, and usually had a keen sense of humor—although he looked awfully serious right now. "Okay, cuz. Why didn't you tell me before what was going on? You were helping a wanted fugitive all this time, and you now have recorded proof of her innocence? I should arrest all four of you, then figure this all out."

"You know I won't run away, so if you learn something different from what I told you—which you won't—you can arrest me then. And I believe that Savannah feels the same way."

She had approached them, and now nodded. "I'm innocent. I said so all along, and you finally have proof. You're taking the man I allegedly murdered into custody, Sergeant Colton. I've already handed Zane's gun to you. And I won't run away again. I don't think I have to. In fact, I suspect I'll need to go to the police station now, right? But you don't have to cuff me or anything."

Grayson couldn't help it. He drew near Savannah and put his arm around her, smiling triumphantly at his cousin. "Thanks to this wonderful lady, you're going to be the primary cop to solve this situation," Grayson told him. "You'll get recognition for it. I think you'll be thanking me soon."

"Don't count on it," Spencer said—but then he smiled. "I gather the two of you are more than first responder and rescued soul."

"Count on that," Grayson said, giving Savannah a kiss.

It finally appeared really to be over. Savannah felt overjoyed.

Oh, she did accompany Grayson to the police station, as his cousin, the police sergeant, insisted. But no one took her into custody then, either, although she did have to make an official statement.

Sergeant Spencer Colton apparently called an EMT, not one of Grayson's employees, to check his cousin out after the car accident. Fortunately, except for some bruising, especially on his head, he apparently was fine.

Afterward, standing in the station's reception area, Savannah was told by the police chief that the situation remained under investigation and she was not to leave town.

"Tell us where we'll be able to find you," said the tall and mostly bald Chief Al Barco.

"I—" Savannah tried to answer, but she didn't know what to say. She would prefer not to return to the bunker or the cabin, and certainly not Zane's guesthouse, which she'd been staying in.

"For now, she'll be staying with me, at the Triple R," Grayson broke in and gave the address. "And here's her current phone number." He provided the burner phone's number to the cop.

His family home? That sounded wonderful to Savannah. But was it a good idea?

"Sounds good," the chief said. He had been regarding her sternly, but now he smiled. "I've got a feeling we're going to have no further official interest in you, but stay tuned. We'll have to let you know."

"Of course," Savannah said. She wished he'd been more positive, but at least there was reason for hope now. A lot of reasons.

"I think you've got some investigating to do," Grayson added. "You have a couple of killers in custody, and one of them's allegedly a dead guy."

Chief Barco laughed. "Let's see how that all works out," he said.

"Yes," said Grayson. "Let's see." He took Savannah's hand and began leading her out of the station.

Sergeant Colton came over to them. "I haven't completely forgiven you," he said to Grayson, but he looked at Savannah and winked.

A cop winked at her! For some reason, that made Savannah feel a whole lot better. She was free now, hopefully forever.

"What'll it take for you to forgive me?" Grayson said.

"Keep me better informed next time, for one thing."

"I just hope there's no next time, at least not like this," Grayson said, and Savannah could only smile and nod her concurrence.

They left the station. But now what? It was dark outside. And Savannah knew her ultimate goal that night was Grayson's home.

Bad idea? Oh, she loved the idea of being with him longer. He had done all he had promised, and it appeared that she was exonerated from the charges that had disrupted her life so horribly.

She really liked the guy. More than that. She had certainly come to care for him, a lot. Probably too much. But in some ways there was no reason for them to stay close together any longer.

Even though she knew she would really like that.

But she had vowed not to get involved with any other men after her ugly divorce —and she wasn't sure she could so easily trust another guy so deeply, after what Zane had done.

Did she dare get even more involved with Grayson now?

They did stop for dinner at a nice restaurant on their way home, an Italian place. And for once Savannah was hungry.

She wished she could pay. She should be able to soon, since she would be able to get access to her bank account and other assets.

But for now—well, Grayson said he would pay, and she let him.

This time.

And next time? There had to be a next time. This simply could not be the end of his being in her life.

She hoped.

But she wasn't certain. And she felt tears fill her eyes as they headed back to Grayson's car.

Chapter 22

Grayson knew his home would never feel the same again.

Savannah and he had stopped for dinner last night after leaving the police station. Savannah had seemed quite happy that her food was warm and fresh for a change, and the restaurant was filled with people—although apparently no one who knew her. At least no one said hi, or pointed at her.

He'd driven them to the ranch after that in an SUV he'd rented temporarily while his car was being fixed.

Savannah and he had walked to his portion of the house and he'd shown her into a guest room.

But she hadn't stayed there. No, they'd celebrated the recent happenings by spending the night in bed together, in the most enjoyable way possible.

He loved it. He loved her. And this simply couldn't be the last night they spent together.

In the morning, they had gone out to a fast-food place for breakfast, and Grayson told Savannah he was taking her back to his office for now.

"I've got something I need to do at the ranch," he said as they finished eating.

"I understand," she said. "Are you going to check with your brothers and sisters and stepmom about how your father is doing?"

"That, too, maybe. But—well, like my siblings, as you know, that wing in the main house where we stayed last night is my own. You are welcome to stay in the guestroom there as long as you want."

"Oh." Her expression, as she looked down at her empty plate, appeared downcast. "You don't need to do that. I'll find another place very soon."

"No," he said firmly and fast, not wanting to even ask where she had in mind—and assuming she didn't yet. "You won't. And that doesn't mean we won't see each other. It simply means we'll each have our own space, so we can decide how much time we will spend together."

Like forever? That was the thought that rolled through his mind. Damn it, he had fallen for Savannah.

Did he want to spend the rest of his life with her? Well, maybe. He certainly felt more for her than he had for any other woman. But she'd just gotten a divorce—was she ready to trust again?

Could he trust that she would stay with him forever if she seemed ready to make a commitment?

He walked her back to his office building and made sure his staff had started to arrive. He was amused at how Winchell demanded Savannah's attention, which she gave without reservation, kneeling on the floor and hugging the smart and skilled search and rescue dog.

He had not been able to bring Savannah here before, not while she was a fugitive, so the people on his staff didn't yet know her. After introducing Savannah to them, he told them her current status: unofficially exonerated from committing a murder.

Of course all of them, Norah in particular, became highly

excited for Savannah and demanded to hear how that had happened.

"Go ahead and tell them," Grayson said to her. "I've got to get on my way. See you all soon."

He drove back to the ranch, half wishing he could have stayed to hear how they all discussed what had happened yesterday—and also get a sense for where Savannah's mind was now, what she thought her future might contain. He would make sure she had a place to stay and anything else she needed, of course, whether or not it was at the ranch. But he had come to know her well enough to feel certain she would make plans for what came next, then implement them.

With his involvement? If so, how much?

He now hoped they would stay in each other's lives, at least a little. Maybe a lot.

He soon drove back through the gate at the Rattlesnake Ridge Ranch and parked in an empty spot near the car he recognized as Asher's. He assumed his other siblings weren't around just then, which was fine.

In fact, his younger half brother was a good one to talk to about how things were going with the family. Asher was actually the ranch foreman.

Of course Asher might be in the stable or out on the grounds, but Grayson entered the main ranch house, planning to go up to his wing on the second floor. But hearing a noise from the kitchen, he figured he had better stop in and say hi to whoever was there, Asher or staff or someone else, rather than startling someone with his presence. He walked through the living room, with its luxurious, floor to ceiling walls and exposed beam ceiling of the open living room. He also passed the dining room, as always taking in how nice this place was, with its wooden floors and lots of trim and expensive decorations.

"Hi, bro. It's a surprise to see you wandering around here at this hour." Asher had just exited the kitchen, a mug of coffee in his hand. "You just picking something up, or—"

"I'll be hanging around here more now," Grayson told him. "And you'll probably be hearing in the news the reason why."

"Yeah? Tell me." They first went back into the kitchen where Grayson, too, got a mug of coffee, then headed into the living room and sat facing one another.

Asher looked like a perfect foreman, Grayson thought, not for the first time. His younger brother certainly looked like a cowboy, with longish dark brown hair, a slight brush of facial hair that included a dark goatee, and a casual denim shirt and slacks that appeared entirely appropriate for horseback riding. All he needed was a cowboy hat, but since they were inside, that wasn't likely at the moment.

Even better, Asher was dedicated to the ranch and to making certain everything went well there—especially important now, with their father in a coma.

"So what's going on?" Asher asked right away.

Grayson told him, keeping the story brief but starting from finding the dead van driver, then Savannah hiding in a fishing cabin, and ending with her exoneration yesterday. "And till she figures out where to go and what to do, I'm letting her stay in my guest room. And—"

The doorbell rang. One of their staff hurried to open it, but Asher headed that way, and so did Grayson, partly out of curiosity.

A man stood there, and he looked vaguely familiar. He immediately looked toward the two brothers while the maid left the entry. "Hi," he said. "I'm Jace Smith and—well, I think I'm your brother, the real Ace Colton. Can I come in? I'd like to talk to you."

Grayson felt as if he'd been hit over the head. Really? He didn't spend a lot of time around here with family, but he certainly tried to keep up with the news about Ace. Sure, they'd been told Ace wasn't their brother by blood.

But it seemed a shock to have someone come in like that and claim to be that real sibling.

"Sure, come in," said Asher, beside him, and they all stepped aside.

Grayson studied the man some more. No weapons—or malice—apparent. If he truly was the real Ace, then they'd have shared a mother, Tessa, along with sister Ainsley. He did have dark hair and blue eyes like they did.

Tons of questions immediately began forming in Grayson's mind. This stranger was his brother? Really? Could he prove it?

The maid returned to the kitchen when Asher asked and Jace said he'd like some coffee, too. Soon, they were all seated in the living room looking at one another—although Grayson noticed that Jace was also glancing at the high-quality decorations around the room.

"So tell us more," Grayson said, taking a sip of his own coffee, forcing his hands not to tremble. This was strange timing, that he happened to be here when this guy arrived. Was Jace for real? Or was he just some guy off the street who had heard about the family issue and decided to take advantage of it?

"Well, I'd been told a little while ago that I might be the real Ace Colton," Jace responded, "and the earthquake made me realize I'd better check it out sooner rather than waiting any longer, before I lose any opportunity to find out." He said he had heard from a friend who was a nurse that there was a switch of newborn babies at Mustang Valley General Hospital on Christmas Day forty years ago—his birthday.

"My mother is Luella Smith," he said, which made both Grayson and Asher sit up straighter. Jace explained that he hadn't spoken to Luella in many years and didn't know where to find her to ask questions, but from what that he'd heard, and what he knew about his own early life, he truly thought he could have been switched at birth. "I'd be glad to take a DNA test," he finished. "I've always felt there was something more to my childhood, and I've been looking for where I belong for as long as I can remember."

Could it be true? Well, they certainly needed to find out.

What would Ace think about this? About this Jace showing up and making his claims. To Grayson, Ace was still his brother.

"Let's get everyone together here for dinner tonight," Asher said, "and we can see what our other siblings think about this. Oh, and Grayson, I think it's time we also met your lady friend that you saved from prison."

"I didn't exactly save her," he said, but he did agree to bring Savannah to join them for a meal here that night as long as she was okay with it.

He didn't mind seeing how she fit in with his family. Not that he was ready to ask her to join it…yet. Would that time come?

And these circumstances certainly weren't the best for her to meet everyone.

Savannah had had quite a morning. There apparently hadn't been any emergencies, so she had gotten to talk with Grayson's first responder employees—Chad, with his dog Winch, Pedro and Norah. They had each told her about their specialties, pasts and how they enjoyed helping other people.

Savannah loved it! She had already been growing somewhat bored with her life, just holding events to collect contributions for the poor and needy. It was too distant and impersonal. What about doing something even more worthwhile, which could directly help people survive? Could she complete what she anticipated to be grueling physical training to become a first responder?

Or was there some way for her to just help Grayson's first responders as they helped other people?

She'd intended to discuss it more with Grayson, and he'd called her to invite her to dinner with his family tonight at their ranch.

That discussion would have to wait.

He had picked her up early at her request so she could buy a nicer outfit to feel more comfortable meeting his family.

She made a mental note of the cost and added it to the amount she'd been keeping track of to repay Grayson when she got access to her own assets.

Now they were nearly at the ranch. Grayson had told her he had related her story to one of his brothers, so he figured the rest of his siblings were now aware of it.

"Plus," he said, "that possible brother of ours is going to be there, too." Grayson had described the situation to her, including the likelihood that the man known as Ace Colton, their oldest brother, was not related to them by blood at all, and that the mysterious Jace Smith now claimed to be the real Ace.

"Do you think, then, that this is the real guy?"

"I guess we'll find out," Grayson said as he pulled in through the gate and pulled into a parking spot. near the entry to the main house. "He's agreed to a DNA test."

Would she ever want to live here? Staying overnight in Grayson's suite was okay, but more? That thought came to her as he strode beside her up the wide walkway to the front door. He didn't knock but opened it.

She was glad she had chosen a dress and heels that appeared elegant enough for this venue, a slate blue dress decorated with white flowers, short sleeved and of a flowing fabric—dressy, yet far from formal. And except for the length of her hair, she knew she looked like herself once more.

Grayson showed her through the living room to the dining room, where most of the seats were occupied. He introduced her to a lot of people, all Coltons—except the guy who was Jace Smith and still, possibly, a Colton.

Some of them had spouses or significant others there, too. Savannah was happy when she sat at Grayson's right side, and to her right were his brother Callum, with whom she understood Grayson was very close, plus his fiancée, Hazel Hart, and Hazel's adorable daughter, Evie, a five-year-old who had long brown hair and a fun, outgoing personality.

The kind of daughter Savannah might wish for someday.

And that thought caused her to look toward her left, where Grayson sat.

At that moment, he was looking in her direction, too—though not directly at her. He appeared to be observing little Evie, as well.

Was he interested in having kids, too? Savannah had never asked him that.

Could she, would she, like an ongoing relationship with Grayson, including a marriage and kids? At that moment, with his family around, and with her own life a whole lot better than it had been, Savannah had to believe she would, in fact, like it.

But would Grayson?

"So what do you think of my family?" Grayson whispered into her ear.

"They seem like nice people," she said noncommittally. "This is certainly different from how I was brought up. My family's a lot smaller."

"Well, maybe you need a larger one," Grayson murmured, then appeared to realize what he had said and took a swig of beer from the stein on the table at the far side of his salad bowl. "Or you should have had one to help you through the mess you just went through a lot better than I could help you."

Savannah was amused at his attempt to back down from what he had said—even as she began to ponder how she really would get along with his family…if.

"No one could have done better than you," was all she said.

She didn't have an opportunity to discuss what he meant any further, since it seemed his family members wanted to get to know the strangers in their midst a bit more. From Ace to attorney sister Ainsley, Rafe, twins Callum and Marlowe, and ranch foreman Asher, they all started asking her questions. Savannah concentrated on their names, wanting to remember them even if she didn't know who else they had brought to this dinner. Her mood was high, thanks to her exoneration—and she had something to announce that she hadn't yet told Grayson, either. This seemed like a good enough time to let him know.

"And it's now official," she said, looking at him. "I received a call from Police Chief Al Barco before. All charges against me have been dropped."

"I knew that," Grayson chimed in. "Barco let me know he'd told you, and it's in the media today, too."

And Savannah could only laugh as the others in the room congratulated her.

They next held a detailed conversation with Jace, who told them about a really awful childhood, where his mother was hardly present. But his attitude, at least, was good.

That led to their last major discussion of the evening—about Payne Colton, who remained in a coma. Savannah felt so sorry for him, and for all his children. She wished she could do something to help.

And maybe she could—at least a little. She would encourage Grayson to go see his dad tomorrow.

So when the time came for Grayson to bid her good-night, she invited him into his own guestroom for a nightcap.

And more. A lot more.

What a night.

It had been enjoyable to spend time with his siblings and their significant others—and that cute little Evie.

Grayson liked kids. Did he want them someday? Yeah, quite possibly—if he ever got married.

And at the moment, after spending the night again with Savannah and having incredible, though protected, sex…

Well, marriage wasn't out of the question. He cared for her. Probably loved her.

But he recognized that, thanks to her particularly ugly divorce and what happened after that, she probably would never want to marry again.

When he left the ranch, he dropped Savannah at his office. She'd said she intended to go talk to his first responder staff again soon. Seemed like she might actually be interested in becoming a first responder, and working for him. Being with her every day like that sounded great. And maybe being with her every night, too?

The thought had definitely crossed his mind. And not just once.

But for now, he was on his way to the hospital. Savannah had urged him, after that wonderful family dinner at which his dad couldn't be present, to go visit Payne.

He'd promised to do so. And now, he was walking through the medical facility's front door again.

He had noticed the Affirmation Alliance Group's table across the street again and ignored it.

But when he ran into Selina in the lobby this time, too, he wanted to turn around and leave again. Instead, he confronted her. "Well, hello again," he said to his former stepmother. "I hope you're just leaving, since I'm coming in."

"Oh, I think you're just leaving, too," she said with a sadistic grin and started to rail at him about being a miserable son and worse—so Grayson turned his back on her and, yes, left.

But this time he didn't go to his car. Instead, he walked around the hospital till he reached another door. He went inside and hurried through the sparkling, crowded hallways, past nurses and doctors in their respective scrubs, to his father's room.

It was a private room, and the door was being watched by a private security guard hired by one of Grayson's siblings. Grayson showed his ID and was allowed in.

It was hard to look at the powerful, egocentric Payne Colton that way, lying unconscious in the hospital bed, hooked up to IVs and monitors.

"Hi, Dad," Grayson said, then sat down carefully at the edge of the bed. His father's skin was pale, his eyes closed, but at least he appeared to be breathing—with help. "Sorry I haven't spent more time here, but I've been busy." Which was true, though not much of an excuse. He talked for a while about the earthquake and helping a woman unjustly accused of a murder and more. Did his father hear any of it? He doubted it.

But Grayson found that the subject he talked most about was Savannah, how she had been framed and how her ex-husband had been at fault—and was actually a murderer himself, or at least an accessory.

The longer Grayson stayed there, the more he wanted his father to regain consciousness and talk to him. Advise him? Probably not, since they had never really agreed on much when Payne was well. But still—

Being in Payne's presence this way underscored the realization that life was too short.

Better to do everything to live it well right now.

Better to do what Grayson knew he really wanted.

He had a goal when he left.

"Bye, Dad. See you again soon."

And he meant it.

Savannah had just had another delightful time talking about First Hand First Responders with Grayson's employees. They were going on a training mission together later that afternoon, which happened often when they weren't on assignment, since they needed to remain fit and smart and skilled.

It sounded enticing to Savannah. Would she be able to undertake initial training and join them soon?

She hoped so. And if she didn't have the stamina to become a first responder like them, she was still determined to help in some way, maybe raising money for his agency so it could grow and help more people.

But at the moment she was waiting for Grayson to come back

to his office and pick her up. He'd called and said he wanted to show her something early that afternoon, and she had of course agreed.

She was watching for him, though, through the window in the lobby of his office building—and saw Norah's amusement as she watched Savannah keeping an eye out for Grayson.

And then, there he was, with his car parked right in front of the building. Savannah didn't wait for him to come in. She rushed out the door and got into the passenger seat of Grayson's rental SUV. "So will you tell me now where we're going?" she asked.

"Nope. You'll see." Grayson shot her a particularly sexy grin, which made Savannah's body react, but her mind was stewing. What was this man up to?

He drove out of town and into the familiar forest. They even passed the site of the destroyed van from days earlier—though it felt like weeks ago.

"Are we going to the fishing cabin?" Savannah finally asked.

"Good guess."

"Why?" was her next question.

"You'll see," was the frustrating answer.

They soon arrived. Savannah got out of the car, as did Grayson. They entered through the window since they had locked the door when they'd left before. There was still no sign of whoever the owner was, so they had the place to themselves.

"Please sit here," Grayson said, moving Savannah's favorite chair out from under the table and taking her hand to help her into it.

Strange. She didn't need assistance, and he surely was aware of that. But she appreciated what seemed like a caring gesture.

She appreciated what came next even more.

"Savannah," Grayson said, sitting down on a chair beside her. "I would never have thought that I'd help to save a woman from being unjustly accused of murder, let alone that it would change my life so much." He was looking straight at her with his emotional blue eyes, and Savannah felt her own tear up. "But it did. And I'm glad I can help. I'm glad I met you. And I want you to stay in my life."

"Oh, Grayson." Savannah's voice choked up, so she moved forward till she stood in front of him. He rose, too, and held her tightly against him.

"You've met my family now," he continued, and she felt his chest vibrate with his words. "And though I try not to get together with them a lot, they are part of my life. They would be…well, I'm hoping you are okay with them, and will remain part of my life, too. Savannah, I love you."

He took a step back. Again he looked down at her, and she responded, "I love you, too, Grayson, Colton family ties and all. And I enjoy families. I want kids someday. Your kids."

Grayson laughed. "And I want yours, too. But, after all you went through, are you willing to trust another man?"

"Yes," she responded vehemently. "If that man is you." She tried to move even closer again, to kiss him.

But Grayson pulled away, making Savannah feel bereft. Only temporarily, though.

Grayson got down on one knee and pulled a small box from his pocket. Savannah heard herself gasp. "Is that—"

"Savannah Murphy Oliver," Grayson said, "Like I said, I love you. Will you marry me?"

Savannah nearly screamed her answer, even though, if she'd asked herself before, she'd have hesitated or worried or—

"Yes," she cried. In moments, after he placed the ring on her finger, she was in the arms of the man who had cared for her, believed in her, saved her life and her future—and now wanted to share his future with her. "Yes, Grayson," she repeated to the man she loved. "I love you, too."

"Now that's the kind of first response I like to hear," he said, and placed his lips on hers once more.

* * * * *

Keep reading for an excerpt of
Texas On My Mind
by Delores Fossen.
Find it in the
The McCords: Riley & Lucky anthology,
out now!

CHAPTER ONE

THERE WERE TWO women in Captain Riley McCord's bed. Women wearing cutoff shorts, skinny tops and flip-flops.

Riley blinked a couple of times to make sure they weren't by-products of his pain meds and bone-deep exhaustion. *Nope.* They were real enough because he could hear them breathing. See them breathing, too.

The lamp on the nightstand was on, the milky-yellow light spilling over them. Their tops holding in those C-cups were doing plenty of moving with each breath they took.

He caught a glimpse of a nipple.

If he'd still been a teenager, Riley might have considered having two women in his bed a dream come true. Especially in this room. He'd grown up in this house, had had plenty of fantasies in that very bed. But he was thirty-one now, and with his shoulder throbbing like an abscessed tooth, taking on two women didn't fall into fantasy territory. More like suicide.

Besides, man-rule number two applied here: don't do anything half-assed. Anything he attempted right now would be significantly less than half and would make an ass out of him.

Who the hell were they?

And why were they there in his house, in his bed?

The place was supposed to be empty since he'd called ahead

and given the cook and housekeeper the week off. The sisters, Della and Stella, had pretty much run the house since Riley's folks had been killed in a car wreck thirteen years ago. Clearing out the pair hadn't been easy, but he'd used his captain's I'm-giving-the-orders-here voice.

For once it had worked.

His kid sister was away at college. His older brother Lucky was God knew where. Lucky's twin, Logan, was on a business trip and wouldn't be back for at least another week. Even when Logan returned, he'd be spending far more time running the family's cattle brokerage company than actually in the house. That lure of emptiness was the only reason Riley had decided to come here for some peace and quiet.

And so that nobody would see him wincing and grunting in pain.

Riley glanced around to try to figure out who the women were and why they were there. When he checked the family room, he saw a clue by the fireplace. A banner. Well, sort of. He flicked on the lights to get a better look. It was a ten-foot strip of white crepe paper.

Welcome Home, Riley, Our Hero, was written on it.

The black ink had bled, and the tape on one side had given way, and now it dangled and coiled like a soy-sauced ramen noodle.

There were bowls of chips, salsa and other food on the coffee table next to a picture of him in his uniform. Someone had tossed flag confetti all around the snacks, and some of the red, white and blue sparkles had landed on the floor and sofa. In the salsa, too.

Apparently, this was supposed to be the makings of a homecoming party for him.

Whoever had done this probably hadn't counted on his flight from the base in Germany being delayed nine hours. Riley hadn't counted on it, either. Now, it was three in the morning, and he darn sure didn't want to celebrate.

Or have women in his bed.

And he hoped it didn't lower his testosterone a couple of notches to have an unmanly thought like that.

Riley put his duffel bag on the floor. Not quietly, but the women didn't stir even an eyelash. He considered just waking them, but heck, that would require talking to them, and the only thing he wanted right now was another hit of pain meds and a place to collapse.

He went to the bedroom next to his. A guest room. No covers or pillows, which would mean a hunt to find some. That sent him to Lucky's room on the other side of the hall. Covers, yes, but there was another woman asleep facedown with her sleeve-tattooed arm dangling off the side. There was also a saddle on the foot of the bed. Thankfully, Riley's mind was too clouded to even want to consider why it was there.

Getting desperate now and feeling a little like Goldilocks in search of a "just right" place to crash, he went to Logan's suite, the only other bedroom downstairs. Definitely covers there. He didn't waste the energy to turn on the light to have a closer look; since this was Logan's space, it would no doubt be clean enough to pass a military inspection.

No saddles or women, thank God, and he wouldn't have to climb the stairs that he wasn't sure he could climb anyway.

Riley popped a couple of pain meds and dropped down on the bed, his eyes already closing before his head landed against something soft and crumbly. He considered investigating it. *Briefly* considered it. But when it didn't bite, shoot or scald him, he passed on the notion of an investigation.

Whatever was soft and crumbly would just have to wait.

RILEY JACKKNIFED IN Logan's bed, the pain knocking the breath right out of him. Without any kind of warning, the nightmare that he'd been having had morphed into a full-fledged flashback.

Sometimes he could catch the flashback just as it was bubbling to the surface, and he could stomp it back down with his mental steel-toed combat boots. Sometimes humming "Jingle Bells" helped.

Not this time, though.

The flashback had him by the throat before Riley could even get out a single note of that stupid song he hated. Why had his brain chosen that little Christmas ditty to blur out the images anyway?

The smell came first. Always the fucking smell. The dust and debris whipped up by the chopper. The Pave Hawk blades slicing through the dirt-colored smoke. But not drowning out the sounds.

He wasn't sure how sounds like that could make it through the thump of the blades, the shouts, screams and the chaos. But they did. The sounds always did.

Someone was calling for help in a dialect Riley barely understood. But you didn't need to know the words to hear the fear.

Or smell it.

The images came with a vengeance. Like a chopped-up snake crawling and coiling together to form a neat picture of hell. A handful of buildings on fire, others ripped apart from the explosion. Blood on the bleached-out sand. The screams for help. The kids.

Why the hell were there kids?

Riley had been trained to rescue military and civilians after the fight, after all hell had broken loose. Had been conditioned to deal with fires, blood, IEDs, gunfire, and being dropped into the middle of it so he could do his job and save lives.

But nobody had ever been able to tell him how to deal with the kids.

PTSD. Such a tidy little label. A dialect that civilians understood, or thought they did anyway. But it was just another label for shit. Shit that Riley didn't want in his head.

He grabbed his pain meds from the pocket of his uniform and shoved one, then another into his parched mouth. Soon, very soon, he could start stomping the images back into that little shoe box he'd built in his head.

Soon.

He closed his eyes, the words finally coming that he needed to hear.

"Jingle bells, jingle bells..."

He really did need to come up with a more manly sounding song to kick some flashback ass.